MINIQUE

ALSO BY ANNA MAXYMIW

Dirty Work: My Gruelling, Glorious,
Life-Changing Summer in the Wilderness

MINIQUE

A NOVEL

ANNA MAXYMIW

McClelland & Stewart

McClelland & Stewart and colophon are registered trademarks of Penguin Random House Canada Limited.

LIBRARY AND ARCHIVES CANADA CATALOGUING IN PUBLICATION

Title: Minique / Anna Maxymiw.
Names: Maxymiw, Anna, author.
Identifiers: Canadiana (print) 20210391197 | Canadiana (ebook) 20210391200 |
    ISBN 9780771096815 (softcover) | ISBN 9780771096822 (EPUB)
Subjects: LCGFT: Novels.
Classification: LCC PS8626.A887 M56 2022 | DDC C813/.6—dc23

Book design by Andrew Roberts
Cover image: CAS Images / Getty Images
Interior image: Ace_Create / DigitalVision Vectors / Getty Images
Typeset in Adobe Caslon Pro by M&S, Toronto
Printed in the United States of America

McClelland & Stewart,
a division of Penguin Random House Canada Limited,
a Penguin Random House Company
www.penguinrandomhouse.ca

1st Printing

Penguin
Random House
McCLELLAND & STEWART

No matter how much you feed a wolf,
it will always return to the forest.

—SLAVIC PROVERB

MINIQUE

Faut aller chercher le loup

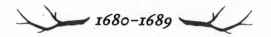 *1680–1689*

Minique curls up in bed, trying to make her body as small as possible in order to stay warm. The night is cold and she thinks she can see her breath when she exhales hard. Sometimes the cold makes her feel alive. Sometimes she hates it. She wishes she could stop thinking long enough to fall asleep, but her head is filled with the day: school lessons and notre père qui es aux cieux and stories about the saints—Saint Giles and Saint Anne and Saint Columba. What fruit is a fruit of the womb? She can see an apple, a pear. She wonders what daily bread might taste like.

Suddenly, she hears something—a voice. A singing. A thin song in the middle of the cold night. Minique sits up and tries to listen harder by opening her eyes wide. She wants to see if it's just her imagination. It's quiet for a moment or two, and then she hears it again, sweet and high. She hurls herself out of bed and shoves her feet into wool socks and then leather boots. Grabbing a wool over-coat and scarf and hat, Minique slithers out of her room, through her silent house, out her front door. It's surprisingly easy to escape.

The night is strange and silver. Minique can definitely see her breath now, even through the scarf. She breathes in and out and feels the wool start to sog. In the dark, frozen puddles glitter across the uneven ground, and the houses look less scuffed and dirty. During the day, everything is grey and drab, but in the dark, it becomes pearly, like she imagines heaven might be. The air feels thin, like if Minique spoke, someone on the other side of town would be able to hear her in their bed. There are no candles in windows. Nothing to show that people are awake or that anyone else has heard what she is hearing. Then she hears it again, and then she turns, and she sees her.

The woman is finely made, like a pretty bird, and her hair is so pale it's nearly white, matching the pearliness of her skin. Maybe that's why she's immune to the cold, Minique thinks—because she's the colour of winter. She's dressed only in a flannel nightgown and some slippers, but she isn't shivering. The moonlight looks almost warm on her skin, the night air making her clothes flutter. This is the ghost of Minique's mother, coming to lure her into the next world.

She floats her way toward Minique, and Minique squares her shoulders and walks to meet her. As she gets closer, she can hear the words to the song.

"Faut aller chercher le loup," the woman hums, "pour venir manger bébé."

Have to find the wolf to come and eat the baby.

"Le loup n'veut pas manger bébé; bébé n'veut pas faire dodo." *The wolf doesn't want to eat the baby; the baby doesn't want to go to sleep.*

We should both be asleep, Minique wants to say, but instead she reaches out both hands. Even through the wool of the mittens, the woman's fingers are like ice.

"Shit," Minique says under her breath, a word she wouldn't use in the light of day. She yanks her mittens off and shoves them onto the woman's hands. "You need to wear more if you're going to go out for nighttime walks!" The woman looks unperturbed; she's humming the lullaby now instead of singing the words, and Minique is glad for that.

"You look like your mother," she says suddenly, and Minique stops her fiddling with the mittens, looks up the woman's body to the calmness of her face, shining like the moon.

"My mother?"

"We were like sisters on the ship, *Le Saint Jean-Baptiste*," she says. "Then I got the good man."

"You knew my mother?"

She smiles like a saint, and brings her newly mittened hands around Minique's face. She's still humming the lullaby, but it doesn't seem wrong anymore; it's soothing. It feels like there's no one else in Montréal, and it's only the two of them, in this moment and forever, touching each other, held in the middle of a song.

"Jeanne!"

Minique jerks away and looks around the woman's body: behind them, Claude, the boulanger, is running down the street, his coat flapping. His whisper-shout has broken the moment. Jeanne doesn't turn to look at him; she continues staring out overtop of Minique's head, out to where the trees would be if she could see that far, through the rows of squat houses and stores and stables and sheds, her hand inching up Minique's cheek to stroke her hair. Minique waves a bare palm at Claude. He looks surprised, like he's only just noticed her.

"Minique?" When he gets to them, he's out of breath. He smells yeasty, which reminds her of the warmth of an oven, and because of that, he seems like an intruder on this moment of cold. Minique unloops one hand from around Jeanne's wrist. She doesn't mention the mittens, only takes a few steps back so Claude can swoop in and bundle what she assumes is his wife into his arms. As the two of them make to leave, Jeanne winks at her from between the flaps of Claude's coat, and Minique can't help but smile before she has to turn around and try to get back into her house without making a sound.

For days after, Minique finds herself humming the lullaby under her breath. She thinks about the wolf, at the edge of the forest. She thinks about the baby, at the mercy of the wolf without realizing it. She adds more words to the song, making the verses longer and longer. *Il faut aller chercher le feu*, Minique sings to herself. *Ce sera de tout brûle.*

Minique lives with her father and her aunt in a small house on the southwest side of Montréal. She knows the direction because her classmates and their parents make it clear to her that it's a worse area than the rest of town. The rich people live in the good houses, in the nice part, and then there's everyone else.

None of the town looks nice to her. In a good part, in a bad part, it all smells like damp wood. She's never been in a house for rich people, but she thinks that the dirt would be just as hard to sweep, that the floors would creak the same. The rooms would be just as dark at night. The bed linens would still be cold. Montréal is dim and muddy and every day is like the one before, slow and sucking. She's heard from other children that Québec and Trois-Rivières are nicer, much nicer. Bigger and brighter, more people. They're closer to the sea, closer to the ships that bring the goods from France. They're not as far inland as Montréal is. If the River St. Laurence is a road, Québec and Trois-Rivières live at the good end. Montréal is where the road is narrow and mean.

But Montréal is the only place Minique knows. She hasn't visited other cities. She doesn't have a father who has to travel there for business. Her father does travel, somewhere, but she's not sure where and her aunt won't tell her. He leaves their house for big pieces of time and she loses count of the days he's gone and when he's supposed to come back. He goes out the door wearing clothes that she and her aunt never wear: hide pants and jacket, fur hat, fur-trimmed boots. She doesn't see men in town wearing those clothes. She doesn't even know what animal has been used to make them.

The first time she asked her aunt where her father had gone, Tante Marie hit her on the knuckles with a spoon she was using to stir a pot of soup. Minique drew her hand back, sucking her skin into her mouth. Her aunt didn't answer; she stared at Minique until Minique pulled her knuckle out from between her lips and wiped it on her dress, looking away.

Her aunt went back to stirring the soup—potato, watery—and Minique went back to tracing the lines of the wood on the kitchen table with one hand, drying her other hand over and over again on her skirt until her skin felt rough.

Tante Marie is hard and thin, and she's tall, even taller than Minique's father. But Minique doesn't think there are soft and warm women in Montréal. From what she's seen of her classmates' mothers and sisters and aunts, women are meant to be tough. They have enough children to fill a house. They can spend hours outside, handwashing piles of muddy clothes in cold weather. They can take a whole day to clean a home and then have to do it all over again the next day. Sometimes, in fairy tales, Minique hears about women who hug like a soft quilt, who smell like sugar, and she knows that those women aren't real. Because the real women are the ones who fight to live every day, and her aunt is one of these women.

When Minique asked about her father again, Tante Marie watched her, still holding the spoon upright, until Minique frowned and took one step back. That's when her aunt sighed and pointed the spoon at Minique's forehead. Minique blinked, as if she'd been arquebused, shot right through.

"Your father is making a living."

Minique didn't know what *making a living* meant. She guessed he was living a life beyond the walls of their house, beyond Montréal. He was making a life away from his daughter and his sister, away from the place they call home, whether they like it or not.

Coureur des bois is an interesting combination of words. To run—like she does when she wants to get home from school and it's the kind of cold outside that makes her feel angry. Running away from the Jesuits and their black robes, running away from the Sulpicians, who always want to talk and talk and talk. Sometimes she sees men striding down the street outside their house, and she knows they're on their way to the auberge, the inn, to see Anne, the aubergiste, who started running the place after her husband died. But the woods are different. *The woods* are that place where people point to but never go; outside the walls of the town, where the dark trees wait, standing like people. Minique can see the tops of the trees if she looks out the window of her attic room; if she crawled onto the roof of the house, she'd be able to see more. *Why are people scared of the woods?* The Iroquois, she's heard. The tribes who'll kill the French on sight. The townspeople must be scared of the animals, too. She's heard some of the boys talk about bears, how they can take a man's head off with one paw. The wolves that look like dogs but can rip your throat out. The moose, taller than a man and stronger, too, able to trample a person in a few steps. And other things. Other things that live there, in the woods.

Her aunt is behind the house, speaking to a neighbour, Marie-Renee, an engagée, a servant for one of the wealthier families. Minique is meant to be doing some embroidery inside. She isn't embroidering, of course, because she hates having to squint at the stitchwork, and she pricks her finger and thumb so much that the sampler ends up with dots of blood on it. She doesn't like the little movements, the way she has to be careful with every pull of the thread. So she loses interest quickly and is now sitting on the ground beside the window, tilting her head up and cupping a hand to an ear. *Coureur des bois.* Wood runners. she knows Tante Marie is speaking about Minique's father from the hushed, odd tone she's using.

Minique imagines her father tall like a tree. She pictures him running across a field, legs like a puppet's. Does he cradle wood in his arms, like a baby? Is he a man made of spruce and pine, branches for arms, leaves at the ends of his fingers?

Sometimes, people make faces when talking about the coureurs des bois. When that happens, Minique can feel the words sitting in her stomach, like they're sour and heavy. She wants to know what it is about the forest that makes people speak about the wood runners from the sides of their mouths.

There aren't many other children in Montréal to be friends with. Compared to the other towns, Montréal seems to be growing slowly. Minique's heard about the filles du roi, the girls sent over by the king. Rumour has it that because Québec was the first stop, the men there got to pick the beautiful girls. Then came Trois-Rivières, where the pretty ones were chosen. Montréal was the last stop for the boat, for the ugly girls, the girls who had something wrong with them. Maybe that's why the population of the town is still so low. At least now there are enough children for schools. The girls have to study at a boarding school set up by Marguerite Bourgeoys, who came to New France more than twenty years ago to help educate the poor; the boys study with the Sulpicians. Minique doesn't have to board; she goes back to her house every night. But there are lots of students who live at the school, including some Indigenous girls. She sees them in the school-yard, but they're taught in a different classroom. She wants to ask why, but she knows she'd be told off by a nun or even strapped on the hand, and she doesn't need to know that badly.

Her classmates are separated into groups based on how much money their fathers earn and how much people need them. At the lowest end, there are the habitants, the families who farm for a living. Then there are the fisherman and whalers, shipbuilders and wharf workers. In another group there are masons and stonecutters and carpenters and coopers. Then there are the blacksmiths, wheelwrights, locksmiths, and armourers. There are the ones who keep people fed, like butchers and bakers and millers, and the ones who keep people clothed, like tailors and weavers and tanners. And finally there are the fancy jobs, makers of items that no one seems to need but everyone seems to want: wigs and gold and art.

There are still other jobs, ones people say are important but Minique doesn't see much of: working in the government, the military. The fur merchants. The lawyers and the judge. Minique doesn't often get to talk with the children of those people. The outsides of their houses are stone, with tall roofs and neat yards. She can't imagine what the insides of their houses look like. It's not like her own house, which is made of wood and is low to the ground, with only two doors and a few windows.

School is miserable. Minique doesn't like being there, but also doesn't like being at home. In the classroom, she is too visible; at home, she is invisible. Sometimes in the schoolyard the other girls point at her and chant *paria, paria—outcast, outcast*—as loud as they can. Any time Minique has tried to tell an adult about it, she's been told to buck up, that bullies only want a reaction. But that's not true. Minique's tried to ignore them for years, and they've never let up. She doesn't understand why they're kept separate from the boys. The boys are supposed to be the wild and violent ones, but girls are meaner and wilder than any boy she's ever known.

It's bad enough when they're yelling at her from across the yard, but it's worse when they're up close.

"Stupid mute," the boucher's daughter, Marie-Catherine, likes to say with a laugh. She's untouchable at school because of her father's job: he's necessary, and so she's necessary. She wears nice dresses and ribbons in her hair, and she likes to call Minique names like *muette* and *stupide* and *lourdaude*. Marie-Catherine doesn't actually touch Minique, but her friends do. They like to circle her and yank at the end of her braid, sometimes so hard that her head hurts by the end of the day. The heftier ones like to kick her in the shins, high enough that it hits her just above the boot.

Minique doesn't know how to win. She can't physically fight a group of them, and she doesn't know what words to say to make them leave her alone. Whenever she's cornered, she panics, and then she can't think properly, and by the time she comes up with a response that sounds good and strong and kind of mean, it's far too late; sometimes she thinks of things to say when she's falling asleep, or the next morning when she's eating oatmeal for breakfast. She'll say the words around the spoon in her mouth and then frown, knowing she'll forget them all over again the next time she's surrounded. So it's easier just to listen to the adults who tell her to ignore unkind words. She stays quiet because she's tired, not stupid.

There are other children who aren't accepted. Maybe their fathers also drink too much, or maybe they also live in an area of town where they have to dodge around sots vomiting off stoops and men fighting each other in the middle of the street. Maybe they don't dress right or talk right or look right. Minique doesn't know why some children escape the meanness of the popular girls, the girls with the nicely braided hair and the clean dresses, and why some children become targets. Maybe it's because her clothes are tattier than those of the daughters of the tailor, the blacksmith, the cooper. Maybe it's because she doesn't have a mother and barely has a father. That one stings the worst. She doesn't mind wearing shabbier clothes, because it feels like there's less pressure to keep them clean. She doesn't mind when her braids come loose. But she doesn't like thinking about having only Tante Marie at home. Thinking about that for too long feels like bruising a knee or elbow, the pain that comes with bending and moving. So Minique tries not to think about it too much; she tries not to let it bother her. If she doesn't react, she eventually gets left alone, and that suits her just fine. Besides, she has Barbe.

She met Barbe Bâby in class, of course. They were stuck with each other right away. Minique doesn't mind. Most of the other children are afraid of Barbe: one of her eyes is a pale blue, but the other is white, like a ball of milky glass. Barbe says it's from an infection she had as a baby, that she doesn't remember what happened, but the other children say it's because she's been touched by a witch.

Sometimes Minique hears people talking about *spellcraft*, in low voices. She overhears it from women walking past the inn. She hears it when men speak with the priests by the water pump in the middle of the town. *Using plants unnaturally*, she hears. *Love potions, poisons on arrowheads.* Part of her hopes they're real things, that witches are alive among them. But they seem like the stories she hears in the schoolyard about ghost boats that look like they're on fire and giant water-snakes that live in the rivers and women who turn into deer and also deer who turn into women.

The fiery ghost boat—the chasse-galerie—is a favourite schoolyard tale, so she's heard it dozens of times before. The story is that a group of coureurs des bois wanted to get back to Montréal to see their sweethearts, and so they made a deal with the devil so that their canoe would fly so they could get there fast. Minique has heard different endings to the story, depending on who's telling it, but the one she likes the most is when the devil tries to steer the boat himself and the men throw him out into the pine trees below in order to save themselves and make it back to their camp in one piece. There's something exciting about that—that people could not only get their hands on the devil, but that they could toss him from a boat and carry on flying.

Barbe doesn't seem to mind that she's lumped in with these fables; she doesn't care about the opinions of others. Minique wishes that she could be more like that, especially when the other girls crowd around her to tug at her hair and sniff at her dress. *You smell like an animal*, they say. *And you look like one too. Guess you never had a mother to teach you how to brush your hair. Guess your father isn't around enough to teach you how to be proper.*

Maybe there's something about her eye after all, because Barbe tends to see things in a different light. When Minique complains about the Jesuits, Barbe looks at her and says: "I like their robes. They remind me of crows." When Minique gets bored with the lessons in class, Barbe tells her: "I like Jesus. He was friends with everyone." And of god: "God is more interesting when he's angry." And of the flying canoe: "Canoes aren't even nice in the water; can you imagine one in the air?" And of the Sulpicians: "They're nice to talk to, because they ask me what I think about the buildings and how they could look nicer. And I want things in the town to look nicer."

If Minique is quiet, Barbe is kind and open. It doesn't make much sense that the two of them are friends, but something about it works. Something about Barbe makes Minique think twice about opening her mouth before her mind can catch up; she finds herself being a little softer and a little less mean. And she thinks that maybe her presence protects Barbe, because when they're together, the girls with the shiny hair and the good teeth and the nice clothes tend to leave them alone. Maybe it's just harder to pick on people in groups.

"Better to be outcasts than part of a herd," Barbe says in her calm voice, and Minique feels less angry. "At least, I think it's what I prefer."

The two of them meet Daniel Nicolet on the way home from school one afternoon, when the sky is the purple and yellow that happens before a storm. Minique's keeping an eye on the clouds, getting ready to make a run for it if she has to. The dim light makes Barbe's pale eye seem brighter than usual, her blond hair nearly white. The two of them are walking hand in hand when they notice someone running alongside them, juggling what looks like paving stones in his hands.

"Who are *you*?" Barbe doesn't sound put off, only curious. And then, in the same breath: "Where did you learn to juggle?"

Minique narrows her eyes at him, but the boy only turns his face to her and grins. He has a wad of something in his cheek, so when he speaks, his words are wet.

"I'm the boulanger and the folle's son. And you're the coureur de bois' daughter, and you're the one with the crazy eye," he says, pointing at Minique and Barbe in turn.

Minique hadn't been expecting that answer.

"Rain's coming," the boy continues.

"You're the lunatic if you think we didn't notice that," Minique snaps, and he smiles even wider.

"You're mean. I like you."

"Well," Minique starts, her face and neck feeling hot. "Well, I don't know if I like *you* yet."

"No one likes me," he says, putting his stones down. Barbe immediately bends to pick one up, holding it close to her face as she turns it back and forth to see the flecks of colour.

"Why?"

"Because my father lets me run around as I please and my mother is crazy."

Something about the way he forms his words seems familiar. When he turns to stare out at the gathering clouds, Minique recognizes the pearly colour of his skin, the way he holds his head. *The boulanger's son*, he said. She remembers Claude running down the midnight street, his coat flapping, and the cool touch of Jeanne's hands in her own. She doesn't know if she should say anything, so she says the first thing that comes to her mind.

"I don't have a mother."

"It's true," Barbe says with a nod.

"Not sure if that's better or worse," he says, swallowing whatever's in his mouth. "I'm Daniel." He sticks out a dirty hand, and Minique only waits one second before she takes it.

"Minique."

"Barbe!" Barbe says her own name with glee, but takes no one's hand, instead walking around the two of them with the rock wrapped up in her skirt for safe keeping. And that's that.

They spend every afternoon together. Barbe is never in a rush to go home; her father is a chasseur de rats and her mother is a lavandière, which means they work long hours and Barbe has an empty house waiting for her. Minique can't bear to be in her own home, and with Daniel, Claude is always busy setting up for the next day in the boulangerie. This means that they have big pieces of time to spend with one another, without the watchful eye of a parent or guardian. So when Minique and Barbe finish at their school, they walk a few minutes east down the street, where they wait at the corner near the seminary in the centre of town. Daniel meets them there after he's finished his own classes, and then the three of them head off.

Minique thought Montréal was boring before she met Daniel. He's the adventurer of their group, and suddenly Minique is seeing the town through a different set of eyes. As the weeks pass and the weather gets warmer, she, too, somehow warms up to Montréal, solely through Daniel's love and irreverence for it. Daniel grabs both their hands and drags them along behind him as he sprints from one side of the town to the other, laughing at the irritated faces of the townspeople. Daniel runs up to the Jesuit quarters and knocks on the door and then dashes away before anyone can answer. He slips in and out of alleys. He blends in, shoves his hands in his pockets and strolls like he belongs everywhere. If he gets told off, he lets it slide like water off a duck's back. The trick, he tells them again and again, is to always look like you know what you're doing and where you're going.

"And if they don't buy *that*," he says, wiggling a loose tooth in his mouth with his tongue, "then you run."

The first time Minique leaves the town walls through the north gate, it feels like a giant achievement. It's summer, and the day is mild and sweet. The smell of pine is in the air—all around her, it seems—so she expects to see the forest right there, right up against the circle of Montréal. But it's not. She's surprised to see that habitants also live outside of the town. There are rough houses, homes that look a little bit like hers. She never knew that outside of Montréal there were other people; she always thought that the town was the hub of life. She never thought about where the crops were grown. But here, life exists in a different way. Families have swaths of land filled with things growing, stripes of green and gold and brown, plants she doesn't have names for. There's a looser feeling the farther away they get from the town. Families are large and loud, with whoops filling the air, the occasional swear word, the smell of tobacco smoke heavy. Minique even sees a child or two smoking a pipe. The forest isn't as close as she thought it was—it stands a ways away, still dark and tall—but she thinks that maybe she can feel its influence, just from leaving the stone and wood of Montréal.

Daniel walks her and Barbe between the different fields—he explains that every piece of land is narrow and long, reaching the small river that runs east to west, to the north of town, so each family has water for growing wheat and maize and peas and barley and tobacco. He tells them that the habitants don't own the land they're on, even though to Minique it looks like each family has made their fields their own, like a signature.

"No," Daniel says around a blade of grass he's holding between his teeth. "They have to pay rent to the seigneur." He spits the grass out onto the ground.

"That's not fair," Barbe says.

"How do you know all of this?"

Daniel shrugs. "I get bored."

If Minique got bored and didn't go to school, tried to creep out and go for a walk along the plots of land, she'd get a whipping from someone. It's easier for Daniel to dart in and out of people's attention. She wonders if it has something to do with him being a boy.

She's distracted from that thought as Daniel stops at the top of the hill. She and Barbe come up behind him, breathing more heavily than he is. They look down, and Minique smiles, because spread out in front of them there are apple trees, shining in the afternoon sun.

The orchard smells dusty and sweet, and the trees are planted in rows they can easily walk between. Daniel grins the whole time: he knows that he's shared a great treasure with them. As with the homes of the habitants, Minique didn't know that the orchard existed. She's eaten apples, but mainly stewed or dried, just once in a while and only as a treat. She never thought about where the apples came from, and now she's here, in the middle of it.

"They're not ripe yet," Daniel says, holding up both hands and jumping to grab a branch. "Not till fall." Barbe and Minique watch as he pulls himself up, kicking his feet up into the leaves, his body following. He's almost completely hidden from view. Suddenly Minique knows why this orchard is so special and why he's brought them here. She's never climbed a tree in her life, but she reaches her hands out and touches the bark. Her palms are sweaty, because she's nervous about looking stupid, and it's probably harder to climb a tree in a skirt than it is in breeches, but she jumps, too, and gets a hold of a branch big enough to take her weight.

"Don't look!" Her voice is louder than she means it to be. She can't even see Daniel, and Barbe is turned away from her, trying to pick a long blade of grass to whistle with.

"I'm not looking at you! You probably look like a capon," Daniel says from somewhere higher up.

"I do not look like a capon!"

"You do, dangling like that. Like a skinny plucked capon, all neck." He giggles. Now Minique *has* to get up in the tree, if only to spit in his face. She growls to herself and does what he did, swings her feet up to try to catch them on the branch. The first swing is a failure, but the second one—which is a little bit more of a walk up the trunk than she'd care to admit—lands, and she scrapes her arms trying to get herself up, but she does it.

Suddenly she's surrounded by green. She can still see the light coming through the leaves, but the smells and the sounds of outside are muffled. It's like she's sitting in a secret room that no one else can find. A bower, like the kind in a fairy tale. She could hide here forever and no one would find her.

"See?" Daniel's voice isn't as teasing. Between branches, she can spy one of his boots dangling, but nothing else. It seems like the tree itself is talking to her. "This is why I come here."

She does see. She does understand. It's not the real forest, it's only man-made, but just being surrounded by the colour green makes her feel better about everything.

"Barbe?"

From somewhere down below them, they hear the honk of a puff of air blown through a piece of grass, and Minique laughs.

There's a moment of silence as the three of them just sit on their different levels, thinking, listening to the breeze in the leaves and the birds overhead.

Then Daniel speaks. "Do you know what I learned the other day?"

"What?" Barbe's voice is faint. There's another bleat from the grass.

"I learned," he says grandly, shuffling around on his branch so much that twigs and leaves shake free and fall into Minique's hair, making her frown, "about the nain rouge."

"The what?" Barbe has stood up and wandered over to the bottom of the tree. Minique can see her entire pale moon of a face tilted up; it's likely that, from his high perch, Daniel can only see pieces of her.

"The nain rouge, Barbe. Nain! Rouge!" He exaggerates the last two words; it sounds like he's cupped his hands around his mouth to make his voice louder.

"What's that?"

"It's a monster!"

Barbe laughs. "Tell me about the monster."

"The nain rouge lives in the forest," Daniel says, his voice floating down. "It's really small, like a child, but it's got a red face, like the devil. And it's covered in black fur."

Minique starts to feel strange. There's a swoop in her stomach like she's seen something scary, except she hasn't, because all she's doing is listening to Daniel tell a story that he's probably picked up from some schoolyard hooligan. Her body feels hot and cold at the same time, and there's spit gathering under her tongue. She swallows to try to make herself feel better.

"A child?" Barbe is still leaning on the trunk, staring up.

There's a rustle, and a muffled swear word, and then Daniel slides down the tree. His hair has leaves in it, but his eyes are bright and wild. He lands on a branch right above Minique.

"Small like a child," he repeats, looking down at both of them. "And it's got red eyes that glow. In the dark. And also big teeth."

"Who told you this?" Minique digs her fingers into the bark.

"Two trappers. They were in the boulangerie and I overheard them talking."

"What does the nain rouge do?" Barbe is still curious about the red monster; Minique wishes, for once, that she'd just be quiet. She wishes both of them would just be quiet and that they could all move on to something else.

Daniel stares at them. "When you see the nain rouge in the forest, you go crazy. They said they saw a man kill and eat his wife and children after he met the nain rouge."

Minique feels like she's trying to remember something that happened in a dream, or something that she knew once, or thought about, and has forgotten. Like a grey, fuzzy kind of thing that she can't quite reach out her hands and catch. Her mind doesn't know why her body is so tense, why her guts hurt, why her skin is sweaty. She wants to ask Daniel more questions, to get him to tell her everything he knows, to tell her who the men talking about this monster were.

But then Barbe sighs.

"Bad things always happen, Daniel."

Some days, they walk through the cemetery; Minique picks up pebbles and balances them on gravestones. She thinks about the first people who were buried here. When people die in winter, the graves can't be dug out because the ground is too hard. They have to wait until spring, when the ground is wet and mucky and the mud sucks at Minique's boots and the dampness in the air makes her itchy around her wrists and ankles. She wants to feel safe in the cemetery, because it's quiet and mostly peaceful and Daniel and Barbe both like it, but whenever she looks around at the graves, she thinks of the people in the earth, and she walks a little bit faster.

Some days, Daniel brings them to the wharf. Minique's never even been in a canoe, let alone on a ship; she feels no pull to the water. Some people have it in their blood, which makes sense if they travelled here, if they still think of their homeland. She can see it in some people, the way they sway a bit on their feet. Minique can't imagine living a life like the people with the sea in them do, one eye looking back at the River St. Laurence and one at their new home.

Minique looks out at where the water meets the sky and imagines her mother coming in on *Le Saint Jean-Baptiste*. Saint Jean, the one who got his head cut off at the request of a woman. She sees his head on a silver platter. She sees her mother's hands curled around a railing or a rope. What does her mother look like? Minique imagines her as dark-haired and sharp-looking. She thinks of her like a hawk. While the other women look nervous, Minique's mother does not. She's standing and watching while the men on shore get closer and closer, and her new life becomes clearer and clearer. What is she feeling? Excitement, fear deep inside? Or maybe her mother wants to keep on sailing, learn to climb the rigging and tuck herself at the highest point of the mast. Maybe she hates the idea of her new life, and hates her husband. Maybe she wants to run past the town walls, into the forest, and disappear forever.

Minique will never know. Time has softened the image of her mother from everyone's minds, and those who might remember her won't reach into their memory. Minique doesn't know if this is because they're afraid of her father, or her aunt, or maybe the ghost of her mother. Maybe the citizens of Montréal are just tired of remembering the past, and want only to look to the future.

As the summer trundles toward fall, they take to crawling up onto Daniel's roof, wriggling through his window and heaving themselves up from where they stand on the sill. They sit side by side and talk. Daniel tells them about his mother.

"She's not scary," he says, shaking his head. "She doesn't get violent or say bad things." Minique watches him as he talks. His face is angles: the point of his chin and the line of his nose. It's so different to the softness of Barbe's cheeks, the little wispy hairs on her forehead. "She just does things that make people uncomfortable."

"Like what?"

Barbe asks the question, but Minique knows. She walks through the winter night. She sings about wolves and babies. She stares right through you and at you at the same time.

Daniel shifts around. "Like she'll recite the Act of Contrition over and over again to herself out in public, or she'll wear the wrong clothes for the weather. Or—or one time, she only wanted maple syrup for dinner. And one time she refused to put her hair up, and then after that she refused to cover it, and then Father Etienne got mad and told my father that he has to keep her inside."

Father Etienne. Minique scowls at his name. He's piggish and mean. Minique doesn't care for the other priests, but she *hates* Father Etienne; she hates the way his eyes roll around in his head when he's lecturing people or giving a homily. He talks so loud and with so much of his lips that he ends up spitting on people. He's short, but likes to pretend he isn't; he puffs up his chest to try to disguise it, and wears cassocks that are too long and cover his boots and drag on the floor. He likes to stand on the step above people whenever he can, whether in front of the church or at the entrance to a store, to be able to look down on them while he talks. Father Etienne thinks the people of Montréal are heathens. He's said so, from the pulpit, his saliva spraying out onto the pews. He complains that the women wear their dresses too low, that the men gamble and drink too much. Minique has seen the habitants grin at each other mid-homily, and then slide to the back of the church, where they play a stealthy game of dice just outside the entrance, clicking their tongues at the altar boys sent out to investigate.

Hearing Daniel saying Father Etienne's name makes Minique's blood boil. She frowns, shaking her head.

"So now she has to be locked up when no one is home," Daniel says, clacking two stones together in his hands. He's not looking at Barbe or Minique. "So she doesn't get out and bother the priest or anybody."

Minique wonders if his mother's nighttime walk had something to do with her being kept at home. If maybe someone else saw them that night. Maybe she did the wrong thing, giving Jeanne her mittens and not immediately leading her to a doorway or an alley, to keep her away from prying eyes. Maybe she should have brought Jeanne right into her home.

Or maybe it's better to be locked away. It's a lesson Minique puts in the dark part of her brain, the part she doesn't need that often but that she knows she'll use at some point. *Move yourself away from the crowd instead of being singled out as an enemy. Go quietly. Hide yourself. And maybe you'll live.*

If the nuns and the brothers and the nosy townspeople think it's odd that Barbe and Minique and Daniel are spending so much time together, they say little. Minique thinks that because the three of them are so strange, people don't mind. People probably say: *Good, I'm glad those simpletons aren't infecting anyone else.* Sometimes Minique wonders if people think they're up to no good, maybe pulling up their skirts and pulling down their pants and showing one another what they have under their clothes; she knows that some of the other boys and girls do this, out of boredom and also just to be disobedient. If you're always told *no*, you want to do the *yes*.

But that's not what this is about. They talk. They explore. Daniel has brought a wash of colour to her life; he's brought the taste of sugar and the scent of an apple tree's leaves on a warm day. He smells like things that are alive and green and dirty.

The nuns and the missionaries like to talk about the father and the son and the holy spirit, and Minique thinks that if she could see the trinity, hold it in her hands like a real thing, then maybe she would want to know more about it. Stories are interesting, but nothing compares with real life. Even the grouchy townspeople can't bring her down—*yes, we know we're not supposed to go out; yes, we know it's dangerous; yes, we know we should go right home after school.* She'll listen to nuns and the Jesuits talk about the bible and she'll pretend to be interested as best she can, but Minique knows that this is the most holy thing she's ever felt.

———

When she gets home just before dinnertime, she notices a large pair of muddy boots by the door, a pack dropped in the hallway. Two voices talking low in the kitchen area. She recognizes the rumble of her father, and she wants to run to him, like she used to when she was younger. But she's learned to move slower around him. To be careful. He doesn't like surprises; he doesn't like quick movements. He doesn't like spending a lot of time in the house with them. She thinks it's been a few months since she saw him last, but it could be more. She used to count the days when she was younger by making marks in the back of her bible, but she doesn't do that anymore.

She doesn't mean to listen or to sneak around, but she walks slowly, trying to make herself small and quiet, and so she hears some of what they're saying to each other. Her father's voice is low; her aunt's voice is stern and has a higher sound to it, like she's upset. That tends to happen when her father comes home. They fight *like hammer and tongs*, Daniel's father would say. Minique puts one foot in front of the other, trying to be silent. A boy at Daniel's school told him the Iroquois walk in a straight line, balancing on the toes, and so she tries it. She imagines herself walking on a rope, trying not to fall to either side.

"Children?" Her aunt's voice is hard.

Her father doesn't answer. Then he says *yes* in a voice lower than she's ever heard, and there's a slapping sound, like someone has hit their hand on the table.

"What were you thinking?"

Minique focuses on being as quiet as she can be, but she loses her concentration and stumbles to one side, grabbing the wall and doorway to steady herself, pulling herself into view of the kitchen. She looks up and sees her aunt and her father both staring at her. Tante Marie has a worried look on her face, her eyes wide and her eyebrows high on her forehead. She's holding her hands in front of her body, winding her fingers together as she watches Minique straighten up.

Her father has a different kind of look on his face. At first, it's plain and indifferent, like a mask, but as she stands and pushes the hair out of her face, he looks fearful. Like he's seen a ghost, some people would say. Like she reminds him of something he would like to forget.

"Papa," she says, shy.

He stares back at her for a few beats, and then Tante Marie bumps her hip into the chair at the table and it makes a sound as it moves across the floor, and her father blinks and then shakes his head a little.

"Minique," he says, and crouches down. She thinks that means he wants her to come to him, and so she does, but carefully. She's learned from the last time, when she tried to jump on him the moment he came through the door and he roared a sound she'll never forget and almost threw her off of him. When she wraps her arms around his neck this time, she takes a deep breath and smells leather, smoke, pine trees.

"I have something for you," he says, removing her arms from around him and rummaging in the leather pouch tied at his waist. He pulls out a soft pair of shoes. "Moccasins," he says. *Moccasins*, she thinks, turning the word over in her mind. She doesn't think she's ever seen anyone wear them in town; she'll have to pay more attention next time she's outside of the walls to see what the habitants there wear on their feet. When she turns them over, she sees that there are decorations on the toes: tiny beads in patterns of green leaves and little pink flowers. The gift is so beautiful and so fine

Minique loses sight of the beads for a moment because her eyes get a little blurry.

"Thank you," she whispers, and her father nods and then pats her hesitantly on the head, turning back to mumble something to her aunt. Minique ignores them and slides her feet into the moccasins. They're too big for her, and she's not sure if that's because her father wanted to get her something she can grow into, or if he lost track of how old she was. When she takes them off her feet and holds them up to her face, she smells how her father smells, something smokey. And she sees flashes of something. Of a woman beading, and then her hand in a large white hand. A laugh that sounds like a child's.

Minique pulls the slippers away from her face and stares at them. At the beadwork that could never be done by a man's hand. At this surprise gift. And she wonders who made them, and how they know her father.

M inique drags her feet as she walks behind her aunt. She didn't want to come on errands with her aunt today; she and Daniel and Barbe had planned to play skittles in the flat field just beyond the orchard. Daniel had spent a week whittling the pins, although he had given up on the ball and borrowed one from one of the habitant families, the Guyons. The three of them were supposed to be outside the walls right now. Instead, she's dipping her head to try to shrink from everyone's view.

There's something particularly unpleasant about walking through the middle of town. It means she's out in the open. To be exposed is to be in danger. Her aunt doesn't like town that much, either. She's scowling in sour displeasure; Minique can almost taste it coming off of her. Tante Marie's frown drives most people away, but those who remain give the two of them looks that range from openly dirty to mildly judgmental. The weight of their gazes feels heavy on Minique's shoulders. It's bad enough when she's at school, trying to avoid the main streets and take the back alleys to get to the classroom on time. But here, now, in the middle of it, it's worse. And yet—also a relief. There's no hiding. At least here, she can see everyone. This is why she hates town.

Her aunt inhales beside her, picking up her pace, and Minique feels a kinship with her. She might be only twelve, but she feels that the closer she crawls to womanhood, the more she starts to understand bits and pieces of Marie. For example, right now she understands that her aunt is only out in town because she has to be. She understands that Tante Marie doesn't want to parade up and down the streets; she understands that there's something weary and heavy about the way her aunt feels, but it's an emotion she can't quite grasp. If Minique were funnier, if she were someone who made people laugh effortlessly, maybe she could find a way to lift her aunt's mood. Maybe she could duck-walk or pull a face or say something that would make her aunt smile. But she isn't, and so she doesn't. The best she can do is tug the basket out of Tante Marie's hands and carry it herself, while it's still light and empty and the impending warmth of the early summer day won't sap her strength. Her aunt doesn't say thank you, but she rests a palm on the top of Minique's head for a brief moment.

Minique and Tante Marie don't hug. They don't touch more than they have to—fingers against a hand when someone passes over a plate, or their bodies brushing past each other in a doorway. Minique's not sure she wants to have that kind of warm relationship anyway. But as they both trudge, their footsteps matching, she grabs her aunt's wrist. Tante Marie falters for a moment, looking down at her niece with her blank face, and Minique feels brave enough to crawl her fingers down and hold her aunt's hand. She can feel her aunt's hot, dry palm against hers. Tante Marie looks away very quickly, but she doesn't drop Minique's hand, nor does she pull away. Instead, Minique feels her aunt's fingers tighten around her own. Minique wants to rub their joined hands on her face, as if she were a cat, to soak up the rare feeling. But instead she sets her jaw and keeps her eyes straight ahead, trying to keep her face as blank as her aunt's. Maybe she understands Tante Marie a tiny bit more.

They make the circuit, picking up all of the necessary items. First they go to the boulangerie, where Minique smells all of Claude's hard work, warm and sweet and pillowy. Tante Marie buys the cheap bread they always get; they're not rich enough to have the clean white loaves made with the good flour. As Claude wraps their purchases up, he looks at Minique, and winks. She smiles back. When Tante Marie turns to leave the shop, Claude tosses Minique a palmier; she shoves it in her mouth before her aunt can catch her, tasting the rich butter and sugar spread across her tongue and into the pockets of her cheeks. Then they go to the boucher, where her aunt buys a small amount of mutton; it's never anything better than that, but at least they can afford some meat. Minique wishes they could eat beef more often, or even pork or goose. If they were any good at hunting, they could be eating dove, maybe even baked into a tourtière. If they were any good at fishing, they could be eating fresh fish. But she and her aunt aren't good at either of those things, and so they have to rely on what they can get in town.

For their last stop, they go to the general store, because her aunt wants to see if she can haggle the shopkeeper down on some fabric she's had her eye on. Minique hopes it's for her, for a new shift, because the one she's been wearing has turned grey and is starting to fray under the arms and around the neck. She makes sure no one ever sees it.

The store is busy enough that Minique feels uncomfortable standing at the counter alongside her aunt, who is gesturing with a strong, raw finger in the general direction of the bolts of cotton and linen. Instead, Minique floats over to the corner of the store where the windows are. She gets her face as close to the thick glass as she can without touching it, and watches the warped figures of people on the street outside. The day seems too bright, the colours of everyone making her eyes ache a little. There's a lady, her skirts splaying out behind her as the bubbles and swirls of the glass catch her clothing. There are two children, running through the divots and the dents. And there's a group of men, tall, made taller by the stretch of the window. As she watches, the men get larger as they move nearer, hats growing bigger and boots getting thicker.

That's when she hears it: a murmur that starts up among the people in the store, like the way birds all rustle at the first sign of a disturbance. Everyone has their eyes fixed on the window, craning their necks to look out onto the street. Minique chances a look back at her aunt, but Tante Marie is pretending not to notice, instead picking through the reams of rough, cheap cloth that the shopkeeper has brought down for her.

Coureurs des bois, she hears a woman behind her say, and that's what makes Minique's head whip back to the window. She presses her face to the glass, to take another look at them, to see the way they walk, the way they move, to see if it's different from the rest of Montréalers. So these are the runners of the woods, the men she's heard about but never seen out in polite society. *Coureurs des bois, coureurs des bois*—the words take on a movement the more the people behind her say them. The phrase slips out of the corners of tight mouths, slithers on the floor. But she can't pay it any mind, because her eyes are on the men and she can't look away.

They're just men. That's her first thought. The wood runners are just men. Not myth, not monster, as far as she can see. Maybe they're a little more muscular than the townspeople, maybe a little rougher around the edges, but they're men nonetheless. She watches as they clap one another on the back as they walk. They're brawny and bronzed and there are deep lines around their eyes and mouths. They wear moose-hide jackets, some with fringe, some with beads. Some of them have leather hats and moccasins. All of them have long rifles, loud voices, bearded faces. She's not particularly frightened because they're like her father, but she's also uncomfortable because of that reason.

She knows there's a difference between men and women. In church, she's been told again and again that the worst of the world has come from women, from that first woman who refused to be only a rib. From the woman who bathed in public, drew unwanted attention, and somehow caused the death of her husband. From the woman who just wanted to look one more time at her town before it was burned up, and who was turned into a pillar of salt. This lesson has been repeated again and again to everyone, but especially to girls. Minique sits and watches Father Etienne spit these words out: his face grows red, his saliva spraying. *Don't you dare*, he says without words. *Don't you dare think of stepping out of line. You are what you are, and if you reach for more, you're damning yourself and everyone around you.*

She watches as two of the coureurs des bois heft their packs over their shoulders and break off from the group, coming toward the entrance of the shop. The people behind her scatter so as not to look so suspicious, but Minique stays where she is. The roof of her mouth feels like something is tickling it. She wants to get a fingernail up there and scratch at the skin. Even before they come in the door, she can smell the smoke and oil on them. And she knows that rolled up in their packs are the furs that New France is built on, the brown pelts that course from here to the continent like blood from a cut.

Minique's heart hammers in her chest as the door to the shop opens, and the room is filled with the scent of pine and fire and something alive and hot. The itching in her mouth explodes, and her head feels like a bee is inside of it, knocking around at full speed. She hasn't closed her eyes but she's also seeing things, almost like when she's about to fall asleep and she's imagining scenarios and watching them play out on the inside of her eyelids. The buzzing in her head gets louder, like there are more bees, and the itching on the top of her mouth is everywhere now, all across her tongue and teeth and the inside of her cheeks, hot, hot, hot. She takes a breath and she *sees* these men in the forest, sees their hands covered in blood as they skin beavers, ripping the fur from the shiny meat. She blinks hard to try to block it, but it doesn't work; there is brown and pink and red on her eyelids and in her mind and bouncing around her head, buzzing, buzzing, buzzing. She breathes harder through her mouth, trying not to be loud, and the sight keeps coming, not all in one go or smooth like when she imagines stories, but choppy, like bits and pieces flashing at her. She sees moccasins and men sleeping under canoes and calluses on the palms of hands and blood under fingernails. Scariest of all, somehow she knows that one of the men is nervous, because he hates talking to strangers and hates haggling even more, and the other one is bored, wanting to get back to the woods and to his family. Their feelings each have a taste to her: one hot and bitter, one cooler and thicker. She panics. Is she being possessed? Has the devil suddenly gotten his hands on her? Or is this the holy spirit? Is this what it felt like at the Pentecost, with tongues

of flame on people's heads and their mouths speaking all the languages of the world all at once? Panic, sheer panic, like she could
open her mouth and something vast and dark would crawl out,
oozing its way around her and into the streets, like the St. Laurence.

Tante Marie's head snaps to look at her, and Minique wonders,
not for the first time, if her aunt can read minds. Minique straightens her spine and closes her mouth, trying to look as proper as she
can, and then the visions stop as abruptly as they started, and she's
left with a gentle hum in her ears and a hot feeling at the base of her
tongue, almost like she's going to throw up.

She breathes shakily, waiting for it to come back. But it doesn't.
Her dress is damp in the armpits and she feels like her face is red,
but no one else seems to notice. Everyone is pretending to be busy
with items in the store, avoiding one another's eyes.

Minique stares at the two men, trying to see her father in them.
She wishes she could walk right up to them and examine them up
close. Instead, all she can do is take one small step forward, and even
that is too much, because no one else in the shop is moving. Both of
the coureurs turn their heads to the right to look at her, their eyes
burning bright in their weathered faces. She is pinned in place near
the window; they stand near the counter, the length of two men away,
their heads and necks and shoulders angled toward her, but their
bodies are frozen almost mid-movement, legs braced in a stride. She
can't see their mouths through the tangle of their beards, but the gazes
catch her in place. She wonders what she looks like, standing stock-
still, breathing heavily through her nose. They turn fully toward her,
staring, and what started out as the expression of a predator when it
sees prey has turned into one of mild amusement. She realizes she's

the only person in this whole store who's looking back at them, and that means they're able to single her out. It takes all of her strength not to blink or look away, but she also finds that she doesn't want to. This is a challenge: *Who are you to stare*, their eyes ask her, *to look so boldly*, and the voice in her head yells back—*I am Minique!*—and the room becomes only the three of them, becomes a forest at the rims of her eyes and around her nostrils and at the back of her throat, the green creeping in from all corners, unceasing and unyielding—

Her aunt drops a bolt of fabric on the floor. Everyone jumps a little, and the trance is broken. By the time Minique collects herself, the men are starting to pull rich beaver pelts out of their packs, taking up so much space that all of the other customers are forced back. Minique looks at the piles of shiny brown fur, but Tante Marie is at her side before she can do anything else.

"Don't," her aunt says in a low voice. As if she knows that Minique is tempted to run her fingers through the pelts like she used to when she was a child and her father was home more often. The softness and the smell of oil remind her of that time.

She glances up, and Tante Marie looks pale and scared. Around her, Minique can hear the whisper of the other people, voices like the slither of snakes. She wants to stay and listen. But Tante Marie pulls at her hand and the two of them are swept out into the street, and Minique is blinking in the watery light, breathing in and out as slow as she can.

At home, Minique follows her aunt around, trying to figure out how to word her question. She's distracted by the taste of Tante

Marie, rough and sour in her mouth. She's confused and scared and overwhelmed by all the things she can sense and see and smell and feel now. It's like a set of doors has been flung open and she's not able to shut them. Her food tastes different: oatmeal's texture is almost unbearable on her tongue, while she can't get enough of the salt of dried meat. The feeling of her clothes on her skin bothers her, like her body is sensitive all over. Things that never interested her—the grain of the wooden kitchen table, the weave of her bed linens, the way clouds spatter across the sky at different times of the day—suddenly start to enthrall her. She wants to cry a little bit, and also jump up and down, and maybe also run outside the town walls to where there are no people, nothing she can smell and see. But for now, she has something to do.

"Those men," she starts, and her aunt turns to her from where she's standing at the stove, makes a motion with one hand that looks like she's chopping at something. Minique can still smell her: angry and, strangely and suddenly, afraid.

"Quiet," Tante Marie says.

"No, I can't," Minique answers like vomit, and she thinks she might actually cry. "Everyone's always keeping secrets, Tante."

Her aunt stands still, backlit by the afternoon light struggling to come in from behind the covered windows. She hums softly. The encounter in the shop has peeled back part of her shell. Minique somehow knows that this is her one chance.

"My father?"

"Is a coureur des bois," her aunt answers, softer than Minique expected. "And a poor one, Minique."

"What?" Does *poor* mean without money? Does it mean bad?

"He thought that he would find glory." The word is brittle; her aunt sighs. "He found something else instead."

"What else?" Minique frowns. "What's *else*?"

Her aunt shakes her head. Whatever it is that Minique's father found—insanity? Drinking? Something without a name?—Tante Marie doesn't want to talk about it.

"What about my mother?"

Her aunt hesitates a little longer before answering this question. She takes a breath before she starts speaking, seems to think again, and then releases it. Takes another breath: "You were dealt a bad hand."

What does that mean? Minique wants to yell. *Why is everyone always talking in riddles around here?* She sees Jeanne in her mind's eye, the unfocused nature of her eyes and the thin lullaby she sang. Was her mother also not right in the head? She thinks: *Is this what New France does to women? Makes them all scared or broken or unwilling to talk about anything?* The thought is almost too much to bear; it makes her sad, the idea of women being shipped across the ocean, trapped, sick, some dying, all of them with no choice but to go to a new land and be married off. She wishes she could see it, see how it felt. It's scary, and horrible, but she wants to know what her mother went through. What her father saw when he looked at her.

Minique wants to sit her aunt down and try to talk to her like she's a grown-up. She wants to say, *Tante, tell me what it was like here as a young woman.* Minique knows that Tante Marie and her brother came over when they were only sixteen and eighteen, but she doesn't know why they left France, why her father married but Tante Marie has seemingly been alone her whole life. She doesn't know what her aunt did before her mother died—if she lived with her brother and his wife, or if she was somewhere else. There's so much she wants to ask her, but she's scared because she doesn't have the words, and she's also frightened of what she might learn.

Instead, she just nods, once, and her aunt returns the action, and then Minique turns around and walks upstairs to her room where she lies down, face first, in her bed, so tired she can barely take her apron off before she falls asleep.

That night, she dreams about the outside. The world that exists beyond the town. *The real world*, the voice in her head says, even in sleep, and Minique knows this to be true. Because what's been done with the town, it's not right. It's not natural to carve out a living in the middle of a land that doesn't want them.

She dreams about the way leaves sound when they rustle against one another. Like a wind has started from somewhere around her ankles, and slowly it rises, rises, rises, until all the trees begin to hiss, speaking a language she doesn't understand. *Tell me*, she wants to say, but when she opens her mouth all that comes out is a growl, and as she tries harder and harder, the wind gets stronger until it's so loud that she wouldn't be able to hear her own voice even if she screamed. The trees bow under the pressure of it, and her hair tangles around her face, her skirts around her legs, and then she wakes up.

From somewhere, she thinks she can hear a howling, like a wind dying. Her father once told her that a wolf's howl can be heard across an entire forest. She thinks of her aunt. She thinks of the coureurs in the store, their animal eyes. She turns over and goes back to sleep.

Since the incident in the store three weeks ago, the world is different for Minique. The first day back at school, she nearly gags from everything that hits her all at once. She has to sit at her desk and taste one girl's nearly-pissing-herself anxiety about being asked to answer a question, another girl's red, spiky anger over her sister borrowing her stockings, another girl's dark, tarry fear about her father. Minique can't stay thinking about that too long because it's so frightening and makes her shiver. She learns, through rocky trial and error, that opening her mouth makes everything glister, the colours brighter and sounds louder and touch harder, while breathing only through her nose makes everything seem normal, if just for a little while. So she becomes even quieter in class, only answering if she absolutely has to.

At home, Minique walks around the house in her boots, stomping as loud as she dares. She does her chores, but not well. She weeds the little garden at the back of their house as fast as she can, throwing the clods of dirt and plants into the corner of their lot. She sweeps the house violently, leaving dust in the corners. When her aunt wants her to help out with the food, Minique chops the onions and the potatoes sloppily, leaving them in uneven chunks. Tante Marie looks at her sideways, but doesn't say anything.

———

One morning, Minique dresses as she always does and leaves the house to walk to school, but instead of turning right, she turns left, and then slips down one of the alleys. It's a sudden relief to be off the main street: there are too many people there and, as a result, too many smells and sensations. When she's outside, the sky seems brighter and the mud smells deeper and the air seems heavier around her head and in her nose, and she can't help but gasp and then lose herself in the storm of whoever is passing by at that moment.

She's gotten much better at finding her way around the town, with all of Daniel's help, and it takes little effort to make herself disappear. *Just look like you know what you're doing*—Daniel's voice echoes in her head. She can't stand the idea of sitting in a classroom today.

She walks faster as she gets closer to the walls, and in the middle of people coming into the town either for school or for some kind of work or errand, she slides out, against the stream. She follows her feet on their familiar walk, past the houses, up the hill, to the orchard. She wants to hop up into a tree and hide for a few hours. But when she trots down the hill, she can see that there are people in the orchard. Two of them: a teenaged boy and girl, walking hand in hand down one of the rows. As Minique squints at them, they lean their heads together and kiss, and then it turns into something else, quickly, something more hurried. The girl presses the boy up against one of the trees, and his hands start messing with her skirts, and that's when Minique sticks her tongue out in disgust and changes course. Instead of heading into the orchard and taking a path that would bring her right by the two of them grabbing at each other, she walks around the farthest edge, where she can't be seen through the apple trees. This path, though, means she's closer to the forest than she's ever been.

The muffled sounds of the couple are far behind her. She's not quite sure where to go now, though, caught between the forest trees and the apple trees. Minique forces herself to look into the woods. For all the times Daniel has dragged her and Barbe around, they've never entered the forest. They haven't even come near to it.

She walks to the edge, where the grass ends and the trees start. It's almost a straight line, and she imagines men, generations before her, clearing the land. The work must have been hard and back-breaking. Unpleasant, blister-making work, to force the land back.

Minique leans her head forward into the shade. She thought that all these trees were almost the same, but up close, she can see that there are dozens of different kinds, with different bark, leaves, or needles. Small trunks, or thick. Branches that sweep low to the ground, or are so high up even Daniel wouldn't be able to climb them. Her body is warm from being in the sun, but the back of her neck and head are cool, sheltered by the forest. She takes a scared sniff, trying to see if her strange new power works here. It doesn't; she sees nothing. But the smell is foreign and familiar to her at the same time. It's green and deep, tickles at her nose. And it's a memory, something that stuck to her father's coat and his hair. It's the same smell that the coureurs in the general store brought in with them. It's snakey and wriggling and almost wet. She takes another deep breath, and steps a foot forward, her boot sinking in green velvet moss. She lifts her other foot up, about to step completely into the forest, about to see if all the stories she's heard in the schoolyard are true, to see if there are ghosts waiting, when she hears a branch break.

Minique scrambles away, losing her footing as she slips on the moss. She trips backward out of the trees, falling onto her ass, her breath knocked out of her. She sits there for a moment, listening, wondering if she imagined it—but she didn't. The sounds are getting nearer, and she has lost the ability to move her body. It could be big; maybe it's a bear or a wolf. Something that could knock her head off with one paw. Or maybe it's something worse. Minique wants to close her eyes, but she knows at the very least not to look away from whatever's coming for her. She stares into the forest, where she sees a flash of red, a movement in between the trees. She curses Daniel for putting that stupid idea in her head. She curses her own stupid- ity for skipping school. It feels unfair that something is coming for her in broad daylight; shouldn't a monster be creeping around in the dark? Thinking about a monster, of Daniel's gleeful words, makes her throat burn, and she's afraid that if she opens her mouth, she'll throw up all over herself—

Suddenly, a woman comes into view from between the trees, a basket under her arm. She has an apron around her waist, and a few streaks of dirt on her face, but her hair is still in its thick, shiny braid, tied at the end with a red ribbon. Minique gapes up at her. The sick feeling in her throat creeps back down. She swallows her spit.

"Oh," the woman says, shifting her basket to her hip to hold it steady. "What are you doing here?"

"I thought you were a monster," Minique says without thinking, and then feels embarrassed for it.

"A monster?" The woman's eyebrows rise a little bit. She thinks for a moment. She looks familiar to Minique. "Some people might think that, maybe."

Minique doesn't ask what that means. She stands up, trying to be as graceful as possible under the woman's gaze. She dusts her palms off on her skirt, shifting her weight from foot to foot, trying to shift enough to the side to see what's in the basket.

The woman moves the basket into view, pulling the cloth off of it, and Minique flushes again, ashamed of being so obvious. But her embarrassment is overtaken by her curiosity, and she leans over to see—

"Fiddleheads, yarrow, cedar," the woman says, pointing first to some plants curled up like little commas, then to some flowers, then to some greens.

Minique says the names to herself. She's never heard of any of them. Why is this woman walking into the woods to collect weeds? When she looks up at her, she finds the woman looking back, as if expecting Minique to ask. Minique just opens and closes her mouth a few times, like a fish, and the woman exhales a little, shifting the basket back to her hip, covering it back up.

Before Minique can muster up the courage to ask something, anything at all, the woman turns and starts walking the path back to town.

As she walks away, Minique realizes: she didn't taste like anything.

She can pick out Barbe and Daniel even through the jumble of jaggedy feelings. Barbe smells like things that are light and airy, like clean dry wool and cream froth, the scent of Claude's palmiers an hour after they come out of the oven. Minique never sees what Barbe is thinking; there are no violent images that flash in her head. She still can't figure out if those are really things that are in people's minds, or if her own mind is trying to make sense of everything and has painted its own scenes.

Daniel, on the other hand, is all image and movement. But it's simple: thoughts about learning to whittle better skittles or climb the highest tree in the orchard, wanting to smoke tobacco even though Claude has forbidden it, wanting to see how far he can piss into the river. He tastes like sweat and green trees, the fat of meat and the salt of saliva.

Both of them are comforting. She can cope with seeing Daniel's scattershot thoughts, his attention bouncing from one item or person to another. And Barbe exists as a thread of calmness, milk and honey, underneath it all.

Daniel tries to see if Barbe and Minique will flinch when he's in their faces, waving his hands around, gesturing wildly, his voice getting higher and higher the more excited he gets. His scent usually whips around them, agitated and hot and prickly in Minique's nose and on the roof of her mouth. It tastes like something too ripe and yet also hard to chew. She tries to keep her mouth closed when he gets into one of his manias, but it's difficult when she has to keep telling him to get away, go away, *get away from me Daniel, you're bothering me!*

Daniel's fancies run from the nasty (a dead squirrel poked with a stick until its stomach bursts; *you should have seen the maggots that came out!*) to the boring (sitting on the wharf watching the men work; *I've never seen so many barrels in one place at a time, you both should come with me next time*) to the spooky (ghost stories that the boys tell each other in the schoolyard when the brothers aren't listening; *Martin swears to god that he saw something in his attic, he's invited me over next week to go searching for it*). If they let him, he'd never stop talking; he'd run their entire conversation, all day every day. He'd let himself be the leader of their group. The older he gets, the more annoying he also seems to become. Maybe it's because he's starting to become more like a man; his voice has started to hit different pitches, sometimes strange and low and sometimes squeaking. He's started to grow taller than them, too, a marked difference from when they were children.

But there's something that hasn't changed, and that's his obsession with the woods and the things that might live in them. Today he's circling Barbe and Minique as they walk, kind of jigging, as he tries to tell them the most recent ghost story he's collected.

"What are you *talking* about?" Minique has to lean her head away from him because he's so close, his oily, excited face *right* there.

"Remember when I told you about the red monster?"

Minique frowns a bit. *The red monster?*

"Oh! The nain rouge," Barbe says, less perturbed at Daniel's shimmying around so close to them. He never seems to be able to stay still, no matter where they are or what they're doing.

Minique grimaces. She hates this particular story of his. It makes her ten times more uncomfortable than hearing about the ghost of some little girl in an attic. She knows that a house ghost could be real, but it's probably not; it's probably made up by some stupid boy who wants to get the attention and awe of his friends. And how can anyone prove a ghost is real, anyway? It's a floating bunch of mist, a nothing fog. But the nain rouge and any of Daniel's other stories about the things that may be living in the woods are harder for her to explain away. They're things that could leave tracks and scat. Even if they're not real, there are still stories that have existed about them for years and years and years. If the Indigenous people say something, it holds more weight for her. The settlers have only been in Montréal for a handful of decades. How do they know what's living alongside them in the forests and the rivers?

Minique shivers. Daniel's smell has turned rich and burred, like how she imagines spices from the other side of the world would taste if she ever got the chance to try them.

"You always talk about the nain rouge," she says, shoving him away from her. He ricochets back, unbothered.

"Yeah, so?"

"It's boring!"

Daniel bounces around on the balls of his feet. "It's not boring, you just don't like it."

Barbe interjects. "Where did you hear about it this time?"

"My friend Luc, he said that his cousin heard it from some of the Iroquois when they came into town. Except they didn't call it the nain rouge, but he can't remember what they called it. But that doesn't matter. It was the same thing, you know? So if we've been hearing years of stories about it, I know it must be real!" He stops and gets a look on his face like he's concentrating, then belches. "Anyway, apparently it can grow as tall as a tree when it's angry, and some Indigenous people have seen it dancing around someone who is sick and going to die." Daniel continues his little jig, fists on hips, like he's doing the devil dance, too.

"Tante, have you heard of the nain rouge?"

Her aunt is stirring a pot of onion soup on the stove. In a rare moment, she let Minique sit with her and help with slicing the onions. Minique dashed away the tears of the chore without saying a word, because she didn't want to be sent out of the kitchen and miss this opportunity.

"The what?" Minique doesn't miss the very slight delay in her aunt's question. "A what?"

"A—the nain rouge. A nain rouge," Minique repeats, feeling embarrassed.

Her aunt turns around and Minique sees that she's composed herself. She sighs, and picks at the tabletop with her fingernail.

"Where did you hear about that?"

"Daniel."

"I'm not surprised," her aunt says. "He's nothing but trouble." Minique notices that she doesn't say anything about Daniel's mother. She doesn't continue the sentence and say *he's nothing but trouble, just like his mother.* "What is it?"

Minique shrugs. "A monster that lives in the woods."

"What kind of monster?"

"Aren't you supposed to tell me monsters don't exist?"

Her aunt braces both hands on the table and looks at Minique. Minique gets ready for a telling-off, but instead her aunt reaches out to grab her hand—softly, not like she's trying to teach Minique a lesson, but like she's trying to reassure her. "Minique," she says, "monsters are real. They're just not always what you think they are."

She looks up at her aunt's face and sees that it's open. Minique parts her lips and breathes in, tasting that sweetness that sometimes is present when her aunt does something out of character.

"But the nain rouge," her aunt continues, her face closing up in an instant, her hands gripping her apron, "is not real. God only knows where Daniel heard that."

"The Iroquois. And the coureurs des bois talk about it, I think," Minique says, and her aunt looks at her, eyebrows raised.

"Stay away from those men. All of you."

Minique falters, fiddling with her fingernail, before deciding to speak again. "Why does everyone hate the coureurs des bois?"

Her aunt sighs, then pulls out a chair to sit at the table, leaving the pot to bubble unattended on the stove. Minique looks at her in surprise. Tante Marie can likely hear her unasked question: *Why do people hate my father and why do they hate me?*

"I wouldn't say they hate the coureurs," her aunt says slowly. "Although I can see how it seems that way to you."

"Everyone acts like they're the devil."

Tante Marie smiles a little at that. "To some, they are." She rests her chin in her hand. "It's a strange time for the fur trade. Coureurs are illegal; the church and the government both have banned them from working."

Minique's confusion must show on her face.

"But—"

"But your father? He doesn't care. The coureurs don't care. They were forbidden at the beginning and they did it anyway, and they're forbidden now and they'll do it still." Her aunt traces her mouth with a finger. "Lately, though, I've heard of something else coming. That there's a new kind of fur trader, a licensing system. So that's why people stare at us. And that's why the customers in the general store were so taken aback by the coureurs des bois. Why it seems like neighbours are at each other's throats sometimes. Change." She stands up. "And you must remember that the coureurs des bois spend time in the forest, with the aboriginal people, and this makes them untrustworthy in people's eyes. Never underestimate the strength of race hatred. Your father—" She stops, shuffles a little. Goes back to stirring.

My father what? Minique wants to jump up and grab at her aunt's arm, to beg her to continue. But she knows that will accomplish nothing. She's been given more than she expected already.

She thinks, for the first time ever, of her father as an explorer, as someone brave. She's jealous of him for that, at least. That he was courageous enough to go out and try to make a living by whatever means possible. That he turned his work into food on the table, wood in the stove, cloth for skirts and blouses. And yes, the porridge is poor and the clothes scratch at her skin and the house feels too cold, but she's under a roof and alive and doesn't feel like she's going to faint from hunger. She can appreciate her father for that. But he's just another thing that lives in the woods. Minique wishes she had a father like Claude, who feeds her cookies and has a laugh that makes her feel warm, and never yells. She even wishes her father lived in town, just so she had someone else to talk to. But her father has left her and her aunt mostly alone, barely bothering to speak with them even when he's back, and she can't find it within herself to forgive him for that.

The sun is touching the tops of the apple trees when Daniel pulls a bottle out of his coat, shouting "Look!" and waving it around like a prize.

Barbe shrieks with embarrassed laughter.

"Daniel!" Minique wants to smack him in the head. It's a bottle of whisky, about half-finished. It's not easy to get liquor. It's mostly imported from other places and so it's much rarer than beer.

"My father got it as a gift a few months ago, and I hid it from him," Daniel says, clinking his nails against the glass. Sometimes, when he turns his head and Minique can see his side profile, she can see the man he'll become. His nose, the edge of his chin, shows a grown-up version of himself waiting to burst out. He's the one most eager to be older. Minique and Barbe know that there's less power waiting for them as adults.

"We're going to get in trouble."

They'll get in trouble for more than just drinking, considering all three of them have skipped school. The day is too nice to sit indoors; the yellow light called to them before they even made it halfway to their schoolhouses. Minique wonders how angry Tante Marie will be with her; ever since their discussion a few weeks ago, they've been warmer around each other, but Minique isn't sure if the detente extends to truancy.

"If he didn't notice it missing three weeks ago, he's not going to miss it now," Daniel says, yanking the cork out with his teeth, and waving the bottle under their noses. A strong smell wafts out, and Minique wants to cough. Barbe wiggles her eyebrows, reaching for the bottle, braver by far. Minique watches as she takes a swig, and the light filters through the bottle and hits her face. Barbe looks like she has a halo, like she's an angel or a ghost, something unearthly and too good for them. She swallows the liquor like it's honey. Minique, thinking it must not be so bad, reaches for it and takes a big mouthful. Her eyes bug out of her head and Daniel claps a hand over her lips, preventing her from spewing it out; he's faster than she gives him credit for. She has no choice but to swallow, and as soon as she does, she retches, feeling like steam is coming out of her ears. Daniel laughs out loud and grabs the bottle for himself, gulping from it.

"That's disgusting," Minique says. "Barbe, Jesus, how did you not cough?"

Barbe shrugs. "It tastes kind of nice."

Minique and Daniel meet eyes, always forgetting the strong, strange stuff Barbe is made of. Sometimes Minique thinks she'll last the longest out of the three of them.

They melt into the branches, passing the bottle back and forth until the whisky goes down and down and down, until there are only a few fingers left. Minique's world blurs at the edges, and her stomach is a pleasant fire. Even her throat and lips feel warm, the same as the skin across her forehead and her cheekbones. She sees why people can fall into this, why her father likes it; it seems like it would be easy to use alcohol to wipe away the rest of the world and all your worries. Everything seems lighter and funnier: the way Barbe is straddling one of the branches, using the bark to scratch an itch on the back of her thigh; the way Daniel is trying to juggle two apples. Minique and Barbe watch him as he unloops an arm from the limb of the tree he's hanging on to, his head tilted back as he concentrates. Minique knows where this is going before Daniel does, and so it's no surprise when he wobbles suddenly, shrieking almost as high as Barbe might, and then falls backward onto the soft grass below, his apples falling down on him, one landing on his chest and the second bouncing off of his head. Minique and Barbe scream with laughter as he scowls up at them, and Minique feels herself slipping, too. She has a little more dexterity than Daniel does, and she reaches out with both arms to grab the branch in front of her, swinging back and forth, the bark digging into her palms until she lets herself down onto the grass. She's still laughing uncontrollably, pointing at Daniel, who growls like a dog and lunges up from his resting place to grab at her, and then she shrieks in earnest as she's thumped back into the grass. Daniel sits on top of her, trying to pin her down, but she's wilier than she looks and she twists in his grasp, kicking up with both legs and getting a knee under his body. She manages to knee him close to the groin, and the close call makes him groan, half rolling off of her. For a moment, she feels guilt, until he rises back up to pin her.

"Say you're sorry or I'll spit in your mouth."

"You're revolting!"

"Say it!"

Minique yells *no, no, no*, and Daniel collects his saliva in his lip, makes a big show of it, and she thinks she's doomed, until a slender arm hooks itself sharply around Daniel's neck and yanks him backward.

"Barbe!" Minique shouts her name like a victory cry. Daniel's eyes are wide and surprised as he goes down, and Minique jumps up, hitching up her skirts, and follows him as he rolls back onto Barbe, who is grinning like a devil. The three of them grapple like six-year-old boys, yelping and howling into the grass, someone occasionally hissing as they roll over an apple.

When they finally tire, the three of them are lying in a circle, their heads touching. The whisky has made its way through them, and they all raise their arms and legs in tandem, testing to see if they still work.

"Daniel," Minique says, reaching out with her hand and patting it on his face as if to check that he's actually there.

"Yes?" The word is slurred.

"What do people say about my father?"

He's quiet for a moment, and she can hear him and Barbe breathing.

"I don't—"

"Please," she says.

He grumbles a little. "You won't like it." When she doesn't protest, he sighs. "I heard he has another family."

Minique sits up, the world tilting for a moment. She stares down at Daniel. "In town?"

"No," he says slowly, like she's a bit stupid. "In the woods."

Tante Marie's words come back to her: *never underestimate the strength of race hatred*. She thinks of the moccasins. Of her aunt asking about *children* in a tired sort of voice.

"Oh," she says. *Oh*, she thinks. *Oh—I'm not enough*. Maybe if she were sober, she would be spinning more, but all she can do right now is just think oh, oh, oh. Oh shit. Oh, maybe that's also why people whisper about her. Oh, is that the secret that everyone's been keeping? Oh, does the other family know about her? Oh, oh, oh.

Minique can feel queasiness creeping in, panic building, when she feels Barbe's hand worm over Daniel's body and grab her own hand in a grip firmer than Minique would have expected. Daniel winds an arm around her neck, holding her in an awkward but fierce kind of a hug, and she feels herself come back to earth through their touch. The world stops whirling around her; the heat recedes. The taste of vomit on the roof of her mouth lessens. The sky looks a little clearer.

She has thoughts to think. She has questions to ask, if she's ever brave enough. But for now, she can smell the green of the grass, an apple that they crushed somewhere along the way, the grease of Daniel's moose-hide jacket, the sugary scent of Barbe's hair. For now, the three of them lie there, waiting for the world to stop rocking back and forth, for the headaches to come and punish them like they probably deserve, for the bees to stop humming and the grass to stop whispering and the sun to start its slow, inevitable sink below the tops of the trees beyond the orchard.

"If you pull that bodice any tighter I'll kill you."

Barbe laughs from behind her but doesn't let up.

"I mean it, Barbe, I'll club you over the head with the basin." Minique stares at the wall, her palms damp with worry. Her breathing feels short, even without the tight clothing. "I don't want to wear a bodice. I *said* I didn't. I don't even want to go to this dance," she continues.

Barbe laughs again, used to her anxiety as gruffness, and with a surprising amount of strength yanks the bodice as tight as she can, forcing Minique to let out all her breath in a sigh. When she's all laced in, she takes a look in Barbe's hand mirror, apprehensively. She doesn't want to go to the dance; that's not a lie. She doesn't want to get dressed up to try to impress people who don't like her. Barbe begged her to, at one point getting down on her knees in the middle of the street as they were walking to the boulangerie, pleading in one big rush of breath: "I won't be allowed to go if you don't, my parents don't trust me, even though I'm seventeen, which is old enough to get married, so I don't know why they wouldn't, you have to come, you have to, please Minique." Minique knows Barbe's parents see her as an anchor for their daughter, and she can't argue with that. Without her, it's entirely possible some man would talk sweet and silly in Barbe's ear, tell her stories about the chasse-galerie or water cats or deer-women, tell her that he could give her everything, and Barbe, in her innocence and her goodness, with her belief in people, would get all wide-eyed and wondering and that would be the end of that.

Dances are rare. Mostly they happen when everyone, save for the highest-class families in town, gets fed up with the bad weather or the newest influx of missionaries or just day-to-day life, and someone offers up the first floor of their house or their shop, and someone else finds a band, and someone else says they'll bring some food, and someone else says they'll bring some beer or maybe some whisky. News of it spreads around the fountains and at the counters of stores and at the inn. This is when Montréalers work best together: trying to keep something a secret from the Jesuits, Ursulines, and Sulpicians. Even the most pious of her neighbours—her former classmate, Marie-Anne, who keeps her rosary clutched in her sweaty hands at all times, praying in an unstable mutter that makes her look like she's always talking to herself; the boucher's wife, Marie-Ursule, who likes to show off her leather-bound psalter whenever she's in a shop and has a captive audience—still look forward to a dance. It shows the two-facedness of the town: very few are completely righteous, and very few are complete heathens. Everyone has two sides to them. People want to believe that god is looking out for them in this harsh new land, but they also realize that their lives are likely to be short and, if they don't make their own fun, mostly unpleasant.

Minique doesn't dislike the idea of dances because people let their hair down; she dislikes the idea because she doesn't want to be paraded around like a prize pig. She feels itchy in her own skin whenever she has to pin her hair up and wear a tight bodice. She hates the idea of standing against a wall and waiting for some man to beckon to her. But this is her first dance, and Barbe begged so plaintively, and she has to admit that a part of her wants to see her neighbours doing a contredanse.

Tonight, the dance is in the back room of the inn, a place Minique and most of the women of the town have never been, which feels particularly illicit and therefore is making people particularly excited. It's the largest space that could be found, and there's a back entrance they can dart in and out of, so no one sees young ladies of at least some repute going through the front door. Minique's heard that the door between the front and back rooms will be bolted, and the curtains will be drawn.

Barbe promised the dance was going to be small, but now it seems as though everyone in town sixteen or older will be there, even though the night is dry and cold. For some of the young women, it'll be a night of husband-hunting. The odds are good for them: men still greatly outnumber women. The town smells like men, tastes like men, teems with men singing in the street and drinking in the bar and standing with their fists on their hips, their legs wide and their eyes searching for the next fortune to be made. Minique panics thinking about a man trying to grab her for a dance, putting his hands on her without her permission. Trying to cajole her into being a wife. A prisoner.

"You look very nice," Barbe says from over her shoulder, where she's tying a ribbon around her own neck. Her voice pulls Minique out of her thoughts; she realizes she's staring at her own reflection with a look of terror.

"I look stupid." She's not used to looking at herself in a mirror. Dark eyes like two holes burned in a sheet, clammy skin. Even her hair, pulled back from her face for once, doesn't impress her; the dark colour only seems to make her look paler.

"You do not, you look good." Barbe shoved her into a chair and insisted on combing her hair out from its usual lazy braid, which Minique normally would wrap into a sloppy bun and shove beneath a bonnet. Tonight, though, Barbe has carded out the snarls and done some sort of magic. Minique pats at the back of her head and feels a glossy bun made of curls.

"Am I going to wear a bonnet over this?"

Barbe shakes her head. She is resplendent, her blond hair pulled back and her cheekbones high and sharp. She has a new dress on, one Minique hasn't seen before, something blue and frilly. She looks so beautiful that Minique thinks her parents' worries about her getting scooped up and spirited away might be well founded. "No bonnets!"

Minique whistles through her teeth. "That's trouble."

"We're going to wear wool hats for the walk over, anyway," Barbe says with a shrug. "And your hair looks nice, and you'll be all hot from dancing, so what's the point?"

"I'm not going to dance."

"You will."

"I don't know the steps."

"You'll learn!"

"No one ever taught me," Minique says, keeping her eyes on the mirror and not on Barbe. She doesn't want to see any pity there. Barbe comes up behind her and puts her hand over Minique's, tilts the mirror up so that they're meeting each other's gaze.

"I'll teach you."

———

They run on the way over, keeping their footsteps light, holding on to each other and trying not to laugh as their shoes skid every so often on a patch of ice. *Perpetual winter,* Claude calls this weather, but Minique likes it in a way because it gives you an excuse to touch people and nestle in. People think summer is the season of love, because women wear fewer petticoats and men have bare calves when they're outside working and forearms gleam with sweat. But really, winter seems to Minique like the real season for love, because in the face of long, dark nights, there's nothing else to do except peel away a person's layers.

When Barbe flings open the inn's back door, Minique is met face on by a wall of warmth, and the smell of exertion: sweat and fire and the yeast of beer and the dust that gets shot into the air when heels hit the floorboards and palms hit the tabletops. She half expects the entire operation to screech to a halt and all eyes to shift to her, but no one stops even for a second. And why would they? Couples reel around each other in measured circles, grasping hands and crossing feet to the sound of a few violins, a few flageolets, a beat-up guitar that seems to be in want of tuning, and more than half a dozen jaw harps. Someone is also playing a drum, the beat deep, not so much heard as felt through the floorboards.

"Close the door!"

Barbe grins and heeds the shout, slamming the door shut behind them before Minique has time to panic.

With the door closed, the music seems ever louder. And it's music like Minique has never heard before: it's not a dirge, nor a hymn, not meant to inspire piety or fear. Instead, it's rollicking, punctuated by shrieks of laughter and whoops when the musicians undertake a particularly complicated run. It swells and grows outward, looping around everyone. She can't help but smile at the feeling of it reverberating up through the soles of her shoes, through her hips and her shoulders. It never ends; when one song seems to be drawing to a close, the musicians launch into a new tune effortlessly. The dancers keep going for as long as they can, sometimes switching partners with the gesture of a chin or a flick of the head, sometimes staggering off the dance floor to grab a beer and press the cool mug to their forehead after drinking half the contents.

And so many people. The room is packed with people, all of whom are *smiling*. This is what surprises her the most—everyone looks happy. The other women aren't wearing bonnets either, so she can see the shine of their hair in the candlelight; the men aren't buttoned up to the neck, so she can see the sweat on their collarbones. She wants to open her mouth and taste them all, but she's worried it'll be too much. Over the past five years, she's gotten better at figuring out how to use her power, this strange curse, but mostly person by person, or in small groups. Large gatherings—like mass, or this, so radically different from people layered into pews—prove to be too much of a storm of feeling. It gets hard to separate people's emotions yarn by yarn, like she has been learning to do. Every time she has to speak to a merchant or a neighbour or a Jesuit, as unpleasant as it always is, she tries to take a little of them in and explore the ridges and borders of their feelings. She's learning what each emotion tastes like, what colours they hold. Everyone is a little bit different, but the undercurrents remain the same, the deep core of each sentiment. Still, it exhausts her, probing into and sorting through people's thoughts and worries and pleasures.

It forces her to feel things she never would and often never wants to. She'll have to be careful tonight not to get so winded that she has to breathe through her mouth.

She sees a woman in the doorway that leads to the front room of the inn. She's leaning against the jamb, arms and legs crossed like a man. Her black braid is pulled over one shoulder, and she has a towel thrown over the other. Couples dance past her, never bumping into her, always keeping her safe, like a filled cauldron, like a holy artifact. The long braid is the same as it was that morning five years ago, but there's no red ribbon tied around the end of it this time. She has an apron around her waist, but there's no dirt on her face and no basket of fiddleheads on her hip.

Minique has seen plenty of women shrink in a crowd, roll their shoulders in and try to make themselves smaller. Men don't do it. And this woman doesn't do it. She keeps her shoulders pulled back and her neck straight, her head tall, as she looks around the room with burning-coal eyes. She refuses to shrink. Minique wonders if this is also what she's like when she's out in town, running errands, being forced to interact with people who silently judge her and talk about her behind her back. This woman holds a majesty in her body, and Minique covets it.

Barbe notices Minique staring. "That's Anne," she says. It suddenly makes sense that Minique has seen her around town only a handful of times since that incident at the edge of the woods. Anne operates on a different schedule than Minique, existing in the night, dark and gleaming like the way the low light is shining off her hair. She must be about fifteen years older than Minique at most, but she looks sharp and ageless, her eyes flicking over the crowd like a bird of prey's but her mouth rounded into a small smile. She's moving in place, swaying back and forth to the music, like she wants to get out on the floor and dance.

Minique knows nothing about dancing. Her aunt doesn't believe in it, as far as she knows, and her father didn't teach her. And she didn't get any guidance from her classmates, most of whom didn't even want to brush against her in passing, let alone hold her hands during a contredanse. She's watched Daniel and Barbe bow to each other as a joke and go through the motions of a bourrée, but she can't remember any of the specific movements they made. And she knows that their pretending has nothing on what's happening in front of her now: propriety melting away into fluidity. The lingering of fingers on someone's wrist, right on the pulse; a woman's heavy eyes and the tilt of her head; the bob of a man's adam's apple as he watches his partner. Everyone's gaze is hot, each stare loaded with a purpose that Minique doesn't talk about or deal with in her day-to-day life but still understands in the basest part of her body.

Before Minique can ask about Anne, or the dance steps, or anything at all, Barbe springs into action, manoeuvring her around the edges of the room and finding them a table that's far back from the action. Not one minute after they've sat, a heavy, sweaty body slams down on the seat beside Minique, a mug of beer frothing over onto the tabletop.

"Daniel!"

Daniel is covered in a sheen of perspiration. His white linen shirt is gaping open at the neck, and he's grinning like a madman. He takes a slug of his beer before speaking, and uses the back of his hand to dash away the foam from his upper lip.

"You dragged her out?" He's looking at Barbe but jabs his thumb at Minique.

"Believe it," Barbe says.

"She got on her knees," Minique grumbles, feeling stupid all of a sudden.

Barbe nods. "I did get on my knees."

"Better keep your wits about you tonight or you'll end up on your knees again, Barbe," he says, wiggling his eyebrows.

"You're disgusting," Minique says. Barbe laughs; Minique isn't sure if she understood the joke, or if she just doesn't care.

"Yes," Daniel says with a laugh. "Do you want to dance, Barbe?"

"Oh yes!" Barbe shoots out of her seat and unloops her shawl from around her shoulders. "Can you hold on to this, Minique?" And then they're off to the dance floor, their faces close as they shout about god knows what, and Minique is yanked back to the past, to them walking together at sunset in between apple trees, murmuring to each other, and she wonders if she's missing something.

She runs the shawl between her fingers as she watches them stand across from each other, Daniel bowing and then Barbe curtseying in a pantomime kind of way. Then they step back, step forward, walk around each other in a circle. They reach out with their arms and grasp hands, turning. The line of dancers breaks into groups of four and they all fling their fists into the centre, turning themselves into a knot, walking and laughing for eight steps in one direction and then eight steps in the other. Not everyone is perfect; there's been a fair bit of drinking so far, so there are stumbling feet and tongues held between teeth in concentration and a few people are walking in the wrong direction but are laughing about it. The real fun happens when people break off into pairs, jigging in place. Some of the twosomes seem to take it as a challenge, spinning the tightest circles they can manage; some slow down and just look at each other, relishing the moment. When Minique looks over at Barbe and Daniel, she sees that they're both laughing, their eyes glittering in the orange cast of the candles. Barbe's hair is glowing like a crown. Even her bad eye has taken on the look of something majestic and otherworldly. Daniel seems as entranced as Minique is, and as he bends to say something to Barbe over the din of the music, Minique feels her gut twist. Worry bleeds into her: worry that if these two cross that line, she will be left behind.

I wish it wouldn't happen. The thought comes hard and fast before she can help it. *I don't want it to happen.* And then she feels guilty for wishing away a potential happiness for her friends, in this town where happiness is so rare and hard to come by, so she shakes her head to slingshot the thought right out of there. Then she picks up Daniel's mug of beer and takes a big sip, resisting the urge to gag. Then another sip. And one more.

Minique knows the beer is already taking effect, because a coureur sits down opposite her and she doesn't immediately get up and walk away.

For a minute, they sit and stare at each other. Minique finds it refreshing to be able to look without compunction, though whether that's because of the beer or the heat or the bonnet-less night, she's not sure. He's broad and bronze, his beard long, his hair longer. She's not sure how she knows that he's a coureur, but she does. Maybe it's the weather-worn cheeks, the callused hands. He reminds her of her father, and something seizes in her chest, but she staves it off by drinking more beer.

Over his head, she sees other coureurs have joined in the dancing. They must have just arrived. She's surprised there wasn't more of a commotion. Doesn't everyone hate them? Isn't that why she was pinched and prodded all of her childhood?

"I don't know how to dance," she says out of nowhere, her eyes still over her coureur's head but her words directed to him. She feels him laugh more than she hears it, and then she snaps her eyes back to his face. She expects to see snideness there, but sees only a wide, pleasant smile.

"Do you want to learn?" His voice isn't that of a monster. He sounds like a man.

Minique opens her mouth for the first time that evening to sip air in. She sees him in her mind's eye, canoeing till his hands scab over and blisters burst and there's blood on his palms. She sees him speaking haltingly to the Wendat. She sees him running his fingers through the lushness of beaver pelts. She doesn't see enough to know if he's a bad person or a good person. But she sees enough to stand, placing Barbe's shawl on the bench, and hold out her hand, and he takes it and leads her to the floor.

It smells of smoked leather and salt. Minique lines up across from her partner and grimaces in apology as she clumsily breaks into the steps, a little behind the others. He doesn't seem to mind; the first time he pulls her in for a spin, his hand is large and sure on her lower back, and she sees the glint of his teeth as he smiles. No fangs there, nothing inhuman. Minique can't help but smile back, even as she trips over her own feet and he has to right her. But no one notices. No one is paying attention, and everyone is focusing on their own feet, their own partners, and their own wants. *This is a freedom*, she thinks, and then she has to stop thinking so much because it's slowing her legs down and she wants to keep up. She's a little distressed to realize that she wants to fit in for a night.

Her partner doesn't let her down. He twirls her with an expertise that surprises Minique, considering he must spend most of his time with other men. He guides her with strong arms, and grins when she apologizes for making mistakes, and then, when the song ebbs to a denouement, he gives a little bow and she's scooped up by another set of arms.

"Daniel!"

"I can't fucking believe you're out on the dance floor," Daniel says, gripping her around the waist and dancing her slowly on the spot, like they're newlyweds.

"Get off, you're all sweaty."

Daniel laughs and shakes his head like a dog, spraying her. She shrieks, pinching his side, and he relents. "Dance with me, though."

"Where's Barbe?"

"Some habitant got his hands on her. No, no, it's fine, Minique," he says as she cranes her head to look. "She's not as dumb as she looks."

"I know that," she says, flushing.

"You don't have to coddle her all the time."

"Oh, shut up and dance, then."

Daniel is a wilder dance partner than her unnamed coureur. Maybe it's the beer he's had, or his general enthusiasm for life, but he flings her around like a rag doll, and she has to flex the muscles in her arms and legs to keep up. But it's fun in a different way, because every time he spins her out, she feels like she's flying; there's a moment where she thinks he might let go or his grip might slip, and she'll ricochet off the tables.

By the time Barbe grabs her, Minique's throat is raw from all the laughing. A mug of beer has been passed up and down the line of dancers, with everyone taking hurried sips, and she has wetness on her upper lip that she keeps trying to swipe off with her tongue. The room has gotten messier and hotter: women are rolling down their stockings and throwing them into the corners, men are shucking vests and scarves. Barbe is grinning wildly and sets up across from Minique like she's a man; Minique looks from side to side but no one seems to care. She sees couples pressing their hands together like a kind of promise. She sees Anne standing on a stool in the corner and good-naturedly yelling out instructions at all the dancers. She sees Daniel by the musicians, talking to a few coureurs, his hands animated and his face lit up.

When they start dancing, Barbe gets as close as she can to Minique on every spin and kisses her on the cheek with moist lips, and Minique can feel the smile against her skin. When they twirl, they put their arms around each other's necks and hold each other close. Minique feels Barbe's heart leaping in triumph against her own chest, and she vows to never, ever forget this moment. That no matter what happens in the future, she will know that at least for one night, they were young and boisterous, vital and present and screaming with laughter just to prove to the new world that they were alive, alive, alive.

Daniel walks home with them, and the three of them weave through the streets, trying to stifle their giggles. They've all thrown their layers back on haphazardly, and so the cold seeps in a little more than it normally would, but they huddle together to fight it off. Barbe's stockings are sliding down her legs and her hair is half pulled out of its bun. Daniel is wearing a hat that is certainly not his own. Minique is trying to feel a little dread for the ire she knows she'll face at the hands of her aunt when she tries to creep quietly back into their house, but she can't dredge it up. It's nothing she can't handle; tonight was somehow, miraculously, worth it.

The three of them stand outside Barbe's house, holding hands in a loose circle. Minique feels like they're preparing to summon some-thing: she's seen people hold hands in prayer, but this is larger than that. They stand and look at one another, smiling. It's like they're sending energy through one another's hands, like it's looping them together, a big gold ring, a binding. Minique squeezes Barbe and Daniel's hands so hard she swears she hears their bones creak, but they don't even grimace. They stay there, standing, steaming in the cold night, together. And when they all turn and go their separate ways, they don't say goodbye.

When Minique gets nearer to her house, she can see Tante Marie standing in the window like a watchful ghost. Minique picks up her pace, marching to her trial.

As soon as she's in the door, her aunt is in front of her with a finger in her face. Tante Marie isn't one for yelling, but she does manage to intimidate regardless. Her face is like stone.

"You better not have been where I think you were," her aunt says, mashing her lips together so hard they start to turn white. She looks angry but also scared, in a way. Minique has no answer for her, because obviously she was exactly where she wasn't supposed to be, and she has no regrets. So she bends over to unlace her boots in order to dodge that finger, but as she does, her aunt grabs the back of her coat and pulls her upright faster than Minique can blink. It's not violent, but it's firm. She's never experienced anything like that from her aunt before; she didn't know Tante Marie could move that fast, if she's being honest. Minique stands by the door and stares at her aunt. For the first time, she sees the similarity between her aunt and her father. And she sees, for the first time, how much stronger Tante Marie is because she can control that anger. It's another tick in the column of evidence for the women in New France being more powerful and more capable than the men.

Tante Marie doesn't touch Minique again. The scared look has melted from her face, and now she looks only irritated. Minique wonders if she's been up waiting the whole night.

"You can't go out and meet with Barbe for a week," her aunt says. As far as punishments go, it's average. Minique nods; she was expecting something like this anyway. "And you have to help me with spinning and knitting for that week, too." Minique groans, and Tante Marie looks triumphant. "Go to bed. You're lucky the governor didn't shut it down and have you all thrown in jail."

Life doesn't become easier after the dance, but it becomes a little more understandable. Minique finds it harder to be angry at her neighbours after she's seen a chunk of them dancing wildly. She starts to understand the value of a facade that is made up of more than surliness. There's an art to arranging your face in order to get what you want. She has insight into that now, why some of the women speak scripture with one side of their mouth and swig beer and hum along to music from the other side. There's a merit to staying unnoticed, to not always answering a question with a snarl. She knows she won't become one of those women who is outwardly placid, but she has learned a lesson from the two faces that her female compatriots wear.

For the first time in a long time, she feels comfortable in public. She doesn't turn her face away if she passes people on the street; instead, she tries to look at them to see if she recognizes them from that night at the inn. Sometimes she does, and the two of them exchange a closed-mouth smile. Something has shifted and she's not the enemy, nor someone to pick on. She's proved herself in some way.

"I'm very, very bad at it," Minique grumbles as she and Barbe walk side by side. They're picking their way between houses, dodging children and dogs. It's late enough in the day that the sun is starting to turn pink at the edges. This is usually the only time the two of them can get away, once there's a lull in their chores.

"I'm also bad at it," Barbe says, popping the rest of her bread into her mouth. Minique has been complaining to her about weaving, which is the newest task Tante Marie has been trying to teach her. Sewing was bad enough; embroidery was silly and she thought it was useless. But weaving has completely stymied her. They can't afford a loom, so Minique has been learning what her aunt has been doing for years: hand weaving, working with a warp and a weft. It can take hours and hours; Minique's lost whole afternoons trying to make a small piece of cloth. It's not that they can't buy cloth—they do for more delicate fabric like cotton, for undergarments. But since there are restrictions on commercial weaving in New France, all the cloth for sale is imported, and therefore more expensive. It saves money to make their own material for the rougher outer clothes. And if it's not weaving, it's washing or carding wool, spinning it out into yarn, learning to knit and crochet. At least Tante Marie has given up on trying to teach her how to make lace.

She and Barbe complain to each other about their new responsibilities. They both left school at about fourteen; after the age of twelve, and their first communion, the nuns stop teaching the girls reading and writing and start focusing on needlework and other skills a chatelaine should have. And by that time, her aunt said she needed her at home, and Barbe's parents were saying the same thing, and so they withdrew from school and started to learn the house-keeping skills in their own households. Minique isn't sure that Tante Marie is a better teacher than the nuns, but she would be miserable either way. She's too impatient for small things like stitching and tatting. Her fingers feel too awkward and too clumsy; her eyes wander; her neck hurts when she bends over her work. Kitchen work is a little better, because she has enough recipes under her belt that she feels comfortable. She can chop wood for the stove, albeit slowly, and over the years she's taken some pleasure in the keeping of their wan little garden behind the house; if they were outside the town walls, on real land, she might have a bigger yield. As it stands, she's learned how to grow beets, cabbage, and pump-kin. Working in the dirt was annoying at first, seeing her nails always crusted with soil, but now she likes it. At least she's outside, in the light, away from the stale house air. She's planning an herb garden, too, where she'll grow thyme, verbena, and marjoram, using seeds she got from Barbe, since Tante Marie saw no use in buying them from the store.

"I wish men had to do this shit," Minique mutters.

"Yes, but men have other terrible chores," Barbe says.

Do they? Minique can't think of much that men do that women don't. Men aren't sewing or weaving or cooking the food or doing the laundry, but she still sees women out in the fields come harvest time, or chopping wood, or gutting fish or cleaning meat. Maybe the fancier women don't have to do these things, but the poorer the family, the more everyone has to work.

"What does Daniel have to do that's so terrible, then?"

Daniel is able to do whatever he wants. It's part of the reason they don't see him anymore. Minique has no idea what he's been doing; he was joining them for afternoon walks, and then suddenly he wasn't. They saw him at the dance just two weeks ago, and now nothing. Barbe surely knows more than she's letting on, since she was the one who suggested that they just continue to walk without him.

"Well, he doesn't want to take over the boulangerie," Barbe says.

That's not a surprise. Claude is so measured and careful in the way he runs his business, and Daniel is neither of those things.

Barbe continues. "He's becoming a coureurs des bois."

Minique stops walking. Barbe doesn't realize it for a step and is snagged on where her hand is wrapped around Minique's arm.

"What?"

Barbe looks back at her, her milky eye gleaming in the afternoon sun. She looks angelic. Minique feels a rush of jealousy. That Barbe has such fine hair, is so delicately formed. Knows all of Daniel's secrets. When have they been finding time to talk? Do the two of them go for walks without her? She's not sure what she's more upset about—that idea, or the fact that Daniel will be becoming a version of her father.

"He said something about it at the dance, that he was talking to some coureurs." Barbe pulls on Minique's arm, but Minique doesn't move. She's seeing her father's face above a flask, her father's hands holding a pair of moccasins, her father flinching when she moves too fast in the corners of his vision. She imagines Daniel in his place, Daniel as a weathered and fragile man. How long has it been since she saw her father? Months, now. The older she gets, the more he stays away.

"It will be alright, Minique," Barbe says, gently. She tugs on Minique's arm again and this time Minique moves with it. She can't bring herself to say all of her fears out loud. Barbe seems to understand, and tightens her grip, pressing her palm to the skin of Minique's wrist. "It will all be alright."

She tries to put little stock in the meaning of dreams, but it's hard not to when every night is an odd landscape of images melting together in a way that makes no sense at all in the light of day. She dreams about things she's never seen, like giant boats or black bears or Indigenous tribes she doesn't have names for. She dreams about things that aren't real, like wheels attached to big metal machines and money that has writing on it in languages that she doesn't understand and oceans that are red and blue and shocking green. If she were to be worried by every dream, she would be anxious all the time.

But tonight, she dreams about her father. He is clear and defined, and she recognizes him. She dreams about the woods like a circle around him and her. She thinks she sees someone in the forest, someone very small, smaller than she is, and she wants to tell her father, but she's in the body of a child, weaker and less able to command attention. She tugs on his sleeve, but he ignores her. She can say *papa* all she wants, but his face tells her that he's not going to listen, that he knows what she wants to say, maybe, but doesn't want to acknowledge it.

The leaves shift in the woods; something's circling them, she can see the little figure through the murky dark. She can't help it; she grabs her father's wrist, because she can't bring herself to grab his hand.

He's murmuring something, his gaze off to the dark edge of the trees. She can make out two words that he's saying, one syllable each, and she wants to know what they are, but she can't quite hear them properly.

That's when she sees it, where his eyes are looking, this thing that comes out of the trees and stands at the edge of the clearing. At first, she thinks it's an animal, a goat or a small bear, because it has dark fur. It grows, suddenly, as tall as a tree. Limbs all stretched out and spindly, reaching far and wide. She can't see its face, but she's trying, her eyes squinting, and then her father lets out a sound like an animal in a trap, almost, and the thing turns its head and she sees red.

Then she wakes up.

It feels like something heavy is sitting on Minique's chest for two weeks afterward. She finds herself clenching her teeth and digging her nails into her palms, always in a state of heightened awareness, like she's waiting for a storm to crack open across the sky or the winter ice to heave apart and break up on the St. Laurence. Something big and full of a sound, something that reaffirms her smallness, her fragility.

She tries to tamp down her anxiety as she cuts lard into a bowl of flour, trying to master Tante Marie's pie-crust recipe. Minique prefers the taste of a butter crust, but lard is more available and less expensive, and so lard it is.

She's kneading the dough on the tabletop, frowning at it, when Tante Marie walks into the house. Minique looks up to greet her, but falters at the look on her aunt's face.

"Tante?"

Tante Marie turns her head to face Minique, slowly, like she's sleepwalking. Minique is immediately scared, because her aunt is always stoic and purposeful, striding from one destination or task to the next. She grabs the dough with her fingernails, feeling the peal of thunder building, feeling the ice warp and shift with the sound of a thousand screams.

"Your father's gone missing," her aunt says, in a voice that sounds like it's underwater, and all Minique can think of is the feeling of coming awake after that dream, her body damp and her heart racing. She feels the stale air of the house heavy around her. She smells the oil and the reek of the lard. She sees her aunt, the emotions of shock and then, even more frightening, helplessness chasing their way across Tante Marie's face. The two of them stand there in stupefied silence. When Minique looks down, the dough is throttled in her hands, and she squeezes her fingers together, feeling it shred to uselessness.

"The other coureurs des bois say he disappeared into the forest in the middle of the night," her aunt says, and her voice isn't its usual stone. It quavers like a bow on a string, and Minique has to remember that her aunt has lost her sibling.

"And they haven't . . . found him?"

"No," her aunt says.

Minique drops the dough, busying herself with wiping her hands on her apron. There were so many questions she wanted to ask her father;

she was waiting till she felt grown enough, big enough and strong enough, to be able to stand up and face him. She wanted to know more about her mother from the man who married her. She wanted to know more about his life before New France. She wanted to know more about the woods, what drew him there, what was so seductive.

Suddenly Tante Marie drops her face into her hands. Her shoulders shake. Minique sits across the kitchen table, frozen for a moment. As her aunt grinds the heels of her hands into her eye sockets, as if to dash away tears before anyone sees them, Minique gets up to stand beside Tante Marie, hesitating before softly placing her hand on her aunt's shoulder. She's surprised at how hard her aunt is, how close to the surface of her skin her aunt's bones seem. Minique spreads her fingers out as wide as she can, willing the warmth from her hand to soak into the brittle bird-like hills and valleys of Tante Marie.

Tante Marie reaches one hand back to cover Minique's. Minique stands as still as she can bear, terrified that if she moves or says something she'll break this tenuous, strange communion. They stay like that, like a dark painting, until Tante Marie shakes her head and clears her throat, raising her head and patting a few times at Minique's hand. Minique takes that for the signal it is and removes her hand from her aunt's shoulder.

"We have furs. We'll be fine for a year or so, but I need to figure out how we'll support ourselves eventually," Tante Marie says. Her voice is rough but still has its mettle.

Minique didn't think about that at all. A dread falls through her body. She forgot that her father was the furnace of the family, some- how keeping them supported from so far away. She wants to be scared and childlike, but she thinks of her aunt and balls the dread up as tight as she can, storing it in a deep, dark place inside of her.

"I'll be able to grow more in my garden this year," she says. "We can use that for food, and barter with what we don't need. I'll get more seeds and try to grow some peas and squash. And—and it's probably time I get a job anyway."

Minique's never thought about her future. In her mind, she's still a child, despite being on the cusp of womanhood. Girls her age are married; there's no want of men in Montréal. But the thought of a man touching her as a husband is repulsive, and no men want to be near her anyway. So a job was always on the horizon for her. She'll likely have to be a blanchisseuse, a cardeuse, a domestique. She's too bad with her hands to be a couturière. The idea of being a maid in her former classmates' homes makes her feel sick, but the thought of Tante Marie poor and starving makes her feel worse. Maybe she can ask Anne if she needs help at the auberge.

Tante Marie rises and turns to face Minique. Minique stands there, her aunt's pale eyes roving over her face. Minique feels assessed. When she was a child, she might have shied away from this, feeling like she was being judged in an unpleasant way, but now she sees it for what it is: her aunt taking whatever she thought of her, and reorganizing it. Tante Marie leans forward and presses her lips to Minique's forehead. It's not quite a kiss, but her mouth is warm and dry, and it feels holier than any sacrament.

Her own feelings about her father are also hidden in that deep, dark place inside of her. They were balled up with that murky dread, crushed in her palms; she tried to suffocate them. She feels

something dull in her body, like the sound when a bell without a clapper is struck. But mostly she feels a morbid curiosity, like if she can find out exactly what happened to him, she might solve the mystery of her woodenness and be able to unball those feelings. But she has no one to ask; nobody knows a thing. Her aunt tells her that no body was found: no evidence of a struggle, no animal sign, no broken branches, no blood, no tatters of skin. She has no physical representation of her father to ruminate on. Nothing to put in a coffin, nothing to leave in the dirt outside the town walls. All she can remember is holding his wrist in her dream and feeling his heartbeat, not panicked, but almost calm, loping and real.

Part of her, the selfish part, thinks that she's free now. That she doesn't have the spectre of a coureur des bois hanging over her, won't have to tiptoe around or avoid him when he comes back from his trips. There is another option: that he's not dead. That he's given up on her and Tante Marie forever, has chosen his other family. Chosen the woods. That option is worse to think about, so in her mind, her father has died. He was stalked by something. He was tracked by something. He was carried off by something.

She does want to feel more upset that her only living parent has gone. But even when she sits on her bed and tries to squeeze the tears out, to think of the saddest things she can, nothing comes. No feeling. No tears. No grief, not like when she thinks of her mother, whom she didn't know at all. It doesn't make sense. But in a way it does, because it's always easier to deify strangers. To know someone up close is to be able to see all of their flaws and problems. It is to love them less, sometimes.

And going missing is such an unfinished way to leave life. It means that there's no funeral for her father. No mourners, no service. No one comes up to her to give her their condolences, and she wouldn't have wanted that anyway. No one pays attention to her beyond the tenuous bonds she's created with those who were at the dance, and something about this feels comforting. As though in something bad, there is also something good, the two nestled beside each other, connected and held fast.

Over the next few days, she tries to feel bad, or—ashamedly—good. She tries to dig deep and see if she can pull out some sort of emotion. She wonders if her aunt is doing the same. The house feels no different now; no one is in active mourning and neither of them has changed their daily schedule. If Tante Marie is crying quietly in her bed at night, Minique can't hear her, and also she doesn't want to. Because it would remind her that she should also be crying, that she should be a better daughter. It would remind her that other people's parents mean something important to them.

But the thing about family is that you can't choose it. Minique isn't even sure that her father chose to have her as a baby. And he made it quite clear as she got older that he was actively choosing not to be around her. That, as he spent more time in the woods, he chose other children, other family. She can't be angry. She simply has to move past it.

And she thinks that maybe she has freedom, that she might see her future open up, clear and friendlier, without the image of her father hanging behind her, snarling and sad. She thinks that maybe life will get easier in Montréal.

Then the fever comes to town.

"Minique."

She doesn't raise her head from where it's resting on the kitchen table. She feels heavy, like her head is made of wood. Her eyes are so swollen. It's like she's been hit in the face over and over again, like she's been dragged onto the dance floor by the devil himself and waltzed around until her throat is hoarse from begging.

"Minique"—this time a bit more insistent.

She wants to keep sleeping, or at least pretending to sleep. She wants to keep her head down on the table, her eyes closed, safe in this world where everything is quiet and dark and none of the bad things have happened.

"Minique." And this time, it sounds like he's crying, and so she opens her eyes slowly and winces at the brightness of the kitchen, at the silhouette of the figure standing in the doorway like a reaper.

"Daniel," she says, her voice rough, and the figure moves closer to her like an eclipse and falls to its knees beside her.

It started quietly. Slowly enough that there wasn't talk of it by the water fountain and in the boulangerie, not in the alley by the school nor in front of the Sulpician seminary. Slowly enough that, at first, no one noticed that Marie-Catherine, the daughter of the boucher, the one who used to corner Minique and call her names, hadn't been seen recently. Slowly enough that no one noticed that one of the Sulpician fathers had a chest cough that sounded like something inside of him was trying to crawl its way out, and then no one noticed that the other Sulpicians all bloomed with the same illness, quarantining themselves so quickly and without warning that one day their door was open and the next it was locked to every congregant and petitioner. Everyone chose to ignore that their hands were clammy and their foreheads were warm until the fever had landed in their bones and taken them down and it was too late except to wait and see.

Marie-Catherine was the first to die. Minique heard from her aunt that it was a quicker and quieter death than everyone expected; as quick and quiet as one could go covered in a rash and begging for the blinds to be drawn because the light burned her eyes. As quiet as one could go seeing demons in the corners of the room, the walls melt away, the linens writhe with thousands of bugs.

The boucher's wife died next, but somehow the boucher did not. There was no rhyme or reason to the people the fever took. It killed three missionaries in a week, left the fourth still standing. It skipped the nuns altogether, but wiped out an entire street, from the babies to the elderly. Whole houses were quarantined, the town doctor working overtime to paint a black mark on the door of each home to be sequestered. Neighbours no longer said hello to one another; windows were shuttered tight and front doors locked. People became suspicious of each other, immediately: *Where did the fever come from? Who brought it to Montréal? How did it decide whom to kill and whom to spare?*

The town became bare and skeletal, with only the most necessary of tasks taking place—the shoeing of horses, the prayers of the missionaries, the baking of daily bread since even in the middle of a plague people still needed to eat.

Barbe and Daniel and Minique took to sitting on the roof of Daniel's house, looking out at the ghost town Montréal had become in the span of only a few weeks.

"It's so odd," Daniel said, his voice lowered like he was in church. "It's not done yet."

"Adèle died yesterday," Barbe said softly. Adèle had been one of their classmates when they were younger; Minique had never liked her because she was generally mean and had liked to bully the two of them when she was bored. She'd had long shiny hair and big shiny eyes, and Minique had mostly been jealous of her. But she had been at the dance, and she had been laughing, and the two of them had even shared a smile. It had felt like a detente.

"Did we do this at the dance?" The question slid out of Minique's mouth before she could stop it. She wasn't one to believe in god's retribution, but the timing felt bad and suspicious. She knew other people were thinking about it, too. Who had they angered? What had they done?

"No." Daniel shook his head, turning to spit artfully off the roof. Normally he would be more careful in seeing where it landed, but with almost no one out doing their daily errands, there was little worry. Minique could see the way he drew his brows together before speaking, gearing himself up to refuse what she had just said. Even if he didn't totally believe his own words. "No," he repeated. "That wouldn't be fair."

"Life's not fair," Barbe said, and her voice was a thin melody. Minique nodded her head; she knew. She knew what Barbe meant. She turned her face up to the wan sun and tried to still her mind. She tried not to wonder if she would be next. She didn't want to know what the fever felt like, nesting in her body. She didn't want her eyes to burn when the curtains were opened. She was scared, but she was trying not to show it; she was being like her aunt, who was keeping the household going without a word of complaint.

"It's not fair," Barbe repeated in that same strange tone of voice, and from the corner of her vision Minique could see Daniel's head turn to look, slowly, like turning to look at something frightening in a dark corner of a room. Minique felt something heavy drop through her body, her breathing suddenly becoming difficult. She turned her head to look at Barbe on her other side, and she watched as Barbe brought both hands up to her face, spreading her fingers wide and then bringing them back together again, as if mesmerized by the motion. Barbe's eyes were overbright, more than usual, large and liquid and completely unfocused. Anyone else might think she was normal, but Minique knew that something was wrong.

"Barbe," she started, reaching out a hand, but Barbe moved before Minique could get to her, and stood up suddenly. Daniel's head tilted up with the movement, and the two of them stared at her, tall against the sun, and so both of them noticed when she swayed once, twice, and then one of her knees bent and she started to fall, slowly, like a tree being taken down in the heat of summer, and when Minique grabbed her, she felt Barbe's skin burning up, scorching her own hands, and she wanted to let go but she held on as tightly as she could even as she opened her mouth to yell for help.

Barbe didn't go quickly, not like the butcher's daughter. Barbe went very slowly. It took two weeks from that moment on the roof. Every day it seemed like there was a new symptom, some new horror to try to combat. If it wasn't pain in her gut, it was her back aching so badly she couldn't be propped up in bed without crying. If it wasn't a cough that rattled her chest, it was vomiting into a basin kept by her bedside. Minique never knew what waited for them behind the door of Barbe's bedroom. Some days she imagined turning around and not walking through the doorway; she imagined running past the orchard and through the forest. Running forever. She imagined not having to watch her best friend's body twist with pain under the bed linens.

But she never would do it. She never could. Every day she took a deep breath and walked through the door. Sometimes she was the first one there; sometimes Daniel had arrived before her. They rarely spoke to each other, only settled into their spots and waited.

She and Daniel and Barbe's father and mother sat a vigil. Barbe's parents had resisted at first. "We don't want you to get sick," her father said. Her mother said nothing, but Minique knew from parting her lips and drawing in that Pierrette Bâby was not entirely concerned about their health; instead, she was filled with a blinding grief and also a white-hot resentment that her daughter's friends weren't ill. There was nothing to be done for that; Minique wanted to draw Madame Bâby into her arms, wanted to share her small reserves of physical warmth and touch with her. But she did not. She respected the dark star of anger and wretchedness that burned inside of Barbe's mother. She felt no ill will toward it, only honoured it, the taste of it like the taste in the air before a lightning strike, the wet ash of a tree felled by a storm.

Sometimes they sat all together. Other times they took shifts in the dark room, dark because toward the end Barbe also cried out if any light came in. The warmth and the dark reminded Minique of confession. *And where was that god now?* How could a good father do something like this?

Minique knew Barbe was going to die. She and Daniel never spoke about it, because saying it out loud would erase the tiny bit of hope they had, but it was as clear as the day they rarely saw anymore. Their lives existed in the dark—in a darkened room, in the night when they finally left Barbe's house to stagger home and fall asleep with their clothes still on, in the dark of their own minds.

The dark taste of the houses in mourning, bitter and sticky. The dark scent of destruction that clung stubbornly to every roof and every eave and every door in the town. Everything she tasted was black and char; for the first time since she had been struck by her curse, all people were the same, all feelings uniform in their grief and exhaustion and illness. The evilness of the fever was everywhere, an ooze as deep and cloying as treacle. It coated her tongue so much that she stopped being able to taste it.

But still they sat. Still they rested their elbows on Barbe's bedspread. Still they helped her father lift her, sponge her to cool her down, change her nightgown. Still they held her mother's hand as they led her to lie down to get some sleep, saying *yes, we will stay up, yes, we will watch over her, yes, you need to get rest*. Still they made their peace, slowly, painfully, angrily, as the days passed and as the nights stretched out in front of them.

The day they didn't know was the last day, all of them were so tired their eyes were sore, their fingers shaking as they held the cup of water to Barbe's mouth, the mouth that didn't want to drink anymore. The eyes that didn't want to open anymore. Minique felt the urge to connect herself to Barbe, to try to memorize the texture of her skin and the rise and fall of her chest. She touched her hands to Barbe's sweaty hair, along her brow bone, along her damp neck and shoulders. Barbe quieted under her touch, instinctively, and Daniel let out an odd sound that was halfway between sob and laugh. Minique kept her eyes on Barbe, but reached out her own hand, blindly, and grabbed at Daniel. His palm was hot and wet, but he grabbed at her, too, and then she saw from the corner of her eye as he groped out sightlessly until Barbe's father clasped at him, and then her mother grabbed her father's hand. The four of them formed a chain, being the strongest they could be as they listened to Barbe's breaths get thicker and harder, as the death rattle reached its way across her chest, as her mother hummed a tuneless, made-up lullaby overtop of it all, as Daniel cried almost silently, as her father prayed beneath his breath, and as Minique sat there, stupefied, too tired to think of anything important to say until Barbe's rattle finally stopped, and then there was silence.

"Daniel," she says, her voice rough, and the figure on its knees beside her lays its head on her lap. She cards her fingers through his hair, such an intimate act, a terrible and close thing they would never normally do. He leans into her touch and she feels the fabric of her skirt grow damp as his shoulders shake.

The house becomes her world: dark, closed in, and protected. She's not scared of the fever; she's repulsed by the idea of having to see and talk with other people. Her skin crawls at the idea of stepping out into the wan, cold sunlight, of exposing herself to the gaze of the other survivors, of seeing who hasn't lived. As Tante Marie buys tea and lard and turbot, Minique dully goes through the motions of keeping the household going. She keeps the fire stoked and makes lopsided pie dough and smokes eels, watching with tired eyes as the oil drips down into the fireplace, screaming and sizzling.

It takes a few weeks for Daniel to be able to persuade her to go for a walk. He comes around three times, his eyes shadowed and red, his face woeful as she shuts the door in his face. On his fourth try, he grabs the door before she can slam it. She wants to fight him, but it's as if all of her strength leaves her in that moment, and she heaves a wavering sigh that feels like torture before she turns to grab her hat and coat.

As the two of them leave the walls, she takes a shivery breath. It feels like they're being unfaithful to Barbe. It makes Minique's gut queasy, and she digs her fingers into Daniel's wrist so hard that he turns to stare at her. He must see the desperation on her face because he sighs and pulls at her arm. He's not diplomatic or delicate like Barbe used to be when Minique would get into one of her moods;

instead, he tugs on her body to force her forward one step at a time until she starts to feel less terrible.

They walk through the dormant orchard. Minique focuses on the sugary crunch under her boots. She can take solace in knowing that with each step she'll destroy an untouched piece of snow, leaving her mark and also ruining something in the process. She focuses on making a pattern with her steps, something like a drumbeat in her head, like the night she let herself get danced around and her skirts whirled around her ankles, the night Barbe's eyes were so bright they looked like two stars.

She stops. Her knees start to buckle and she doesn't want Daniel to have to hold her up. She knows that he's suffering his own breed of grief, something that he's never put into words before but that she's almost certain of. Or maybe, she thinks, grief is just the same for everyone, deep and dark and sly, ebbing to make you think you're fine and above water, and then sliding back in to take you under, arms wrapped around you like a sweet and bitter kind of embrace, when it's least expected.

She doesn't fall. She can't bear to fall, knees damp in the snow, and leave her imprint of weakness for everyone after her to see. Minique makes a promise to herself, right there and then, that she can't ever fall. If she was alone in this dead orchard, she would scream as loud as she could; she would get on her hands and knees and rub the snow along her neck and cheeks and into her hair; she would make a noise that would get all of the officials in town running, all of the Jesuits and Sulpicians sprinting with their skirts held up around their knees, all of the nuns turning their heads at once like they were hearing something out of a horror story. She would make the sound of all of the monsters she's ever learned about, the things that dwell in the woods, the sound of red, of scaredness, of realness.

She stiffens, or maybe her legs sag a little, because Daniel stops beside her and squeezes her arm. She appreciates it, but wishes he would grip her a little harder, just enough to hurt. She thinks the pain would serve as something corporeal, something that fills her lungs like a cold gasp.

He doesn't speak; he doesn't need to. He can't even look her way; she doesn't need him to. He just holds on to her upper arm as tight as he can bear, and she stands there taking it, and the two of them stare past the orchard into the skeletal thrush of the forest. If it were another day, everything would be oddly and coldly beautiful, the world clean and calm in all of the best ways possible. Instead, Minique hopes that the cold brings down the fever of the town. She assumes by now that she and Daniel have not gotten the disease, though nothing is for sure. She doesn't know what she hopes for.

She doesn't know where to direct her sadness. All of the grief she never felt for her father is now raging and bubbling inside of her. It feels like a real thing, something solid that lives beneath her breastbone and hurts if she bends too far or moves too quickly. It pulses when she wakes up, after she comes to and realizes that everything is a nightmare. It moves in her when she tries to eat, making her feel sick. It's there when she turns and when she adjusts her skirts and when she braids her hair and when she murmurs good morning to her aunt, when she goes to the privy and walks up and down the stairs and when she tries to read a book to take her mind off of the bleak, bleak world she's living in.

The words vault out of her without any thought.

"How is there a god?"

Daniel's hand doesn't change its grip on her arm; he doesn't flinch. "They say god has his reasons," he says, and his voice sounds tattered.

"Who says?"

Daniel turns to her then, his eyes red-rimmed. He says nothing.

"Who?"

When he still doesn't answer, she pushes at his jacket with her other hand, and then twists her arm out of his grip and pushes with both palms. He feels weak; his body sways with each of her thrusts. As she shoves at him, she jostles tears loose from his eyes, and they run down his face in cold misery, and she knows she should feel bad but she can't bring herself to. She knows that she's crying too, but she doesn't make any sounds like sobbing. Neither of them do. Instead, they grapple with each other, the trees and the occasional crow standing witness to their stupid bodies, and Minique feels like she could throw him to the ground, pin him with her knees and her elbows, and speak right into his face.

She doesn't. Instead, she grabs him by the collar of his jacket and pulls him sharply close to her, right up to her face, so he can probably smell the sour tang of her breath, of a body not taken care of, and she hisses right into his mouth.

"I will never ask god for anything," she says. "Because god doesn't exist, and now we all know it." All she can hear is the branches of the trees clinking like glass in the breeze, the caw of a crow far away. Daniel's ragged breathing.

"Minique," he says, "you can't say that."

"Why? Don't tell me you believe in god after this?"

There's nothing in his face to show what he thinks, but his deep unease curls into her mouth, and for a moment she can see herself through his eyes, her dark hair tangled and wild around her face, her mouth crusted at the corners with old spit, her teeth pointed and shining as she snarls into him. She lets go of his collar, momentarily ashamed of her surge of anger. He places a hand over hers where it lingers on his chest.

"You can't say that," he repeats. He takes a breath and looks around, thinking. "People want something to believe in, Minique. Otherwise they worry that their lives are in vain. You can't rip that away from them, especially not now."

She shakes her head stubbornly, her eyes swimming with painful tears.

He continues. "And I worry that—I worry about you."

"What do you mean?" Her voice sounds thick and stupid to her own ears, but at least her eyes have dried.

"People already think you're a bit funny," he says hesitantly. "I don't want you going around town saying . . . saying that."

"But I know there's no god."

"You don't."

"I do, because—" She stops, slamming her teeth together to cage her tongue in her mouth. She was about to say *because god can't exist in the same world as this curse*—her palate. Whenever she starts to think about it as her power, as even remotely freeing, all she can see is Father Etienne's face, purple and shiny, full of rage; all she can hear are his words, his spitting about sin and hell. She may not respect him, she may hate him, but it's men like him who run the town, and part of him speaks for all of them. To be different is to have the curse of Cain.

Minique feels exhausted by her secret, this thing that burdens her from her mouth like a bit, like she's a horse with her tongue lacerated. She wants to share the emotions she's absorbed from everyone. She wants to unload those worries so she can uncrook herself and breathe like there isn't an imp sitting on her chest. But she can't tell Daniel, not in her weakest moment, not ever. He might be her best friend now, but she can't trust anyone with this. "Because," she finishes lamely.

"Ah, Minique," he says, his voice choked, and he brings a hand up to the back of her head, to pull her into an embrace.

"Don't," she says. "Don't cry, don't cry," she repeats, and her voice swells to what could be called a yell, and then Daniel shakes his head and continues to cry anyway, and their knees don't buckle but the two of them cling to each other in the middle of nowhere, in the middle of a god-forsaken country, and they weep.

Minique paints her grief all over her face: her eyes are red and painful from crying, her cheeks damp. She doesn't try to cover herself with a shawl or a hat; instead, she stalks through town bare-headed and bare-faced, dragging her skirts, disregarding the dirty snow that splatters up her boots. She likes to see people dart out of her way when they see her coming. She likes to think everyone's afraid of her, of the sadness inside her and the way it might swell and devour Montréal to leave nothing but a hole in its place.

Today she walks down the main street, in the middle of the road. She remembers Daniel's words—*people already think you're a bit funny.* Her grief has blossomed into something so beyond funny, so beyond just a little bit off, a little bit strange. She might have tried to control it if she cared at all what people thought about her anymore, but she doesn't, so she didn't. She knows Tante Marie worries for her, but if anyone understands the strange and winding paths of grief's fire and how they manifest in people, it's her aunt. So Tante Marie lets Minique do what she wants; there's no longer a struggle for propriety.

When she comes to the main town hub, she watches people beetle into houses and stores and dart into back streets. She wants to laugh, but that feeling dies in her mouth when she sees the familiar squat figure of Father Etienne swivel out of a doorway. Bile rises in her throat like a hot tangle of ribbons, red appearing at the corners of her vision. She hates all of the religious men even more now, knowing without a doubt that they're selling fraud. She can repel most of them with the cut of her eyes and the nest of hair that rests around her face like a dark cloud, because men are scared of an unkempt woman. It's a small power, but a power nonetheless. Most of the Jesuits and Sulpicians stay out of her way; even the ones she used to tolerate are the enemy now, and they seem to smell it on her like she can smell their unease, and so an agreement is reached without words.

Father Etienne deems women as so much less worthy than men that there is no detente to be respected. Maybe he sees her as an animal to break. Whatever it is, it leads him to approach her, with such a smug look on his face that she's sure he's been lying in wait.

"Minique."

She doesn't appreciate the way her name is familiar on his tongue. It doesn't feel paternal or kind; it feels like ownership. She stares back at him, unmoving but not trying to make herself look like prey. She lets her eyes go unblinking and hard.

He's been speaking, and she's let her mind wander away, beyond the walls, beyond the cemetery, away. She's drawn back by the sharpness of his voice, the slice of his hands through the air as he gestures like he's in the pulpit.

"It's not proper," he's saying. "It's not proper to drag yourself around town like this. Be wiser; be more ladylike. People are talking."

"People always talk about me," she says, interrupting his aggrieved flow. Her voice is low, but not quiet.

His face hardens even more, somehow, and twists into something uglier. His thick lips are slicked with a froth of spit, so much that he looks rabid, and the web of veins across his cheeks is red and purple, flaring with his effort. He smells like sheer hatred, something that's hard to describe. It's like a mix of cow shit and river scum and the scent of the air before a bad storm, all prickly and strange. He holds a finger out at her, jabbing like he's brandishing a sword as he speaks.

"Mark my words, connasse: you're destined for a poor end."

She doesn't blink at it, doesn't sway in the face of his righteous male anger. Because she's refused to wrap her grief up, to be maudlin in the face of the church, she's the enemy. But Minique is so bruised inside, so heartbroken, that it means barely anything at all. How can she care?

She brushes by him, worried for a moment that he'll follow, continue pointing at her through the web of her hair, but somehow he stays where he is, his eyes narrowed and his mouth twisted, and she leaves him in her wake as she follows only her feet, not her mind nor her eyes, turns herself over to the animal movement of her body.

Because sometimes Minique walks and isn't sure where she'll end up. Sometimes she walks and then realizes that she's on the other side of town, or sitting outside of the Sulpicians' door, on the ground, or in the orchard, staring into the forest beyond the apple trees, one hand wrapped around a branch and her nails digging into the bark. She doesn't always know how she got to where she did. It should bother her, but it doesn't. Instead, it feels like a relief, to let her brain relax and her body take over. It's a quiet respite from the sadness.

She often ends up just outside the walls of the town. Minique likes this; she hates people seeing what she's doing. It doesn't matter if they're friendly or not; she knows that her every move gets catalogued by other Montréalers and stored in some mental ledger. Everyone here natters about everyone else. But eyes on her make her skin itch and the hairs at the bottom of her neck prickle. She can taste curiosity, and slyness, and it has the flavour of apples that aren't quite ready, like bread that has too much flour and not enough leavener. It tastes like the one time Daniel's father forgot to add sugar to the biscuits he was baking that day. Like touching your tongue to something you know isn't pleasant and waiting for the shock to course through your body and the saliva to flood your mouth. She can't stand to be around that for too long. Outside the town feels like the safest place for her, despite all of the stories that spill out of the missionaries' mouths about white people getting their scalps cut off and their skin peeled back and their bodies boiled and split and chopped. Minique thinks about the pain that might bring, compares it to the pain inside her body, the grief that has no place to go because no one in the town is talking to one another and no one is becoming a place of refuge for anyone else.

She's never believed the missionaries. She sees them for what they are, men grasping at some form of power. Those men taste piss-acrid on her tongue, save for a few who seem simpler than the others and seem to believe in some great benevolence floating in the sky. There isn't comfort for her there. There is barely comfort anywhere, but she feels the least distressed when she's outside of the town. She feels closest to human when she lets the rawness of the uncontained whip across her cheeks and through the mess of her hair. She never looks at the forest for movement, because she doesn't care. She knows she means nothing in the face of all things, and it's likely that no one and nothing will come for her.

She keeps her eyes closed when she stands with her back against the town's walls, and that's how she misses the minute scraps of red that sometimes weave their way through the trees when she's outside, when she's thinking, when she's letting her grief eddy wildly inside her. She doesn't get a chance to see the way luscious crimson braids itself into the spruce and pine, and then disappears like the trail of a shooting star.

Minique trudges back into town. She keeps her head down, not wanting to catch anyone's eye. Gone is the hard-jawed grit she showed when facing down the priest, the joy she took seeing her neighbours flee from her. Gone is the reckless wildness of a few weeks ago, the freedom of the dance. Now she is just tired. The sadness, the anger, they both come in waves. As she pulls her exhausted body through the street, a commotion catches her attention. She raises her gaze slowly, worried about what she'll find. She doesn't know how much else the town can take. She's surprised there are enough people willing to go out to cause a commotion.

When her bleary eyes focus, she sees Anne, the aubergiste, being marched down the street by six men, Father Etienne at the head of the group. The little priest is marching the hardest and with the most determination, his head tilted up with pride and his knees rising high with every mincing step. The other men look nervous, their eyes darting around to see their audience. The street is mostly empty, but there are a few people watching, like Minique. There is a cantonnier, wide-eyed, his hands tight on his wheelbarrow's handles; the meunier, his ruddy face folded with a frown as he looks on; some habitant children, dirty-faced and peeping out from behind barrels; two married women, holding their loaves of bread with one hand and clutching each other's arms with the other.

The men seem frightened to touch Anne; every so often, one will brush his hand at her elbow and then snatch his arm back as if he's been burned. But they surround her like a pack, like they're worried about her running off. Anne looks less scared than the men around her. She seems calm, her gaze steady, her hands down by her sides instead of twisted in front of her. She looks around in a measured way, her eyes landing on the windows, the stray dog, the back of the priest's head—and then on Minique, who is standing half-behind a corner of a house.

Minique feels a jolt when she meets Anne's gaze. It brings her back to the feeling of sitting on her ass and staring up at the woman with a red ribbon on the end of her braid. Except this time, she feels a muddle of things all at once: fear for Anne, wherever they are taking her; anger on Anne's behalf, a rage that flowers for the cocky little priest and his cocky little steps; and, most of all, kinship. She doesn't know why they're taking Anne away from her business, but she can hazard a guess; why does any man try to take down an independent woman? And Minique knows that in another world, it could be her standing there in the middle of all of those men.

Anne's footsteps slow as she turns her head to look at Minique, and Minique feels rooted to the spot. They're in a moment of communion, more moving than anything Minique has ever felt in church—*so this is higher power*, she thinks.

Father Etienne feels his group of charges slowing down, and whips his head around to glower at them.

"Come on, witch," he snaps at Anne, and she slowly turns her stare away from Minique and to the priest, who valiantly meets her gaze for a moment before turning back around. Minique can see red spots on his cheeks as he picks up the pace once again, and the ragtag group of enforcers stumbles away from her, down the street.

But Minique follows. Maybe once she would have turned tail and gone home, but she's seventeen now, basically an adult, and she's braver than she was. She feels like she's tracking something in the woods as she zigzags down the street, from doorway to doorway and corner to corner, trying to stay back a distance but keep Anne's dark head in her sightline. She follows them through the centre of town, past the church and the seminary and the nunnery hospital and the sisters' gardens. She knows already where they're going to end up, and so it's no surprise when she has to hide a few toises back from the jail door. The group clusters around the door; they're waiting on something, their bodies conveying a reluctance. Father Etienne gets purpler and purpler waiting until he finally grabs Anne's upper arm with a fat-fingered grip, and yanks her into the building behind him. Minique can see the faces of the other men as they turn from the door. They look bewildered and tired. She wonders if they wanted to be part of this group of enforcers, or if the priest press-ganged them into his service. The men shift from foot to foot and then slowly disperse one by one, walking off in different directions.

Minique waits, her fingers cold and her feet numb, as she watches the door. It's a decent jail; the town needs it, considering Montréal accounts for most of the crime in New France. People say it's because of all the men here: coureurs, soldiers, sailors, all unmarried and running wild. Usually people are thrown into jail because of things like theft and assault and, sometimes, murder. Minique's also heard of people locked up for things like setting fire to a neighbour's house or duelling with a rival or killing their own child. If the crime is very terrible, the prisoner gets shipped off to Québec, where the colony's executioner lives.

But how could Anne have done any of those things? Did Anne murder someone? Did Anne set fire to a house? Minique smells no smoke and hears no weeping. Anne's dress was clean and her hands had no blood on them. And Father Etienne, calling her a witch in that tone of voice. Minique stands there until the cold creeps up from her feet to her calves and from her fingers to her wrists, and then she has to give up before the numbness takes all of her body. She slinks away, back to her home, to wait for the gossip to filter through the ranks of the town and make its way to her.

Sure enough, it only takes a day before she learns all the details. All she has to do is linger in the alley near the general store and listen. Anne's been charged with a slew of things: promiscuity, running a brothel, and, most serious of all, witchcraft. *Witchcraft!* people say in the store and around the hitching post. *Witchcraft*, in an unbelieving tone of voice, followed by *promiscuity? A brothel?* Anne may be an outsider in Montréal society, but everyone in town knows her, and therefore everyone knows that she hasn't been seen in the company of another man since her husband died years ago, and that she certainly doesn't run a brothel.

As for witchcraft, people say, certainly Montréalers would know if sorcery was in their town. Surely the milk would be curdled and the eggs would have blood in the yolks and people would be waking up in the middle of the night with the weight of the hag on their chests. True, there was a fever. True, so many died. True, Anne did host a dance in her auberge against the wishes of the religious authorities. But maybe that's not witchcraft; maybe that's just the bad luck of living here.

Minique is curious to know what Tante Marie thinks of it all. What she doesn't expect is for Tante Marie to clap her hands at the mention of Father Etienne's name as if trying to rid herself of something. Her aunt is making dough for a pie crust, and so flour clouds out into the still kitchen air.

"That priest," Tante Marie says, miming spitting three times over her left shoulder.

Minique gapes at her. Her aunt has always been about propriety and staying within the lines. But Minique supposes she's never asked her directly about Father Etienne. Minique just assumed Tante Marie would denounce Anne and fall in line with religious authority. But then again, that's the mercurial nature of Montréal. People can pray out of one side of their mouth and insult the clergy with the other. Part of it is keeping up appearances, and part of it is keeping things interesting when people's day-to-day life is full of drudgery.

"You don't like Father Etienne?" Minique sounds relieved even to her own ears.

Tante Marie looks up at her from where she's focusing on rolling out the dough. Their pies are never made with enough lard, so the crusts are always dry and finicky to work with.

"He's a stupid little man," her aunt says.

Minique can't help it—she starts to laugh. It's the first time she's laughed since Barbe died, and it doesn't feel like a real thing; it's a little bit unhinged, not as pure as it should be. But it's a laugh nonetheless, something that unties her chest and loosens her from the inside out. She laughs until there are tears in her eyes and she has to stop for a breath. Tante Marie is startled, but Minique can't help it. It's the relief of knowing that she's not alone in her hatred for that pugnacious bully. Her heart feels a little lighter. She also feels a little ashamed of assuming about her aunt, but if Minique's face is flushed, Tante Marie says nothing.

"I hate him," Minique says under her breath, reaching out to play with a piece of dough that's come loose. She doesn't tell her aunt what she wants to: that the priest called her a name in the street, that he felt bold enough to be able to come up to her and upbraid her in the light of day. That he made her feel scared and sadder than she already was. That she wishes he would drop dead.

Tante Marie takes the little ball of dough out of Minique's hand and slaps it back into the rolled-out sheet in front of her.

"Anne is one of the smartest women I've ever met," she says. "Never underestimate how far smarts can get you, even when you're a woman. And never underestimate how much people actually hate being told what to do by priests."

Minique doesn't know what to say. But before she can ask *when did you meet Anne?* her aunt claps her hands again.

"Make some use of yourself and go get me the pie tin, Minique."

The judge sets the trial quickly, because prisoners have been known to escape the jail when left to linger. Within two days of being arrested, Anne is in the courthouse; the dozens of onlookers who can't fit in the building stand outside the windows and by the doors, hoping to catch a glimpse of the proceedings or overhear something salacious. The trial will pit the accused against the accuser, and whoever has the more convincing case, the better argument, will win. Those arguments have been known to get heated, even explosive. Lots of the town's gossip is churned out of the courtroom, a whisper network of vulgarity passed mouth to ear.

Minique is also in the courthouse. She got up before the sun rose to wait by the doors in order to be the first spectator let in. The seats are hard and splintery, and she feels her lower back going numb as she sits and waits among the whispering. She wonders if some of the whispers are about her, sitting like a wraith in the front row of the onlookers' seats, her hair coming out of its braid and her feet tapping nervously on the floor. Usually she'd be stalking around the town or sitting in a field, so to see her inside a public building, in the middle of a group of people, must be shocking.

She doesn't care. She feels a pull to be here and to witness whatever's coming. She knows from the look in Anne's eyes that something is going to happen. And for the first time in a long time she feels something other than sad: she feels angry on Anne's behalf, repulsed by the priest, and, most of all, riveted for the spectacle that's to come.

Anne walks down the aisle like she owns the place. She doesn't swagger, but her boots make solid, measured sounds and her head is held high. She doesn't look around at the chittering onlookers who sit in rows to either side of her, only sits at her table with her back straight and her hands folded. The tables are so close to the crowds that Minique can see that there's no sweat on the nape of her neck; her fingers don't shake.

Father Etienne, on the other hand, storms to his seat like a rabid dog. His ears are already tipped with red, a sign of the growing rage inside him. His cassock flaps around him as he turns to glare at the courthouse before thudding into his seat. The onlookers titter: he doesn't realize it, or maybe he does but doesn't care, but he's not well liked among the congregants. Behind his back, people call him everything from a bigot to a misanthrope. People hate that he calls them out by name during his sermons; they hate that he sometimes refuses them communion if he thinks they're dressed inappropriately.

Montréal's governor, the Marquis de Vaudreuil, isn't in the court. That's all the better, since the few times Minique's caught a glance of him, de Vaudreuil has looked nothing but haughty, as if the town is below him. Instead, the town major, Jacques Bizard, is sitting in for him. Bizard is about two decades older than Minique, and is neither adored nor hated by Montréalers. He turns a blind eye to alcohol smuggling and drunkenness, and is known to enjoy a party himself. Crucially, Minique has heard that he dislikes Father Etienne: Bizard has been known to call the priest a *surly creature* for his efforts to admonish and mortify his flock into submission. As Minique watches Bizard, the town major looks at the priest and then rolls his eyes back into his head so much that Minique can see the whites below his irises.

The judge heaves his way into his seat, placed on a dais so the court can see him. Justice Cabzie is an old man; sometimes he falls asleep in church, not quite snoring but making little *puh-puh* sounds with his lips. He's portly and has to use a walking stick. He rests that stick by his chair as he creaks back and forth, getting comfortable, and then rubs his hands all over his face, groaning. The courthouse giggles once again. Bizard yawns so wide his jaw cracks. Father Etienne quivers in place like a pudding.

"Father, state your accusations before the court."

The priest launches himself from his seat, clearly having been waiting for this moment of glory.

"I bring before you today a *witch*," he hisses, spreading his arms wide and waiting for a beat, as if to see if the courtroom reacts. It does not. People stay silent, watching. Minique twists her hands in her skirt. The priest clears his throat and continues. "Anne Lamarque, aubergiste, is accused of promiscuity with her lodgers, running a brothel, and *witchcraft*." Again he puts the emphasis on that word.

The court is silent. A chair creaks; someone's stomach makes a sound. Bizard yawns again. Minique feels something like hope.

This time, Father Etienne isn't deflated. He's worked his way up to a lather. "When my men searched her inn, we found herbs and potions; we found feathers; we found wax for poppets. And we found this," he shouts, pulling a book out of his cassock and smacking it on the table in front of the judge. It's a notebook, worn with age but innocent-looking enough. Minique cranes her neck to try to see if anything is written on the cover; she's a little too far to be able to see.

Justice Cabzie squints down at it. "It's a notebook."

"It is a witch's grimoire. Read it and see!" Father Etienne whirls around as Cabzie thumbs through the pages. "She has been seen coming and going from her auberge at all times of the night; her windows have been seen lighted when all should be asleep; men have been seen arriving at the witching hour, and she has been seen in her nightgown greeting them. Tell me, is that not the evidence of a harlot and a sorceress?"

The judge grunts, closing the book in front of him. "This seems to me to be a book of herbal remedies," he says. "Like our herborisateur's. Perhaps Madame Lamarque just didn't want to pay his exorbitant prices."

"No woman should have autonomy over her own body," Father Etienne nearly shrieks. He's looking now like he does when he gives a sermon, spittle flying and face oily.

The judge sighs and looks at Anne. "Madame Lamarque, what is your rebuttal?"

Anne stands. She looks at the priest, his trembling jowls, his spit-flecked mouth. She doesn't turn to speak to the court, because for a woman to do that would be seen as unseemly, not humble. Instead, she talks directly to the judge and to the major, her voice calm and clear, her hands clasped in front of her.

"Sirs, I was an herborisatrice back in France, so that book is a remnant of that time. I brought it with me in case it could be of service here. There's nothing in there that could harm or hinder anyone. As for the coming and going—" She shrugs. "I run an inn.

Sometimes coureurs des bois or sailors get in at late hours and I have to get out of bed to greet them. That is likely why I've been seen in a nightgown."

Father Etienne is almost jigging in place with holding back the urge to speak, but he lets loose as soon as Anne pauses to take a breath. "So you deny having relations with all these men?"

"Of course I do," she says, turning slowly to face him. "I run a business; I make my money fairly, without begging for it."

A murmur goes through the courtroom. Anne is essentially telling the priest that he's a beggar for alms.

Father Etienne yells, "Liar! How can you, a woman, be so successful in your business without whoring yourself out, without running a bawdy house? We all know that women's minds are not so developed as men's, and therefore your auberge should have been run into the ground years ago."

"I was always the business owner," Anne says quietly. "My husband was the one who was better with the customers. I know nothing of women's minds as compared with men's, except for what the courtroom is witnessing today. And speaking of the courtroom—" Here she pivots smoothly on her heel, facing the rows of onlookers. Minique wishes that Anne's eye would catch on her, but it doesn't. Anne is staring down the aisle, her sight like an arrow. "Maybe we should ask the people of Montréal if any of them have been at my 'brothel,' either as customer or employee."

The room is quiet. No hands are raised. Anne nods once, sagely. "I thought so." She turns back around to face the judge. Her voice dips low and modest, but has an undertone like honey. "I'm just a woman trying to make a living; I've been targeted by a priest who has repeatedly rebuked the people of Montréal to the point of refusing them sacraments and driving them away from his church. I beg the court to see that."

Father Etienne opens his mouth as if to speak, but the judge raises a hand and his voice. "Sit *down*, Father." His voice rings around the rafters; Father Etienne is startled into thumping back down into his chair. "The major and I will discuss this. We will be back in a quarter of an hour."

When the door at the back of the courthouse closes behind the two men, the room erupts in noise, a buzzing of words and exhortations and people talking to their neighbours as fast as they can. Minique has no neighbours that are willing to talk with her, so she sits in the middle of the melee and tries to pick up on words. She can hear *waste of time* and *poor woman* and *where would we go to drink* and *ridiculous man*. The taste of the room is wild and whipsaws between scandal and intrigue; people smell so interested and so riled up that it makes the roof of her mouth prickle. Minique always assumed that the town would be eager to condemn someone accused of witchcraft. Settlers in New France are bloodthirsty: public punishment for crimes is common, with people being caned, flogged, and even branded, or put in stocks to be shamed. She's even heard that the general can order the accused to be tortured.

Anne is acquitted. It happens quickly: the judge and the major come back in after their break, and Justice Cabzie announces it to the court. Minique's eyes snap to Father Etienne as the courtroom erupts in whoops and jeers—he's rigid, his mouth hanging open and his eyes rolling around the room like a mad dog's. Either he over-estimated his power in the community, or he overestimated the esteem Montréalers have for him. Either way, the verdict is a boot on his back. Anne, for her part, doesn't gloat, but when she gets up to leave the courtroom, her grimoire back in her hands, her cloak pulled tight to her throat, she leans over to the priest's table. Since Minique is in the front row, she and a handful of other spectators can hear Anne's voice, low and full of vitriol, as she bends close to Father Etienne.

"You aren't worthy to say mass, you sinner. And if you ever come near me again, I'll tear your cassock off and whip you in the street like the dog you are."

Minique's jaw drops. The other people in her row look at one another, unsure if they heard Anne correctly. But Minique knows she heard what she heard. Father Etienne's apoplectic face and shak-ing hands tell her so. The smell of him tells her so: angry and fecal, but also shrinking, becoming smaller by the minute as the people around him grin at Anne's cheek. The small smile on Anne's mouth tells her so. The smell of victory rises in the courtroom, satisfying and filling like burned sugar, swirling around the trim of Anne's cloak and chasing at her heels like the sounds of the jubilant Montréalers as she walks down the aisle and throws open the doors of the courthouse, a free woman once more.

Minique stands there, blinking in the sunlight streaming in through the doorway. All around her, people are talking; their voices aren't scared or disappointed. Instead, the Montréalers who sat to watch the trial sound delighted. She can hear Tante Marie's voice in her head: *never underestimate how much people actually hate being told what to do by priests.* She can hear mutters of *good* and *riddance* and *useless* and *go for a drink*. People want their auberge to stay open; they want their aubergiste to remain solidly in her place. The room tastes like new honey, sweet and rich and delightful. The mood is rising, rising, and the sweet taste spreads across the roof of Minique's mouth as it does, rolling in waves down her throat like nectar.

Minique thought her neighbours were all mostly pious, following along with the church and only deviating when there was a worthwhile opportunity for it, like a dance. But now she wonders if, all along, the people of Montréal have had sheer gleeful disobedience in their hearts, if their facades are slipping to show their impish selves underneath. And that thought makes her breathe easier, standing there in the eddy of their laughing, wild, two-sided voices; she lets her body fill with air, feels it travel to the soles of her feet and lift her high, high, higher.

Pour venir manger

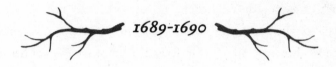

1689-1690

Minique stands outside the inn. She reads the words on the sign over the door: *La montagne du loup*. She's never noticed the name before; now all she can see is a lean, dark wolf stalking the edges of town, something feral and hungry. She feels light-headed for a moment and has to put her hands on the door to steady herself. The grain of the wood is warm from the weak midday sunlight, and this makes her brave enough to reach for the handle and walk inside.

The room is dim. It takes her a while to adjust to the darkness, the chairs and the tables and the bar slipping into her vision. The light from the windows slices inside in sharp yellow wedges, and ignites all of the specks of dust that have been stirred up by her arrival, like she is stepping into a place filled with stars, or like this place is somehow secretly, silently on fire and she never knew.

She's never been in here during the day before, and perhaps she expected it to be shut down, or for the door to be locked. But maybe the aftermath of the fear and the fever has driven people out of their homes, or maybe there have always been people looking for a drink at all hours of the day. Either way, there are men positioned around the room, stock-still, like they're subjects of a painting. The gloom gathers around them, obscuring their features, but not in a way that feels threatening. Instead, they feel like ghosts, their eyes tracking the flutter of her hands at her sides but their bodies motionless.

As she moves farther into the room, the men relax their gazes one by one, disinterested, and this reassures her more than anything. As she passes them, they start to mumble among themselves again, shapeless words that provide a comforting background noise. It seems that nobody is here to judge. She tries not to make eye contact with any of them, not wanting them to feel that she's going to expose them in some way, but her gaze catches on one of the men, who tilts his head away from her, staring with unfocused sight at something she can't see, and she's reminded of Daniel.

Daniel, whom she has not seen for a few weeks. She had hoped they could be harbours for each other, but he has withdrawn completely from the public. She doesn't know if he's helping Claude in the shop, is busy with his life, or is just avoiding seeing her. He doesn't come knock on her back door; she's stopped expecting him to. She plays back their last interaction in her head, wondering if she did something to drive him away, wondering if she worried him with her outburst. If maybe he decided that she was too big of a risk. It stings, but she can't bring herself to go knock on his door. She can't bear to see Claude's big, pitying face. If Daniel needs to deal with his sadness on his own, like a stupid man, she'll deal with hers any way she likes.

As she cocks her head from one side to the other, assessing her options and considering whether to just turn around and leave, she notices one of the men moving. He's holding up a hand, pointing her in a direction: toward the back of the inn, near the room where they danced. She shivers. His eyes aren't outright looking at her—he seems to be focusing on a spot over her shoulder, toward the streams of light that are hitting the wooden floor—but he's sensed her intent and she's unsettled and also grateful. She follows the strong line of his finger to a door that is ajar and needs only a light touch from the tips of her fingers to swing open without a creak.

Anne must hear her anyway, because without even turning away from her workbench, she says "hello Minique," and Minique almost doesn't cross the threshold because it's so queer and welcoming at the same time. Still, she jumps a bit, relieved that Anne can't see her quailing like a child. She looks around the room in a bid to distract herself. It's just as dim back here, but there aren't any windows; instead, the light comes from a lantern Anne has perched on a table in one corner, and a few candles that are now guttering with the draft. It's the smell that hits Minique the most: it's green and vegetal, dry and sweet at the same time. It smells like when she and Daniel and Barbe used to run through the fields. Minique feels her eyes prickle hot and mean at the thought of Barbe, and then the thought of Daniel holding his own grief so hard and bad inside of him. She presses the backs of her hands to her eyes, briefly, and then whips her arms down to her sides. She might be able to wear her sadness all over her face up and down the streets of Montréal, but here, in this room, she has to be brave. As brave as Anne was in the courtroom. It's a feeling she hasn't experienced in weeks, and it surprises her.

Anne turns around, wiping her hair back from her face with both palms, and with that action she goes from a sentry to the aubergiste.

"Are you here for a drink?"

Minique shakes her head. She's thinking about what it was like to have a female friend in this hard town full of men, a friend so precious and so important that she can never be truly replaced. She's thinking about how Anne is the opposite of Barbe. Anne is solid and strong, with dark hair and dark eyes. She has sense and her feet are planted on the ground. And yet—

The moment their eyes met as Anne was being marched down the street, Minique felt something. She doesn't have words for the feeling because it's only new and fluttering, a baby of a thing. It feels grotesque to be searching for a replacement for Barbe so soon after her death, but Anne's strength, mixed with that strange bit of otherworldliness, reminds Minique of the women she's known, and she wants to chase it.

And anyone who can stand tall and proud while being arrested, while in court, is someone she wants to be around. If only off to the side. If only for a moment. She'll take what she can get, whatever scraps Anne is willing to toss her way. Just for a change. Just for something to do.

Anne pats a stool and Minique thumps down onto it, a bit stunned. Anne disappears into the main room for a few minutes, and when she returns, she places a cup of tea in Minique's hands.

"Better for you than beer," Anne says, and Minique can smell chamomile. She takes a grateful sip. "Though beer has its place." Minique has a moment where she sees Barbe's pale silk hair whipping around in the middle of a dance, hears the laughing scratch of a bow on a string, and she feels like someone has socked her in the gut. She forces the feeling back down with a second sip of tea and scalds the grief right out of her body for the time being.

Anne sits down across from Minique and watches her. It's rare for Minique to feel cowed in the presence of someone, especially now that she's not a child anymore, but Anne's even gaze makes her feel like she's ten years old again. Minique wants to stammer and fill the silence with something, but that's not the right action. Instead, she opens her mouth slightly, trying to breathe Anne into her palate. Trying again to see if she has a flavour. She tastes the garden-like smell of the room, the sweetness of the dust mixing with the candle wax. She tastes the tea on her tongue, and even the faint bitterness of the men beyond the door. But Anne—Anne is nothing. She is like porcelain or glass. She has no taste, no mood, no scent, and Minique is left there with her mouth hanging open. She's never met someone who didn't immediately waft their intentions to her; every person has had a taste, and that's how Minique has started to define her interactions in her daily life without even thinking about it. Now, she has to revert to what normal people do in situations like this, and she's suddenly aware that she's probably not very good at it.

Instead, she starts to examine the rest of the room more closely. When she first bumbled in, it was too dim for her to make out the details. Now, she can see that Anne was bent over a thick book, writing. She can see the ink smudged on Anne's wrist bones and the edges of her hands. She can see that the herbaceous smell is coming from bundles of herbs hanging from the beams, that the ceiling is feathered with dried plants. She can see a mortar and pestle at one end of the table, and a few bowls at the other end. Anne has a cluster of bottles and jugs on a shelf behind her, but they're unlabelled and Minique can't make out what's inside them. There are also a few books behind Anne's body, but she can't read the spines. There's a bouquet of feathers—black, maybe crow—hanging from one of the beams. There's a knotted rope hanging beside it, with rocks tied into it.

Anne follows her eyes, turns her head a little to see. Then she smiles, reaching a hand back to touch lightly at the rope. Minique waits for her to explain, but Anne stays quiet. There are lessons to be learned here, like the way her aunt taught her about the power of being silent and drawing the question out. So she knows what she's doing when she cedes.

"What is it?"

Anne keeps her fingers on the rope but her eyes on Minique. She's not hard or critical-looking; she just seems to be observing, giving Minique time to expose herself if that's what needs to happen. Minique sits, trying to look as placid as she can. This might be a moment where she finds an ally, if not a friend, and she doesn't want to ruin the peace she's found in this sweet, dim room. She doesn't want to be sent out of the pub, doesn't want to have to squint her way back home through the harsh midday light.

Minique takes another sip of tea. For the first time in a long time, she's calm. She closes her eyes and takes in a deep breath, letting the warmth spread from her throat to her stomach to the lines of her thighs. She feels it travel down her legs and pool in the soles of her feet, where it ebbs into the ground, beneath the wooden floor, and creates the perfect line: tea and mouth to body to floor to earth, again and again and again.

"A magic ladder," Anne says, tugging on the end of the rope so that her nails click against one of the stones.

Maybe Anne thought Minique would balk at the term *magic*, especially in the wake of the trial, but Minique doesn't care. Magic is believing that god lives in a building or a cross or a string of beads. Magic is believing that holding your hands a specific way means that good things will come to you, and dancing and singing and laughing and having a good time mean that bad things will happen. Magic is the forest, the places her father hunted and lived, the world beyond her ken. Magic is the stupidity that brought them all here, the ship sailing down the River St. Laurence, dropping off women at every port. It doesn't matter to her that Anne believes in one specific form of magic over another; when it comes down to it, they're all living in a world of stories and sorcery. *Magic* is just another word for something men don't comprehend; she understands that now. If this is magic, so is her ability.

"What does it do?"

"It grants wishes," Anne says.

Minique shakes her head. "Nobody gets what they wish for."

Anne stands up and unloops the rope from the rafters. She touches a finger to the first knot.

"By knot of one, the spell's begun." Her voice is low, the same kind of low it was in the courthouse, but with none of the demurity she showed to the judge. Minique feels the hair on the back of her neck stand up, and for a moment, she wonders if Father Etienne saw something in Anne that no one else was able to.

Anne's finger moves. "By knot of two, the magic comes true. By knot of three, so it shall be. By knot of four, this power is stored."

Minique keeps waiting for the panic to set in, for the warmth and calmness to dissipate, but it never does.

"By knot of five, my will shall drive. By knot of six, the spell I fix. By knot of seven, the future I leaven. By knot of eight, my will be fate." Anne looks up at her, wraps her fingers around the final knot. "By knot of nine, what's done is mine."

Back on the continent, from what Minique has heard from Tante Marie, women are getting killed by the dozens, even hundreds, for all kinds of reasons: sorcery, reading a book, using a poultice, speaking big words, making a tincture, walking a different route home on the night of a full moon. Using plants and animals to cure themselves or help others. Using knowledge passed down through generations of women who came before them. For this, women are hanged or dunked underwater till they drown. They are tied to stakes and burned alive. She doesn't know why New France is different. Maybe cutting down enough trees to build a pyre would be too hard here. Maybe there are so few women that the men just want to keep them all alive. Maybe it takes too much energy, and that's energy that the men in charge of the colony don't have, because they're too busy trying to keep themselves warm, keep tabs on the tribes they want to subjugate, keep their ragged little towns running and their ragged little people alive.

"Can anyone make this?" Minique's voice sounds thick, but she reaches out and gestures to the rope. She doesn't know if she's allowed to touch it. She wants to touch it.

"Anyone can make this," Anne says with a small smile. And then, as some sort of kindness, she asks: "Are you ready to try?"

Because Anne owns her own business, she's able to up and leave in the middle of the day. All she does is tack a piece of paper to the front door, lock up, and they're off. The first few times she did this, Minique goggled at her.

"What about customers?"

"They'll always come back," Anne said to her with a laugh. "Vice is forever."

Now Minique is used to them leaving the town gates in the middle of the day. It mirrors her own desperate walks, except with less wretchedness.

Today, the two of them are walking through the cemetery. They've already passed the orchard. Minique tried not to look at any of the trees, especially not the one she and Daniel and Barbe used to heft themselves up into.

Spending time with Anne has been like jumping into cold, clear water: sharp and edifying and somewhat dangerous. There was no preamble, no friend-courting like she's seen other women do: the dance, the bowing of heads, the painfully big smiles. Instead, it was like when she met Barbe and Daniel—immediate and immersive, with no excess pleasantries. She wouldn't call Anne warm, not even particularly friendly, but there is kindness and also patience, and that's more than she can say for many people.

"There's not much that lives here during the winter," Anne says. "Usually I collect during the spring and summer. But if you know where to look, there are still some things to be found." Minique has no idea what she's talking about, but she nods anyway.

They've reached the woods, and Minique looks back at their path through the dirty, hard snow. The bare, skeletal apple trees, the graveyard. Sometimes it seems as though there are more people dead and buried than there are making a successful life in Montréal. She looks to Anne, who is standing with her hand on the branch of a pine tree, running her thumb over something glistening. Past to present to future, looking back to forward. It's not an easy choice to take another step toward the forest, but Minique does it because she can't think about the graveyard anymore.

"Sap," Anne says.

"Like for syrup?"

"From a maple tree, yes. From a pine tree—" Anne digs a fingertip into the sap and holds it up. It catches the sun and gleams. "You can use it to stop cuts from bleeding. You can make it into a tea to help a sore throat. You can make it into a soap and use it for rashes." Anne bites the sap off the end of her finger and rolls it around in her mouth, chewing. "You can use it to settle the stomach. Also good for lighting fires, for making torches, for waterproofing, for making glue."

"How do you know all of this?" Minique is gobsmacked. One tree, many uses—and how many times did she stare out at this forest and not know all of that?

Anne shrugs. "That book you saw in the courtroom. And I ask the Iroquois."

Minique blanches. She's immediately brought back to sitting in the classroom, listening to the nuns talk about how violent and terrible the Iroquois are. "That's why we were sent here," Sister Marie-Marguerite would say. "To save them." At lunch, in the yard, the girls would talk about what would happen to you if you were captured by the Iroquois: "First they peel off your scalp and then they cut off your fingertips and make you eat them and then they cut off your feet and then they peel off your face, and then they shove hot coals down your throat, and you better just hope and pray that you die some time during it all so you don't have to bear all the pain." Minique never thought to ask where her classmates, young girls who knew nothing about the world beyond the town walls, were getting this information. It sounded more like something Daniel would tell her and Barbe to try to make them squeal, but when she relayed the details to him, he rolled his eyes. "That's not true," he said. "The brothers say things like that all the time. But they're so annoying I'd want to kill them, too!"

Anne sees Minique's face and laughs. "Yes, the governor and the religious idiots are always keen on giving Montréalers a bogeyman, aren't they?"

"Haven't they killed so many—"

"But you'd defend your home if strangers came and tried to take it away from you."

Of course Minique would, or at least she'd want to. How has she never thought about it that way? It's all the French have done since landing here: tried to take over more and more land, when they clearly can't even handle the land they currently have. Montréal still isn't growing; it's a stagnant cesspool full of men who are constantly getting arrested for fighting and killing one another. Women don't want to live here, and children get sick and die here. It's a rough, mean town, and people often leave for greener pastures.

"Sometimes the men come into town for the fur fairs, and I pay someone to translate. Or I try to speak myself, but I find it hard, the languages." Anne makes a complicated, fluttering hand motion near her mouth. "The Iroquois know plants better than anyone else. The French say they want alliances, but they antagonize them because the Iroquois value their women and they don't give a shit about our religion."

How can Anne be so brave? Minique hates talking to people, especially men of any kind.

"I've never been to a fur fair."

Anne looks at her sharply, leading her deeper into the forest. "That surprises me, considering what your father did, but I suppose your aunt is strict enough that it was never an option. The markets aren't as popular as they used to be. The trade is dying down. But there's one coming up in the summer. We'll go. It'll be good for you to see."

Minique makes as if to say something, though what it is, she's not sure. But before she can get any words out, Anne continues. "You can't be cloistered forever."

I don't think I'm so cloistered, Minique wants to say. She's eighteen, a grown-up now. She doesn't believe in the religion that's always being pushed onto her, and that's a start. She has something that no one else has, something that sets her apart, and that's the next step. She's out here in the forest getting her palms sticky and her hair mussed in the middle of winter, and that's more than anyone else in the town can say. But she's missing a large swath of knowledge because she didn't know trees could be used as glue or as a dressing for wounds, and she didn't know that she could go to the fur market, and she didn't know that she would want to, either.

Anne moves on to another tree. She crushes some of the foliage between her pointer finger and her thumb, and the sharp smell of cedar blooms between them.

"Boil this in a tea and your teeth won't fall out in the winter," Anne says. "Helps with coughs, helps with fevers." She stops, considers something, tilts her head up to the grey sky they can see through the treetops. "It also must be said that half of the power of healing someone lies in the mind." She brings her hands up to either side of her head, taps once, then twice, then three times. "If someone thinks they're drinking something that helps them, if they think they're taking a medicine, they're more likely to get better."

She turns to Minique. "The mind is the most powerful tool we have. Among other things." And then she levels Minique with a scrutinizing look. Minique freezes in place, pinned under the heaviness of Anne's stare. She feels, all of a sudden, like Anne is peering through her like she's a piece of fine glass, that Anne can see beyond all the warps and dents into the marrow of her. Minique can feel the words in her gullet, hot and liquid: she wants to grab Anne by the arm and anchor herself to her, tell her how she's different, how she can taste change on the wind and rage from the heart and lust coursing between two mouths. Minique wants to confess everything, to lift the weight of it from her body and force someone else to share in her dire, maybe deadly, secret.

But she waits perhaps a moment too long, standing there wide-eyed and choke-throated, and Anne turns from her without saying anything more. She continues walking, and Minique follows behind her, trying to put her own boots into Anne's footsteps in the snow.

They walk for a few minutes more, the cold air soothing Minique's flushed face. The forest undulates around them with the sound of winter: the scrunch of their boots in the crispness of the snow, the creaking of trees in the wind, the pipping calls of tits above them.

"Is this sorcery?"

Anne doesn't stop walking. "Is what?"

"This?" What is *this*? What are they doing? Is there shame in trudging through the snow and tearing the tips of branches off of trees?

Anne turns around. Her face is placid. "Do you think sorcery exists?"

Minique stands and looks at her, looks at the woods around them. The forest sounds like the highest note of a stringed instrument, the wind a tumble of notes through the branches. She feels clumsy, like a stain on the landscape. Like she's facing some sort of test and will fail. But Anne is a calmness in the wildness and anxiety, and she stands there, dark-haired, dark-eyed. Minique has the sudden thought that she's looking at a version of herself from years down the road.

"I think—" What does she think? "I think."

Anne smiles. "You don't have to answer now. There are some questions that need time. But just remember that this place is terrible; it's astonishing. Sometimes it seems like it's nothing but badness. It's death and grief."

Minique nods, feeling that grief threaten to come out of her throat and fill her mouth.

Anne goes on. "We have to find beauty somewhere. We have to find pleasure and beauty. Somewhere. And for some of us—for some of us, that comes from agency. Do you know what that means, *agency*?"

Minique shakes her head.

"It means to have power. It means to be in control of your own life."

"That's something they don't want us to have." She doesn't have to specify who *they* are, because Anne laughs a little.

"It's true. You saw that in the courthouse that day. I knew it was coming. Etienne, that fool. He doesn't realize everybody hates him. The new world is so far removed from France in so many ways; religion doesn't have that much power over people here." Minique frowns at that. "I know it seems like they do, but they don't, not compared to the continent. There is room for more wildness here. Especially in Montréal, as unruly as it is.

"Sometimes you have to find agency through something like this," she says, a hand gesturing around her. "Through something that confuses or angers other people. Minique, if you make a life for yourself—if you make it so that you have knowledge no one else has, can offer a product or a service that nobody else can—then you have agency. You can have power."

It's like a siren's song, the idea of power. The idea of striking just a little bit more fear into people's hearts. The idea of being able to feed and clothe herself, to live alone, to earn a living without having to rely on a man or a family member or the church. Minique can see that Anne is offering her something, and she knows already what her answer is. Because all parts of her are screaming *yes, yes, yes*. Because she knows that if she wants to thrive here—not just live, not just survive—she has to do something.

"I want that," she says.

Anne isn't a perfect teacher. She has gaps in her knowledge, and sometimes Minique suspects she's making answers up on the spot.

By virtue of being a settler, Anne will never know as much as Indigenous people. A few French people have naturalized some plants that used to grow only on the continent, and there are some plants growing already in New France that have cousins in Europe, but most of the knowledge Anne has cobbled together was either brought over or has been picked up from the Indigenous tribes, whether observed directly or absorbed second-hand from the coureurs or the missionaries.

"And then I write it all down," she told Minique. "That's the book you saw in the courthouse.

"That's your first lesson," Anne said, "listening." Minique opened her mouth to protest, *I've always been good at listening, I had no one to talk to*, but Anne raised her eyebrows and then a hand, continuing. "Listening for the information that everyone else thinks is worthless. And, often, listening to people who are treated poorly, or people who drive you crazy, who you'd rather ignore."

After years of being talked at about things she finds useless, it's easy to be talked at about something fascinating. It soothes her to watch Anne glide around her workshop, touching items with the tips of her fingers, explaining how to decant or julienne or macerate or extract. Anne doesn't get angry when Minique asks her to repeat something so she can write it down; Minique has taken to carrying around a notebook and a pencil stub to scratch out messy notes. Anne doesn't get frustrated when Minique picks up the little glass bottles herself, holding them close to her face. She doesn't get impatient when Minique smells all of her varieties of tea with her eyes closed. She lets Minique learn things by touch and scent and taste, which is to say slowly; it takes time to build the image of something in your mind through all of the senses that aren't sight. But Minique knows that once she learns all of the things like this, they will forever be in her head; they'll never slip away.

Minique begins to understand Anne's blunt honesty and the way she wields it like a tool, not trying to harm but only trying to make her own life easier. She appreciates Anne's stoic demeanour, the way she carries herself like she's playing a card game. Even in the face of a belligerent man in the murkiest corner of the inn, Anne is implacable. Minique appreciates Anne's criticisms of New France, of Montréal especially, and the measured way she distributes them, and conversely the way Anne will stop to talk with anyone who wants to speak with her, even if they're a Jesuit, if they're drunk, if they're someone she's rolled her eyes at before. She's judicious and calm, and this makes other people want to be pulled into her sphere.

After the trial, Minique expected people to be more scared of Anne, but it's gone the other way. People stop her in the street to ask her how she's doing and where she's going. Her inn is busy. She's always at the brasseur to restock her stores. People make way for her in the shops she goes into, moving to the sides to form a pathway. Minique doesn't know if they're scared of her or admiring her. Maybe it's both.

Minique finds herself wanting to know more and more about Anne's life. "What is running the inn like?" she asks one day, and Anne explains that it's constant, it's tiring, it can be depressing to see people piss away their fortunes, but at the same time it allows her to talk to men, to have eyes everywhere, to be able to offer people a shelter if they need it.

"Were you worried in court?" she asks as she's helping Anne sweep out her storeroom, and Anne says she really wasn't; maybe she ought to have been, but she knew in her heart of hearts that Father Etienne didn't stand a chance. "Never interrupt somebody you hate when they're making a mistake," she says. Men like that, she says, you just need to give them enough rope and they'll hang themselves; you don't need to do anything except sit back and wait. "Do you want to stay in Montréal for the rest of your life?" Minique asks her on a morning when Anne is putting shims under some of her wobbly tables. "I don't know," Anne says. "Maybe there's more out there."

Spring arrives with a lushness that surprises Minique. She thought that after the horror of the winter, a thaw would never come. But the world has woken up. The snow melts fast and fiercely, leaving giant, foul-smelling puddles in the middle of all the streets. Green shoots start to poke up through the mud that sucks at Minique's heels. The air tastes damp, not the dry, sharp pain of winter. She starts to wake up earlier and earlier, the daylight dancing in around the edges of her window. She dresses in the quiet of the house, avoiding Tante Marie, holding her boots in her hands until she's outside in the sweetened air, where she can sit on the stoop and lace up before starting the walk to the inn.

It's the start of the busy season for Anne.

"Why so busy?" Minique is toying with two tins on Anne's work-table in the back room. Anne is taking down bundles of herbs and sorting them, occasionally mumbling to herself as she unties the strings keeping the bunches together.

"Because plants are growing," she says, sounding distracted.

"What do you do with them?"

Anne points with her head at the notebook on the other side of the table. The *witch's grimoire*, Father Etienne had called it. Minique's seen it sitting there, day in and day out. Sometimes it's closed, bound with a cord. Sometimes it's open to a well-worn page. She's never been bold enough to peek at it.

She asks, hesitantly: "Can I touch it?"

Anne nods, a string between her teeth. "You can touch anything in here; nothing I have is off limits to you."

Minique feels a bit foolish for having thought she wasn't allowed, but she reaches for the book, carefully opening it. It's the size of a bible, saddle-stitched with a thin leather cover. The pages crinkle satisfyingly as she thumbs through them. *For coughs and colds*, reads one title at the top of a page. *For toothache and bleeding gums*, reads another. The pages are filled with remedies for sore throats and warts and infected wounds and headaches and cramps. Some are written in a fainter, lighter hand; some are written in a bold one. At the back of the book are dozens of empty pages.

"Were you expecting it to be magic spells?"

Minique startles, shuts the book. Anne smiles at her. The rafters have been cleared of the dried bundles; she's packed them away into various tins and cloth bags with carefully written labels.

"Where did all this come from?"

Anne takes the book, opening it to the first pages. "These were written by my aunt. She learned some of these remedies from her mother and her own aunts. I think it's likely that some of these were added by other female relatives as well." She flips through to the second part, in the clearer, stronger handwriting. "These are my additions. A lot of the recipes had to be adjusted for the plants in the new world, so I tried to revise them as best I could."

"And there are those empty pages at the end to add more," Minique says. Anne gets a puzzled look on her face, and then smiles.

"Yes, that's what those pages are for."

Maybe it's because the summer seems brighter and wilder after the horrible winter. Maybe it's because Minique wasn't sure she'd live through the new year. Maybe it's because she never really stopped before to look at all of the green. But there is green. All around her. The world smells ripe and fresh at the same time, like an ending and a beginning. Winter is a time of quiet, snow like a heavy blanket muffling every voice to a murmur and lulling every human and animal to sleep. But the cusp of summer from spring is a time of sound; wind in the grass, a finger dragging softly on a rich pattern of moss, mud squelching.

She and Anne exist outside, work outside, breathe outside. Minique's hands have started to brown from time spent in the sun; her hair has lighter strands in it. She and Anne shuffle around on their knees and in half-squats in the meadows, in the scrub around the cemetery, in the woods, trimming and uprooting and picking and snapping. Anne explains that if they don't collect plants now, they won't have ingredients for the rest of the year. It's lucky that the summer is the busy season for the rest of the town—for habitants, farming their fields; for coureurs and the Iroquois, preparing for the August fur fair; for farriers and rat catchers and diggers and postmen and road menders, seeing business boom after a period of hibernation—and that the whole place thrums with activity and no one pays attention to them going off together every morning. In the hive of summer chores and morning-to-night work, everyone minds their own business.

Before this, summer was always just another season for Minique. A series of months in which she had to wear lighter dresses and braid her hair with more care to keep it up out of her face. Maybe she was too young to understand the joy that summer can bring for people who have had to work the whole winter to stay alive. Or maybe now the town needs a season of kinder weather. But never before has Minique noticed the way people let their guards down in the warmth. At the end of a day, when she's walking back to town, habitants sit on their front steps with mugs of beer, glowing with pleasure, their boots off and their children playing in the shallows of the river. In town, people walk with a little more sway, bonnets dangling from a fingertip more often than they should be, faces turned up to the sun.

And the woods grow and rustle alive. Even on days when there's no wind. Even on days when the trees should stand absolutely silently. Even then, the woods crawl with life, swarming and pulsing and swaying. As a child, she never thought of it. Now she spends most of her days in between the trees.

Anne and Minique collect thistle and sage and sweetgrass and primrose and nettles and fireweed; one time, Minique came home with her hands covered in welts, to Tante Marie's dismay. Her aunt shook her head and told Minique to keep her hands in a bowl of cold water.

Anne and Minique cut stalks and bind bundles to be taken back to the inn and dried. They snip tender buds and nip petals and pour them into little silk bags, to be eventually made into teas—for sleep, for calmness, for fatigue. They stain their fingers with the purple blooms of violets and dye the backs of their hands a violent orange from the dusty innards of lilies and their palms smell strongly of wild onion by the end of each day. With every plant they remove or bisect, Anne makes sure to tell Minique what they're doing, why they're doing it, how best to store it, what best to use it for. Minique keeps her ears open and tries her best to remember, to write it down later that night, when she's alone in her bed, for herself: *Mayapple to ward off insects. Sarsaparilla for earache and nosebleed, and also for a good drink on a summer day. Ginger for an upset stomach. Bloodroot for sore mouths and bleeding gums. Peppergrass for stubborn chickens that don't want to lay eggs. Flax for hair loss and skin so beautiful it will stop a coureur in his tracks.* The list goes on and on and on, and Minique finds herself murmuring plant names and cures and side effects under her breath when she's not with Anne: when she's about to fall asleep, when she's washing her face in the basin, when she's counting her steps on the way to the inn. It probably doesn't lend well to the reputation she has in town, but who there does she care about anyway? Who does she have? Tante Marie. Daniel.

Sometimes when she thinks of Daniel, she has to hit a fist against her chest, just to thump some sense back into herself and alleviate that strange ache. She hasn't seen Daniel for months. It's really no easy feat in Montréal, but with the grief and the fever, she assumed everyone was staying in their own homes. When the sickness was finally gone, and people were brave enough to venture out, she never saw him; he never came and knocked on her back door like he used to do to collect her for a walk. And Minique got angry. She thought *how dare he abandon the one friend he really has*, and the longer she thought about it, the more tightened up with rage she got. She didn't have pride when she was haunting the streets full of grief; she didn't have pride when she defied the priest and wore her sadness ugly and mean for everyone to witness. Sometimes she thought about marching over to the bakery or the Nicolet house to pound on the door till her hands got bruised. But pride held her back. How could she go out of her way for a friend who clearly didn't want to be a friend anymore? Whenever Tante Marie came back from the bakery, Minique left the room. She didn't want to hear anything about Claude or his wife or his son.

She never considered that while her grief was outward, his might be inward; that he might be drowning in it. She never considered anything at all—she only considered herself.

While she's with Anne, Daniel's out in the real woods, the deep woods. Tante Marie eventually tells Minique that she heard from Claude that Daniel's learning how to portage, how to skin and tan a hide, how to read the rivers. Will his sadness send him out into the forest forever? Will he become a shade like her father? Or will he be able to master his own emotions? She tries not to let him take up too much space in her mind, despite that ever-present pain rolling around in her chest, withered and dry. If the two of them have to come through this tunnel by immersing themselves in the forest, then maybe they'll see each other on the other side.

She keeps herself busy. It's not hard with all of the things Anne has for them to do. Minique learns how to dry, how to mash, how to extract, how to pulverize. She becomes deft with a mortar and pestle and with the tins and jars used to decant. She also learns how to wield a knife with the most delicate of movements. Anne keeps her knives sharper than any Minique has used before, and so she suffers more than a few bleeding fingertips and palms before she becomes used to the motions; she gets familiar with her skin on her tongue, the taste of blood in her mouth, rich and metallic. She learns how to skin and flay a stalk, how to stew for hours while skimming the scum off the top, how to finally avoid blisters and rashes on her hands when harvesting the angrier plants and then how to use plants to give someone else blisters and rashes, if need be.

While she does all of this, she's also trying to make her own tiny additions, altering recipes minutely to see if it changes the outcome. If she macerates instead of mashes. If she dices instead of shreds. If she boils it on high or simmers it on low. She's remembering and noting and logging the changes, in her head and in her notebook.

Sometimes, Anne watches over Minique's shoulder, murmuring the words aloud as Minique writes them. Minique curls a hand around the notebook, wanting to shield it from Anne, not really knowing why.

"You make your own notes," Anne says, smiling. Minique nods. "Don't you trust me to tell you everything I know?"

Minique is fiercely certain that Anne is absolutely not telling her everything she knows. She doesn't know whether it's because Anne wants to withhold a few key pieces of wisdom that make her indispensable no matter how skilled Minique becomes, or whether it's for some other reason. It doesn't matter. Minique has to learn in her own way; she has to manoeuvre around whatever tests Anne is laying down for her.

So she starts to build her own knowledge base. She tests ointments on her own wrists. She streaks her own ankles and calves with

ANNA MAXYMIW

oils she's made, seeing how her skin reacts. She goes around smelling herbaceous, of a greenness that wafts its way out from underneath her sleeves and her hem. It announces her: *Here I am, here is my power.* For the first time in a long time, she has something that levers her out of bed in the morning, that makes her want to put her feet on the floor and get dressed and face the world in all its frailties. And in those frailties, she can see the beauty: the bee saddled heavy with pollen like gold dust, the bead of blood starkly red like a gem on the tip of her finger when she catches herself with a thorn, the whorls of hair stuck with sweat to the back of Anne's neck like writing in another language she's so close to deciphering. The world shows itself to her, the bad side of it she already knew intimately, and the good side, the side dappled with light and life, that she was so sure didn't exist and couldn't be hers.

And there is beauty in having a friend. She thinks Anne is her friend. Anne doesn't voluntarily touch her like Barbe did, doesn't lean into her body so much that Minique can feel her warmth in her bones. But Anne is a steady, constant presence. Despite running an inn and being dragged before a court and having made an enemy of the priest, Anne has a life remarkably full of order. She keeps her workplace clean and organized; she makes Minique wake up early every weekday to meet her; she never raises her voice nor gets particularly sharp if something is done slowly or incorrectly. Minique finds her soothing. For someone who was accused of being a witch, there's nothing shocking about her. That isn't to say that Minique isn't a little bit scared of Anne: she is. Anne doesn't volunteer her feelings; she doesn't talk about what's going through her mind; she never really shows emotion on her face.

Today, she's perched beside Anne on a log, drinking cooled sassafras tea out of a canteen Anne carries at her side. Minique tilts her head and looks up at the canopy above her, the whispering of leaves on leaves like a lullaby. Crows creak in the trees. A rabbit bobbles, unafraid; Anne follows it with her eyes. Minique's arms and legs are strong from the weeks of clawing through the underbrush. Her hands have new calluses that she wears with pride. She feels tall and healthy and, mostly, emboldened.

"Why did you come here?"

As far as Minique can tell, people don't ask each other this question. The truth is, the settlers are a ragged, strange crew, built from violence and sadness. Some people came willingly, but many people had to be persuaded or, in the case of those convicted of poaching or smuggling, forced over as a life sentence. And then there are those who wanted to escape poverty, lured with the promise of land or ship passage. People were sold on the idea of a new country, fierce and free and easy, with soil to turn into farms as far as the eye could see. That was a lie, but by the time everyone realized it, they were all stranded in the new world, shivering in their miserably thin jackets and their piss-poor shoes and left to figure it out for themselves.

Anne looks sideways at her.

Minique decides to offer up a little of herself. "Because I didn't. Come here. And I always wonder why people—why people do."

"Does it make you feel lesser than?" This is her specialty: answering a question with another question. Minique stores that in her mind, alongside Tante Marie's blank-eyed silences. These are tools that women use to dodge inquiry or to turn a conversation on its head. But right now, Minique wants to bulldog her way through.

"I asked first."

Anne laughs. "You have no guile." Minique opens her mouth to maybe whine, and Anne holds up a hand. "Yet. You have no guile *yet*."

"Do I need it?"

"We all do." The *we* holds the unspoken meaning: the women, we, us, the reluctant sisterhood. Minique turns her face to Anne and watches her ear until Anne smiles and relents. "You'll have to get better at asking things without making it sound like you're asking them, you know." She caps the canteen. "My family died."

It's not said with a tremulous voice, but that's exactly what makes Minique feel bad. Anne catches the look on her face and shakes her head. "Don't make that face. It happens, Minique. It happened with my family, and it happened with your mother and your father.

"I wasn't married—I wasn't even betrothed yet. It was a rash. Terrible thing: blisters all over. Fever, shitting. Father, mother, two sisters, one brother. All dead within two weeks. But I didn't die. I didn't even get sick." Anne meets her eyes. "Here, Minique, people are more focused on living than they are on making other people's lives a particular kind of hell. Be thankful for that. It's why I was acquitted. But back on the continent, it's worse. Men, they believe that a woman who's strong is unnatural." She wipes her hands on her apron, twisting the cloth around her fingers more than usual. "I thought they wanted to send me to the pest house, to see if I'd eventually get the pox, but it was worse than that."

"Worse?"

"Have you ever seen a person burned alive?" Anne is no longer winding her hands in her apron. They're steady in her lap. Her voice is clear and strong. No shake, anywhere in her. Minique wishes she could turn on a power like this, at will.

"No." Her voice is very small.

"The screams—I've never heard anything like them. Not even when I've heard women forced."

Stop, Minique wants to say.

"The skin splits open and the fat spills out and all you can do is pray that the person is dead by that time, so they won't see their body leaking into the flames. The bones shrink. The ashes are greasy afterward, and people dig around in them for teeth to keep as souvenirs."

Without warning, Minique gags, turning around and retching off the back of the log. Bile strings from her mouth. She hadn't even felt the vomit coming—it had barrelled right through her. She's red with surprise and embarrassment and nausea.

"I never wanted to see that again. And I didn't want to become that woman at the stake. I got on the first ship I could find, and I met Alexandre on the way over, and we pretended we were married because we knew we would get better treatment in New France if we seemed proper."

"*Pretended*? You never married him?" Minique wipes her mouth with the back of her hand. She's shocked. Alexandre died when she was young, but she remembers flashes of him. Tall, slender, with blond hair. A voice that carried a melody even when just speaking. He was kind, she thinks, too kind for this place. She's heard from Claude that Alexandre and Anne were inseparable. That sometimes they finished each other's sentences, reached for each other's hands at the exact same time. When he died, everyone expected Anne to turn over the auberge and live off of the proceeds till she became old and grey. Or maybe to move elsewhere. Even go back to France. But Anne did none of those things. She wore black for a year, refusing to speak to anyone. She gestured to flour and eggs and sugar in the store and conducted her business without opening her mouth. She stayed quiet behind her veil, kept the auberge doors closed and the windows dirty. And then, a year to the day after Alexandre died, she cleaned the glass and lit the candles and opened the door, and suddenly she was back.

"Alex was my friend, but not a lover," Anne says, her cheeks the slightest bit pink.

"Why not?"

"He didn't prefer the company of women." Minique blinks a few times, unsure of what this means. Anne sees her stymied look and smiles. "I forget. I mean that he loved men but knew that he would be safer if he married a woman. And I needed a protector, too."

Minique wants to ask *how do two men love each other?* But she won't press Anne like that. Instead, she asks: "Do you miss him?"

"Every day," Anne says. The rabbit is back; it nibbles on the grass and clover, unaware that the two women sitting near it could kill it and skin it in a handful of seconds.

When Anne breaks the silence, her voice startles Minique.

"Do you want to go to the fur fair?"

The day of the fair dawns hot and sticky. Minique wakes up feeling like she has a fever; her sleep was patchy and odd, with dreams she can't quite remember. She wipes a wet cloth over the back of her neck, under her arms, and between her legs before she dresses. When she touches a tongue to her own wrist, she tastes salt. She resists the urge to bite into her skin, to confirm that she's actually awake.

She can't bear to wear heavy clothes today, so she ties herself into a cotton shift and a worn blouse with a loosely laced bodice overtop, and pulls on her thinnest pair of stockings, her oldest petticoat, and one of her lightest skirts. She rejects the idea of a shawl, and can't bring herself to wear a bonnet that clings to her head, but she does take a wide-brimmed hat that once belonged to her father, an artifact fished out of his wardrobe in the hazy, strange days after his death. Wearing it will draw scrutiny, but it will at least shade part of her face from onlookers. How long has it been since she threw herself into the press of a crowd? Since she walked among throngs of her neighbours? She remembers Father Etienne spitting into her face, his rage at her unabashed emotion, and she wonders if the other men in town are in his thrall at all. If anyone else will shove their way into her personal space.

By the time she slides as quietly as she can down the stairs, she's sweating again, her collar already damp; she tugs her hat lower to try to cover her shiny face. As she walks down the front hallway,

Tante Marie pivots out of the kitchen, and Minique startles. She and her aunt have been dancing around each other ever since the outbreak of the fever; it's likely her aunt has no idea how to deal with Minique's grief, and maybe doesn't want to, and after watching Barbe die, Minique doesn't want to try to pretend to be anything she's not. It's like the two of them have made a pact, and if she's honest with herself, Minique prefers it. There's no useless worrying over her appearance, no trying to learn silly skills that will make her a good wife one day. It's a live-and-let-live existence, two women circling around each other through different rooms, tracing each other's footsteps but rarely, if ever, meeting.

Now, the two of them look at each other. Minique hadn't realized how much older her aunt looks, how her skin seems thinner, her eyes cloudier, and her hair more brittle. In Minique's mind, Tante Marie has always been a force to be reckoned with; now, she's surprised to see that she looks like an old woman.

But her eyes, more clouded they might be, are still sharp enough to snag on Minique's hat.

"You look like your father," she says. Her aunt doesn't say it with any kind of particular malice, but Minique still shivers. First it was her father cursing her, saying she looked like her mother, and now this. *Why can't I just look like myself?*

Instead, she hurries out the door before her aunt can attach any more ghosts to this day. Now Minique is carrying the presence of her father with her, on the way to this place that would have been his purview, and it sits heavy on her shoulders. It's a yoke and it's armour. For so long she's been trying to forget him. What did he add to her life? What did he do for her? It was nothing tangible, or so she

thought. But now, with more age behind her and life in front of her, she can see that he was the force behind everything. That without him, and his necessary absence, she wouldn't have had a house to live in, food on her plate, dresses to wear to school and boots to wear in the winter. It's an odd mix, feeling bitter and wistful about someone long gone. But today, she can wear his spirit like a cape.

Anne is waiting a little way down the street. Even after so much time spent together, Anne is still that little bit removed, aloof like a cat. She won't comment on Minique's appearance or ask how it was getting out of the house or question her about what her morning was like. Right now it's business, the two of them moving toward a goal.

The fur fair is in the west end of town, on the common land, so they have a distance to go. Normally, Minique would shy away from walking right through the middle of Montréal. But today, the town is wildly alive. It's vibrating with more people than she's ever seen before, and in the masses, Anne and Minique are just two women. People are spilling out of doors and hanging out of windows, waving to one another. The crowd tastes light, a veil of happiness cast over everyone with a vein of greed running underneath it all. Anne laughs out loud at the look on Minique's face as she takes in the joy around her.

As they get closer to the site of the fair, the noise changes to the musical yell of hawkers, the clang of blacksmiths and metal workers, the seesaw of haggling. There are stalls everywhere, merchants shaking out beaver furs and rabbit pelts and even what she thinks is a moose hide. There are bodies, bodies, bodies: white bodies and brown bodies and male bodies, mostly, but also some female bodies. There are hands flying over tables, pinching and prodding fur, running through pelts, making choppy motions to refuse a price, turning a palm up to placate.

There are tents and lean-tos and carts, and the innards of people's lives leaking out of doorways and windows. There are babies on cradle-boards and on shoulders and in the crooks of arms. There are more Indigenous people and coureurs des bois than she's ever seen in her life. There are people she's never seen before, people who aren't from Montréal or anywhere even close. There are people who smell like patience and people who smell mercenary and people who smell bored. The mix of scents is too overwhelming for Minique almost immediately and she has to snap her mouth shut and breathe only through her nose. Anne's hand on her wrist is an anchor, but she's not being pulled along; she's being allowed to dawdle, to look, to see the way the fur glows rich in the sun, the way a runnel of sweat traces down the back of an Iroquois seller, the way a buyer touches her fore-head with the tips of her fingers in a thank-you gesture when language is too great of a barrier.

She thinks of Daniel. She's learned from talk around Montréal that Daniel isn't in town any longer. He's officially decided to become a coureur and is on an expedition to the pays d'en haut. This fair, all these young men—she's reminded of him. She has to stop herself from whipsawing her gaze around to look for a tall blond head, to listen for a rowdy laugh. If she's learned one thing, it's not to beg for emotion from other people. To not become a drooling beast for love.

But it's not just Daniel; she also finds herself thinking of her father again. Feeling his presence, the idea of him, big and terrible but also jovial. Throwing himself into this life. He would have been here, bar-tering and laughing and trying to be as cutthroat as he could be. Did he think about her and Tante Marie as he accepted a price that was maybe too low, maybe too poor? Did he fight for every coin?

As she loses herself in that morass of thoughts, Anne senses the change in her, and tugs her wrist, pulling her over to a table she's been slowly leading them toward. Anne makes a gesture of greeting to the Iroquois men behind the piles of furs, smiling genuinely for once, with her teeth showing, and the three of them gesture back.

Minique tries not to stare, because she knows she'll show her naïveté, but she's never been so close to anyone Iroquois before. Her body prickles all over; she feels the base of her tongue swell and get hot, almost like she's about to throw up from the way her gut is churning. She can hear her stupid classmates' shrill voices in her head: *First they peel off your scalp and then they cut off your fingertips. They peel off your face. They shove hot coals down your throat, and you better just hope and pray that you die.* She thinks of the sour mouths of the nuns as they talked about conversion, about the divine missions that drove them and the brothers to New France. She feels those memories deep in her bones, like they're part of her foundations. She wants to cleave to them solely because they are familiar. She wants to give in to the fear because it's what she knows best. But here, in the warmth of the day, with Anne holding her wrist in an iron grasp, she finds that there's less and less room in her for that fear. That a man is a man: he's likely someone to be scared of because of the weaponry he has between his legs, but maybe that's it.

If the coureurs are dressed far too warmly for the weather, in itchy linen shirts and trousers and high boots, the Iroquois are dressed exactly the right way. Minique can see where Montréalers have stolen their ideas for dress. The Iroquois men are in deerskin breechclouts. One of them wears hide leggings underneath, but the other two, who are closer in age to Minique, have their legs bare, skin shining between their hips and their moccasins. Minique sweats in all of her layers, her mouth watering at the idea of getting the breeze on her own sticky body.

Two of them have long hair, worn loose down their backs, and one has a scalp lock, the sides of his head shaved bare. Up his arms and along his chest, he has marks that look like ink burned into the skin. When he raises an arm to Anne, his muscles ripple and the marks jump and sway.

Minique can't stop looking. She knows she's being rude, but it's so rare to see so much of men's bodies, and she finds herself eyeing the ridges of thighs, the dimples of knees, the edges of collarbones. She takes her chance while she can, trying to commit everything to memory. One of the men starts laughing at her, at her big eyes and the way she needs to swallow her spit with a heavy motion. She feels her face turn red at the timbre of his voice—warm and liquid, like the way the sunlight is pouring down around her shoulders and across her body—and she looks away, and then back, and then away again, and then finally back at his face. He continues to laugh, but there's no malice in it, and she finds she doesn't feel so ashamed. She only feels out of her element, a bit stupid, a bit slow. Anne has let go of her wrist to talk, and Minique hangs back, feeling like a child watching her parents. She wants to run her fingers through the fur. She wants to run her fingers through their hair, feel the muscle under the leggings. She wants the coureurs to take off their shirts in the weighty light. She wants to crawl out from her clothes.

Instead, she turns to watch Anne. Anne runs her hands through one of the rabbit pelts that's on the table as she talks in what Minique can tell is very, very rough Mohawk. She can see the faces of the two men speaking with Anne, can see that they're smiling at Anne's efforts, but as with the laughter, it's not malicious. Because Anne knows that she's close to useless, but she's trying, and so she is smiling, too. The man in front is nodding, looking the most focused out of the entire group, and is pulling out a pouch for her, loosening the strings to let her sniff at what's inside, handing it over as Anne passes over a good new knife at the same time. It's the smoothest kind of bartering, the kind that comes from an already established relationship. Minique watches as Anne gestures emphatically with her hands; if she had to guess, Minique would think that Anne is showing how a plant is growing, from the way she's fluting her fingers upward, pinching her fingertips together to show some sort of bud or blossom. There's a frenetic energy in the way she's miming whatever problem she's trying to fix, and Minique is so enrapt watching the two of them talk that she doesn't immediately notice that the man who laughed at her is gesturing at her. *Come here.*

If he had laughed cruelly at her earlier, she wouldn't at all consider moving her feet. But she realizes that of all the things that have made her body feel warm, her tongue thick and stupid, it's kindness that seems most important. She wants to lean into kindness like a cat leans into an outstretched hand, like a snake leans into a slice of sunlight. She wants to trust her instinct.

All of her schooling and the wails of the nuns and the Jesuits would tell her not to move. She can hear their dusty voices in her head. But they lived inside lives; Minique doesn't want to live her own life pressing her face to rippled glass and inhaling stale air. And an outside life means being brave. She steps forward.

If she's being honest with herself, she's mostly shy because she's face to face with a man who isn't a family member or a friend. She's shy because the sun is so hot and his teeth are white, and because for the first time in a long time, maybe since she danced with the coureur at Anne's inn, a thing that feels like it was several lifetimes ago, she feels attraction, which surprises her. She thought that after Barbe's death she wouldn't feel anything like that ever again. That she didn't deserve to. The man keeps gesturing until she's close enough to smell him, but she keeps her mouth closed, breathing in and out through her nose.

He leans in. She's hypnotized. Can't move, wouldn't want to. Anne is rattling away in the background, being corrected by the man with the tattoos, and the third man has moved on to talk to a coureur, near the far corner of the table. Minique feels prickly all over. She wants to tear her dress off, wants to roll around in the furs, rub her body hair against the rabbit pelts.

"By the way," the laughing man says, in French, and Minique's eyes snap back to his, "we can speak your language."

She can't help herself: she snorts, hard and sudden, at the incongruity of listening to her mentor limp her way through the conversation, and then the fluent French. The reservations she had about the fur fair—fear of waking her father's ghost, of standing out like some sort of imposter, of having to meet people and be subject to their scrutiny—are struck out of her, like a bird flying away at the sound of hands clapping. She laughs at her mentor, at Anne being willing to embarrass herself in her efforts to learn more. She laughs at the fact that the people of Montréal are so eager to call the Iroquois primitive, but here she is, only able to speak French, while the man in front of her can speak at least two languages, if not more. As she laughs, he grins, too, and then starts to laugh alongside her. She doesn't notice that she's breathing through her mouth until she becomes fully aware of the sweetness across her tongue, the calmness of the taste. That their table, the three discussions going on, the hand gestures, the patting of the furs, the exchanging of goods—all of it tastes like tranquility, with the whisper of focus. It tastes like family history; she can sense herself as a base note in all of it, the salt of her blood, the flavour of her breath, like her father was before her. Like he did; like she is now doing. Anne slides her eyes over to Minique mid-conversation, sharp and knowing, and Minique wonders if she can sense it, the turmoil gone quiet. Wonders if it was all part of Anne's plan. But Anne's eyes slide back to her conversation partner, and the man beside Minique leans in again to say something to her, and the day clicks back into place.

The fur fair lasts for seven days. Every night, Minique walks back to the grounds. She doesn't enter; she just lingers at the edge of the action, trying to absorb the feeling of it all. She doesn't venture in to find the table of men Anne talked with. She knows that Anne came away with new tobacco, some new information about sundews and violets and how to better use them, and a bag of wild carrot seeds; she bartered with a new knife and an axe head. Minique, who can barely talk to a shopkeeper when she needs sugar or tea, keeps the seamlessness of this interaction with her as she walks, wanting to learn from it.

On one of her nights out walking, she sees a stocky figure in black pacing up and down the rows of the market. It's the time of the

evening where the sun is low enough in the sky that a purple light
has cast itself over the earth. It softens everything with a hazy brush,
like living in a watercolour painting, and so his angry little smudge
of black on the landscape stands out in harsh contrast. Maybe she's
better able to notice Father Etienne now that the fair is close to ending and some vendors have gone back to their own camps or cities.
Perhaps he's been out every night, like she's been, except he's been
spying and frothing with rage while she's been observing and thinking about her own role within the fur trade, how it's part of her
blood. But she stops in her tracks and slides back behind a hitching
post, watching his figure grow smaller as it moves away from her.
Father Etienne's hands are up, as if he's giving the sign of the cross
or casting some sort of protective charm. People ignore him, or turn
away; a handful of coureurs openly roll their eyes at him, while
another man tosses his head in a movement of irritation, and some
of the vendors make gestures back at him. Minique wants to laugh
at the priest getting openly mocked, but she also knows how his
anger and pride run deep. She worries.

She mumbles some words that she tries to imbue with the most
power she can muster. She pictures the priest being bound by red
ribbons, shouting angrily. She pictures his tongue swelling in his
mouth until it's impossible for him to spew his terrible rhetoric. She
thrills at the thought of this, her insides filled with a dangerous joy.
Anne has told her that if she's putting intentions out into the world,
whatever she feels will come back to her threefold. It's the law of
return: do as little harm as you can, and be prepared for hurt to come
back at you if you cause hurt to someone else. But in the moment,
imagining the hateful priest rendered still and speechless, imagining

him as helpless before her, Minique only feels a fruitful kind of joy. Even when he turns on his heel to face in her direction—far enough away that she's not sure it's actually her he's looking at, but near enough that she can see the revolting outlines of his person and the way he holds his body—she can't help but laugh out loud, over and over again, feeling so free and so malicious and so, so happy at the idea of him impotent.

Summer's final act is so beautiful Minique can almost forget that winter is coming once again. The days aren't as long as they were in June, but they're still painted with purple and orange. She sees how the summer sunsets loosen up the people of Montréal, inside or outside the walls. How sleeves are pushed back, and skirts tied up and shoes flung to the side. She wishes Barbe was still alive to witness Minique allowing herself to enjoy life in New France, for once.

In the mauve, in the gloaming, with Anne guiding her, she's been able to see what she couldn't before. Maybe she had to cry the scales off of her eyes to be able to see the beauty of the curl of a fern balanced in her palm. The rich smell of cedars and pines after a rainstorm. The velvet of a new shoot against the back of her hand. Maybe the coureurs had it wrong, to charter a flying canoe and avoid all of the forest beneath them. She wonders, after this summer of growing, how she'll feel at the first snow. If she'll still have a sense of wonder when the days are only a handful of hours long and the cold seeps in through every crack. Even as summer starts to melt into the early days of fall, she tries her hardest to keep that wonder in her.

"Do witches really cast spells naked?"

Anne cranes her head around to stare at Minique. The two of

them are getting the auberge ready for the day: Minique is dusting off the tables, and Anne is setting chairs up.

"How should I know?" Anne puts a chair down on the ground. "Do you think I'm a witch, Minique?"

Even after all these weeks, she's not sure what Anne is, deep down. Her logical side tells her that witches don't exist, and that the women being accused of sorcery are women who understand plants, who track the cycle of the moon as it relates to their bodies, who can survive outside in winter and know how to use the power of the summer. But the superstitious side says *maybe there's something else at play.* She doesn't want to admit that, somewhere deep inside her, she wants witchcraft to be real. Because wouldn't it be amazing to be able to have strength like that? To be able to soar over the treetops in a bowl or on a broomstick; to drink a tea to fall asleep without dreams, to wake up feeling lively; to be able to kill a master with something so sly and secret that no one ever realizes you're guilty? To be able to keep yourself safe?

She says none of this. The only thing that comes out of her mouth is an extended hesitant sound.

"Are you a witch, Minique?"

The easy answer to that is *no.* If she were a witch, wouldn't she feel powerful?

Anne stands with her fists on her hips. Her gaze flicks from one part of Minique's face to another. That thing about casting spells naked—it was only something Minique heard, once or twice, either passed around the schoolyard or mumbled in the back pews at church when Father Etienne was droning on and everyone was bored. She's heard whispers that overseas, they can grind up human flesh and herbs to smear all over their bodies, and then they turn back into the young, beautiful women they once were. That they're seducing girls to come join them, and they all take off their dresses and shifts and dance in the forest around a fire stoked by the fat of dead children. That they feel the moonlight on their skin, and then they all rise, holding hands, into the night air. The story is always the same: women as consorts of the devil, wreaking havoc on the innocents, meant to be killed in the name of god.

"No," Minique says. "I'm not. But I heard—you know, that women, they—" She flutters her hands in front of her body, nervous about sounding stupid. "They take off their clothes and go—go flying," she finishes, swallowing hard, her voice getting higher at the end like she's asking a question.

"Who the hell is telling you all of this?" Anne mutters, uncurling her hands and wiping her palms on her apron. "Flying, is it? Christ," she says under her breath, and Minique startles at the words. She's never heard Anne speak like that.

"I didn't mean to—well, you just hear things. Other children, when we were younger—it doesn't matter," she says, turning to grab her shawl. She wants to smack a palm to her forehead. To believe schoolyard tales like that? To believe the men who show up to church still drunk from the night before? To ask Anne, who came from the continent, about these things? *Stupid, stupid, stupid.* She wraps the shawl around her shoulders, ready to bolt.

"Wait," Anne says.

Minique stops, standing for a moment, facing the door. She turns to Anne, who has a strange look on her face.

"You want to fly?"

A trick question, surely. But one more easily answered with a wavering *yes*. In a canoe, in a bowl, on a branch. To save yourself, to extract yourself. To fly away home.

Anne sighs a little. "In a week, on Friday. Meet me at the edge of the apple orchard, at an hour to midnight."

Of all the things she expected Anne to say, a midnight meeting outside the safety of their homes wasn't it. But Anne has her head tilted, as if to say *you wanted it, so accept it*, and so Minique nods once, and then scuttles out the door, her lessons for the day abandoned.

She wiggles out the window of her room instead of risking the door. She's not sure she makes less noise trying to drop gracefully to her feet in the yard than if she had tiptoed across the wood floors, but she feels safer, her shawl wrapped around her head and her face, her boots already tied.

She's never been outside of the gates at night. There should be guards on a night like this, with the moon so full and bright, but there aren't. Maybe there never are. She didn't have a plan to get by them except to beg, or threaten, or try to sneak past. But she needs to do none of those things, and only pulls her shawl closer as the moon illuminates her completely. It even gives her a shadow, another Minique walking alongside her, looking more confident than she feels. She's vibrating with a potent mixture of fear and excitement; thrilled at having unfolded Anne just a little more, being made privy to yet another of her layers, and yet also deeply, darkly afraid of whatever it is that lurks in the woods at night, whatever rustles through the silent grass, lurks behind the gravestones, the things of her childhood stories, things told to give people nightmares. She practically sprints to the orchard, weaving behind the habitants' houses to avoid being seen, trying to be as light on the balls of her feet as possible. She wishes she had the moccasins her father gave her, to be fleet-footed and stealthy. To be able to dart in and out of the trees like her own shadow. To be able to surprise Anne where she is standing, her back to the orchard, tall and strong and staring out at the forest. But she can't surprise Anne, who seems to know and hear everything; she turns to meet her, a basket under her arm. The basket is already full of what look like mushrooms, and Minique squints to try to see. Anne shrugs the cloth over the basket, points into the trees, and then they're off.

They walk for about an hour. Minique has never gone this far into the woods, not even with Anne. And most definitely never at night. She feels frightened for the first few minutes, trying to whip her head around to hear the different sounds in the dark: hooting, clicking, chirruping. But eventually she has to focus on Anne's back in order to have a hope of keeping pace, and so she follows dutifully, turning her eyes forward. The branches that grab at her ankles and wrists don't feel threatening, the shadows of the canopy cast from the rich light of the moon aren't sinister. She concentrates on one foot in front of the other, keeping her breathing steady, in and out, to the rhythm of their steps.

They're spat out of the forest into a clearing that seems familiar. The space looks unnatural, a wide circle of shin-high grass ringed by trees. She wonders how it came to be, and who or what it was cleared by. The grass in the moonlight looks like the river, liquid and silver and rippling in the gentle wind. If the woods were filled with chattering, this clearing is quiet, like all sound fell away the moment they stepped out of the trees. Like they're hidden from the rest of the world.

Anne walks toward the centre of the clearing, but Minique hangs back, at the edge. Full moon. Fairy circle. Two women walking in silence. All of the elements for something sorcerous are in front of her. She wanted to know, and now that she's here, she wonders how it would feel to turn around and head back to the orchard. But she couldn't do it on her own; she doesn't know the way back, and she doesn't want to risk walking in the forest alone at night. It seems better to take her chances here.

Anne stands in the middle of the clearing, rustling around in her basket. Minique walks through the undulating grass, wondering what it would feel like on her bare legs. What lives there, in it, furrowed through it. What travels across it. As she draws closer to Anne, she sees that Anne has untied her apron and has flung it to the side; now she's starting on the buttons of her skirt and her bodice.

"What are you doing?" Minique doesn't mean to sound so alarmed, but she can't help it, not as Anne's outer layers fall and she's left in her shift and petticoat. She's already removed her stockings and her moccasins.

Anne looks up at her as she unfastens her petticoat and it joins the pile of clothing at her feet. Next, she grabs at her glossy braid, and starts to unwind it. Minique draws in a breath; it feels so intimate to be able to see another woman's hair unbound. She's never even seen her aunt with her hair down. Anne's hair comes undone and slithers out across her shoulders, like dark water.

"You want to know what it's like to fly," Anne says, and then she does something Minique rarely sees her do: she smiles with her teeth. "And it's been a long time since I've gone flying." As she says that, she pulls her shift up over her head and tosses it to the side.

Minique's face feels like it's on fire. She's never seen another naked person; she's rarely even looked down at her own body. With no full-length mirror, she doesn't quite know what she looks like. For Anne to be standing naked in the middle of a clearing, in the bright moon-light—it feels like the world has turned on its side. It makes the hair on her arms prickle and the base of her tongue feel hot. She tries not to look at Anne's body, but she doesn't succeed; she sees the long lines of muscle, the strong thighs, the curve of breasts, the length of her neck. It doesn't help that Anne is standing with her legs apart, her hands on her hips. Not afraid at all. Not ashamed.

"If you want to fly, you have to join," Anne says, nodding her chin at Minique. "If not, you can watch."

Minique still doesn't know what Anne means by *flying*. Surely they're not going to leave the earth?

Her hand comes up to the tip of her braid. Anne turns around and rummages in her basket, drinking from a water skin, clearly trying to give Minique a moment to decide.

She pulls at her braid, relishing in feeling the crimps come undone and dragging her fingers through her hair up to her scalp, where she presses her fingertips into her tender skin. She follows Anne's method, with shaking hands: apron, skirt, stockings and boots, pet-ticoat. When she's just in her shift, shivering with the chill but mainly from the terror and excitement pounding through her body, Anne turns back to her. She has a jar in her hands.

"What's that?"

Anne holds the jar up. "Flying ointment."

The way she's holding the jar, Minique knows it's something important.

"What's in it?"

"Back in France, it would have been belladonna, mandrake, wormwood. Here, I've had to change it a bit." She opens the jar, tilts it to show Minique. "Cannabis, water hemlock, poppy juice, aconite."

As inexperienced as she is, even Minique knows the danger of these ingredients. Aconite she's never heard of, but cannabis she knows. Settlers grow hemp for the fibre for sails and rope, but she's heard of some people who smoke it. Poppy juice, the flower that can make you drift into oblivion. Hemlock, a poison.

"Do we eat it?" Her voice shakes.

Anne laughs. "No! Thank god. We'd die on the spot."

"Oh," Minique says, and clutches her shift.

"People call this the poison path," Anne says, "tinkering with plants that shift your consciousness."

"Am I going to be poisoned?"

"No," Anne says. "I've been dealing with flying ointments for decades. Longer than I've been here. It's not just women who want them, either. You'd be surprised who wants to talk with the devil."

"The devil?" Her voice is a squeak.

Anne shrugs one shoulder. "It's not really the devil. People just use that term to describe anyone or anything that's even a little bit threatening. The devil was the first dissenter, remember. But before *the devil*, he was the Old God. The Wild Adversary." She puts two hands up to her head, mimicking horns like a stag's. "Cernunnos, the Goat, the Horned Snake, Baphomet."

Minique's skin starts to tingle and feel tight, like her body wants to escape.

"Baal," Anne says.

Anne's hands do look like horns, like she could dip her head and charge at Minique and knock her to the ground. Her fingers seem to be lengthening and twisting in the light. Minique makes a sound of distress, and Anne drops her arms.

"People just want to vilify what came before Christianity," she says, no longer the Horned One, just Anne again. "And sometimes some people want to talk to the Adversary again, just to see." She walks in a small circle, her fingers coming down to touch the taller stalks of grass. "Just to remember."

She dips a finger into the jar and brings the ointment out into the moonlight where it shines. They stare at it for a moment until she rubs it between her hands, bending down. "Between your toes." She starts to move up her body, applying it as she goes. "Behind your knees. The base of your spine." She has to dip back into the jar. "Between your legs. On your belly. At your elbow." She straightens up and Minique can see her body gleaming with the grease. "Neck. Behind the ears, temples." Anne pauses for a moment and closes her eyes, takes a breath. When she opens her eyes, she looks far away, like she's imagining another time and place. For once, Minique wonders, really wonders, about Anne's history. About why she survived the sickness that killed her whole family. Why she knows so much about plants that can kill someone or drive a person crazy. Why she knows how to anoint herself like this. Why she looks like Artemis, standing naked and tall and shining in the middle of this meadow, this clearing that nags at Minique's memory and looks like it was carved out of the forest by a giant's hand.

"Forehead," Anne says. Her hands move from her brown hair to the top of her head, along the line of skin where her hair parts. "Crown."

Crowned like a queen, Minique thinks. Anne looks at her, her gaze steady and calm. There is a question there, though, and her eyes flick down to Minique's shift, and then back up to her face. *Will you go all the way?*

Seeing Anne coat her body in the ointment makes her feel less anxious about it, though the hot fear is still racing up and down her limbs. She tries to ignore that and focus on the excitement. The feeling of doing something bad, something that would get them punished if found out. She balls her hands in the cloth of her shift and then, in one violent motion, rips it off over her head. She doesn't look to see where it lands. She doesn't look to see Anne's face. She doesn't look down at her own body. Instead, she reaches out a hand for the jar, which Anne drops heavily into her palm. The ointment feels warm and alive when she dips her fingers into it and she rubs it on her feet, legs, back. She hesitates for a moment before she reaches between her legs, trying to be as perfunctory as possible. Stomach, arms, neck. Behind her ears, the dips of her temples. She tries to picture this as a meditation and tries to pull her breaths in and out in deep bellows. Without thinking, she marks her forehead in a cross, like worshippers are marked with ash on Ash Wednesday. It feels wrong, but also right, like she's twisting that symbol into something new.

When she reaches up to her head, she struggles to find where her hair is parted. The nerves are making her hands shake. Anne steps close to her and does it for her, a strong finger down the line of her scalp. Then she steps back, and the two of them stand there, looking at each other.

Waiting for something.

"What's going to happen?"

Anne turns in a slow circle, stretching her arms and her legs. Minique watches the muscle ripple under her skin. "People think witches fly on broomsticks. But there are other ways to fly. Think about it. The ingredients."

Opium torpor, the smoke of cannabis, the knife's edge of hemlock.

"I feel strange," is all Minique can manage. Her tongue is too big for her mouth, her skin prickling like ants are walking all over it.

"That's because you're flying," Anne says, tilting her head to let her hair fall down her back. "Let your feet come off the ground."

She doesn't need a broomstick. She doesn't need a bowl or a mortar or a pot. Not a plate, not a cauldron, not even a canoe with the devil in the bow. All she needs is the body she prowls around in. The hair that never gets to swing free, and the skin that never gets to feel the air. She's aware of the bone and blood and guts that make her. She feels all of those parts now, every inch of her skin, the parts inside her, the fluid, the solid: it makes her vision swim at the corners of her eyes, her tongue circle around in her mouth, the soles of her feet damp and the back of her neck hot.

She can't see Anne but that's because she's on her hands and knees in the grass, and it's too tall around her, stroking at her cheeks and her shoulders and her belly. She rolls onto her back, panting, and all she can see is the moon, bright and unblinking, and the stars, and the blanket of the night sky, all seeming like they're coming closer and closer and closer to her face, her wide-open eyes. It's not just her feet leaving the ground, it's her whole body, carried on the ocean waves of the grass, warmed by the glittering of the stars. She wants to be eaten by the moon, plunged into the warm dark waters of the sky. She wants to disappear across the treetops, a trail of fire in her wake. She wants to become the stag that Anne became, the bear that rumbles through the trees, the wolf that rips throats out. She tilts her head back and cries out into the night air, a loud, harsh sound she's never made before. A moment passes, and then, from across the clearing, she hears the guttural reply. It could be Anne; it could be anyone or anything. It could be the monster that lurks at the edge of the clearing, watching; it could be the wolves that wait. It could be that she's the monster now. If they want to believe that she's the monster, shy away from her in the streets because of her sadness and her strangeness, because the priest has cursed her, then let them. Let them, let them flee from her. She can extend her jaw and turn her skin red, grow scales, grow dark hair across her shoulders. Let them run. Let them run from her. She prowls the clearing, she prowls the air, she crawls on her hands and knees. She grows horns and she drops them; she hears the symphony of the watchers in the woods, humming and sighing at the sight of her. *One of us*, they say, maybe. *Finally.* Finally, she realizes. Finally, it comes to her. Finally, she gives in to it, closing her eyes and seeing the trees rush under her, her hands on the paddle and the hot-breathed adversary in the back of the boat, panting on her shoulder, his red body pressing closer and closer and closer as she howls with laughter.

Minique blinks awake.

She's on her back in the grass, her body covered in dew. Her throat aches and her muscles are sore. Her hair is matted to her face and her neck, and her head feels like it's been battered around. The corners of her eyes are gritty. It hurts to draw breath too deeply. She tries to speak but she can't, so she groans instead, a whisper at first and then a hitching sound that grows as she starts to move her fingers and toes, to take inventory and see if she's still alive or if this is some purgatory she's been sent to.

Anne comes into view above her. She's dressed again, and for a moment Minique wonders *did I dream it all?* But Anne's hair is undone and heavy on her shoulders, and she has circles under her eyes, so Minique knows that she didn't. Anne is holding the water skin in one hand and Minique's clothes in the other, and Minique slowly sits up even though her body is screaming at her. The sun isn't quite up yet, the sky burning orange on the horizon, the moon sinking out of sight.

When she's dressed, when Anne has wet a corner of her apron and wiped the visible smears of dirt off of Minique's hands and neck and cheeks, the two of them stand quietly in the clearing. Anne turns in one more circle, her arms stretched out.

It hits Minique then. The clearing: it looks like the one she dreamed about, with her father. A cold feeling trickles down her back.

The previous night was momentous somehow. It all feels too fresh, too blurry at the edges. She wonders if she's still feeling the effects of the ointment, in the way that things in the corners of her eyes seem to be moving too fast or too slow and her skin feels hot all over. Or maybe it's that she's changing form, slowly and surely. Undergone a baptism.

She shakes her head. Strange, tricky, sacrilegious thoughts. Ones best kept trapped inside her, at least for now. She can keep them buried for a while. But she can't ever forget the feeling of lifting out of her body, of the weight of horns, the freedom of being able to cock her head back and yowl to the night sky. She hopes no one from the town heard her; she wonders what they'll make of her and Anne staggering back in the early morning. She has no plan to be stealthy, no ideas for how to get back into her house, how to slither past her aunt.

As if she's heard Minique's thoughts, Anne picks up the basket and flips the cloth off of it: it's filled with mushrooms.

"For when they ask us what we were doing. We just say it's cooler to forage for them at night, it better preserves them. They don't know."

When they get back to the inn, Minique's so tired she's seeing double. She's considering slinking home and crawling into bed, maybe going up onto the low roof and through the window if she wants to completely avoid Tante Marie. But Anne thumps her basket of mushrooms down onto the table and pulls out her grimoire, opening it to the blank pages at the back.

"Now you're ready."

"For what?"

Anne ignores her and goes to her cabinet, pulling out a jar of a purple-red liquid and a small brush. She sets them down in front of Minique.

"Paint it."

"Paint what?" Minique wonders if she's still feeling the effects of the ointment. She has no idea what's going on.

"This." Anne points at a page Minique thought was empty.

Minique picks up the brush and opens the jar. It smells familiar, like something overcooked in a kitchen. She dips the brush into the liquid and hesitantly swipes it over the page.

Minique stares at the damp paper, completely confused. She thinks Anne has maybe lost her mind. She turns her head to say that to her, and Anne jabs her finger back at the book. Minique looks at it, and nearly drops the brush in shock.

There are words on the page. They're faint but slowly getting clearer. For a moment, Minique thinks *is this magic?*

"Cabbage water," Anne says, tapping the jar. "Reveals words written in vinegar."

"Holy hell," Minique breathes, and Anne laughs. Minique reads the words in front of her: "*To end an unwanted pregnancy.*" She snaps her head around to look at Anne.

"This is why I wasn't charged in court. It's a trick the women in my family have passed down for years. Every time you need one of the left-handed or more dangerous remedies, you reveal it. When you're done, you rewrite the remedy in vinegar on a fresh page, and then cut the old one out and burn it. This book has been rebound five or six times to add more paper."

Minique is reading words she's never seen before: *cohosh, pennyroyal, pessary.* If the priest or the judge had been able to reveal these hidden pages, Anne would have been killed. She knows how big of a risk Anne's taking, showing her this.

"What else is there?" She wants to read all of it.

"We can't reveal everything, because then we'll be here all night rewriting them. You're already going to have to rewrite this one,"

Anne says, "which is good practice for you. But I keep a list in code on the inside back cover."

Minique flips it open. There's a numbered list written in tiny hand near the spine. It goes sixteen, twelve, sixteen, six, nine, on and on.

"P is the sixteenth letter of the alphabet. P for pregnancy. And L for love tinctures, that's number twelve. Sixteen again for poisons. Six for F for flying ointment, and then nine for intoxicants. It takes some memorizing. And if you take a page out, you have to make a little mark next to the number so you know where to start next time you're searching. But for the most part, it's always kept us safe."

Us is the sisterhood Minique is now officially a part of, between the night in the clearing and this, the power of the delicate red thread between life and death that she holds in her hands now.

"It's yours," Anne says.

Minique blinks. "The book?"

"The book is yours."

A few months ago Minique would have nodded feverishly and thanked Anne and not thought anything of it, but after so many days spent with her, she knows this comes with a catch. For Anne to give away this precious thing—

"Are you leaving?" The words tumble out of her as her hands tighten on the book. She wonders if the grimoire is a gift, or maybe, maybe, it's a burden that Anne has been trying to get rid of for some time.

"I've heard that Trois-Rivières is down an auberge," Anne says.

"So you're leaving." She isn't surprised. This is the pattern of Minique's life, after all. No wonder Anne kept her at an arm's length; this was always in her plans. She feels wooden.

"I think . . ." Anne stops for a moment. "It might be better for you."

"You *leaving*?" Minique feels anger flare up through her body. For as long as she's been alive, people have made that choice for her.

Anne touches the book in Minique's hands. "With this," she says, and then presses her finger to Minique's forehead, "and this, you'll be able to have freedom. Without me as a ball and chain. That stupid priest will think I took the grimoire with me."

Minique looks down at the book and back up at Anne. "Freedom," she says.

Then Anne does something she's never done before. She pulls Minique into a hug. Minique is rigid at first, surprised and stiff, but Anne wraps her arms around her and squeezes with the strength of a woman who moves barrels and fills taps and stacks chairs every night. Minique nestles her head into Anne's chest, her forehead on Anne's shoulder. She breathes in the smell of her, cool and green. She wonders if she'll ever have a friend again. Her anger is gone; she only feels tired.

Anne lets go of her. She bends over and opens a drawer, coming up with a handful of stones. She moves on to the tables next, picking through her pouches and boxes with a delicate speed. She looks to the rafters, pulling items down and examining them. The tools assemble on the tabletop: Pebbles. Feathers. A skein of string. It's then that Minique knows what Anne is doing.

"Ladders are from France," Anne says, turning to her. She measures out a length of string and cuts it carefully with a knife. She ties a loop at the end of the cord, testing its strength with two sharp tugs. Holding the string by the loop, on her pointer finger, she turns to face Minique. "My mother taught me, and her grandmother taught her, and that's how it went."

She keeps the string hooked on her finger as Minique reaches out for it and runs the length of it through her palm. How can something as simple as string do something for her? She closes her eyes for a moment and allows herself to breathe, and she measures the space in between each breath and each pulse of her blood that she feels in her ears. Within herself, she finds the push she needs to be spurred onward; she has to trust that she's making the right choice, that she'll put the right emotion into this. She opens her eyes, Anne nods, and Minique begins to tie.

"By knot of one, the spell's begun." Her fingers move up the string, tying in a little white stone: white for clarity, for protection, for the ability to open herself up to the forces that may be and to see as far and as long as she can. That she can ask for.

"By knot of two, the magic comes true. By knot of three, so it shall be." She picks up some crow feathers: for the most knowledge she feels the world can spare her. For canniness and brashness.

"By knot of four, this power is stored. By knot of five, my will shall drive." Now pieces of pine bark, for the ability to last through every season and grow even when everything conspires against her.

"By knot of six, the spell I fix. By knot of seven, the future I leaven. By knot of eight, my will be fate."

With each of these knots, she feels a prickling, hot urge to wish for an equal. In her mind's eye, she sees them as a giant who stands alongside her, not in front of her, not hiding behind her. She doesn't know what this means, this concept of a similar, an equivalent, someone to fly over the trees with her, but she knows that it's something that's pouring out from her mind and down her arms, that it's too late to pull it back into herself, and so she gives into it and sends it forward, imagining it with every loop and pull of her fingers.

"By knot of nine, what's done is mine." *Mine, mine.* What has she had that's been hers and only hers? Not Barbe, not Daniel. Not her father, and not her aunt. Not her home, not her town, not her life, not really. So here, in the back room of an inn, she makes her final promise to herself: that she will turn her life to the direction of *mine*, to the sweetest form of selfishness.

She exhales and lets the ladder fall from her hand.

With Anne gone, Tante Marie is the only person Minique has left. At one time, this might have been horrifying to her, but now it has the feeling of comfort, familiarity. The two of them spend their mornings at the kitchen table, their hands cupped around mugs of tea. This winter feels milder than the last one. The cold air still slices in around the doors and windows, but it doesn't chill Minique down to her bones.

There are still some bridges that are never crossed, and that feels good in the way that slipping on a worn boot feels good. She and her aunt don't ever talk about the fever. They don't talk about Anne. Just once, her aunt says, "I'm glad you're home," and Minique stares at Tante Marie for a moment before nodding slowly. She can't bring herself to say *so am I*, because she's sad. But there is a solace in being around her aunt's predictable actions. She sees a lot of Anne in her aunt. She wonders if Tante Marie might have liked Anne if they had ever gotten to know each other.

The first morning Daniel visits, he knocks at the back door while she's stoking the fire to make a second cup of tea. Minique doesn't want to go to the door; the only people who ever use that door are dead or gone.

His hands are shoved in the waistband of his pants and his eyes are big; a patchy beard covers his face, and his skin is more tanned than she's ever seen it. She stares at him like he's a ghost. They stand there, silent and stunned. They stand there, separated by the doorstep. Minique can see the questions scrawled across his face; she can also, horribly, see some fear.

Daniel, this is Daniel, this is Daniel and he's finally here, her mind yells with joy. She feels a rush of happiness that she immediately tamps down; the void is filled with anger, then, and bitterness that it's taken him so long to come see her. She pours that anger into herself. And there is also wistfulness, because he looks like a man even though just a year has passed, and she's worried that there might be too big a gulf between them now to be anything other than strangers.

She says nothing, because his eyes are big and liquid, and so she pushes the door open and jerks her head to beckon him in.

He shuffles inside as she pours him a cup of too-strong tea. He smells different now: he smells like her father. If she breathes through her mouth she is overwhelmed by flashes of pelts and tobacco and a pipe hanging from a colourful wool belt and the smell of a fire made from damp wood. She tenses, expecting that same terrible note that her father always had, something burnt and mean underneath, but it doesn't materialize. Daniel's scent is only full of wonder, like Barbe's used to be, with a note of sadness and something wary.

When she sits down across the table from him and raises her eyebrows over the rim of her mug, he turns red, and then starts talking in one big blurt of words. First he explains his months in the woods—"I barely had time to say goodbye to anyone, my father was so mad at me, he wants me to take over the bakery"—the trip up to the lake, the weight of a canoe on his back—"Easier than you'd think, actually, I couldn't believe it"—and what it was like to finally escape the confines of Montréal. "Freedom," he says, with a dreamy tone in his voice. Minique can barely keep up with him; he's bouncing from one subject to another frantically, like he's trying to fill the silence with no room for her to interject. He asks questions without expecting an answer. First it's how she's been in his absence ("Papa told me that you took up with the inn witch, watch out there, eh?"), then it's asking how her aunt is ("Where is she?") and then it's what the weather means ("Mild winter means the sap won't run, bad year for sugaring"). Her anger simmers stronger and stronger the more he talks, as he pretends that nothing is wrong, pretends that he didn't have time to say goodbye to her, pretends that she's stupid and believes him. Like Barbe never died. Like they never clutched at each other in the orchard and were mired in their grief.

The year away has made him look like a man, but he's still a child. She always thought of Daniel as the brave one, but now she sees that he was only brash. Maybe she's taken that mantle for herself.

When he finally tires himself out, he takes a slug of tea, grimaces, and then sits there staring at her.

Minique supposes he wants her to say something, but she finds she has nothing to say. *You left me* isn't helpful; neither is *why didn't you even come to say goodbye?* She has no choice but to use the lessons she's learned from Tante Marie and Anne: she sits silently, looks back at him with a face wiped of all emotion. She tries to soften her gaze to look at his face unfocused but keep her eyes hard enough to pin him in place.

After about twenty seconds, he cracks.

"I'm sorry," he says.

His voice is so plaintive and wretched that Minique feels her anger fall mostly away, like when Anne had her in her arms. She wishes she could be better at remaining angry but she can't. She wants to have a friend. She wants at least one person. So she can do nothing but reach a hand across the table. She thinks of women, of the complicated love between women, but Daniel is Daniel, and she'll take what she can get. She can't erase the memories of spitting off roofs and the taste of whisky and the sound of his raucous laughter. When he grabs at her, she feels that same jolt of togetherness and rightness that's propelled them through their entire lives. She knows they're different; she knows she hasn't forgiven Daniel all the way, and she might never, but to have a familiar face back in her life when she needs it most is something she can't turn away.

Daniel comes to visit at least once a week, but usually twice, while he's back in town. The coureurs take advantage of the warmer weather to go up to the Upper Lake area; they return near fall. Her father's time away makes so much more sense to her, the fact she wouldn't see him for what seemed like ages. Daniel brings bags of baked goods from Claude—*these ones didn't turn out the way he wanted; he says these are too dry at the edges*—and even Tante Marie will sit at the table to talk with him for a bit, a blessing that Daniel has no idea is so rare.

Daniel has never asked about her time with Anne. The town thrums with rumours always, and lately, she's sure, some of those have been about her. If they said it about Anne—strange, inappropriate, unseemly for a woman, so much time spent at the tavern—she's sure it's been said about her. Anne was able to dispel so many of those rumours through her magnificence in court, her poise against Father Etienne, and yet still, even after her victory, people talked because gossip is a hobby in Montréal. Minique has none of Anne's magnificence; she's sure her neighbours mutter things about her when she passes by, even if they're usually cordial to her face.

But sometimes, when she's talking to Daniel, she sees that same look in his eyes, the one from the doorstep: a little bit of fear, a little bit of far-offness. It's like there's something alive between them, a tree with branches slowly pushing outward, outward, outward. But at least it's something they know well, how to dig their fingers into the bark and look for the sturdiest limb to tuck themselves into. As long as they can do that, they can adjust to whatever else is going on beneath their bodies, the changing and moving nature of their friendship. At least they have each other.

Minique is starting a fire to make the first pot of tea for the day when she realizes she hasn't seen or heard Tante Marie. Her aunt is usually up before she is, and even in the grey world of half-dreaming and half-awake, Minique registers the sounds of her footsteps on the first level of the house and something about that will lull her back to sleep for a few more minutes. Today, she was out of bed earlier than normal, her eyes itchy and her face puffy.

The silence hits her.

When she goes to see if her aunt is still asleep, she finds Tante Marie in bed. Minique knows already, she knows, but she still says her aunt's name, first normally and then louder. She presses her palm to Tante Marie's forehead, and pulls her hand back at the feeling of her aunt's skin, cold to the touch. A slow, inky dread spreads through her; her gut churns as a hot prickle of sweat starts on her upper lip and in the palms of her hands. She wants to open her mouth and scream. She wants to beat her fists against the bedspread. But then she looks at her aunt. There's no rictus to Marie's face, no image of suffering; it's the most fitting end for her, something private and silent. Outside, the cold wind, carrying with it the smell of snow, sharp and clear, whips around, trying to crawl in under the door and around the windows. It sounds like a person shrieking without a voice, a giant sigh, and Minique pulls her shawl closer around her body, huddles herself against the idea of winter, the long nights of cold dark alone in this house in this town.

As the undertaker carries the body away, Minique can't find it within herself to cry, even though she feels more sadness about her aunt's death than her father's disappearance. At least Tante Marie stayed. At least she cared enough to chastise Minique, to try to teach her a lesson or two. She and her aunt were different, but they were together by necessity, and they forged a connection from that. Still, Minique stays dry-eyed. She wore too much grief with Barbe; she can't bring herself to scoop out her insides once again. Three deaths in a row: bad luck in trebles. She has nothing left to give.

It's only when Daniel knocks on the door that she heaves a juddering sigh.

"I want to sell it all."

Daniel looks at her, his cup of tea halted on its journey to his mouth. "What?"

"All of this shit." She gestures to the furniture, the drapes, the cutlery, the plates, the trappings of a life. She sees how people in town define themselves based on the things they own, and yet the items are all just weights that pin somebody in one place.

And Anne has given her a gift. With the lessons in the woods, the passing over of the grimoire, she's given Minique a lifeline out of becoming a blanchisseuse, a cardeuse, a domestique in her former classmates' houses. Anne has given Minique freedom. Now she has to make the jump.

"And the house?"

"And the house," she nods.

Daniel says nothing, but he puts one hand to his heart, his lightly curled fist resting on his chest. Minique sips her tea and sits in her silent, cold home, her mind a flurry of questions. Where she can go. What she can do. How she can shuck this town. Over Daniel's head, out the window, she imagines she can see the line of trees where the forest begins.

Le loup veut manger

1699-1701

Minique surrenders to muscle memory, letting her brain float free. Place a piece of wood on the stump, swing, wrench. Stop to press the back of her hand to her forehead to mop up some of the sweat, and feel the breeze cool her armpits, her nape, the damp line running down the back of her blouse, her coat abandoned on the woodpile despite the winter cold. Stop to close her eyes and listen to the white-throated sparrows singing in the trees around her, crooning their same refrain: *Po-or Sam Peabody, Peabody, Peabody.* Not poor Minique. She's here, isn't she?

There's something about chopping wood that she likes. She can see the efforts of her labours, the immediate—if not always sightly—results right before her eyes, the halving and quartering and splintering, the smell of oak as it yields to the axe.

After her aunt died, she sold all the belongings she'd never need. She kept only her bed, Anne's book, her clothes, some items from the pantry, a few pots.

"But where are you going to go?" Claude had asked. It was spring, and they were burying Tante Marie's body. Only she and Daniel and Claude were at the cemetery. Her aunt had kept to herself by choice. Minique felt that it would be a betrayal to have a big funeral. So they watched the gravediggers fill the hole back in;

the earth was so dank from the disgusting thaw of spring that it was nearly mud, hitting the wood of the coffin with a liquid sound.

Minique kept her eyes on the coffin slowly disappearing under sloshing earth, but pointed out at the woods.

"But Minique, that's crazy. You know that, right?"

Claude was the closest thing she had to a father figure, and so she didn't snap back at him. She knew he was doing it out of kindness. She also knew that if this was his reaction, the other people in Montréal would be vehement, even more convinced she had lost her mind. Former classmates, the nuns who taught her, the people she had to queue with at the boucher, the boulanger, the épicier. The people who saw her walking to and from the forest with Anne, and walking to and from Barbe's house with Daniel. The people who wondered at the dirt smears on her hands, the green smell around her neck, and the fact that she and her coureur friend were untouched by the fever despite spending days inside a sick house. Maybe they would call her a sorcière behind her back; maybe they would just call her folle, démente, insensée.

"But Daniel lives in the woods part of the year," she said instead, looking up at Claude.

He sputtered a bit, settling on: "But he's a man, chère."

She didn't answer him, afraid she would say something rude. Daniel remained silent beside him; she couldn't tell what was in his head. Instead, she looked out past the sweaty backs of the men at work and tracked the dancing tops of the trees with her eyes.

She knew Claude didn't tell anyone about their conversation in the cemetery; it was either Daniel or the gravediggers. Either way, the rumours that abounded about her, that Daniel reported back to her, became petty and strange: that she was heartbroken now that her lover, Anne, had moved away; that she was moving out to the woods to be closer to Daniel, her other lover; and, worst of all, that she was the one to poison her aunt so she could sell the house and make her escape. People scattered from her as she walked. Storekeepers were too nervous to meet her eyes.

But money talks. Her inheritance from selling off all of the family's belongings was meagre, but the town was still suffering after the fever and there were men—habitants' sons whom Daniel used to play with as a child, whom he was still friendly with as an adult—who were looking for work. Alone, Minique would not have been able to get them to help her build her home. But Daniel, who despite living in the woods for half of the year never lost his silver tongue nor his ability to make small talk, was able to persuade four of them to build her a cabin.

Aubin, Jacques, Mathurin, and Tugal didn't like to be around her at first. Whenever she came near them, to see what they were doing, to try to learn, they would shy away, like dancing away from a wild animal. Daniel had to stay on site to keep them from being too uneasy. Minique wasn't sure if he was nervous about her safety around four men, or if he was trying to reassure the men that she wouldn't harm *them*.

It took a week for them to warm to her. It was only by sheer will, her insisting on helping with every step, as best she could. If there was a log to move, she tried to shoulder as much weight as the rest of them, despite their gritted teeth and trying to shoo her away. If there were branches to shear off, she would clumsily hack at them with Daniel's hatchet as he watched her from a distance, laughing behind a hand, the other men looking aghast at her technique.

Eventually, they realized she wasn't going anywhere, nor was she going to hex them or poison them, and so they grudgingly started to teach her so she wouldn't kill herself. She watched as they felled trees and figured out where a pine would fall and what angle to wedge into the trunk. She learned how to use a drawknife to separate bark from logs; she picked splinters out of her hands at the end of each day. She learned how to level land, how to notch a log and assemble a wall. By the end of it, after the weeks of planning and preparing and finally building, she was just another member of the crew, sweaty and covered in sawdust.

At first, the four men had tried to talk her out of the location. "It's too dangerous," Aubin told her. "So far outside the town," Jacques said. "Not even close to the river," Mathurin said. "The Indians will get you," Tugal warned her. She had just shaken her head, knowing that they were wrong. None of the men asked her why she chose the clearing. She knew they wanted to, but something made them hold back. And she was never going to tell them that once, here, she had been free, if only for a night. That this place, of a dream, of a nightmare, was the only place she was going to be able to make a life.

It's been nearly ten years since she chose to leave town. There are days when she regrets it, when she thinks about what it might be like to look out her window and see other people instead of her chicken hutch and her stable and her smoking shed, be able to walk out the door and have amenities at her fingertips. There are days when she feels scared by the woods and by being alone. If she dies out here, how long will it be before someone finds her? If she disappears like her father, will anyone mourn her?

But mostly, she's happy for the space she's carved out for herself. Here, she can be as loud as she wants, and no one hears but the grey jays. She can walk around without a bodice. She can roll in the grass of the clearing just to feel it on the skin of her wrists and her ankles. She can tip her face up to the sun-setting sky and yip and yowl. She can wear her hair down around her shoulders if she wants, pull it to her face to smell the pine dust that's permanently settled into all parts of her body. Here, she can live a life where she doesn't see another human face for days.

She does see people on occasion, though. It started with one woman, Aubin's wife, Marie-Madeleine, whose daughter had croup. In exchange for a slice of pigeon pie, Minique sent her home with ivy tea and instructions to feed the child raw onion and hold her head over a steaming bowl of hot water. Whether it was her own knowledge, accrued from her time spent with Anne and the grimoire, or whether it was dumb luck, it worked. Aubin's daughter coughed up all her phlegm the next day; Marie-Madeleine was convinced that Minique, while probably not right in the head for wanting to live alone in that awful clearing, was useful; and Minique's reputation as a sage-femme was forged.

Now she helps soothe colicky babies or heal a nasty bruise or chase a fever away; she keeps a store of salves and teas so she can trade them with people. Those are the easier tasks to complete. Those are the people who come to visit her during the day, when the sun is bright and nothing needs to be hidden. She sees these same people over and over again; she rears their families from afar.

Then there are the people who show up at her door at night. Sometimes they try to obscure their faces with scarves or kerchiefs. Sometimes they stand as bravely as they can, even as they flinch from the candle she holds in her hand.

Often, she knows what they want before they even open their mouths. It'll be a young woman huddled against her jamb, her face drawn and the skin under her eyes dark.

"I need to start my bleeding."

Minique doesn't ever ask why, or if the woman is sure. It takes work and bravery to come to her cabin, especially with the sun setting and the edges of the forest pulsing with dark. She knows that whoever stands on her step wants what they want.

"A spoonful of this under your tongue every hour," she'll say, holding the tincture she's made from equal parts black and blue cohosh. "If nothing happens in a week, come back to see me. If you bleed for more than two weeks, come back to see me. If anyone asks about this, you tell them it's for a toothache." Sometimes she's tempted to threaten them: "If you tell anyone that it was me, I'll curse you so you never walk straight again. I'll bring monsters to you in your sleep. I'll show up at your window, flying on a pestle." But she doesn't have to threaten them. They're terrified enough.

The by-dark requests run the gamut from things she can actually help with (something to help with a flagging libido, something to put a violent husband to sleep earlier than normal) to things she can't promise any result for (a love potion, a curse) to the things she won't help with (a poison). Either way, she tells them what she can or can't do, and then leaves it up to them to decide if they want something anyway. If a woman comes to her begging for a love tincture and won't take no for an answer, Minique sometimes sends her on her way with wild columbine oil, or catmint tea if she's really distressed. When it comes to matters of the heart or of hate, Minique makes no promises and has no guarantees, and so no one ever has the guts to come back in a fury if something doesn't work.

This is how she supports herself: people are willing to pay to get what they want, or what they think they want, and so she can afford periodic trips into town to buy lard and sugar and thread and cotton. When she does go, she keeps her eyes up, but never lets her gaze linger too long on anyone, never gives away the secret of who comes to her door in the evening and who comes to her door in the day. She never stays in Montréal long enough to overhear anything about herself, but she hopes she's feared rather than pitied.

Mère Minique, they call her. There's hurt in that, since she'll never be a mother, and she's not old. But when she hears people say it, she thinks they say it with a little bit of respect.

She sinks her axe into another piece of wood and it splits cleanly down the grain.

"Minique!"

The shout comes from beyond the edge of her clearing. This is their routine, him calling out to warn her so she can make herself presentable—but she jumps anyway, reaching for her coat. She gets herself into it in just enough time to see Daniel striding down the path toward her. He looks a little more worn, his skin more leathered than the last time she saw him, his beard a little more tangled—but that's the way it is now. He raises a palm in greeting and she returns it, and then he smiles and she remembers a younger version of him, like when they first met. She expects him to be holding an apple in each hand.

She hustles into her cabin, leaving the door open behind her, already moving toward the tea kettle.

"Ah Christ, I hate your tea," he groans, shifting his pack off his back and dropping it by the door.

"It's that or nothing."

"Should opt for nothing."

She grins. "What's the news?"

"Who says I have any?"

"Wouldn't have left your wife and come here to see me if you hadn't any," she says, fiddling with the mugs.

"Just came from town," he says, thumping himself down in a chair so heavily that it creaks. She resists the urge to roll her eyes.

Minique relies on Daniel for a number of things. When she first settled here, unsure of how she would support herself once the money from the house ran out, he's the one who first told the people of Montréal what she could do and where to find her. If they refuse to enter the woods, he acts as the middleman until they're brave enough. If Minique doesn't want to go into town, if the anxiety about being stared at gets too great on some of her bad days, he brings her necessities to her. But mostly, he loves to feed her information about the town she hates to visit. He tells her about who has taken over what post—who has become the town major, who *wants* to become the town major, what terrible decisions de Vaudreuil is making as governor of Montréal, what cases are before the court. Who has married whom, and who is sleeping with whom. It's easier to be a man and get details just by standing around and listening than it is to be a woman, especially a woman like her.

The last time she visited town, to get a new pair of boots from the cordonnier, people nearly ran to get away from her in the street, and the shoemaker and his assistant froze in place like rats when she walked into their store. Daniel is her link to the other world, and it's a link she doesn't want to give up, as much as it pains her to admit it. As much as she wants to leave Montréal in the past, it's in her blood.

"And?" She fiddles with the kettle, hissing as she burns herself.

"You ever heard of Fort de Buade?" He drums his fingers on the tabletop so aggressively that she looks up at him and notices the look that's playing across his face—a mix of weariness and worry. It's something she doesn't often see on him.

She nods. She's heard of it. It's on the Mackinac, farther than she's travelled before, and she's never had reason to go there. She hates dealing with men anyway. She makes a humming sound to let him know she's still listening, but he doesn't mind—he'd talk if she were or if she weren't.

"It's shut down now, anyway," he says, taking the cup of tea she slides across the table. "It was a real mess before they closed it, though. They brought in some asshole to run it a few years ago. Cadillac. Fils de garce." He takes a sip of tea, wincing. She steeps it with at least three times the amount of tea other people might normally use just by virtue of keeping the pot on the stove all day and reheating it and adding to it when she sees fit; it's dark like rich lake water, and tastes like it, too. It keeps her alert and makes her feel like fire is coursing through her veins on the mornings when it's so cold she can hardly bear to peel herself out from under the blankets.

She shrugs an apology at Daniel. He blows into his mug, uselessly.

"Anyway," he continues. "Antoine Cadillac. Real connard, couillon. It was like Sodom and Gomorrah."

"That bad?"

"La Durantaye was fine. He kept the fort under control. But when Cadillac was brought in it all went to hell. He started selling brandy to the Odawa and the Wendat, which is already a problem. People were getting sick, all sorts of shit. A fever took out about half of the Wendat, probably from one of Cadillac's men. And then the Jesuits got angry, because of the brandy, and Cadillac threatened to kill one of the missionaries if they didn't back off. The traders were all running wild, doing whatever they wanted with whatever women were around." Daniel shivers a little. "He either couldn't get a handle on his men, or didn't want to. People think the frenzy was a tactic to keep the English traders in check. You know, make as much money as you can, any way you can. But that's what happens when you have a criminal in charge."

"Who appointed him?"

"Frontenac," Daniel says, his mouth twisting wryly. "May he rest, of course."

They both lean over at the same time to spit crackling streams into the fire. She's not an expert like Daniel, but he's taught her enough for her aim to hit with a satisfying sizzle. Frontenac has been dead about a year, and while much of New France mourned him as some sort of noble patriarch, there were others who saw him for what he was: a turbulent, bloodthirsty man who insisted on making a name for himself through ill-advised channels. If he's the one who installed this Cadillac—she doesn't like the thought of it. That's the incestuous nature of New France: it's all the same men lauding one another, a never-ending circle of back claps and plaudits.

"Have you met him?" Minique spares a glance at Daniel, who is digging something out of the seams of his boots with a knife.

"Cadillac? In Montréal," he grunts. "He got himself sent to France after Fort de Buade imploded, but now he's back." He pries the clod of dirt loose, holding it up on the tip of his knife and examining it before flinging it out the door.

Daniel did what her father did, except he did it right: he has what people in town would call a mariage à la façon du pays, a country marriage. Two years ago, while on his yearly expedition to the upper country, he met a Cree woman named Danis and began living with her. Minique's never met her, since the two of them live too far apart, and she wouldn't be physically able or even allowed to portage north to Danis's territory.

People in town don't talk much about mariages à la façon du pays, but they happen often, from what Daniel tells her. A marriage is a marriage, he says, and some of the coureurs spend so much time living alongside or with their hosts, of course someone's going to fall in love. It's not technically legal in the eyes of the town or the church, but when has that ever stopped anyone in Montréal from doing something they want to do?

"But this is what you *don't* hear in town," he told her once. "That the women are smarter and truly even stronger than most of the coureurs, and *they're* the ones to ask when it comes to the fur trade." Danis is both wife and business partner, directing Daniel to find the best pelts, making sure he doesn't die in the bush, and improving his fluency in Cree, which is a crucial asset for a coureur.

Claude is still partly holding out hope Daniel will marry someone in Montréal, but when Minique ducks into the bakery to check on him from time to time, and to drop off chanterelles, he likes to brag about his daughter-in-law, "Denise," despite never having met her, even if he does lament the possibility he'll never meet his grandchildren. Minique's not sure what Jeanne thinks—she hasn't seen her in years—but Daniel says she's just happy that he's happy.

Now Danis is expecting, should be giving birth in about four months. Minique knows it's hard for Daniel to be away from her for the winter season, and she wonders if soon he will be spending even less time in Montréal. Perhaps the two of them, Daniel and Danis, thrive living like this, together intensely and then apart, being their own people. There are sadnesses, she assumes, being away from the person you love, but to be independent and have your own power, without anyone else's influence, is heady.

All of these things—a life partly in the woods, outside of the harsh grasp of Montréal; a partner who can match him; a child on the way—have smoothed out Daniel's harder edges and made him smile more in the past year or so than he did for all of their late teens and early twenties.

Minique snaps in his face to get his attention back to her, like she would with an unruly dog or cat, and he clacks his teeth at her.

"What's he like?" She always asks this of the men he tells her about; she wants to collect details.

"Cadillac? I've heard he's . . . odd. Actually, that's not the right word." Daniel screws up his face in concentration. "Unpredictable. That's more it. At de Buade, they said he was always going out on expeditions to try to make maps. Half the time you couldn't find him because he'd be out on the straits. He spent a lot of time with the tribes, surprisingly." She knows what he means by *surprisingly*, considering most French men deem the local people to be not worthy of time or consideration. "Apparently he writes a lot. Very strange. People say he's putting together a journal of his time in New France." Daniel tilts his head toward Minique, as if to say *can you believe it?* "But I don't buy it. I think he's reporting back to the chancellor, Pontchartrain, in France. Or to someone."

Writing during all of this. She clicks her fingernails against the mug. "Why'd he come here?"

"From what I heard, he had to flee accusations back in France."

Minique raises her eyebrows. She's heard rumours of people in New France who left behind some sort of past they didn't want to cart across the ocean. Left behind families with young children, left behind their religion. Or like Anne, left behind suspicions. "What kind of charges?"

"Rumour has it he killed someone."

"Who?"

"I haven't found out yet," Daniel says. "Apparently the body was . . . hard to identify."

She shivers.

"Anyway, he's back from France now, and he has some big plans," Daniel says.

"What plans?"

"Before he died, Frontenac asked that Cadillac be made lieutenant commander. Cadillac wants to make a *new* fort, as if he didn't run the old one into the fucking ground."

"Where?"

"River Détroit."

Minique frowns. "But that'll give him a monopoly on the fur trade."

"Exactly," Daniel says, twirling his knife in his fingers. "Yes, exactly." And then it clicks. That the coureurs des bois and fur traders would see their lives be ruined by that, if one man squeezed his fist to choke the life out of the competition. It's always the men who come over from the continent who thirst for dominion, dragging their families along for the terrible ride. Many of them crawl back home with their tails between their legs, the spectres of dead children or wives hanging over them, the shame of being rejected by the virginal new world they wanted to plunder oozing around them like a miasma. It happens again and again, and no one seems to learn from it.

"And has no one spoken up about it?"

"Oh, everyone has." Daniel is up and rummaging around in Minique's larder, and she rolls her eyes at his back. He turns around with a fistful of moose pemmican, a wad of it already in his mouth. "It's a madhouse. All the coureurs are yelling at one another about what we should do next, but no one has any ideas, and everyone will probably just yell until they tire themselves out and no one does anything in the end. But some people are saying it'll ruin Montréal, maybe even Québec."

She sees worry in Daniel's face, despite his best attempts to hide it. She can smell it on him, a tang that wafts toward her whenever he gestures. It tastes like sour, like salt, and she doesn't like having it spread across the roof of her mouth. It makes her feel anxious and sweaty. She wants to get rid of it. She wants to help solve this.

She feels a strange knot in her gut. She wonders if Daniel came here to cajole her into doing anything, but she's not sure he has enough guile. Besides, what would she actually do? He hears things around town, reports back to her as the two of them laugh in her kitchen. The rumours of her being able to turn people into toads and spiders and cats; that she rides a branch around the woods on every full moon; that she's the one who lures men into the flying canoe and then causes them to fall to their deaths. She likes that last one the best, that people think she's powerful enough to usurp Satan. Daniel tells her the things he overhears, or directly solicits, and he recounts them all with a giggle.

The thing is, Minique isn't sure what she's capable of. If she had been given a longer time with Anne, if she was brave enough to ask the Iroquois more questions, maybe she'd know. There are times when it feels like she could do more than just make a draught, when she thinks that if she wanted to bind or charm someone, she could. She thought she felt it when she stared at Father Etienne walking through the stalls of the fur fair. She thought she felt it when she knotted her ladder. But mostly she feels mortification, hot and nauseating, which ripples through her when she thinks about sorcery, because it feels like she's constantly playing pretend at being not only an adult but a sage-femme and also the sorcière people think she is. She wants to tell Daniel that maybe there's some truth in the rumours he brings her from town. She wants to tell him what it was like to prowl through the tall grass like a horned one. But they're not children anymore, guileless and open-mouthed. They're adults who have their own secrets, their own cards held close to their chests.

She knows, somehow, that this is what will drive them apart one day.

She looks over at Daniel, steadily eating through most of her pemmican. She's drawn from her thoughts as he noisily uses the same knife from before to pick at a piece of meat between his teeth.

"You're still so revolting."

He grins back at her, his teeth white in the gnarl of his beard. He's still so handsome, actually, and she sometimes wonders what life would be like if the two of them had given up and just gotten married. She knows he harbours no secret love for her; maybe she could have brought herself to love him if they had paired off. Her life might have been easier with a decent man by her side, a man she mostly understands and mostly enjoys spending time with. But she also thinks about her cabin, her independence, the power she takes from living by herself. She'll chop all the wood in the world on her own if it means no one looking over her shoulder, judging her, asking questions, invading her space, for every day of her life.

"What is Cadillac doing next?"

"There's some big bullshit banquet in his honour next week," Daniel says. "On Saturday. The governor is putting it on at the inn."

"Are you going?"

"No," Daniel says, grimacing. "It's only for Cadillac's men, and the fancy men in town. Part of me wants to see if I could sneak in, but I'm going to be out on the water." Daniel still dislikes convention and spending time shaking hands. As a child, it was about perching on rooftops and in branches; as an adult, it's about removing himself to his canoe, to a lifestyle that is more difficult than living in town but, he would argue, more rewarding. There's no other person who understands this better than she does.

Minique takes another sip of tea and lets it burn its way into her to prevent herself from opening her mouth and flicking her tongue at the air. There's something twanging inside of her, muted, almost indistinguishable if she weren't able to sit in silence and divine herself, like she's gotten used to doing over the years. It's a plucking, like something she forgot or willingly pushed to the back of her mind has turned its head and opened one of its eyes, using the tip of its finger to nudge at her, as if to say *you didn't forget, you didn't erase me*. She doesn't have the words for it, so she takes stock of the feeling and promises to come back to it later.

"That man thinks he's some kind of giant," Daniel says, shaking his head. *Giant*—Minique is brought back to twine in her hands, a hot urge ringed around her neck. From the corner of her eye, she sees the rope ladder twist where it hangs from the rafters. What an odd word for Daniel to use, that word that she carved into her mind when she stood with Anne and tied all her knots—

"Oh!" Daniel raises his hands in exclamation and then starts rummaging around in his pockets, moving on to his bag when he doesn't find what he's looking for. He curses under his breath until he grins, pulling something out and flipping it to her across the table. It bounces, makes a metallic sound, skitters to a rest at her own hand curled around her mug. It's a ring.

She frowns. "Proposing?"

"Fuck off," he laughs back. "It was at the trading post last time I was there. Who else would I give it to?"

Minique picks it up and sees what he's talking about. It's an insignia ring, bigger than what people normally might think pretty, and the letter is a stark M. It's not flowery nor looping; it's strong font, clear lines. She loves it.

"I wonder who it belonged to," Daniel says through another mouthful. "M for Montréal? Marie?" He shrugs. "Happy birthday."

"My birthday isn't for another five months," she murmurs, staring at the ring up close, admiring its form.

"I'll take that as a thank you."

"Thank you," she says, looking up at him. "I've never had a gift like this before." She has to blink hard a few times to keep from crying. It's the most thoughtful thing she's ever been given.

When he eventually leaves, balms for bruises and burns tucked into his pockets and more pemmican in his bag, Minique waves from the doorway, and then slips the ring onto her middle finger. She is immediately reassured by the weight of it and the way the metal warms to her skin. The letter there, announcing her before she can even open her mouth. *I am Minique*, it says. *Be aware.*

She doesn't sleep well that night. She's plagued by patchy dreams in which she's playing cat's cradle by herself and can't seem to pull her hands from the string, which wraps itself around her fingers and her wrists. The pressure gets to be so tight that it hurts; when she yells out, the cord bursts into light, like fireflies. She dreams about apples that are so red they look as if they've been dreamed up for a fairy tale; she holds them in her palms and they're heavier than they look, like stones. When she drops them to the ground, they bounce once and then turn to liquid like blood but more viscous, and she falls to her hands and knees and watches as it slowly seeps into the moss and pine needles. She smells columbine and catmint there with her face so close to the forest floor, and something else, something that tastes to her like a plan for victory, an urge for glory, something that upends everything purposefully and with strategy. She hears boots on branches, the sharp cracking familiar and yet frightening, and she wills herself not to look up as the sounds get closer. She'll keep her eyes on the underbrush for as long as she needs to, because this is what she knows, and this is what she feels most comfortable with. This is what she's chosen for herself.

Minique wakes up to the sound of steps. She curls around herself for a moment like an animal before she fights back against those instincts and straightens her spine, flexes her fingers as if she needs to furl them into fists. The footsteps hang in the air; the dream starts to lift its tendrils from her, and the sound—it's not boots, it's the creaking of the trees in the wind and the sound of her cabin settling as the heat from the fire dissipates. It's not someone coming to her. Coming to get her. Her whole body feels silvery with relief. For now, she's still alone. Her chest is billowing, and she has to sit up and put her forehead between her knees, cushioned on the stretch of nightgown, to get her breathing back to normal.

Still, throughout the day, she can't help but remember that emotion she woke up with: the idea of something impending, the taste of change. Beneath her wrists, she can feel the steady drum of her heart. She feels determination. She remembers this emotion, how it flourished in her when she was out in the woods with Anne, how it was in her fingers when she held the rope.

"It's nice to have you back, old friend," she murmurs, pressing her arms into her breasts and feeling the beat of her blood.

She lugs bucketfuls of snow into the house, dumping them into her tub and watching them slowly melt in the heat of her cabin. She puts a few pots' worth on her stove, waiting for them to reach a rolling boil before carefully pouring them in. When the bath is ready, she throws handfuls of salt and birchbark and blackberry leaves into the tub. *Protection*, she thinks. *Curse-killing. Prosperity.* Anne's words come back to her: power lies in the mind. She waits until the water smells vegetal and then she steps in, right leg first, left leg next, lowering herself down until she's submerged to the neck. It's been a while since she had a proper wash, so she can feel the layers of dirt lift off of her, helped by the handfuls of salt she's running along her skin. She scrubs as hard as she can bear, until she brings tears to her eyes, because if there's one thing she's learned, it's that pain grounds her more than any plant, any partner, any other way humans make roots for themselves. When she feels pain, she knows she's alive.

She leans her head back, getting her hair wet, and scrubs at her scalp. Tonight isn't necessarily about looking good or clean. It's not about smelling nice. It's about smelling like she came straight from the forest. It's about looking the part. It's about rattling some cages and raising some hackles. It's going to stir up trouble, too, but she wants to see this Cadillac herself, take him in, try to sense what he wants and where his ambitions go. *Giant slayer*, she thinks. That prickling feeling spreads from her neck to her mouth; she can feel the saliva pool in the pouches of her cheeks and under her tongue.

She holds her breath and then she slides under the water, hearing the crackling of the fire fade away. She stays under for as long as she can, pinching her nose shut, pretending she's baptizing herself, able to wash away all of the bad memories. Goodbye father, goodbye death, goodbye jeering, goodbye fever. Goodbye world that is changing whether she wants it to or not. Goodbye normalcy. Minique shoots up in the bath, water streaming down her neck and clavicles, little flecks of bark stuck to her forearms and chest, blackberry leaves freckling her breasts and stomach, all giving her little scales like some sort of half-formed beast.

After she towels off, after she yanks a comb through her hair, sitting close to the fire to let it dry as best it can, she starts from the inside and works her way out. She pulls on a garter, and then dark-blue wool stockings. She puts on a cotton shift, and then her petticoats. Next is a black wool blouse, buttoned up to her neck, fastened at the wrists. A black wool skirt, long enough that it covers the blue of the stockings except for when she's taking the biggest of strides. She puts on moose-hide boots that Daniel got her, the ones that go halfway up her legs and are trimmed with rabbit fur. Danis beaded blue and white circles along the toes, and Minique is reminded of Barbe every time she looks down, somehow, the blue like the unforgettable blue of her eyes. She forgoes a bodice but wraps a black shawl around her shoulders and then winds it around her torso.

By now, her hair has dried enough that she can braid it. She knows other women in town tend to wind their hair up into some sort of bun and cover it with a bonnet, or some sort of hat, depending on how wealthy they are. But Minique doesn't want to stick pins into her scalp, not today, and what propriety does she have to protect anymore? In the forest, bonnets get dingy quickly. She could wear a breechclout out here and no one would ever see it; she's been considering it for some of the muggier summer days.

After her hair is braided back, she binds it with a piece of blue ribbon and tucks the plait down into her collar; it's still damp enough that it'll freeze otherwise. She pulls on her black wool coat, long enough to cover her skirts underneath. In the left pocket of the coat, she puts a small piece of birchbark, something to grab at and dig into her palm when she needs to centre herself. She wraps a black wool scarf around her face one, two, three times, until her eyes are the only part of her that isn't covered.

She grabs her moose-leather hat and gloves, both also lined with rabbit fur. She shoves the hat on top of her head, on top of the shawl, securing everything in place, and then wedges her hands into the gloves. Minique stands still in the middle of her cabin, silently sweating. She breathes in the smell of pine, and grounds herself with it. She wonders what the hell she's doing, what kind of situation she's willingly putting herself into. She has the strange urge to laugh. She's in a fugue. Like the clearing. Like the tall grass. Like the way her mind set when she tied the ladder and she poured all her emotion into it despite knowing it was a poor idea. But all she wants is a look at the giant, even if that means she has to suffer the stares of the people in town. She knows the dangers of putting herself into the sights of ambitious men; she opens the door anyway.

The night is the kind of sharp, clear cold that is nearly pleasurable, where everything is silver and silent. The snow squeaks under her boots, and the moonlight is just enough to not need a lantern but not enough to banish the shadows that line the path she's cleared for herself over years of walking back and forth with a hatchet and swinging until her arms were so sore she couldn't lift them above her head.

Minique has about an hour until she reaches town. Sometimes the walk is drudgery; sometimes it's a meditation. Tonight, it's the latter. It's the kind of winter darkness that's good for thinking, where the rhythm of her footsteps echoes her pulse and each inhale burns a path straight to her mind.

As used as she is to the forest, she still doesn't love nighttime walks, at least not when the moon is waning. Even the hardiest of people can see their imaginations run wild with the shape of the branches, the snap and scrape of the snow underfoot. In the dark, it's possible to see things that don't exist, or maybe do exist, or maybe live in the dusky space between worlds. It's possible to have her mind run askew through the trees, hooking its fingernails into the bark and marking its way. It's possible to think about tales told decades ago, to keep her eyes open for a flash of colour in between the pines. Minique tries her hardest not to give in to the temptation to unspool the direst parts of her imagination, instead focusing on the satisfaction she takes in marking the path with her footprints, carving her claim in the most temporary way possible.

Montréal glows strangely from where she stands, where the forest meets the bald land that surrounds the town. From some angles it looks beautiful, like a piece of stained glass, but closer up, it looks monstrous, like it doesn't belong. It's a puzzle, welcoming and foreboding, a promise of some semblance of safety and also a prison.

Before begging for entry at the gate, Minique likes to walk through the cemetery outside the walls for a few minutes. She likes the silence, the oddness of the shorn land and the silhouettes of the graves. She avoids Barbe's grave, although she knows where it is. She's not ready to have a chat with her yet. Instead, she silently asks Barbe to help her tonight. She taps her fingers on her aunt's grave, the marker they put out for her father. *Live by the forest, die in the forest*, she thinks.

The town streets are emptier than normal. The soft hide of her boots seems to ring off of every facade. She's sure that her breathing is echoing up and down every street, that it'll announce her presence at the party long before she arrives. She thinks that someone will be able to sense her fear and will barrel out of a doorway, reaching for her.

But she runs into no one. She sees no faces at the windows, no knuckles curled around door frames. Montréal is a ghost town tonight. Minique lets the silence fill her ears until she comes to the door of the inn. Even if the windows weren't lit up with a red glow, she'd have known that this was the place because she can taste it on the air: the sourness of the beer and the sweetness of the wine, the odd smokey lick of desire that she always senses when men are in close quarters with one another.

She's tempted to knock but she knows that she's timed it perfectly: they should all be so drunk that there will be no one guarding who's leaving or who's arriving, and so she pushes the door open and she's inside.

Being a woman in Montréal means living in danger. The threat exists around every corner, at any hour: going to the store, passing a man in the street, walking after dark. Walking at any time of day. Just being seen. Dancing with anyone and being considered a tease; forgetting yourself and smiling at the forgeron, who leers back. If it's not a man who means you physical harm, it's a man who means you spiritual harm. If it's not a man who wants to get you, it's a woman who wants to take you down a few pegs. Minique has sensed the bad, the mean, the malicious, the traitorous. They've all traced their way across her tongue and she has spat them back out and tried to move on.

But this—the light cutting a way for her like a path, the noises spilling around the corner as she moves farther inside—is something else altogether. This is a storm of rollicking, cruel male energy, and it's like a wall as soon as she steps into the main room. All of her senses are assaulted at once. There's the smell: like grease and burnt wax and hair, like something a little bit rancid, a little bit sweet underneath. She can taste it at the root of her tongue, like the way that part of her mouth swells right before she's about to vomit. Then there's the candlelight, the way the flames are throwing shadows onto everything: the smaller tables in the corners, the long table at the centre set up for the most honoured guests, the ones who will drink the most wine and eat the most meat and talk the loudest in a bid to own the conversation. There's the noise, the yipping that calls to mind the smaller wolves, the ones that aren't quite as majestic as the warier, bigger ones. The coyotes, slavering when they're half-starved from the winter.

As she steps forward, a man making his way to the front door stumbles into her, knocking her back. She hisses. The man lurches on his feet, eyeing her up and down, and Minique curls her lips, showing off the points of her teeth. There must be something threatening about her face, because he backs off, and she strides around him. She knows where she's going: it's not the tables of little coyotes, although she knows that the underlings are the most dangerous men in the room because they'll do anything to be lauded. She's headed to the main table, to the big wolves. The ones who watch and wait.

The men notice her immediately. All of their heads turn to her. It's like standing in front of a jury. Part of her wants to recoil from them, but part of her wants to grow twenty feet tall, fling out her arms, grow claws, become the witch everyone thinks she is.

Instead, she keeps her face as implacable as she can, letting her gaze settle only for a second on each man—but definitely, solidly on each, so that none could think himself excused or safe. Or special. She flicks her eyes over what from far away looks like suaveness and richness, and is, up close, lanky hair, pocked cheeks, cracked lips, dirty fingernails. Well-fitted coats over stained shirts; well-made shoes over dirty stockings. Nothing here is impressive to her: Is this what the old world has sent to divide and conquer? Are these the best men they could find?

"Hey poussin!" A man half gets up out of his chair. He has oily brown hair and a poorly groomed beard. She can see that he's missing teeth. "I got a seat for you!" He smacks his thighs with both hands.

She resists the urge to roll her eyes. The men around him laugh uproariously, whistling through their teeth and repeating his joke, chortling.

Another man nearly dances into her path, that's how drunk he is. He's weaving on his feet, his eyes unfocused. He reaches out as if to grab her by the waist, and her heart races. It was easier to imagine this when they were all sitting at their tables, but now she realizes how monumentally stupid her decision is. She pivots out of his way and he sways forward instead of correcting his course, catching himself on the edge of a table before he falls on his face. He snarls like he wants to come after her again, but his legs don't cooperate, and he slides to the floor, spitting vitriol, his head lolling around.

She resists the instinct to swing her head around and check to see if the other men are getting any ideas from their addled colleague. She knows what danger it is to look like prey. Instead she cocks her head and tries to listen, to hear for the scrape of more chairs and the heavy plod of more feet. She won't open her mouth, not yet; she can't risk becoming overwhelmed by the sheer stupidity of the people in this room. While she listens, she keeps her own feet moving, walking toward the wolves.

And then she comes to him.

There are two kinds of men she encounters: those who ignore her, and those who shrink from her. Minique doesn't command respect among the former, and doesn't stoke any lust in the latter. But this one in front of her doesn't seem to fit into either of those classes.

In the maelstrom, he's a glittering eye, still and predatory. Despite only now making eye contact with him, she knows that from the minute she walked in, he's been appraising her. She supposes this is how he earned his reputation as the world-eater. He notices people, takes stock of their weaknesses and their whims, and catalogues them for later.

He's odd-looking. Aquiline and angular, with a face that's hard lines. A nose that's too big, a mouth that's too thick. Lush black hair that hangs in waves, should be tied back while he's eating, probably gets caught in the greased slash of his lips. Worst of all, he's staring back at her without compunction.

This is no different than facing down a young male trouble bear: the same musk, huffing, cock of the head. She imagines him as ursine. That black hair becomes a pelt; the meat-slick mouth a maw; the broad nose a snout.

"You're staring," he says.

She opens her mouth just a little, tries to breathe him. What can he tell her from the way he'll feel across her tongue? She clicks her teeth together rhythmically, trying to bring him in, trying to plant him inside of her. He watches, silently, and she notices that his face begins to mirror hers, his lips dropping open, his four front teeth pressed together, grinding back and forth.

"So are you," she says, and she knows her voice isn't as strong as it could be. She hopes he thinks that's what she always sounds like, scratchy and hoarse. As if the forest had wound itself around her throat.

He slips one hand across his mouth, like he's smiling into his palm. His other hand slides across the table, toward her, palm down. He splays his fingers wide. She feels a thudding at the base of her spine.

"I know who you are," she says. Her voice sounds strange to her own ears, like her throat is scaled. Wood against wood, nails sunk into a trunk. She wants to reach out and touch his forehead, dip into his mind if she can, try to see his future, where he's going to dirty the ground with blood next. That's what is emanating off of him— copper and gore, the saltiness of hard work buried somewhere, but underneath it all, some bite, a twanging vein of decisiveness. It's a nauseating mix, potent and pressing.

"Do you?"

As if woken up by his voice, the men on either side of him react like dogs, rolling their heads blindly toward the conversation, their nostrils flaring and their tongues darting out to flick at the corners of their mouths. Minique has to stop herself from recoiling at their blank eyes and addled faces.

She looks at Cadillac, tilting her head to the side for a moment. *What do you want me to do,* she asks him with the angle of her neck, *with these filth mongers looking on like this?* She hopes the men are so drunk already that none can see her trembling.

Cadillac holds up his big hand, then, and the baying stops. Minique can hear the spittle-thick click of their canines as their mouths snap shut like traps. They all stare at her for a moment, all the sullen, smug faces.

"And how does a wild woman know of me?"

Those words—*wild woman.* She's still for a moment as she turns them over in her head, the familiar curves of them. Since she's not fuckable, they've picked different words to cut her into pieces. *Wild. Disgusting. Rough.* No *whore* or *slut* for her, not often. It's a different brand of violence, not as shame-based, but designed to hurt nonetheless. *Dramatic. Controversial. Deserves what she has coming to her.*

But wasn't that why she stalked in here? To bring the drama, to gaze on the giant? To be foolhardy for once? And maybe, maybe, to stake her claim on this land just like he has?

"A wild woman has her ways."

Cadillac smiles, revealing more of his sharp, crooked teeth. *Faut aller chercher le loup,* Minique suddenly hears in her head, the thin thread of Jeanne's song from long ago. *Have to find the wolf.* Find him, so he can't sneak up on you. Know him.

"Ma bonne mère," he says, and his voice is taunting and sweet all at the same time, and the hair on the back of her neck rises at the same time her hackles do. "Why are you here?"

"To tell your fortunes, sirs," she says, making sure that last word doesn't sound at all deferential.

Cadillac's smile widens; his eyes are still on her. She takes two steps forward, bringing her body to the table. This way, he's forced to tip his head back to look up at her.

"See what you can tell me of the future. I don't care about the past," he says in a voice so low it feels intimate. And then he holds out his hand.

As she looks down at his face, which is somewhere between mocking and curious, something inside of her urges her not to take his hand. *Touch this man*, it warns, *and something will happen.*

But she grabs at him, perhaps more aggressively than he expects, because his fingers curl around hers, tightly, in—what? A warning? She shoots him a look, and he lets go, relaxing enough that his fingers curl open and the back of his hand rests in her palm.

She wishes that she had brought a deck of cards for fortune-telling; at least that way, they'd be safely across a table, not having to touch each other. Instead, the weight of his hand is stoking a tendril of something starting to uncurl in her gut, a tenuous thing, treacherous and ripe. It's disgust at the men around her; disgust at the man sitting in front of her, at the blood she can smell on his hands. And it's disgust with herself, at the heavy heat that's unfurled along the muscles of her inner thighs, animal and profane.

Men who destroy aren't men to be loved. She knows this. She knows that men who are constantly hunting, wanting, and consuming are men to be avoided. There's always a deep hunger that gnaws at them, that urges them to take more, take more, take more. These hungry men keep their eyes on the tree-line; they search for fur, wood, something unseen. She knows this. She knows this because there's a part of her that wants the same things, moans with the same hunger.

Cadillac stares at her silently, almost sulkily, as if she had been ignoring him. She's reminded of a boy pouting, and she can't help the smile that spreads across her mouth. His eyes snap to her lips, and he inhales, as if he's about to start speaking, but she tightens her hand and her nails dig into the skin that covers the hardest bones. His eyes narrow, but she bows her head, her breath across his palm. If she wanted to, she could lean her body a little bit forward and the tips of his fingers, now rigid with surprise, would brush against her collarbone, the tops of her breasts. The muscles of his wrist tic, and she runs her tongue across the ridge of her teeth. *Don't feed the wolf,* she thinks, but her brain is flooded with fog and hotness.

She closes her eyes and inhales for a moment. She can taste him still, sweet and metallic, like biting your tongue while biting into a candy. He looks hot. He looks feverish with need and appetite.

"What are you *doing*?"

She opens her eyes; he looks disgusted, but she wonders if that's a cover for unease. There's a coating of sweat on his upper lip and he's moved his head incrementally back, away from her. She wonders how long she had her eyes closed for.

He's staring at her with narrowed eyes, waiting.

"Gathering my thoughts," she says.

His eyes get narrower, like he doesn't believe her. But what can he say? This is her realm and her town.

She notices that his palm is shimmering with a light coat of sweat. She purses her lips and blows, and his fingers jerk.

This she can do. If he won't be scared of her, then she'll make him feel something else. The whole banquet has slowed down around them, gone from loud and glistering to muffled and shimmered at the edges of her vision. She doesn't want to look from side to side, because she doesn't want to take her eyes off of him, but she wonders if she did whether she'd see the men frozen like gargoyles. It's just the two of them now, two masters of their own domains. She's no longer a woman, fragile at the hands of men. Instead, she's an equal. Tall. Strong. The creator of her own world.

"What do you see?"

She keeps her head bent, refusing to drag her eyes up to him and let him dictate her pace. Instead, she takes her right hand and lays it overtop of his, palm to palm, her fingers reaching down his wrist.

That's when she does meet his eyes. He's staring at her, so she lets her vision go soft, the edges of her eyes blur in a familiar way. She opens the corners of her mind, opens the corners of her mouth, and breathes it all in. Starts to unfold the specifics of his life, sharpening her focus, spreading herself over the map that shows his peculiarities, his particulars.

"Wife," she says. "Where is she?"

"Beauport," he says, quietly.

"Children, too."

He nods. If he's ashamed or proud of his family, she can't tell.

"What else do you want to know?"

He sits still, moving air around in his mouth so that she sees his jaw working. It looks like he's chewing gristle, and she recognizes it immediately for what it is: a tell. She slots it away in her mind, to use later. *Later?* She knows from how he sweats in her grasp, although he pretends not to, that there will be a later for them.

"Glory," he says.

"Glory, yes," she says, squinting. They all want to know about glory. Except it's usually couched in terms of *fame* and *fortune*. Not that word—not something that evokes victory. She traces a fingertip across the lines in his hand, and he follows the action with his gaze. "Riches to be won," she says, wrapping her pointer finger around his ring finger and pulling lightly. "You'll be successful in your goal for glory," she says. "So much that people will name cities after you." He preens here, rotating his head on his neck. "Not just cities, but things." She can't really see this part. It's beyond her ken. "Your name will be household. But," she says, frowning a little.

"But?"

She presses her pointer finger into his flesh. "You could lose it all. Your notoriety, your health, your happiness."

"Happiness," he says, softly. *Doesn't he know what happiness is?*

"If you don't respect those around you," she says, pressing in harder. Abruptly, she brings his hand to her mouth and reaches out with the tip of her tongue. He makes a strangled sound, moves as if to pull away, but she tastes him before he can and then drops his hand out of surprise.

Because Minique sees, behind her eyes, a flash of red. She tastes it before the image reaches her brain, the dream she had as a child, the nightmares that come sometimes—hard and bitter in the back of the mouth. Something that has the scent of rotting leaves, the unworldly. She almost retches, but staves it off by pressing her knuckles to her top lip. She stares at him, knowing that the whites of her eyes are showing, knowing that she looks, all of a sudden, like prey. He stares back, stock-still.

"The red—" she starts, but he gets an odd look on his face, and whatever spell she has woven is broken.

"The what?"

She tries again, tries to put words to whatever she just saw, but he's shaking his head.

"Do you believe that shit?"

She's not sure what he's talking about, or maybe she doesn't want to admit it, but his hand is back in his lap. When they held hands, when she touched his skin for the first time, something was burned into her. She digs her nails into her own palms, bites her tongue and shakes her head, and those things snap her back into her body. Cadillac is sitting as far back in his chair as he can, and before he can say something else, before his acolytes can ask for their own fortunes, she turns as smoothly as she can on her heel and walks out.

The trip home goes as quickly as she can make it go. There's a sensation crawling along her wrists and her ankles, and she's not letting herself recognize it for what it is. *Bondage*, she thinks, and she repeats that word to herself with every step.

Something has found her and tethered itself to her.

"Run," she says, to whom she doesn't know, and she lifts her skirts in her hands and starts to sprint.

———

Back in her cabin, Minique loses herself. She goes for the kindling first, letting loose a sound like a bugle and a shriek as she grabs the pieces of wood and flings them across the room at full force. When that's not enough, she goes for the bedding next, ripping it off the mattress and trying to tear it with both hands, failing, throwing it on the floor instead. When that's not enough, she picks up one of her stools, holding it over her head. She wavers for a moment, and then plunges over the edge, slamming the furniture down as hard as she can with a yell. Wood splinters; she has to shield her eyes with a forearm, panting, and only then does she feel the storm has passed. When she regains her breath, she looks around at the disaster she's created. She falls face first onto her bare mattress.

She's back in the forest, sprinting down the dark path. The thing that's chasing her is no longer a figment of her imagination: she can feel a reverberation in the dirt from something heavy and broad. She can hear the snapping of twigs, the *thwip* of branches being shoved out of the way and flying back into place. She won't look behind her, but she doesn't have to, because as soon as the lights of her cabin windows come into view, as far off as they are, she's grabbed around the waist, and she can't even scrabble for the trees to anchor herself as she's pulled back farther and farther into the woods.

Minique wakes up with a sharp inhale, smelling dust and dirt and daytime, the sweet scent that comes when the sun hits the wood of her cabin. She's drooled in her sleep, and it's covering part of her face. She knows that she has indentations on her cheeks and neck from the straw ticking of her mattress. She knows she looks like a mess. She feels like one, too. She slides her hands under her shoulders and pushes her body up and the day begins again.

Except the day isn't normal. Her legs shake as she tries to go about her chores: restocking her kindling pile, darning the linens she ruined last night, sweeping up the debris left on the floor. She tries. She gets the cabin cleaned and the bedclothes on the mattress. She opens the windows but locks the door because she wants to feel the breeze yet also has a strange sense of foreboding. She manages to drink a cup of tea and gnaw on some bread. And then she has to drag herself back to bed, even though it's the middle of the day, because there's an ache rattling around in her head and something that feels like a fever crawling its way up her body. All she can hear is Anne's voice, her old refrain: *be in control of your own life, be in control of your own life.* To work in a liminal space, to exist as a woman surveilled by men of faith and men of little faith, Anne warned her to always be in control of herself: of her emotions every time she picked up the book, of her greed when choosing who to help, of soft-heartedness and pity.

When she wakes up next, it's the middle of the night. The fire she made has burned down to just embers, and the cabin is cast in an orange glow. When she shifts to prop herself up on her elbow, her whole body twangs, pulled tight from her thighs to her collarbones, and all she can do is shove a hand between her legs to try to fight the heat out of her flesh and bones before the sun comes up.

———

The desperate heat fades into something that only chews at her edges when she stands up too quickly or turns her head at a certain angle. It's not that she feels sick: she's upright, she's breathing. It's more like something has crawled into her, stuck in her skin like a burr. Like there's an itch in her body in a place she can't identify and can't reach; if she had claws, she'd be tearing into herself right now. Anyone else might not notice, but alone, with no distractions, Minique knows that something has changed.

Still, she tries. If valerian or hemp tea won't do it, she'll try to chase it away with other, less reliable measures. She fishes out black candles and sets one in every window, lights the wicks and watches the flames flicker. *A guttering flame means there's something in the house*, Anne's grimoire says. So Minique takes handfuls of salt and draws a line around her whole cabin, even going so far as to border the paths in the woods, making another circle around her house farther out. She makes the third circle around her bed, so that the last thing she'll feel every night is the salt against the soles of her feet. If she were a pious person, she'd be kneeling in it, the pain a tithe. But she's not.

Minique holds off on going into town for as long as she can. She tells herself it's because she's lazy, but the truth is she's terrified of running into him. She's not even sure if he's in Montréal anymore, because the town is a shithole compared to Québec. But Montréal is closer to the world that Cadillac wants to build, deeper inland on the St. Laurence, that vein of the water that connects everyone and everything. So Montréal is necessary, in this way. A shitty, indispensable stopover for those who think they're going on to bigger and better things. If someone were to ask *why don't you all just leave*, they'd be met with a scoff. *Because this is our place* would be the answer. Minique admires and rejects that sentiment all at once.

But it makes for intense visits. After living alone for so long, she finds the storm of emotions in town difficult to cope with, and the more time passes and the longer she stays away, the harder it gets. Still, she's low on sugar and completely out of salt, and she needs more thread, too, which means that it's time for her to be brave. As she pulls on her layers, she sends up a little prayer to whoever's listening, asking that the trip be as painless and fast as possible. The entire walk into town, she repeats this request to the beat of her boots, as the afternoon light glimmers into her. Her one consolation is that it's always a little easier to go into town during winter: there's so little of her distinguishing features visible, hidden behind her tuque and her scarf and her mittens and her giant coat, that some people don't even notice her.

The town rises in her vision like a gloomy stronghold, so different from the violent beauty of it on the night of the banquet. By day, it's mottled and dowdy. Even the streets look dimmer and sound more muted. The continent doesn't have winters like this—that's what she's heard from other people, the ones with long-enough memories. This winter, this snow, this never-ending cold: it's not natural, it's not normal. It feels like punishment, those voices say: it feels like we're going to die here, deep in it. It's not an idle thought—people *have* frozen to death, found curled in a snowbank as if sleeping. Death is the only certainty anywhere, but in the new world, it's like an old friend who comes to visit a little too often.

For Minique, winter is the cloak that protects her. Not everyone in town wears moose hide and rabbit fur. They cling to the fashions from back home, but a wig lets the bitter wind whistle through it, and snow seeps into leather shoes and freezes the buckles. She knows her father didn't invent this and that he took the idea from the people he traded with, but she can't help but feel grateful that she was always dressed in hide, not cotton; wore fur, not linen. Now, as an adult, it means she can pull the weight of winter around her body and let it cradle her. It seems like a small gift, but on this dire land, it's so much bigger than she could have known as a child.

When she enters the general store, unwinding her scarf as she steps inside the doorway, she sees the shopkeeper's eyes widen. Minique sighs as she walks toward the counter, readying for another day of stilted transactions and retailers trying to hand things to her without touching her skin with their own fingers.

"Sugar?"

As she asks, he scuttles off to a shelf, keeping his head down, and she's reminded of why she stays away.

The sun is starting to dip in the sky by the time she's finished all her errands. This is the time of day that Minique likes: it's bruised and strange. It casts a purple-yellow light on everything and makes shadows warp and stretch. It also means that people start to hunker down for the night. Because of that, the street is nearly empty. She sees the backs of men as they disappear into doors, the flap of skirts turning around corners. She can hear the satisfying crunch of her boots on the dirty snow lining the street, the creak of her hands on the handle of her basket. It's calm now, after a harried afternoon of trying not to taste people's fear when they see her. Here in the gloaming, she can finally take a deep breath.

When she turns to head out, she sees a figure at the end of the road. She stops moving on instinct, standing where she's able to observe. She doesn't know if they've seen her, or what their business is, but as they start to walk in her direction, she can tell that it's someone tall and male, dressed in silly boots and a jerkin that seems inadequate with the wind picking up.

Minique has a tight feeling in her throat, like the scratchiness that comes with every spring. She doesn't move toward him, nor does she retreat. The sun is setting behind her, so she can see her shadow grow lean and long, stretching out toward the man, who's walking to her at a measured pace. She breathes deeply inside her scarf and does what she thinks he won't expect: she walks toward him, too. His features come into clearer focus: that distinctive nose, the dark eyes that click around like a bird of prey's do. She wonders what she looks like to him—if her eyes are similarly sharp, if she holds herself like a predator might.

"I would address you properly, but I don't know your last name," he says when they're a few feet away from each other, and he punctuates it with a puff of laughter that turns into a wisp of breath. He is trying hard not to shiver now that he's stopped walking, and it's evident in the way he's positioned his body. He's attempting to appear bigger than he is, with the way he's thrust his chest out and crossed his arms, but the effect is lost somewhere around his jaw, which is clenched against the cold, and his temples, where she can see beads of sweat. Some of his hair has escaped the tie at the back of his neck, and it's clinging to his jaw and cheeks. In the banquet hall, he was cosseted and powerful; here, she can see the fine lines of weakness.

By contrast, she's unreadable and swathed. This is her town, for better or for worse.

"With the amount this town talks about me, I'm surprised at that," she answers, her voice even.

"You just have the one name. Like a god."

"Like the devil," she shoots back. He smiles a little at that, and the curling of the corners of his mouth surprises her. *A god*, she thinks. *As if the people here believe in more than one.*

"I'm just coming back from a meeting," he says, filling the silence in the way people do when they're not comfortable. *Thank you, Tante*, Minique thinks, *for the gift of learning to wait someone out.* "Do you want a drink?"

That pulls her up short. Firstly, it's not proper for a married man to ask an unmarried woman for a drink. It's not proper for any man to ask any woman, really, unless there are family members around or it's a public place filled with people. It's also not something people do with her, in particular.

He must see the way her brow furrows, because he holds both hands up in a gesture of placation.

"As a thank you for telling my fortune the other night," he says, and the beginning of a smirk is on his face, like he's regaining his footing. "And to ask you about this place."

Minique wants to sigh. Men think they're so sneaky; he thinks he's pulling one over on her. If he sees her as an outcast, he might think she'll tell him information about the town, about its weaknesses. Especially if he thinks she might live outside the town walls and has a relationship with the Indigenous people or the coureurs des bois.

Still, she's forgotten how good it feels to talk with someone who's not Daniel, someone who doesn't know her every whim and can't predict her every mood. This is what normal people do; they chat, they drink, they socialize. She ignores the hand that he's holding out for her and instead walks alongside him.

He's not staying at the inn; that would be too lowly for him, somehow. Instead, he's staying at a house owned by a relative of the governor. The family has moved out to live with other relatives, meaning Cadillac has the whole place to himself. It shows—it's clear that he's not actively using some rooms, which are cold and coated with dust. The place smells like frost and distance. There's hardly any human scent for her to pick up here.

They're not alone, though: he has a cook and a housekeeper, one lighting the fire in the drawing room, one bringing out a dish of biscuits, though both women melt into the wallpaper with the practised ease of people who have been serving others for years. Cadillac overlooks them because of his pedigree, but Minique recognizes the sister of one of the girls she went to school with, and the aunt of a former bully. These are the people who see and know everything, and she's learned over the years to respect them, no matter what the history is between them, because all information is important information. Men like Cadillac don't know that, or don't value it. Minique nods to the two women and is surprised when they both nod back before disappearing into a series of doors like magic. The presence of other people in the house is both a relief and a disappointment. Being alone with any man, save for Daniel, is a threat that she feels in her marrow. They're all animals at heart, searching for their own pleasure and sustenance in whatever form they can find it, regardless of permission or propriety. Or pain.

Being a woman in the new world means pain, it seems. Even as removed as she is, she's still part of the sisterhood of heartache. She sees the misery of an unwanted pregnancy, the desperation of losing a pregnancy that *was* wanted. She sees the bruises, the bite marks, the shadow of memory that crosses their faces as they sit in her kitchen and try not to tell too much of their story. But they always fail; either they tell it with words, or the purple that edges out from beneath their sleeve tells it for them. From that, Minique has learned that to be married is to mostly be unhappy, that love here is mostly a fairy tale. And that tethering yourself to someone is a danger.

Cadillac watches her as she walks around. He doesn't follow when she opens doors and looks into rooms to see dust held in the air like unspoken thoughts. She noses around blatantly, lost for a moment in her own mind. She sniffs at corners and lingers in doorways, trying her best to get a handle on the place and the man. He stands in the corner of the drawing room when she comes back in, and he doesn't move toward her as she chooses a chair that's farther away from him than she thinks he would like. It means her back is to the door, but it also means he's always in her sightline. She takes off her coat, but no other layers. When he turns to a cabinet to get two glasses and a bottle of what she guesses is brandy, she watches his hands as he pours, making sure his fingers are in view and that he's not palming anything. When he brings the glass to her, she takes it without touching him, and she holds it in her hand until he takes a sip from his first. Only then does she sip in kind, feeling the lush burn of good alcohol wind into her belly.

It's pleasing to be able to exist in silence with a person. She and Daniel can accomplish it sometimes, but he likes to chat, so mainly she becomes a reactor, someone grunting or cooing at the right moments. Here, Cadillac lies on a chaise longue, toeing his boots off as he does. He turns his head to look at her, the fan of his black hair spread out around him. Even reclining, his gaze is pointed and deep. She understands why men fall over their own feet to follow him.

"So, Mère."

She shakes her head, taking another sip of brandy. It's so good, coating her tongue with goldenness. She wants to drink it all down.

"It's never been Mère," she says. "It's just Minique."

"Why do they call you Mère Minique, then?"

"I don't know how it started," she says. "I don't have children, and I'm not that old."

"No, you're not," he says, and there's something about his timbre that makes her look at him. The gaze is still on her.

"If they turn me into an old woman, they take away my dominance." That's the most she's said about the townspeople in a very long time. She feels a bit shaky, like she's disclosed some part of her she can't claw back. But Cadillac only nods and turns his eyes up to the ceiling. The room is getting warmer, whether because of the brandy or because of the fire, Minique isn't sure, but she unwinds the shawl from around her shoulders.

"You and I are not so different, I think." He punctuates this thought with a sip; his glass is already nearly finished. She's surprised to find that hers is, too.

"I think we are very different."

"But we're not." He turns to face her, the firelight casting a pretty glow on his big features. "We're above and beyond this trou à rats."

Lord knows Minique doesn't love Montréal—it absolutely is a backwater compared to the other colonies, or so she's heard—but she also doesn't love an outsider calling it a shithole. Yet she knows this is some sort of test, so she says nothing.

"It doesn't have to be like this," he says, thoughtful.

"What do you mean?"

"If I were in charge," he says, his fingers at his chin and his eyes looking at the ceiling again, "I'd run a tight ship."

Minique wants to laugh. She already knows he ran a very loose ship at de Buade. Instead she makes her face look serious, and she nods along with him.

"The justice system here is lax. Not like France. That has to change. Can't have people accused of witchcraft and sodomy and other vile shit being let go. Not that fortune-telling act you did, but the demonic acts. Spells written in blood and poppets and charms worn around the neck. Abortions and miscarriages."

He takes a drink. "And you need a new fort. One where you make the Indians work for you. Keep them on the land near you where you can see them. Have them work the land, and also buy their furs. For cheap, you know. And they can't marry the French, but the French men can have relations with them if they please."

Minique would like for him to stop talking. She thought he would want to keep all of his grand ideas secret, but he's so confident in himself, and likely thinks so little of her as a challenge to him, that he's gladly telling her.

"And people need to be outside more," he's saying. "Less of sitting around in church and more of people working the land and going out to hunt and trap. We should be getting younger boys out with their fathers to collect more furs. And they all have to be registered as voyageurs. Not coureurs. There has to be a system in place. And the voyageurs should be going farther inland and farther north. If people in this town focused less on what wigs they were going to wear and more on learning the land and learning how to take from it, Montréal might not be such a limping hellhole. It's nothing compared to the other colonies, truly."

Minique throws back the rest of her brandy. Cadillac, in his eagerness to get her drunk, mercifully shuts up and gets up to get the bottle, refilling her glass and then refilling his own. In one breath, he's threatened Daniel's livelihood and his marriage, the sanctity of the untouched places of the forest, the Iroquois, and also her, as well as any other woman who seeks power over her own body.

They sit in silence for a while, the arrogance of his diatribe done and dissipating. He seems to burn hot and then cool fast. He's not wrong about Montréal likely needing a firmer hand, but the rest of his plans are garbage; they sound like something he's writing in his diary, big, grandiose ideas, like how a child tells a tall tale to whoever happens to be listening. Minique's not going to make the mistake of assuming he's a simpleton, but she at least can smile behind her hand at his simplistic outlook on turning Montréal around. This place is complicated; it's dark and dangerous and full of crime and sickness and apathy, but it's also spirited and strange. The people here are sharp-toothed and hard-hearted, smarter than people give them credit for. She supposes she should thank all her bullies and detractors for toughening her up.

The fire kicks up, and Minique feels her breathing slow. This is dangerous. When she spent time with Anne in the inn, mostly the men were good and let them be, but sometimes the men were bad. When people are left alone with alcohol and their thoughts, things can happen. And sometimes Minique was on guard, all her skin prickling with it, with the taste of men plotting on the air. But the room is finally warming, the walls the colour of yolk from the flames in the fireplace, and the brandy glows inside of her. Minique knows that every situation can turn in an instant, and she knows her escape route if that happens. She knows the words she'll yell to get the housekeeper and the cook, the door she'll take, the reason she has her boots on while his are off. But for now, on the cusp of the second drink, unbuttoning her sleeves and rolling them up her arms, everything feels good.

"The thing is," Cadillac begins, holding the glass with two massive fingers. Minique winds one arm out of her sweater, and then the other. She still has her dress on underneath, but the wool is starting to make her feel itchy and contained. "The thing is, I think mostly everyone here is stupid."

Well, sometimes I do, too, Minique wants to say. She realizes she might be a little drunk. "Why?"

"Because they are," Cadillac says, laughing, and sips. "Did you come from the continent?"

"No."

"No, right. Of course not."

"My mother was a fille." That's as much as she's going to give him.

"I can see it," he says, and his eyes slide over to her.

She doesn't ask what he means. "Why do you think we're all stupid?"

"Not you, Minique." The way he says her name: it makes her uncomfortable and pleased at the same time.

"Do you say that to everyone you're trying to get in your pocket?"

He laughs, and it surprises her. "You're sharper than most of the people here, and yet they keep you out in the woods."

"That's *why* they keep me out in the woods." She's surprised enough that he knows where she lives. He doesn't need to know anything else; he doesn't need to know about the fever or Anne or Daniel or the house or her father. Nor the fact that she was the one to put herself out there, that she wanted to keep that clearing for herself forever. And nothing about her heart. Her alone, wild heart. It thumps now, excited, anxious.

Cadillac makes a sound of assent. He throws back the rest of his brandy, gets up for the bottle once more, groaning as his knees pop.

"Not cold like this in France," he murmurs as he moves. "No matter how long I'm in New France, I never get used to it. My body never gets used to it."

"Because we're not supposed to be living here," Minique mumbles as he fills her glass. The world is liquid in a nice way. She knows that she needs to slow down and that the walk back to her cabin will be stupid, dangerous. But how long has it been since she's had a little bit of fun? "So why are you here?"

His answer is swift, and one she's heard before. "Glory. There's not much of that left in France."

"Is getting kicked out of de Buade glorious, then?" She didn't mean to say it, but she felt the urge, red and luscious, in her throat.

He freezes while raising the glass to his mouth. Neither of them has touched the biscuits; perhaps that's what they should be reaching for instead. He sits up on the chaise longue, looking straight at her. She wants to laugh at his miffed expression.

"First of all," he says, "I'm amazed that a woman living in the middle of fucking nowhere could know something like that."

"The trees talk," she says, hopefully mysterious enough that he might believe it. Lord knows some people in town probably do.

"Second of all. I was doing what I had to do."

"Abusing the local tribes?"

This, strangely, makes him angry. Colour comes up on his cheeks. "Abuse? Abuse is what the Jesuits do—" He stops himself, puffing out his lips in that tell of his.

She doesn't push it. She agrees with him, in fact. Minique tries to communicate that with her eyes, softening them a little, but she's sure she just looks bovine.

"Me giving adult human beings alcohol—that's not abuse." He clenches his free hand into a fist.

"It is if those people don't know what alcohol is."

"It isn't." He sounds like a child.

"Then why did you get sent away for it?"

He makes a sound that's close to a growl. But she's heard the growls of wolves, the chuffing of bears, and she's not scared. She wants him to know that she knows about him. That he's not the only one who keeps an ear to the ground.

"Sometimes people can't see genius when it's staring them in the face," he grinds out at her, and she does the only thing she can think to do: she laughs.

He stands up, very suddenly. She thinks for a moment that he's going to grab her, rush over, but he stalks over to the bottle and, instead of filling his glass, drinks straight from it. She still has a little bit of brandy left in her own glass and she swirls it around, dipping a finger in and tracing it across her lips to feel it burn in all the cracks from the cold weather.

"You men, you always think you're geniuses." She can't stop herself. "Here, no one is a genius. Here, we're all going to die." She laughs again because it's so funny, the look of irritation and horror on his face.

"What?"

"Everyone comes here thinking they can make the land theirs. Do you know how many people I've seen die here?" Minique has to take a breath, her throat starting to get tight. "You're all idiots. And you want to use us, the *stupid* ones, in the trou à rats town, to advance your agenda. You want to take away our livelihoods, our fur trade. Want to choke us out. Because we're simple to you." She stands then, to match him. Strides over to where he is, happy she doesn't wobble. She takes the bottle from his hand and swigs from it, maintaining eye contact all the while.

He takes her wrist in his hand, the arm that holds the bottle. She had forgotten that she had rolled the sleeve up, and now his palm burns against her bare skin. That feeling in her hips comes back, and she has to straighten her spine to prevent bending into him. Her body wants something that her mind doesn't yet know, or approve of.

If he knows this, he doesn't let on. He just holds her arm as she lowers the bottle from her mouth. She smells him, and she knows that he's aroused. It's like green cedar boughs thrown onto a fire, apples sweltering on the ground on a hot day: sweet, sharp, strange. If her mouth wasn't brandy-scented, maybe she would have picked up on more. But instead the two of them stand there. The longue is so close, inviting. If she makes one move, if she bends forward, she could push him back onto it. She could hike up her skirts and press her body to the thickness of his. She could straddle him and pin him under the weight of her ladder and her wish.

That's the thing about isolation. It means that Minique doesn't know touch the way other people do. She doesn't get embraced, doesn't have a friend grab at her hand when they're walking down the street, doesn't brush fingers when exchanging plates at a dinner table. Her life is narrowed down to the occasional back clap from Daniel and her own touch, her own fingertips along the ridges of her thighs, her own palms pressed to the back of her neck or the shelves of her collarbones. Cadillac's palm—broad and scorching—is foreign to her. A touch imbued with want and intent.

Cadillac slides his hand up her wrist, circling his hand around hers, both of them holding the bottle. The twingeing in her body gets louder, harder. She tries to control the flush that rises to her cheeks. Her mind is stuck in the moment that feels like a sticky web stretched into something longer. Those appraising eyes are focused on her, the pupils bleeding into the dark irises. He's staring at her in a way she can't quite decipher, in a way that frightens her, that makes the feeling deep inside her intensify in a way she thinks is equal parts thrilling and unpleasant.

Minique starts to pull her hand away, forcing Cadillac to take the bottle from her. She turns slowly, forcing herself to break their tableau. He stands in the corner, part in shadow, as she slips her sweater back on, as she winds her shawl around her body. As she picks up her coat and her fur hat, her mittens. As she methodically armours herself once more and picks up her basket of things bought in town. As she stands in the doorway, a figure obscured by wool and hide and a faint miasma of shame. He's still in the corner, silent, drunk, and she doesn't want to open her mouth. She doesn't want to know what he's thinking. She might burst into flames. Instead, she bows her head for one moment, subservient if only in appearance, and then turns around and walks down the sad, dark hallway and out into the night.

On the walk home, surrounded by the bitter clasp of cold but hot on the inside, she takes her right hand out of her mitten and holds her fingers to her face, breathing him into her mouth and realizing, with every slightly wobbly step she takes on the path that is so familiar to her she couldn't lose her way on it if she tried, what is building inside of her, behind her, all the way into the town she always tries to leave behind.

It's months before she sees him again. At first, she tries not to think about it. She knows how a connection can debilitate a person, how a tether can be a chain. Like when women are in love with one man but are made to marry another. When a mother loves her baby and can't save it from dying. When your friend is tossed into jail, leaves town. Connections to other people have given her strength, but they've also weakened her.

For the first few weeks, she has to dig her fingers into her windowsill to keep herself from lacing up her boots and going back into town. She isn't familiar with this weakness, the kind that makes her desperate for even a look at somebody, and it's scary to her, the way she feels possessed. She tells herself that she's starved for human interaction, with no one to sit at her table and chat. It would be easy to make an excuse to stop by the general store, for a thimble or a pair of scissors.

Instead, she digs in her heels. There are fewer chores to do in winter, but they're crucial. She turns her focus to her traps, on trying to get better at skinning rabbits to save as much of the fur as possible. She always feels guilty before she has to break their necks, but she tries to do it as quickly as possible, thankful that it means something to eat. There was a time when gutting an animal made her sick, but Daniel whapped her on the back of the head as she retched, and from that moment on, she knew she had to sort herself out if she wanted to live on her own.

She organizes her seeds for her vegetable and herb gardens for the spring. She checks on her chickens and makes sure that the layer of straw at the bottom of the coop is thick and warm. She seals up the chinks in her stable, where her one mulish cow lives. She makes candles: black ones with dye made from oak galls and rusty nails, red ones with dried chokecherries, yellow ones with burdock. She goes out and forages for frozen rosehips, leftover acorns, cattail roots, and chanterelles. She makes jam out of hawthorn berries, taking extra care to make sure every seed is picked out, and tea out of wintergreen. She cleans her chimney and fireplace, makes trellises for the summer's plants, and sharpens all the tools and knives she has in her cabin and shed. She wishes she had more experience fishing, but sometimes people trade her smoked pike or muskellunge or eel, which goes into storage alongside the salted bacon that's a key winter staple. She cooks bean soup and rabbit stew and makes frybread in her skillet; she eats pickled spruce tips for greens and carrots stored in her shed for vegetables, and when she wants something sweet she can make her own maple sugar, though her tapping skills are not very good and she only has one or two trees that she works on. And in the evenings, when it's been dark for hours and the tasks of the day start to wear off, she sits in one of her kitchen chairs and she reads Anne's grimoire, taking it out from where it's stored in a drawer wrapped in a cloth, or she sews her stockings, or she stares off into the middle distance and thinks. It's easy to spend time thinking, even easier now that she has a face to focus on.

As the winter passes its peak, as the shortest, darkest day comes and goes, Minique tries to keep herself from feeling desperate. She doesn't get guests in the colder months; she knows that. She doesn't even get that many customers, and if people in need of a cure won't come to her for fear of the weather or the woods, how can she expect anyone to visit for pleasure?

Winters are very hard in New France. The deep and dark expanse of the woods, the wild blanket of the land, is unforgiving and cruel. It wants the settlers off of it. And so people die when they get lost in a blizzard, or they get hit on the head by snow falling off a roof, or they fall through the ice into the river while trying to fish. They lose their toes and fingers and sometimes parts of their noses or cheeks. Their skin turns black or blistered. They die of winter sickness, their teeth falling out and their breath coming short and their bones aching with fever. Their mouths bleed and their eyes bleed and their bodies cave in on themselves.

Sometimes people lose their minds. She's heard of it: someone gets such a terrible case of cabin fever that they step out into a blinding snowstorm in nothing but shirtsleeves. They walk out into the night and never come home. Bodies have been found curled up naked in the snow, their clothes scattered around them in a circle like a nest. A feebler brain would call it some sort of demonic ritual, but the older habitants and coureurs know it for what it is: when someone is in the process of congélation générale, they think they're burning up and they strip down to try to save themselves.

Sometimes, when the nights are so long and the days so bleak, when it seems like the cold is everything and everything is the cold, that life will never exist outside of the bitter, biting maw of winter, people take their own lives and then those of others around them, too. Those people aren't talked about much. People who kill themselves are sometimes charged with a crime after the fact, since it's a mortal sin.

"At least it's not like the winter of 1608," people will say while making small talk behind their scarves, swaddled in wool. Not that any of them were alive a hundred years ago, but the horrors live on in people's minds, passed down and warped through generations. Rivers and lakes completely frozen over, unable to be fished. Birds froze to death, falling out of the sky. Cows and sheep and pigs all died standing. Gardens and crops all perished from frost. The wine in every church was frozen solid, so communion couldn't be given. People starved to death. People ate other people. *At least it's not like the winter of 1608!*

For Minique, surviving the winter boils down to one thing: stoicism. There are days she doesn't even want to get out of bed, let alone check on her animals and traps, but she does it because she knows that if she doesn't catch at least a scrap of the watery winter sunlight, scour out her lungs with the severe air, she won't feel right. She won't sleep right. She has to absorb at least part of the day, a little bit of the cold, unadulterated. Sometimes when she's chopping wood, she'll even strip down to her dress and roll up her sleeves— not enough to get frostbite, but long enough to feel the gnaw. To remind herself that she's absolutely alive.

And there is incredible beauty in winter. People forget that, mired in dirty wool and greasy furs, with the taste of blood in their mouths. But if she's dressed right, if she drinks her cedar and rosehip tea, if she keeps her root cellar clean and her woodpile stocked, her animals fed and her knives sharp, there are delights to be found even in the harshest season. Summer seduces people, with the luxurious heat and the rolling, rich sunsets, but on a good day, when her mind is right, winter might be her favourite season. The forest becomes a skeletal cathedral, the icicles the church bells, the feathery white branches the thuribles. In winter, everything is silent; sounds are softened. Light slithers, silvery and mercurial like a snake. The entire season is beautiful in its wanness. And Minique, surviving alone year after year, with no one to help with the chores or stockpile food or keep her company during the long nights, is the strongest of all.

There is also something precious about the time winter affords her. Like the bear, she can hibernate, cushioned under the layers of snow on her roof, her blankets on her bed. She doesn't have to run around gathering plants and flowers for her customers. She sleeps more, since the sun rises later and sets earlier. The dark lulls her, but that's only because she's already comfortable with the dark. She's danced in it; she's crawled in it; she's found it inside herself and dipped her fingers into it. She's not scared to be alone with her thoughts.

It happens the same way every year: The season changes fast, somehow. It's still a little ways off from full spring, but people get sick as soon as the dry cold of the winter gives way to the dampness of the melt. As soon as she starts to smell the muck on the wind and notice the dripping off her roof, customers appear looking the worse for wear after winter.

She goes from spending hours alone cosseted in her warm cabin in the dark to accepting dried fish for licorice syrup for a sore throat, a bag of flour for clover and honey for a wet cough, salt and sugar in exchange for coneflower tea for a stuffy nose. And with every transaction, every flash of skin she sees through the trees, every cleared throat to get her attention, she secretly hopes it might be one person.

Minique is having breakfast, smoked eel on toast with tea, when she hears someone lumbering down the path. Male, certainly: she's heard enough women slinking to her cabin to know what they don't sound like. Clumsy, definitely: she can hear the scratch of branches on a jerkin. It's usually the women who take care of a household, and know what tinctures are needed when a sickness gets too out of hand for them to deal with on their own. The sound of a man heading her way has her on guard. For a moment, she has a disgusting shred of hope, but she gets rid of that thought as soon as it slips into her mind. Instead, she shoves the rest of the crust in her mouth and grabs the small hatchet by her bed. With its weight comfortably in her palm, she opens the window that faces the path and waits for her visitor to be spat out of the forest.

He tumbles out gracelessly, hands over his head. He looks around like he's completely lost, gape-mouthed and shivering. Minique raises her axe to set it down on the windowsill, and the motion makes him notice her. He doesn't raise a hand in greeting; he smiles instead. It looks oily and rehearsed, which fits well on his face. He's short and broad, stocky like a coureur but not nearly as fleet-footed. She thinks she could outrun him if she had to. As far as she can tell, he doesn't have a gun, and even if he's armed with a knife, she'll get to him far faster with an axe between the eyes. Her aim is good enough.

"What do you want?" Her voice is crisp.

He holds out his hands as if in supplication. "I'm here on business."

She taps her fingers on the windowsill, watching his breath puff out in rancid curls. "It's rare that men come to me."

"What makes you think they don't want to?" His voice is lecherous. He dips his head a little as he rummages in his pockets, pulling out a bag that she can hear is heavy with something.

Her curiosity and mercenary nature win out. "What for?"

"Something for bruises." He throws the bag to her and she catches it with two hands. Minique knows the polite thing would be to ask his name, but the less she knows about him the better.

"Stay there." She closes the shutters, ignoring his mutter. She keeps small pots of salve of consoude ready for simple requests like this, and she grabs one, holds it in her palm, and wonders whom it's going to, whom it's going to heal. Her mind goes to the image of purple fingertip bruises across the striations of a haunch or the muscled wing bone of a shoulder. She flings open the shutters again and lobs the pot at the man without warning. To his credit, he catches it. He doesn't say thank you, but dips his head once and then trudges away, still shivering. Minique shakes her head and latches her window and doesn't think too much of it.

Until the next one comes.

Two weeks later, she hears a throat being cleared somewhere outside the cabin, and starts up from her fire where she is boiling down a spruce tea.

When she opens the window, it's a different man standing there. This one at least is dressed in enough wool that he's not quivering with the cold. He's taller than the first one, and older; she can see streaks of grey in his beard. He looks more comfortable in the woods, a hatchet at his hip and a hat on his head. She reaches for her axe, not lifting it up onto the windowsill like last time, but keeping it in her hand below the ledge.

The man bows a little, straightening up and tossing her a bag with more money in it. Money is an odd thing in New France; for the most part, they tend to use notes to mark out who owes whom and for how much. People trade more often than not, but when money is used, all money is used. Minique has seen coins from France, from England, even doubloons from Spain. They change hands and no one is really sure what to do with them. Gold and silver can be melted down, but for what? Still, she takes the pouch in her hand and hefts it, hearing the satisfying jingle. If she ever had to leave, she supposes. If she ever had to pay her own passage.

"What this time?" She's still looking at the bag, thinking of a ship with many masts and the taste of salt in her mouth.

"Something for a cough," he says.

"Sticky or dry?"

He flounders for a moment. "Dry?"

Cedar syrup is one of her more popular cures, probably because it doesn't taste like shit and seems to help with so many things. He's paid her too much for it, but she doesn't offer to count out change. She makes him come to the window to retrieve it, and he tucks it into his jerkin, nodding his thanks. She watches his back, wondering at it all.

The third one comes two weeks later, and Minique isn't surprised by him. In fact, she's been keeping her window open in expectation, having marked off the days on a piece of wood with a pocketknife.

He's young, no beard. Face like a boy's. His eyes dart around from the door of her cabin to the grey jays in the trees to the way her fingers are tapping on the sill. Her axe is on the floor by her feet; she knows this one won't do anything. She can practically smell his fear.

She is gentler with this one. "Hello," she says, and he straightens up like he's about to jump into the air.

"Hello," he says, and his voice quavers.

"I don't bite, you know."

He frowns, as though remembering he's a man, and meant to be brave. "I'm not afraid."

She laughs out loud at that, and he looks surprised. Maybe he's shocked that her laughter doesn't sound like a hag's cackle.

"I thought you would be older," he says.

"They all do."

"I didn't get a good look at the banquet."

Cadillac's men, then. There are so many things she wants to ask this man-child. *Why are you here? Were you forced over to the new world? Do you like it here? Are there people back in France waiting for you? Does Cadillac talk about me? Does he deride me, or is his voice tinged with wonder?*

"But I would have remembered your face," he says, nodding a little, like he's saying something groundbreaking.

"My face?"

"It's pretty." He flushes, the tips of his ears red. "It makes sense now." This last part is said under his breath.

This guileless idiot doesn't realize he's let something slip, and Minique doesn't give him time to. She hopes her cheeks aren't pink, and if they are, she hopes he's far enough away not to see it.

"What do you want?"

He fumbles around, taking a piece of paper out of his pocket and squinting at it. "For sadness?"

Minique, who is half turned to look at her stores, stops. *Sadness.*

"That's an odd request," she says nonchalantly over her shoulder. "Are you sad?" The piece of paper in his hand tells her a lot: that he's not coming of his own accord, that someone has sent him. Someone with money. Someone is testing her.

He shrugs. "It's what I was told."

Did Cadillac pick this boy to send to her because he knew he would let things slip? She doesn't know what kind of a leader he is. She just puts this information into her brain and tamps down whatever is blooming inside of her.

Sadness. Sadness can't be cured with a draught. She could send him off with something to help with sleep. Or something that could cause a short-lived euphoria. Something that could make a person want to eat more, want to have sex, want to dance. But all of it would be temporary, and it would fade, and the thing deep down, the seed of melancholy, would remain. If Minique knew how to cure sadness, she would be the most famous and sought-after woman in New France, maybe in the entire world.

And if there's one thing she's established for herself in this role she's created, it's that she's been honest with everyone who's come to her. She might not like the people who show up at her door or her window, but she won't lie to them. She couldn't bear it. So she turns to him and looks him straight in the eyes.

"I can't cure that."

He balks, his hands tracing the edge of the paper. She holds out her hand and he trots over, dropping the note into her palm. It's nondescript paper but the handwriting on it is big and slanted. Black letters, one word: *sadness*. She resists the urge to hold it to her mouth.

"Tell whomever needs this to come to me themselves."

He shrugs, having fulfilled as much of his duty as he could. He doesn't realize what's going on, or if he does, he doesn't care. There's something refreshing in that; she wishes that she could care less. She watches his skinny back as he walks away, the jerkin fading into the verdant lace of the trees, the branches swallowing him up piece by piece.

Two weeks later, Cadillac is on her doorstep.

Minique is ready. She's been up since before the sun, sweeping out the corners of the cabin, cleaning the floor, clearing off the table. Anything personal, any item that can tell a story about her, has been hidden under her bed or pushed into a cupboard. She's drinking the tea she was able to buy with some of his money; it's better than what she's used to, and she's thinking about how Daniel will appreciate it when she hears the birds around the cabin trill agitatedly. She waits a few moments, counting in her head, sipping, and then, without looking, she nudges her front door open, sitting back down at her table when she hears the wood catch in a leather-gloved hand.

"So this is your lair."

She's sitting with her back to him, which is a gamble, but also she wants to show him that he has no power here. She drags the second cup she set out on the table that morning over to her, and pours the tea into it, pushing it back into place for him.

His body comes into her sightline in pieces: first a hand at a hip, a big thigh, the belt, the jerkin, the collar, the relaxed jaw, the wide mouth. The face she's thought about throughout the winter. He's clear-eyed and loose-mouthed. She hopes her expression mirrors his, and she takes another sip to keep herself from flicking her tongue out at the air. If she had been a man, brought up to search out her fortune in a new land and meant to lead other men, weaker men, she would have more experience in this: the schooling of features, the wide set of the body, the cock of the head. Women have their own language of the body, and the two dialects don't often intersect; men fall prey to women's closed-mouth smiling and head-bobbing, and women fall prey to the hands on hips and squared-off shoulders.

He slouches in the chair, immediately at home, raking his thick hair back from his face, brushing the side of a gloved finger down the slope of his nose. His eyes are rolling around from thing to thing: the pot over her fire to the herbs hanging from her rafters to the stones on her windowsill. She watches as his gaze settles on the sun-bleached piece of rope hanging in the farthest corner, the feathers moving slightly in the air. He wants to get up to look at it, she can tell. She sees it in the brief tensing of his muscles. What will happen if he puts his face close to it? If he reaches out and touches it? She keeps herself from reacting, and the moment passes. His hand comes up to the cup of tea instead, and he moves his face back to her, eyes finally settling.

It's not like his house, where he was looking at the ceiling and she was focused on the brandy. It's not like the banquet, where they were posturing. They're really, truly alone. No chaperones. No bootlickers. Minique lets her gaze rove, taking in the breadth of him, the arch of his eyebrows, the way his fingers drum lightly on the cup. The fur hat on his lap. The way he is starting to look more comfortable in New France.

"Sadness?"

He smiles. "I had to pick something you wouldn't be able to solve."

"But the other two?"

"To lower your guard," he says, taking a sip of tea. His honesty is refreshing.

"How did you find me?"

"It's not hard to extract information from the idiots in town," he says, grinning. "And they are idiots."

"They can be." She allows herself this one admission.

He laughs at that, and she is taken back to the warm room, the fire, the brandy. The brush of his finger against hers. She keeps her mouth closed.

"Why are you here?"

He drains his tea before answering, and she sees it for what it is: a delay. When he puts his cup down on the table, he looks her straight in the eyes.

"I need to see more of the land."

Whatever she was expecting him to say, it wasn't that.

He continues. "I want to go out on another expedition. My old canoe was left behind at de Buade; god knows what happened to it. But I've commissioned a new one, and it should be ready in a few weeks or so."

She expects him to ask her for a stack of simples and salves. That he'll raise his eyebrows at her and tell her that he's already paved the way with his pouches of coins and he wants all the things that will keep him as physically safe as he can be in the bush. She puts both of her hands on a thigh, making to push herself up, to move around the cabin and start pulling items from the shelves to see what she can arm him with. But his leg shoots out, his foot hooking around the leg of her chair, and she's reminded of how quickly he moves for such a big man. He pulls the chair toward his body, and she moves into the motion.

He leans forward. "And I want you to come with me."

She's stunned for a few seconds, thinking that she perhaps misheard him.

"No," she says, reflexively.

"I think your answer should be *yes*."

"Why would I go out into the bush with you, someone I barely know?"

"Have we not talked more, you and I, than you've talked with some of your neighbours?"

Minique winces. Cadillac catches the motion like a big cat, and leans closer toward her.

"And have you not always wondered what your father did? What he saw?"

She feels a chill run through her; she freezes in place so as not to physically react again and feed him the delight he's clearly looking for with his prodding. She'd been so focused on gathering her knowledge about Cadillac that she had neglected to think about whether he was collecting his own information. Asking about her. Prying answers out of her reticent former neighbours and classmates. She can only imagine what they're saying among themselves now that the man from the continent has been sniffing after the witch.

"You have no guile." Each word is like a heavy stone pulled from her.

He smiles. "Come," he says. "Less than a week. To the falls, just west of here. Less than a week away from your cabin. For someone who makes it a point to live in the woods," he purrs, looking up at her from under his eyelashes, "it seems you haven't seen that much of your surroundings."

His words rankle, but she's heard worse. "You can do better than that," she sniffs.

She expects him to sigh and chide her. What she doesn't expect is for him to laugh, look thoughtful, look predatory. "You're right," he says. Before she can ask what he means, he reaches out and takes both her wrists in his hands. She instinctively pulls her arms back, but he holds tight, his fingers like hot shackles on her skin. He tugs a little, and her chair scrapes across the floor as her body moves the tiniest bit toward him with his effort.

"You're very brave, to be out here all alone." His tone has dropped to something velvety, but there is also an inference there: *we're alone now.* Minique forces herself not to lean away from him, which her mind is screaming at her to do. Her body, however, is completely under whatever spell he's weaving. *Is he magic?* She has an image of the full moon and naked bodies howling in the grass, except it's not Anne with her this time. She breathes in and out through her nose as he brings his mouth closer to her ear. When he speaks, a shudder goes down her spine.

"But I think that underneath all that bravery"—he pauses to look around at her living space—"you're lonely. Too afraid to live in town with the people who are so scared of you, but too afraid to be here, alone, forever."

Her eyes have slipped closed. She can feel the heat of his face radiating onto her cheek, the breath of his words on her ear. He surely must be a sorcerer, if he can turn her into this.

"Come with me," he says, his lips so close to her ear he's almost touching her. His voice is soft. "And let us be not lonely together."

When he lets go of her wrists, she opens her eyes. She was so close to turning her head to the side and slotting her mouth over his. She chose the aloneness. For thirty years, she's been in control of her loneliness. And now, within months of meeting this selfish, strange man, she's not in control anymore.

He turns his head to look at her, and she moves her face back.

"Was that better?" His words break the spell. "I'll be back in three weeks," he says, "to get you." As he's walking out the door, he turns back. "It would be a good cure for sadness, Minique."

If she were a smarter woman, she'd stand up and hurl her axe at him as he walked away. She'd curse and lock the door behind him. But her treacherous body keeps her sitting in the chair, her mouth slightly open, as she watches him amble down the path.

Six for F for flying ointment. She can't make the decision about Cadillac on her own, and she remembers moments of glittering clarity in this very clearing, the freedom of letting her mind wander as her body lay immobile in the long, soft grass. She paints the red water over the page, watching as the words come to life. She's never used this recipe before, because who in Montréal would ask for it?

Her eye scrolls down the page, catching on terms like *bat's blood* and *soot* and, most horrifying of all, *baby's fat*. She sees *belladonna* and *mandrake* and *fine wheat* and *smallage*. This is not the recipe Anne rattled off to her at midnight in the clearing. This appears to be an original, from the continent. She shivers to think of how baby fat is procured and how its properties differ from wax, which is what she's going to use for her own version.

Minique hisses in irritation and fear, thrown off course. She had assumed that Anne would have written her own recipe down. But Anne was a sly one, and Minique isn't surprised that she kept something for herself. She closes her eyes and tries to picture the silvery grass of the clearing, the smell of the night air, damp and rich. She tries to picture Anne standing naked, the jar in her hand, her mouth forming the words. *Water hemlock.* Minique writes that down on a new page. *Poppy.* She knows she's missing some things, but the long-ago shade of Anne in her mind turns away from her, smiling from one corner of her mouth, hiding the jar from Minique's sight and refusing to cooperate.

Minique adds nightshade instead, and the seeds of some poppies she's dried, and water-hemlock sap. She boils it all down with three cups of oil, making sure to keep her windows and door open to create a cross breeze in her cabin. The grimoire doesn't say how long to cook it for; she lets it simmer for hours, until the oil is green and the herbs fall apart as she strains them. She adds beeswax one knob at a time until the consistency is thick like syrup, and then she pours it into a jar that she leaves in her root cellar to cool.

The jar sits there for a week. Truthfully, she's terrified to try it, and also far too excited. She doesn't particularly want to die naked and alone in a clearing, but she also doesn't want to have such a good high that she becomes addicted. She doesn't drink much, she doesn't smoke tobacco, but she still remembers the feeling of horned knowledge, the looseness of the body, that flying ointment brought her, and she wants to experience that again, to let herself be taken over by the basest part of her. To give up thought and see if she receives clarity in its place.

Finally, on a day grey and silent, the air so still she can hear the squirrels dancing in the underbrush and the crows sharpening their beaks on branch bark, Minique takes the jar of ointment from the cellar. Her hand is damp as it wraps around the pottery, and she has to make sure she doesn't drop it. She puts it on her table, and there it sits till nighttime, when she peels off her dress and shift, releases her hair from its braid, and rubs the mixture on herself. She massages the salve into the crooks of her arms, behind her ears, her neck, along her hairline. Opens the windows of her cabin and feels the night leak in.

Her tongue lolls in her mouth and the back of her neck is hot and cold. All parts of her body have been tuned and tightened. She can feel the invisible, the minuscule: a fever's whisper before it blossoms into the sickness, the legs of an ant at a standstill, the thousands of grains of salt pressing into the backs of her legs. Pain at the front of her head, like she might grow horns at any moment. Pain in her chest, like her heart is struggling, trying to break free of its bonds.

What is the cure for sadness? She wishes she knew. She closes her eyes but she feels the wetness under her lids anyway, tears leaking out, unstoppable. She hasn't cried and cried and cried for years, maybe not since Barbe died. Not when her aunt died, not when she left the town, not even during the first few months alone, when she was terrified at every yip and every creak. Her head pounds; her heart pounds.

The ointment has taken her over now. The high is different from the last time. She was stupid to think it would be the same. This time is meaner. Instead of flying, she feels like she's falling, over and over and over again. Like she could plummet through her wooden floor and the earth after that, all the way to hell. Her head is spinning and her body feels heavy. Vomit rises in her throat and she swallows it back down, until she can't anymore and she runs to an open window to vomit out of it. She wonders if Cadillac did something to her. She wonders if she's managed to finally poison herself after all these years. She staggers to her bed.

She dreams about trees. She dreams about the woods like a circle around her. She thinks she sees someone in the forest, someone very tall, bigger than she is. She can hear them walking, and she has that same feeling from running home on the path that night, after she touched her tongue to Cadillac's palm, after she tamed all the wolves of the banquet.

She knows that she's supposed to be scared of whomever's in the woods, but she isn't. She rolls her shoulders back, squaring her body. There's no one to protect her: this is her fight. The leaves shift; something's circling her. She can see the tall figure through the fence of trees.

He's getting nearer and nearer. She can hear the footsteps, heavy and determined. Maybe she should run, but as his body comes closer and closer to where the clearing meets the trees, as she hears the birds agitate, she doesn't run. Instead, she waits a few moments, counting in her head, sipping, and then she opens her arms.

Two weeks later, Minique's standing in front of her cabin when he crashes through the woods, emerging looking like a hopeful puppy. She can even imagine his tongue rolling out of his mouth, swiping around on his chin. He sees her outside her door, a pack over her shoulder and her

hat on her head. If he wonders how long she's been waiting outside, swatting away the bugs and ignoring the laughter of the jays, he doesn't show it. He doesn't dare ask it. Instead he grins and holds out his hand to her from across the clearing.

The dip of the paddle is a rhythm she could melt into, if it weren't for the fact that being in a boat makes her uneasy. Daniel took her out in a canoe a few times, and it was ever the same: Minique sitting with her hands white-knuckled on the gunnels, Daniel laughing at her as he manoeuvred them around eddies and rocks and things that looked like they would be able to take the whole boat down.

She has a paddle in her lap, but she wonders if Cadillac only gave it to her as a token, since he's the one doing all the work. He's not as nimble as she imagines all of the coureurs des bois to be, but he's capable, and that surprises her. She knows, from Daniel, that Cadillac went on plenty of solo trips into the New France waterways. To make maps, as if the land here could ever stay still and tame for long enough to be written down. Still, it surprises her to see him removed from Montréal, from the bureaucracy.

"The gunnels won't come off if you let go, you know."

She shoots him a dirty look over her shoulder, as far as she can bear to turn. His hair is loose in the breeze. She can see gems of sweat along his cheeks and in his eyebrows, but he looks happy. Genuinely, oddly, freely happy, out here on the water. It wouldn't matter if she were here or not; the realization hits her in the chest, but also reassures her. He shakes his hair out of his face like a dog, and smiles at her in a smug way that shows the points of his incisors.

"Shut up," she mumbles, and turns back around.

"Never took you to be afraid of a canoe."

Minique sees, in her mind, plumes of fire like wings in the night. The devil in the back. She sees the things that live under the surface, things that pull and sink you.

"I don't trust the water," she says.

"Why? It brought us here." He always forgets that she was born in Montréal, or else he wilfully ignores it.

She doesn't answer. She doesn't want to tell him *but it took people here, it didn't bring them, not everyone wanted to be separated from the continent by a sea*. Instead, she chooses to look around at the cathedral of budding green. It's rare for her to be able to see the forest from the vantage point of water, so she allows herself to at least marvel at that, at the way the tops of the trees reach overhead like buttresses. The way the branches are reflected in the river, rippled and reaching. Cadillac's paddle makes a thick sound when it enters the water and strokes, and she can feel the boat move with each of his efforts. Out here, there is nothing else for her to scent: Cadillac is downwind of her, and there is no one else around—or at least no one who wants to interact with them. She can just sit and close her eyes and feel the wind, enjoy the way it moves over her face, skimming over her body. Like flying, this movement. She understands why the coureurs got in that boat.

It took two days to get here. There was little portaging to reach the river, le Rivière du Nord, though Minique's arms are strong and lifting a boat over her head was not as hard as she thought it would be. Especially not with the way she was dressed.

She had sat in her cabin and thought for a long time about what to pack, and especially what to wear. The part of her that still feels like a child wanted to wear skirts, but the older, smarter part of her knew that while it was fine to wear a dress and apron when gathering spruce boughs or cedar tips, it wouldn't suffice for the movement she needed to move a boat through the forest. She ended up choosing the pair of loose knee breeches she had wheedled out of Daniel years ago, for chores that needed more nimbleness. Wearing them around her cabin, she realized how much of her legs they showed and it thrilled and worried her, so she put a breechclout overtop. She added woollen socks that came up to her knees, tucked into the hem of the pants, and then her moose-hide boots over that. Then there was the chemise, a big linen shirt that she tucked into the pants and laced up to her neck, and a men's vest that she had sewn ages ago, intent on wearing it at times when she was sick of her bodice. She put a blue shawl over it all, to wind around her face if she needed to. Instead of a tuque, she had her wide-brimmed hat, and instead of pulling her hair up, she left it plaited down her back; she could loop it up under the hat if she needed to, but the rope of hair kept the blackflies away from her nape.

When she got close enough to Cadillac, where he stood at the edge of the trees, he had stared at her. The heat that flickered across his face and ended up strong in his eyes made her stand in place, her hands on her hips. He broke the moment by clapping a hand on her back like he might do for one of his men, and barking out a laugh about her appearance. *I've never seen a woman back home dress like this.* She almost buckled under the strength of his palm. *This is the new world after all*, she murmured.

Minique shifts in her seat, looking down at her breeches. She was nervous about them, but she's happy she made the choice she did. If she hides her braid and bows her head, anyone watching the canoe might think they're two men. There's something freeing in that, in not being deemed a target right away.

Skirts are voluminous but someone could pin her and get an arm up between her legs with little effort. Wearing breeches makes her feel like there's a layer between her and the world, her and the man sitting behind her, even if it's a flimsy one. That if she had to, she could kick her legs and run fast instead of drowning in layers of fabric, skirts pulling her down, down, down.

She didn't even tell Daniel about her trip; she can only hope he doesn't come to her cabin during the days she's gone. As she stares down at her breeches, her palms damp against the cloth, she thinks about how nobody knows where she is or whom she's with. Her little flicker of excitement warps and grows, starts to flame out into worry. She hasn't been in control of her emotions at all lately, and it's hard to tell the difference between the two: both wrap their hands around her throat, both make her breath come uneven and ragged, both make her body prickle with an odd sweat. She thought her choice to come with him was about taking power over her own actions, but with each stroke of his paddle, as they get farther and farther from the cabin she knows and feels comfortable in, she thinks about how he goaded her, the deep satin of his voice as his breath stained the side of her face, the way he leaned into her. She digs her fingers into her breeches to centre herself.

She turns her head to the side. "How much longer?"

Cadillac doesn't even sound winded when he replies. "Till the sun starts to set."

For a man who Daniel swore made notes and wrote letters and was fastidious as a priest when he wanted to be, Cadillac hasn't told her much of his plan, and that worries her. He swore that he learned about this route from some coureurs, that they'd end up at Lachute falls and they'd get to see a part of New France that so few people are brave enough to see, but she knows nothing else. Maybe he travels like a berserker, all action and little thought. Maybe he's planning to take her somewhere and leave her there. Or maybe he's plotting something worse. She wants to turn around and grab him by the jerkin, ask him to explain himself to her. But that would mean betraying herself and the decision she made. She can't bear to second-guess herself, not after each new step of bravery she's climbed up: leaving her clearing, leaving the clutch of woods she knows best, leaving her skirts behind. The two of them ended up in this boat through hard-headedness: he wanted to feel like he had won by making her come with him, she wanted to prove she was courageous enough to explore the place she calls home and makes her living from.

It makes Minique uncomfortable, sallying forth, up the river without a clear-cut plan that she knows and can turn over in her head. What if they capsize? What if they get lost? What if something happens to Cadillac and she has to figure out her way back home? What if they run into other people? At the very least, she's mostly learned to shake off the lurid, the drivel the nuns spouted about the Iroquois, all those exaggerated horror stories of her youth. She has a very tenuous grasp on some Mohawk words, learned from Anne and from the fur markets, and from necessity. That's not to say that she shouldn't be scared. She should have a healthy fear. She only lives outside of the town walls at the mercy of the people whose land she's on. She's heard stories from some of the coureurs about tribes torturing captives, terrible things, stories sticky with blood. She doesn't know if they're true or not, because wood runners have a propensity for exaggeration. And she knows that the French and English would be more than capable of turning around and doing the same thing. Doing worse things, easily covered up under a long black robe. But it means Minique is always walking around with a kernel of fear, the kind of fright that she can mould into a respect and a distance. She imagines Cadillac barrelling his way into a group of Iroquois, writing god knows what in his notebook. She imagines him getting his head bashed in. She imagines trying to talk her way out of that situation, with her bad Mohawk and her strange clothing. Her heart beats and her head aches and she feels like she has to close her eyes to ground herself.

I am brave, Minique tells herself as she fingers the paddle in her lap. *I am brave, and I am here*. She hates it, but he's right, in his proprietary way. This is a part of New France that the settlers don't—or don't want to—see. To be able to eat up all the scenery, to know that she'll be able to save this experience for later, brings back that note of excitement, the thing that chases the worry out of her body and fills her with a silver singing.

When the sun starts to sink in the sky, Cadillac steers the canoe to the bank, and Minique watches as the land comes closer and closer, her heart rate picking up pace by pace. The boat hits the earth with a solid *thunk*. She doesn't wait for Cadillac to help her; she hops out as gracefully as she can with her pack on her back. And then she can do nothing but stand and listen.

All around her the forest is talking. Minique thought she knew the woods. But here, in the wild of it, she realizes she doesn't know it at all. The forest mumbles, swells, chirrs back at her, at her silent, stunned body. It laughs in notes of bird, in the buzz of insects in the shells of her ears, in the suck of the riverbank beneath the boat. She is struck silent. She could stand here forever and absorb it all. And she would, except—

Cadillac launches his way from behind her, canoe over his head, and lumbers up the bank, elbowing his way between the trees and eventually disappearing. The birds pause. The chatter ebbs away as this giant stranger pushes into the forest, brushing back branches with the width of the boat. Minique exhales and follows.

They set up camp in a glade that Cadillac expands using his axe. Minique has her own axe, but prefers to watch. She uses the small knife at her hip to cut a few shoots of yarrow and put them into her pouch. She doesn't realize she's circling him until he looks up from where he's bent over a young tree and raises his eyebrows.

"You're making me feel like a hare."

"Wolves don't usually eat hares," she murmurs, not stopping her feet.

"A buck, then."

"Of course."

The worry and the excitement war within her, making her feel sick. She thought he would go after her as soon as they were alone and away from everyone else. She curls her hand into a fist and feels her ring cut into her skin. She could hit him with that hand, if she needed to, the extra weight guiding her fist.

Instead, she decides to approach it head-on. "Did you bring me out here to have sex with me?"

He lowers the axe and brushes the back of a hand across his forehead, breathing hard. "No."

"You could take advantage of me easily." She brings her hand around to the haft of her own axe, a motion he tracks with his eyes.

"The answer is still no."

"So why then?"

He rolls the question around in his mouth. "I think we could be allies." There's a slight pause before the final word.

Minique doesn't answer. She stares at him, hand still on the wood of the haft. He's never seen her turn and throw in half a second. He doesn't know how good she is with a target, how Daniel taught her using chunks of spruce balanced on her woodpile, from ten paces, from twenty, from thirty. But she can see that he senses it, at the very least. He stares at her, his face slightly smudged with dirt, his chest rising and falling with exertion, before he slowly turns to the trees he's clearing. He has his back to her, and she can't help but feel that it's a deliberate choice. As if he's saying *here is my weakest part, put a blade in me if you need to.*

She unclasps her axe, watching as his neck stiffens at the sound. And then she turns, too, to chop down the saplings that are in her way.

Minique rarely looks at the sky at night. When she's out in the dark, she's looking at her feet, or at the woods around her. She's never known this thick blanket of dark, dark blue that spreads above her now. She always thought that the night held shades of only black. But it's more alive than that; it's like a deep lake lapping out above their heads, undulating between the pinpricks of the stars.

Cadillac had suggested sleeping under the propped-up hull of the canoe, if she wanted to. She didn't want to. There's no rain, no need to hide. If she's going to prove herself, she's not going to take any shortcuts.

Now they lie in their bedrolls, heads near the canoe but not under. There's at least seven or eight feet between them; she put her roll down first, and he dictated the distance. If they both reach their arms out, it's unlikely they would touch even fingertips. Nighttime fell fast, like a cloak dropping around their shoulders, and they hurried to finish setting up camp. Cadillac got the fire going, while Minique dug into her pack, pulling out handfuls of pemmican and dried apples; they chewed in a silence that was mostly companionable.

Minique shifts in her bedding. She wants to be focused on Cadillac, on the idea of his body so near to and yet so far from hers, but she's distracted by the woods, the sounds so much more amplified than they are in her own clearing. She thought Anne had been the queen of the forest; she didn't know. It's Cadillac who has brought her here, into the maelstrom of it. The idea of ten thousand eyes, talons, tongues. The idea of her body supine, flat to the earth and with the dirt between her fingers. Dust to dust, dirt to dirt. She's mostly clothed in dark, the light of the embers coming just up to her hips, nudging at the undersides of her breasts. So she can stick her tongue out into the night without worrying if he'll see her. She can lick at the soft dark, tasting nothing but sap, cedar haze, dying light. Fire that smoulders comfortably. The even in-and-out breath of him, close enough to hear but far enough to be able to trace her hands up and down her arms without him seeing, to be able to tug at the end of her braid, run her tongue along her lips. If he can hear her moving, the whisper of leather on linen, he doesn't say anything.

It's easier to start a conversation when they're both staring up at the sky.

"Why did *you* come here?"

He shuffles; she hears him sigh. She went to sleep in all of her layers, wanting to be able to jump up and flee if she needed to, but he stripped down to shirt and leggings before crawling into bed. It means she has to strain to hear him move, cloth on cloth.

"Grew up in shit circumstances," he says. She can hear the way he pauses, imagines him rolling air around in his lips.

"How shit?"

"Very shit."

There are a few beats of silence. She can hear him breathing in a tempo that's too measured to be natural. She doesn't speak; she'll wait for him to continue, or they'll both roll over and go to sleep. Her eyes get heavy as she listens to the breathing, to the way it matches the trees. She imagines trying to count all of the stars, to number her way into a dream. How long would it take? How long could she lie here, at the mercy of the sky?

His voice slices into the cool quiet. "I didn't like my father and he didn't like me. It got worse as I got older."

Minique nods in response, not willing to interject just yet.

"We grew up in Gascogne, in a small town. My father was out of the house for large periods of time, so as the eldest son, I often had to step into his role. And I despised that, because my siblings were greedy and spoiled and I hated having to interfere in their fights.

"I wanted to stay in school, to finish studying agriculture and botany with the Jesuits. But studying and trying to run the household was too much for me. So at seventeen, I enlisted at Charleroi, in the Dampierre regiment. From there, it was pretty easy to persuade them to promote me, so I ended up with Clérambault, as an officer, in Thionville, and then it was on to Albret."

He's saying these words, these places, like she knows them. "Why didn't you stay with the army?"

"I could have," he says. "But I didn't like how long it took to accomplish something. The jump to officer was fine, but higher than that would have taken years and I didn't want to wait. I already knew I'd be good at leading, but it would take too long for everyone else to catch up."

"And?"

"And," he says, "I didn't really like being told what to do."

"Of course."

"You know what that's like, at least," he snipes back. She's chastened; he's right. She hates being ordered around by men who don't know what they're doing, who can't see the person inside of her.

"Eventually," he continues, "my father lost my entire inheritance. We were wealthy enough; my mother was the daughter of a merchant and my father was a lawyer. But he was also a gambler, and he had terrible debts. I would either have to work it off, or escape. So I chose escape. I bribed a boatswain I knew from the local inn, and he got me onto his ship without putting me on the passenger list. And here I am."

"Here you are," she echoes.

They lie there, staring up at the sky.

"What is France like?" Her own question surprises her.

"It's . . . rules-based," he says, slowly. "It's fancy, and the churches are all corrupt, and the king is a fool who only wants to focus on frilly clothes. And everyone is focused on what they look like and what they smell like. Most beautiful people you'll ever see, most beautiful women in the world, powdered and cinched and wigged."

Minique's angry at herself for feeling a jag of jealousy as he talks about the beautiful people. She doesn't want to be entranced by this description of France, of the vanity, but she is. She can smell the perfume, the sweetness of the powder and the incense. She can see the gold. It's so different to this grime and grit. To the leather boots and the fur hats that always smell like firewood.

"It doesn't sound that bad," she says.

"It is. Because underneath it all, people are manipulative. And cunning. Because they're bored, and they're trying to find ways to escape or trick the church. And the church is too bloated to do anything."

"The church here is—"

"The church here is a different kind of bad," he says, firmly. "Not bloated but hungry."

"Anything is better than here," she says, and her voice is bleak. She doesn't even try to hide it.

"No," he says. "Because this is a new world. Anyone can escape their past here. In France, on the continent, they can't escape shit. There are hundreds, thousands, of eyes, and there are people willing to enforce the rules and ruin other people's lives."

"Did you ever see someone get burned?" She can't get that image of Anne's out of her head, even after all these years.

He makes a sound. "Yes, once. I was young. Three people for heresy."

"How long did it take?" She doesn't know where these questions are coming from.

The answer is immediate. "Too long."

"They don't do that here."

"No, they do not. Because the people in New France are focused on living. There's opportunity," he says, and his voice drops a tone, is a lullaby, a prayer, some sort of syrup that she can taste on the tip of one finger. "There's hope."

"Hope?" It's not the word she'd use.

"Hope for a new life. This land, to be used. To be taken, if one has the means, the guts, the power."

What he's saying—it's wrong. She disagrees. But the way he's saying it, with the tone of his throat pitched low, peeled bare and open, it makes her feel like she can't control herself. She's not brave enough to crawl over, to throw a leg over him and press up against his body—so, very slowly, she slides one palm down to the cusp of her breeches. She feels the cool metal of her ring against her skin, like a warning.

"Not everyone is brave enough to come here, Minique."

Her name in his mouth is treacherous. Her fingers creep under her breeches, between her legs. She's slick already, like fish scales, like thick sap. She doesn't dare to slide fingers into herself; she's worried he'll hear the sound of her arousal over the crack of the dying fire. Instead, she quietly rocks against her hand, tiny movements that don't make her bedroll shift.

"I didn't come here." Her voice sounds thin, but she hopes he won't realize.

"But you're here, at least." She hears a movement, like he's spreading his arms open. Does he mean New France, or does he mean here, by the fire, in the woods? "And you're brave."

It's still uncomfortable to hear someone be complimentary to her. She and Daniel are past the niceties; they've gotten to the place where old friends live. Barbe was the one who was freest and easiest with the kind words. Occasionally Minique gets a nice word or two from the townspeople she helps, but it's usually given in a moment of desperate thankfulness, and she thinks that that means less. It's like touch: a rare commodity in her life. She doesn't want to turn into a beggar for it. But she can't help herself.

"I am brave," she murmurs.

He makes a sound in assent, and she wants to lean into the lowness of his voice. "Yes, you are. You're brave because, of all the people in your piece-of-shit town, you're the one who opens her eyes to the place she's living in."

Not always by choice, Minique wants to say. *I wanted to belong.* She wants to explain that she didn't start out brave; that she still might not always consider herself brave. But she thinks about his voice and his words, and she nods to herself. "Yes. Yes, I try." *I try so hard; tell me I'm good.* She doesn't want to say more because she's afraid her voice will give her away, but she has to keep talking to mask the sound of her hand between her legs. The words seep out. "I try so hard."

"I know you do," he croons. It's like he's casting some sort of spell again; maybe he does all his work by ember light. Just the rumble of his words, and she's a mess. "That's why I chose you; that's why I want to learn more about you. Of all the people in Montréal, you're the only fascinating one."

At the praise, Minique bites her bottom lip as she comes around her hand, her thighs locking, her fingers wet, her eyes wide and staring at the star-spatter above them. He's silent; she thinks he could be listening. Maybe he knows what she's doing. She doesn't care.

Both of them breathe for a few seconds, echoing each other. Breathing up to the stars and the apse of the branches. Minique slides her hands out from her bedroll and reaches out with them on either side of her body, the dampness mixing with the dirt. She plants some of herself back into the earth. She hears Cadillac shift, turn to face her, his voice louder.

"Sleep well."

Strangely, she does. She didn't expect to sleep so soundly, to be lulled by the pulse of the woods. But she wakes up to the watery light of day like she's coming out of a death, well-rested and reborn. She's up before he is, so she slips down to the shore and rinses out her mouth, rebraids her hair, splashes water on her face and hands and arms. When she comes back to the camp, he's still asleep, so she has a moment to examine his face when it's completely unguarded. Without the facade of the leader or of the burly coquet, he looks younger. Some people look softer in sleep, but that's not the right word for him. There's a bird-like sharpness to him that makes it so he'd never be deemed soft, not even if he gained weight and grew jowls.

She turns away when he stirs, the corners of his closed eyes tensing and the muscles of his cheeks twitching, and by the time he's fully awake, she's kicking dirt onto their embers and lobbing the circle of firepit stones back into the woods. She hears the creak of his back as he sits up behind her and rotates his neck to begin the day. He doesn't say anything to her, but she can feel his presence, glowing like when she looks up at the sun for too long, burning a bright hole in the fabric of her consciousness.

As they pack up the canoe for the day, she expects them to be awkward with each other. They aren't, though. They move in the kind of silence that comes from calm. It's only once that her heart seizes: she reaches for the gunnel of the canoe, but he grabs her hand before she can touch the wood. It's not a hard grip, but it's firm. His thumb briefly rubs over the bone of her wrist, and then he pulls her palm toward his face. It's too fast of a motion for her to jerk back, and so she lets it happen, knowing that it's the hand she used on herself last night. His nostrils flare as he holds her skin right in front of his mouth, and then she feels the brief wet touch of a tongue in the centre of her palm; it's so like the night she read his fortune for him she can't help but bark out a laugh. Something about that sound jostles him, and he drops her hand but runs his tongue over his bottom lip.

Minique keeps her face impassive but wipes her hand on her breeches. She grabs the gunnel, scraping her palm back and forth over the wood, as if trying to erase the memory of the night before. Or trying to grind it further into her skin, to keep forever.

The second day of paddling doesn't feel as worrying as the first. She's already used to the motion of the canoe, the lurch of hopping in with one end pinned to the earth and the other loose in the water. She does it without looking back at Cadillac, trying her best to keep her balance as she crouches down along the length of the boat. She glances over her shoulder to see the way he shoves off from land, his shoulders leaning into the wood, the one-two pump of his legs in the dirt before he swings his lower body up into the canoe with a grace she can never hope to have. He barely makes a thud when he lands, almost in his seat, the paddle already called to his hand.

The day smells fresh and wet; as the sun gets stronger, a sweetness fills the air, the scent of daylight on pine. When she listens past the thick burble of the water, she can hear the far-off *rat-a-tat-a-tat* of a woodpecker drumming on a tree, the gleeful shrieks of blue jays. The river narrows and widens with each bend; she's sure at some point they'll have to get out and carry the canoe over rocks.

"We're about a day out," he says from behind her. "Depends on the current and the weather, but it's a fine day, so I'm not worried."

She flexes her hands on her paddle, thinking about how it would be faster if she joined in.

He must see the movement. "You can, you know."

She flushes, hoping the blush doesn't crawl up the back of her neck. "I'll slow you down."

"You won't," he says. If he laughed now, she'd never do it. But he sounds solemn. She hears him stop paddling. Since they're travelling upriver, they start to move backward almost right away.

Minique looks back over her shoulder, startled. "You're undoing all your work!"

"Then you better start," he says.

"I don't know how!"

"Like the letter J," he says, holding his paddle above the water, stroking down the side of the boat. When the shaft reaches where his body is, he turns it, rotating one side of it up. In his hands, the whole motion seems effortless.

"What if I—" She hesitates at the stupidity of her question.

"What?"

"What if I get pulled out of the boat?" She knows that the blush is all over her face, and then he does laugh a little. *It's more than that,* she wants to say. *I don't know how to swim, because I wasn't taught. I didn't have someone to show me things I should know, here. I didn't have someone who would save me if it went wrong.*

"Minique," he says, "if you go over, I'm coming in after you." He hasn't stopped smiling, but it doesn't feel cruel.

"Fine." She faces forward, holds the paddle with both hands, slides it into the water. It's hard—the pressure, the drag. She knows why she's afraid of going under: Who knows what's under the surface here? Who knows what's waiting for her? But the pull against the blade isn't so strong that she can't do anything with it, and so she waits till she hears Cadillac's own paddle slip into the water and then she strokes. It's clumsy, but the boat moves, because he's picked the opposite side and stroked at the same time as her.

"People think that paddling downriver is easy," he says conversationally. She's already feeling the skin on the palms of her hands start to chafe. She's afraid that when she talks, she'll be out of breath. "But actually, upriver is what I prefer."

"It is?"

"It's a fight," he says, grunting a little when he manoeuvres them around a rock that she hadn't even seen. "But a fight is always my choice."

"Why?"

"I can control more. I'm using it the way I want."

She didn't think of it that way, but now that he's said it, it's all she can see.

"Imagine, Minique," he says. "Imagine being the first person to canoe this river."

She wonders if he's talking about one of the Indigenous people. Men like Cadillac don't think a land is completely explored until a white man comes and stakes his claim all over it and names it after some other white man.

"What a glory that must have been," he continues, not waiting for her to add anything. He doesn't need her in order to have this conversation. Cadillac has this way of talking like he's speaking in front of a group of people, a constant performance. Minique notices it in the way he says her name, like he's trying to make her feel like she's the only person in the world. She wonders if it's a mask he puts on and takes off and has gotten used to wearing nearly all of the time, or if it's become part of his personality. She also wouldn't change it, wouldn't change the sound of her name between his lips, the tone of his voice when he thinks he's drawing her in. Wouldn't change the fact that he's somehow persuaded her to pick up a paddle, to be out alone with a man in the bush, to be working at pushing down her worry in favour of excitement. She can't recognize herself in his company. It feels good to shed the skin she's worn for her whole life.

They stand, looking up at the falls. The sound of it is overwhelming, the thunderous groan of water colliding and tumbling. It fills her ears and the cavern of her chest, shaking up between her teeth and into the bones of her head. She's struck dumb by the fragility of the two of them, so tiny in the face of it. She feels the urge to reach out and take Cadillac's hand, as if to complete some sort of chain and share the roar of power. But before she can do that, or decide not to, he reaches his own hand out and grabs at her. He misses on the first try, snatching at the cuff of her blouse, but then their hands connect, palms slapping slick together from the mist of the falls. It's immediate, a feeling of rightness. It's always better when he's not talking, because when they're silent and side by side, they could be anybody. She could be a normal woman in town, maybe a tailor's daughter, maybe a blacksmith's cousin, and he could be any man, a habitant, a furrier, a wig maker. In the silence, they are just a woman and a man, not two figureheads of two different worlds. They're not at odds. They're not trying to undermine or trick each other. It's peaceful, and Minique tightens her hand in his, closes her eyes, and takes a big, bracing breath, feeling the mist on her cheeks and in her nose, feeling his hand wrapped around hers.

After, they set up camp far enough away from the falls that its thundering growl is only a whisper. Neither of them talks about the way they held hands on the walk away from the falls, helping each other over moss-lush rocks and through puddles, only to unclasp when they had to lift the canoe. Now, Minique is building a fire and Cadillac is sitting on his bedroll, unlacing his boots. She blows on the flames, watching his figure through them. The fire takes, crackling kindly, and she sits back on her heels, rearranging her own bedroll.

"What a day," he says, rolling his shoulders. "Have you ever seen anything like it? I'm glad I brought you."

He sounds like he's speaking to a child. Minique frowns. She's always trying to sort him into different versions. There's the seducer, the one who waits till the sun goes down and the fire is lit to pitch his voice low. There's the silent, strong one who held her hand at the waterfall. And then there's this one: the campaigner. This is the one she likes the least; it's the version she met at the banquet. It's the version Daniel wanted her to rise up against. Oh, god, Daniel—in all of this, she's nearly forgotten about his unspoken plea to her, his worry over Cadillac choking out the fur trade. Her face flushes, and it makes her words come out sharper.

"Why do you always talk like you're speaking to an audience?"

His fingers still on his boots. "Pardon?"

"Even when it's just the two of us, you talk to me like I'm one of your men or someone you want to trick. Isn't it tiring?"

He narrows his eyes. "Why does it matter?"

"Because I don't like it," she says. "I don't like feeling like you're trying to put on a production."

"It doesn't matter what you like or don't like, Minique."

"See? Like that, like saying my name all the time."

"You don't want people to use your name?" He's incredulous.

"It's not comfortable. It's—people don't do that." Somehow he's turned it on her.

"That's what normal people do, Minique. Just because you live like a wild animal and never talk to anyone, it doesn't mean the rest of us have to abide by your strange set of rules."

"Why won't you just talk to me normally?"

"Why won't you give me what I want?" He's laughing as he says it.

"What do you want?"

"I want you to tell me the weaknesses of every small-minded moron in Montréal, Minique. I want to know everything about anyone who might challenge me on the way to becoming governor of New France. I want you to make me strong, make me invincible, through whatever you make in that sad little kitchen in that sad little cabin you call a home."

Never mind that he thinks she's an actual witch, or that she can give him some sort of draught to make him—what, strong? All-knowing? A god? The more startling thing is his plan for power. She didn't know that he wanted to be governor of New France. She doesn't think Daniel knows about that plan. What would de Callière think of that? It seems to her like the men who become governor campaign forever, are all enmeshed with each other and fight and then become friends and then fight again. She doesn't think Cadillac can bull his way into this one. And it raises a question: what is he running from if he's trying so hard to make a life here?

"I think you wish you could live in a sad little cabin in the woods, away from all the people you think are idiots," she says.

His face changes, like he was expecting something different. She can see him getting ready to mount another attack, so she decides to mount her own. She drags her bedroll over, settling it so it's just a foot away from his. He looks up at her; his eyes are wary.

"You couldn't even handle de Buade," Minique says.

He explodes off of the ground in one pounce, grabbing her around the waist and rolling her. He ends up on top of her, their two bodies thrown on an angle across the two bedrolls.

"Bitch," he hisses.

"You'll have to do better than that," she says, rolling her eyes. "The priest has been calling me a bitch since I was a child."

As he looms above her, she finds herself grinning. It's the combination of the victory she feels in goading him into action and the feeling of his body weighing down on hers. She shifts her legs a little, widening them, and his pelvis sinks into the void she's creating, pressing them together even more solidly. The snarling face he had on slips immediately. He makes as if to pull back, and she locks her legs behind his and rolls them herself.

Before he has time to open his mouth and say something annoying or smug, or even say no, say *leave me alone*, she puts both her palms on his shoulders and shoves him, and he lets her. He doesn't fight back, but he also doesn't meet her movements. He's just a body to be positioned how she wants.

And she wants. She settles down on him quickly, pressing her front to his like a cat, rolling her spine, flexing her fingers where they sit digging into the skin of his chest. He's completely clothed, but his face is naked, just a few inches from hers.

Minique doesn't slow down to let her brain catch up to what she's doing. He's warm, like he cradles fire in his hips and heart. She can feel that heart thudding in the barrel of his chest, the only sign that he's affected. Her thighs are spread wide over his hips, and she moves her hands up from his shoulders to the juncture of his neck and his hairline. She doesn't do it smoothly; it's halting and jerky. But once there, touching the softness of that black hair, she curls her fingers into it. She holds his head in place with a grip she's sure is painful, but it lets her keep his gaze centred on her. Still, he's not reacting, just letting her do what she pleases. They're almost forehead to forehead now.

"You've got a mouth on you," she says. She meant to say *you're mouthy and you need a firm hand, because you know nothing*. But instead, she sounds overcome. Like she's thought about his mouth before; like she's wondered what it could do.

"And?" He's also speaking in an almost-whisper.

"And it's why you will never be governor of New France," she says.

She expects him to buck her off, maybe to backhand her, but he does something stranger. He sits up and then he kisses her. He licks his way into her mouth as soon as she parts her lips to make a surprised sound. His hands finally wake up, and they clutch at the back of her head, holding her in place like she's holding him. She tastes the want he has, the desire muddled with confusion and guilt. It's more potent at the source, along the ticklish ridges of his tongue and teeth.

"Never?" He sounds wrecked.

"Never," she says back, confident like she's casting a spell. She tugs at his hair to kiss him again, pulling as hard as she dares. He doesn't make a sound but his body tightens under her.

"And you won't help me?" He winds her braid around his hand once, twice, until her neck is like a bowstring and her mouth is the arrow. Minique turns her curled-back lips into a smile and shakes her head. Then she spits into his mouth.

He rears back. She chases the path of his body, tightening her thighs around him, using the strong body she's built by living alone. Then he tips his head and starts to laugh. A rich, unfolding laugh that dances up to the tops of the trees. He kisses her, forcing her saliva back into her own mouth, and then they sit like that for a moment, breathing into each other. Tasting like they're dazed, like they're upset they didn't go further, upset that they went too far.

When he pulls back from her, she's snapped back into her own body like a whip crack.

"I won't," she says.

"Not even a little bit? Won't turn on your neighbours and enemies just a little bit?" She shakes her head. "Won't do to them what they did to you for so long?"

No, I can't, she thinks. *I can't become a bad thing, because then I'm no better than they are.*

"No," she says.

"No," he says, nodding, and then he unwinds her braid and shifts her off of his lap. She's confused at the fluidity of the motions, of the way he rolls gently and gathers up all his bed linens, nestling himself within them. "No, then," he says, and he settles on one side, staring at her.

She also goes to gather her bedding, pulling it over, setting up just a few feet from him. She wants to ask him if it was good. If he liked the taste of her like she liked his. Instead, she settles onto her side, too, facing him. They lie there, looking at each other. Minique feels like the waterfall, like there's a roaring inside of her that's been woken up after decades of dormancy. She wants to open her mouth and let it all out. She wants to talk and keep him awake all night, scared that when the morning light comes this will have disappeared. But he closes his eyes and, somehow, uncannily falls into a deep sleep, leaving her behind.

The next morning, they pack up in silence, passing things with a fluidness that can only come from a release. He doesn't prattle on in that practised voice, and she doesn't snipe. Instead, they get the canoe ready in record time, push it into the water without even asking each other if a final visit to the falls is needed. It's not, because that was one moment in time, one pause in each of their lives. It's best to leave it on the wet rocks, lost in the maw of the river churn.

It takes them exponentially less time to get back to Montréal, travelling downstream and with Minique paddling instead of sitting like a lump. The late dusk is falling as she grabs her pack from the carcass of the canoe, the absent sun casting a mauve hue on their faces.

"Thank you," she says. "I never get to live like a man."

"You're not a half-bad co-pilot."

"What now?"

He reaches out both hands to her, pulling her into his body and wrapping his arms around her in a firm embrace. It's reassuring to be held like this, hard and purposeful. He leans his head down to hers, putting his mouth up to her ear.

"I'm coming for you," he says, low and steady, and it's both a promise and a threat.

Daniel watches her root around in her herb garden. Minique's pulling weeds, using a dull knife to cut down to the roots. She has dirt streaked up her arms and across her knuckles; in comparison, Daniel looks almost pristine sitting on a stump nearby, using a piece of wood to clean under his nails. He's in some sort of mood today, taciturn and looking off into the trees.

Minique frowns up at him. The sun is in her eyes and she's grumpy. She might make her living from plants, but she hates growing her own. She loathes the feeling of dirt on her hands and the way her watering can leaks and gets her wrists and ankles damp. She hates the itchiness of rooting around in the earth. She'd rather deal with the wild than the meticulously planted.

"Are you going to help at all?"

"No," Daniel says, still not looking at her. His voice sounds like a sulking little boy's. He twiddles the piece of wood in his hands, flicking at it before abruptly speaking again. "All of Montréal's been talking about Cadillac, you know."

Minique keeps her head down as she yanks at a particularly stubborn clump of crabgrass. A bead of sweat traces its way down her back.

"How would I know that?" She wonders if she sounds defensive.

"Seems he's lied about his time in the army," Daniel says.

The clod of grass comes free so quickly that Minique lurches backward, dirt spattering on her dress. She swipes at her cheeks with the back of her hands and looks up at Daniel. His eyes have a strange sort of gleam.

She tosses the weed to one side and wipes her knife on the grass to clean it. "His time in the army?"

"Looks like his rank keeps changing depending on who he's talking to. Turns out he told a clerk he was an infantry captain. And then told Frontenac that he had been a lieutenant. And told the Ministère de la Marine back in France that he was a cadet." He laughs. "And someone told me that he stole his coat of arms from another family, and barely changed it at all. *And* his name might not even be real."

All of the things told to her in what she assumed was confidence, in the dark, under the thick, intimate bowl of the sky—she feels them slipping away from her, falling through her fingers. She boils inside, with embarrassment and anger at Cadillac for seemingly lying to her and also anger at Daniel for telling her all of this.

Daniel continues, looking almost delighted. "One of the shop-keepers told me that he heard from one of Cadillac's men that his name wasn't even Cadillac back in France. That it was Laumet. Antoine Laumet. And then when he came to Acadia he changed it to Antoine de la Mothe Cadillac. To escape a criminal charge." Daniel takes a breath here. "Of killing a woman, back in France."

The knife nearly slips from Minique's grasp. She tightens her hand around it as much as she can, feeling the handle make indents in her palm. She has to ground herself, to feel something that pulls her to the earth and this moment, because she feels like her head is about to float away, like her blood is rushing out of her heart, out of her body, leaving her weak, leaving her stupid.

"A woman?" Her voice is thick and hesitant.

Daniel's jaw juts forward. "I always wondered why they never whispered about him killing a *man*," he says. "I told you about the state of the body . . . it's hard to know what's truth and what's hearsay, because information takes so long to come across the ocean. I can only tell you what I've heard. And it's nothing good."

When she was younger, when she still lived in town, one of the habitants went missing. When they found his body in the forest, a week later, they brought it inside the walls so Montréal's major could look at it to try to surmise what had happened. Minique wasn't there. Tante Marie would have never let her see such a thing, a broken body being paraded through the streets as a form of sick entertainment.

But Daniel was there. And afterward he told Barbe and Minique of the mutilation: the missing eyes, the skin hanging in ribbons, the gut chewed open and spilling its rotten contents. The major had declared it a bear attack, the habitant was buried, and Daniel had a gory tale to tell for months. Sometimes not seeing a horrible thing makes it more haunting: Minique carried the image of that body in her mind for years afterward, the carnage on fragile human viscera and bones.

Minique thinks of that body now: skin in tatters, eye sockets weeping, a human being so far beyond recognition. She thinks of the mind of a man who can do that to another human being. She thinks of worse things that can happen to women before they're killed.

She's sitting there on her knees, staring at Daniel, the knife held limply in one hand and her other dangling at her side, when he leans forward and puts his forearms on his thighs. His eyes are narrowed, focused on her and her open mouth and her slightly dazed expression.

"Heard about your trip."

For a moment she doesn't know what he's talking about. She's still thinking about Cadillac lying to her, about Cadillac killing someone, so her mind scrabbles around like claws on a wood floor. "What trip?"

"With Cadillac. Sorry, *Laumet*."

Her guts drop further into her boots. Maybe Daniel came here when she was gone and figured it out. Or maybe Cadillac is talking in town. She assumed he was keeping it a secret, but maybe he's going around telling his men that he tamed the witch and took her on a trip like a pet.

She grimaces. "And?"

Daniel raises his eyebrows as he flings his arms out wide, his voice bursting out of him at the same time. "And? *And?!*"

She mirrors the gesture back at him, getting more irritated and less dazed. "I'm doing what you told me to do."

"I didn't tell you to do anything!"

"You *hinted* at it. You came to me knowing what you were asking without asking."

"I did *not* tell you to become his—his—" Daniel sputters for a bit, trying to find the right word. "His femme du pays!"

Minique rolls her eyes. *Woman of the country.* Like she's a forest bride.

"*You* have a mariage à la façon du pays," she says, balling some weeds in her hand.

"With someone who's my equal!"

"Are you saying that Cadillac is below me? Or are you saying that I'm below Cadillac?"

Daniel flounders, confirming which option he was leaning toward. Minique sighs. The fight leaves her in one big ebb. She wipes her hands on her apron as she packs her knife away. The garden can wait.

"What have you heard?"

He shrugs as he speaks, back to acting like a little boy who's been told off by a parent. "That he's been visiting you. That he's been here three or four times."

"Well, that didn't happen." She doesn't specify that Cadillac *has* in fact been to her cabin.

"And that the two of you went on a canoe trip for a week."

"It wasn't a week."

Daniel gestures with flat palms, an aggrieved look on his face. "See!"

"See what? You told me about him, I'm doing something about it."

"Yes, but what are you doing?"

"Information-gathering," she says, hoping her cheeks aren't pink. It can barely be called that, but that's the best thing she can come up with.

"Are you writing it all down in your little book?"

Minique frowns at the nasty burr in Daniel's voice. She doesn't like it when he talks about her grimoire; she doesn't even like it when he notices it. When he comes to visit, she usually keeps it out of sight, wrapped in a cloth and slid in its drawer. There's something about it, about the things she does using it, that makes him uncomfortable still, even after all these years. He's never been able to get over that idea of her harnessing a power outside of herself, whether it's the kind of power that makes a canoe fly through the night air or the kind of power that lets women control their bodies using what grows around them.

She continues to pack her basket, ignoring him. If he's going to have a tantrum, she's not going to play a part in it. He sighs, and when he speaks again, his tone is less aggrieved.

"Well, what have you learned?"

"Why are you so upset about this?" It's best to counter with a question, because she's not sure how she should answer. *I've learned that I'm likely some sort of pervert who wants to act like an animal around a man who is certainly lying to my face every time I see him. I've learned that the only man I've felt is my equal is mendacious, slippery, and likely also some sort of pervert. That he carries violence in him wherever he goes.*

"Because people are talking about you!"

"So what?"

Daniel huffs and shakes his head. "No, it's a different kind of talking. A nasty kind."

She knows what he means now. "I don't care."

"You should!"

"When you were—gone, or ignoring me. I used to walk around the town after—" She takes a deep breath, always uncomfortable speaking about this, speaking her name. "After Barbe. I didn't know where else to go or what to do with myself."

"Minique—"

She holds out a hand. "No, no," she says, because she doesn't want to know which one it was: if he was gone, or if he was ignoring her. She's not sure which one would hurt more. "I didn't have anyone back then, and that's when I needed it most. Not now."

Daniel looks miserable. She doesn't want to shame him for whatever form his grief took, she really doesn't, but she's never forgiven him.

"It doesn't matter," she says, because maybe if she says it out loud enough it really won't matter and it won't sting. Barbe died and Minique's father never stayed long enough to get to know his daughter and her aunt held her at an arm's length and Daniel escaped to the woods the first chance he got and Anne left town. Is it so much to want something for herself? Just one person whose attention is only on her?

She's not sure if she expects him to apologize, to become chastened, to look ashamed, but he doesn't. And she won't bend. The two of them stay there, frozen, him sitting and her standing, like statues, in the setting sun.

"Daniel," she says with a sigh. "Don't worry about me. I've never cared about what people say. And if I've dealt with Father Etienne, I can deal with Cadillac." It's not a fair comparison: one was blustery and outward with his intentions, and the other is sly like a fox. But Daniel doesn't need to know that. "I'll learn about how he's planning to set up his fort, what Indigenous tribes he wants to make alliances with. And then I'll tell you, and you can try to head him off at the pass. From what I've heard already, he wants to become governor of New France, so everything he's going to do next is going to lead to that."

This is her extending an olive branch: not an apology, but a bridge built tenuously over the river of fire that has just widened between them.

Daniel grimaces and then barks out a laugh, which she recognizes as his own form of a peace offering. "Governor, fuck. Terrible idea."

Minique nods. She can at least agree with him on that.

She's lived so long with her abilities that certain people's scents have become rote to her. She rarely notices Daniel, his bark and earth smell such a part of her daily life. But there's something spiking in his scent. It's feverish with worry, so much that it tingles across the top of her mouth and she has to close her teeth to keep it out.

Daniel tugs at his beard as she rises from the ground and takes the basket from her hands to carry it back to her cabin. Now he wants to help, when the dirtiest work is done.

"Just—be careful. I keep hearing things about how he wants the witch on his side. Like he has some sort of plan for you. It could just be idle talk with his men, or it could be—I don't know. It makes me uncomfortable. Like he means to have you."

He probably will, she thinks.

M inique picks up a wedge of wood and puts it on the old
stump. She hefts the larger axe in her hands and sets up.
When she brings her arms down, the blade lodges in the wood with
a dull thud, splitting the log about halfway. Instead of prying the
axe loose, she thumps it down, over and over and over again, until
everything gives way. She's still worn out from Daniel's visit last
week. She had wanted to leave her exhaustion in the garden, dis-
carded among the clods of weeds and earth. To step out of it like a
skin to be shed. But it had come back that night, and then the next
morning, and the day after that and the day after that. She's not sure
if she should feel anger at Daniel for speaking that way to her—as
if she's never been talked about in town; as if she's never dealt with
murderous men—or at Cadillac for his silver tongue. Or perhaps she
most deserves the anger, for falling into the thrall of two men who
both want to use her to advance themselves.

So she throws herself into her chopping, channelling all her confusion and self-loathing through her meat and bones, the plant of
her feet on the earth and the ferocious cleave of her arms.

Like this, axe held high, arms strained, breath coming in quick,
sharp pants, she has enough brute force for ten men. And every
time she stops to catch her breath, she thinks about large hands
cupping the backs of her arms, the taste of surprise in Cadillac's

mouth, the pattern made by their two paddles. Her nails in the leather of his jerkin and the smell of her palms against the gunnels, the feeling of his tongue against the skin of her hand. She remembers the taste of his spit.

And then the drag of her heart from her chest to the ground when Daniel opened his mouth, the flashing cold pulse at the idea of being lied to. And the disappointment in herself: for believing a man, for waiting for a man.

She takes a break for a few seconds, throws the pieces of kindling into a pile nearby, and turns around for the next log, and her heart nearly explodes.

Cadillac is standing beside her woodpile, twenty feet away, silent and still. Watching her. She keeps herself from jumping, but her pulse picks up, galloping into her throat. She's distressed she didn't hear him, even over the shearing of the wood. She's distressed at her own burgeoning anticipation. They stand there, looking at each other; he's so still she wonders for a moment if she's hallucinated him, if she forgot to drink enough water and is in some sort of sweat fever.

She calls out across the clearing, to see if he's shade or man.

"What do you want?"

Cadillac doesn't burst into a thousand insects at her voice. He doesn't shriek and melt into the shadows that cluster at the base of the trees. He's real, alive and come for her. He stands and stares, looking bewildered, and this she finds the most unsettling of all. Minique wishes Anne was here to tell her what to do—but she knows that this moment is for her alone to grapple with.

And she's going to put up a fight, just like he knew she would.

"Leave, then," she says, shifting the axe to her right hand.

He smiles a little, the bewilderment suddenly gone, and takes a step closer. She feels her knuckles creak as she tightens her grip. If he notices the slight movement, he doesn't give any indication. His gaze is only on her face. Hers bounces everywhere—to his mouth, to his hands, to the trees behind him as if expecting to see someone else. A witness.

"Minique," he says, and his voice rasps. Pine trees in the wind.

She shifts her body.

"Minique," he repeats, like someone would to an unruly horse refusing a bit.

There's something in his eyes that she doesn't like, but not because it speaks to violence. Instead, it's soft. *Tenderness.* She shakes her head once, hard, to dislodge the croon of it. She tries to remember hardness. She brings the axe up to rest on her shoulder as a warning.

A warning he doesn't catch, or ignores, because he steps toward her again. One of his hands is outstretched, not quite parallel to the ground, his palm down. She recognizes it as a gesture to soothe.

"Settle." His voice is firm, and there's a small expression that flutters across his face; if she were to name it, she'd call it excitement. She opens her mouth a little bit to try to scent him, but all she can catch is the taste of the pines, sugary and dry, and the wood dust from her kindling. Everything is green and sweet across her tongue, alive.

She thinks about what Daniel told her and she loosens her tongue from where it's stuck to the top of her mouth. "So are you Laumet? Or are you Cadillac?"

He stops. "What?"

"And were you an officer, or were you a cadet?" She rotates the axe handle in her palm.

"Minique," he says, almost chiding.

"I gave you plenty of time to tell me the truth." He tries to interrupt but she doesn't let him. She's working herself up, still smarting from the interaction with Daniel and the days spent alone, smouldering. "This'll be your downfall, this need to make everyone feel like they're not as smart as you. But what you don't know is that everything you have, you'll lose. Because you're a liar." She seethes the last word at him.

His face does an interesting thing—he seems to quickly gulp for air, like he doesn't want her to see. She can see his hands are flexed at his sides, his neck is pulsing, the tendons stark. And then he moves. In about a half a dozen steps, he's thrust his body into her space, and she's backed up as far as she can, butting up against the wall of her cabin. The length of his body presses against hers. She sees it for what it is: both a threat and an enticement. The thing she's feared for decades; now it's happening because she invited it into her clearing and into her house. The Minique of ten years ago wouldn't recognize the Minique of now, the Minique who, underneath all the roiling and rage, is filled with an unmistakable thrill. It sits heavy in her, preening, slicking its way across her body and making her mouth fill with saliva.

She can't help herself; she starts to laugh, her anger boiling the strange glee—of relief, of anticipation—higher and higher, hotter and hotter. She wonders if she's lost her mind, finally, like everyone has said for so many years. She can't hold her laughter in; she can't compose herself. She can't keep her body from flushing and her heart from beating double-time in a frantic mating dance.

He looks surprised and then mistrustful at her sudden change in demeanour. "What's so funny?"

Cadillac is better as a commander when he's far away; when he's up close, he's open, almost childlike in the odd, lantern liquidity of his eyes and the wide slash of his mouth. She can see him becoming more and more aggrieved, and she's pleased she's managed to unmoor him.

She can't answer him for her laughter at first. What can she say? That every man resorts to this, using his body as a weapon and menace? She has to take a minute to slow her breathing, hiccuping, struggling to get herself under control.

"I expected better from you," she finally says, her tone warbling.

"What would you know about what to expect from a man?" She knows he wants to sound cruel and flippant, but he's again rolling a mouthful of air around his lips, and she knows she's caught him flat-footed.

"Any man can force a woman."

He grins, finally back on his own turf. He dips his head close to her ear and croons. "Who said anything about forcing?"

She shivers.

"Or maybe you need to feel like I'm forcing you?"

Minique thinks about what it would feel like to be made prey, to be able to tell herself in the darkest parts of the night that she tried, she fought, she was overcome. It's tempting to give in and hand over her power, to turn off her mind and lean into the subdued animal part of herself.

But she also thinks about what it would be like to go into it as two equals, two forces coming together as teeth and nails and clash and heat.

"No, I don't want that," she says.

"Then what do you want?"

She has no experience with men, it's true, but she doesn't know of many who ask their woman what they want.

"I don't know what I want," she says, a little ashamed. "Like you said. I don't know what to expect from a man."

His brow crinkles a bit as he looks her up and down. "Are you a pucelle?"

A virgin. "You'll have to find out," she says.

Before he can react, she turns her body quickly, slipping partly out from under his arm and driving an elbow into his ribs.

He makes an *oof* sound and starts to double over, but before she can get free, his left arm snaps out and he grabs her right wrist like a shackle. She drops the axe as she moves to bring her mouth to his hand, to bite at his knuckles and force him to let go, but he's already recovered enough to grab at her skirts with his right hand, turning her so that her back is to his front. With her facing away from him, he can't see her smiling, nor the way she brings one arm forward and then snaps it back to plant an elbow in his gut this time.

"Fuck—fuck!"

She immediately drops all her weight, her knees buckling, as she becomes like a sack of potatoes in his arms, and it takes him enough by surprise that the both of them end up on the ground. Before he can grab her hips to yank her back to him, she twists and kicks at him with one foot. She wishes she weren't wearing her moccasins, wishes for the first time in a long time she had fancy wood-heeled boots, something to make an impact.

"You little bitch," Cadillac says, but he's almost laughing, which mirrors the smile she's desperately trying to hide. She doesn't understand it; this is the thing of her nightmares, being cornered by a man, all alone, with no one around or willing to help her.

And yet—

She's faster than he is simply because she's smaller and lighter, so she drags herself away a few paces to where her axe is, scrabbling at it as she heaves herself to standing.

She's faster but he's still fast, and he's on his feet almost as quickly as she is. She makes to bring the axe up but, as he's moving toward her, he brings his right hand out, across his body, and pushes the axe haft down with just his palm.

"Apologize," he says, closing the space between them and this time pinning her to the cabin wall by her shoulders.

You fool, she thinks, noticing how her arms have been left free.

"No!" She yells like a child would, with a half-smile and too loud.

"Apologize for calling me a liar."

"You *are* a liar!"

"Minique," he says, almost exasperated. "*Everyone* in New France is a liar. You let women think you're a witch and can sell them potions to make men fall in love with them. I let people think whatever they want about me. If it helps us, it helps us. If it doesn't, we control the story. Apologize to me and we can start this all again."

"No!"

"Apologize and maybe then I'll fuck you."

She lets out a laugh like a mare's bray, right into his face. He sees her movement coming, but it doesn't make it easier for him to dodge; she sweeps the axe sideways from where it's dangling at her side, and the butt of it makes contact with his flank. She pulls back and hits him again, in the thigh. She brings the axe close to her body, meaning to flick it up between his legs and hit him there as hard as she can, but he reaches down at the same time she draws the axe up, blade facing toward him this time, and he grabs the haft before the metal makes contact between his thighs.

Minique can taste him now. Ripe like seasoned wood, leather oil, and the way fur feels under a palm. Panting for something, wanting, wanting so much that her own teeth start to ache in sympathy.

She drops the handle, and the end swings into his leg. He throws the axe off to the side, as far away from them as he can manage without moving his upper body too much. She shifts to try to see where it's ended up, but as soon as she does, he moves forward, putting his forearms on either side of her head.

Minique shifts her jaw, trying to sweep up enough saliva with her tongue to be able to spit in his face.

"Don't," he says. "Don't you dare."

"Or what?"

"Or I'll whip you," he says, but it sounds like a smile.

Cadillac brings his knee up, then, and Minique jolts as the solid warmth of his leg is wedged right up against her crotch. Her eyes widen enough that he notices, and that's when he brings his face close enough to hers that she can't see him properly anymore, her eyes crossing and blurring, and just when she thinks he's going to kiss her—or maybe bite her—he rolls his head to the side and licks the side of her face.

"What?" His voice is just a whisper but it's still too loud.

She presses her lips together, and he rocks his knee forward again, up into her, and she remembers that she has hands, and tries to push him away until he has to grab her arms, pinning them by the sides of her head. He leans forward, thrusting his knee up, over and over. She knows she should be struggling to get away, but she wants to chase the feeling between her thighs. This fat heat, this thing that's going to change her in some terrible way. It tastes like brandy. She curls her hands into fists and he tightens his own hands around her forearms, and Minique makes a sound in the back of her throat like an animal caught in a trap, like a cat in heat.

Then he sinks his teeth into the place where her neck meets her shoulder and moves her body back and forth across his leg, and she comes so hard she sees red in the corners of her eyes. Cadillac makes a sound like a snarl into her neck, and then releases her skin from between his teeth, her arms from his hands, her body from his leg. She puts her full weight back onto her feet as he steps away as quickly as he got her against the wall. She watches as he runs his tongue over his incisors, tasting. His own taste is muddled now, twined with what she assumes is her own, and she's finding it hard to figure out where she ends and he begins.

Her hands are shaking when she reaches out to him, but she hooks her fingers in his jerkin. His head tilts in surprise.

She's been alone for so long. She's done her own chores and she's walked the path to town and she's sweated out her own fevers and she's created her own world. She's lived a life of being untouched, and mostly she's appreciated it. And now someone has touched her in a new way, and she feels like her skin is burning with it. If this is her chance to show a little bit of weakness, then it's her chance to take. She twists her hands in his jerkin as hard as she can.

Cadillac responds by wrapping his arms around her waist and half carrying, half dragging her through the door of the cabin. Minique can hear the crunch of her salt barriers underneath his big boots, and she wants to laugh at the uselessness, at the weak witch she is, as he closes the cabin door and locks it.

She didn't hold on to her virginity because of any sense of propriety, religious or otherwise. In fact, she didn't really ever think about it. At best, it was a hindrance, and at worst it was a weapon to be used against her. It's why she doesn't tell Cadillac she's never done this before, any of this; it's something he could use against her, and she feels vulnerable enough already with only her blouse being unbuttoned.

He's the kind of man who stares while he does something, and so while his hand is flicking open her shirt, he's looking right at her, and Minique hates it and she loves it, too. She knows that he's not pretending she's anyone else, maybe a woman in town with a beautiful hat covering beautiful hair and beautiful gloves covering beautiful hands. And she isn't able to pretend he's anyone else, either, because there has never been anyone else whose skin she wanted to see so badly.

Night is starting to fall, and so the cabin gets the glow it always does at this time, like everything is traced in gold leaf, and it lights him up from behind and shines through the black feathers of his hair. He shrugs out of his jerkin and half unlaces his shirt before it seems like he changes his mind and then yanks her toward him again, kissing her.

Minique reaches to anchor herself with the waist of his breeches, which makes him mumble something she can't understand and push against her harder, moving the table she's leaning against. They gleam orange in the setting sun, and Minique knows that this is the most powerful spell of all, this, entering willingly, letting her animal self take over. Fuck the boundaries. Fuck the salt on the doorstep.

Fuck the black candles and the birchbark and the blue wool. When Cadillac tears off her blouse and then shoves the straps of her shift down, she can't even feel shame. She feels only heat, like her hands are burning him as she fumbles at the ties of his breeches and he has to help her with the one arm that's free of his own shirt. When his breeches fall, he kicks a leg out of them but leaves them hastily crumpled around his other ankle. She only has a moment to admire the big, pale sweep of his body before he's reaching between her legs and making a low, animal sound of pleasure at what he finds—he holds that hand up like a trophy kill, and she sees that his fingers are wet, and then he's putting them into his mouth and grunting.

Wordlessly, they move in an eerie tandem: Minique lies back on the table even as he pushes her belongings off of it, and then he's gripping her thighs so hard she thinks she feels bruises forming already. He steps forward, notching himself, and when he pushes into her she has a moment to watch his face, the cold facade of the world-eating leader finally loosened and the normal features of a man in the grips of pleasure coming through.

Cadillac makes a sound of surprise and Minique is brought back to the moment, to the cleave between her legs, the odd, dull feeling of someone inside her mixed with the sudden pain that she assumes is the loss that everyone in town always warned her against. His head is down and he's watching, and when he withdraws a little, he brings his hand down and back up, and this time his fingertips are wet with a red tinge. He looks up at her, questioning, and Minique doesn't say anything. Instead, she uses the insides of her thighs to pull him flush to her once more, forcing him back inside of her, and she lies back completely on the table, her body open like an invitation that he cannot, will not, resist. He is still for one moment before taking his hand and splaying it on her chest, making a pale pink smear between her breasts, and then he leans over her and he moves.

Minique wakes up in the middle of the night, thirsty, feeling like her mouth is filled with sand. She has to stop for a moment, frozen with fear, because she hears breathing that isn't hers—but then she remembers, looks down at the hulking figure asleep beside her. Cadillac sleeps like a giant child, selfish and spread out, one hand under his head and one fisted in the linens. She has only a nook of the bed to curl up in, and must have been covered by his torso and arm, which explains why she's so warm and why the back of her neck is damp.

She slides out of bed, inhaling at the ache between her legs and inside of her. She wobbles over to the water jug and drinks straight from it, shaking enough that she spills some of it down her front and onto the floor. She feels like she could drink forever and never be satisfied, and she knows it's because he's near, and the two of them are tinder. It's frankly dangerous, and she's almost glad that he has a wife that he will have to return to, because if he lived here, with her or near her, at all times, she'd turn into some kind of beast. She's seen animals in heat, and she knows that she's more than that. She wants more than to be bred and ripened, kept in dresses made of stupidly expensive material, worrying over china patterns and the cleanliness of windows and the consistency of sauce. Still, there's a shameful secret pleasure in imagining it, if only briefly.

When she turns, she nearly drops the jug, because Cadillac is awake and sitting up, those dark eyes like two stones, absorbing all the wan light of the moon. Minique holds the jug up in a wordless offering, and he nods, touching his mouth. When she brings it to him, though, he takes the jug out of her hand and places it on the floor beside the bed. He pulls her forward by the hips, bending his head, and she jolts as he presses his mouth between her legs, keeping her in place with one hand opened like a wingspan across her lower back and one wrapped around her bruised thigh and with the lash of his tongue suddenly inside of her, and Minique plants her hands in his hair and imagines it, imagines this other potential life, lets herself go.

The next time she wakes up, the light is leaking into the cabin under the shutters. It spangles the bed and his hair, stark against the sheets. She traces the sharpness of his nose with her eyes, not trusting her fingers to do the job, not wanting to wake him.

It doesn't matter; he wakes up regardless, as though he can feel her eyes on his body. He shifts, groaning a little, stiff with the morning, and the scent of him washes over her like a blanket.

"You smell like pleasure," Minique says, her voice rusty with sleep. She might not be awake, held in that gold, sparkling moment before the day settles properly and there are things to be done and responsibilities to face.

He props his head on his hand. "What does that mean?"

Maybe it's because she feels caught in that magic moment, like nothing is quite real, like it's a dream. Maybe that's why she lowers her guard. Maybe it's because he smells curious to her, not malicious or probing. She wonders how to say it. Maybe there's no way.

"I can sense people's intentions" is what she goes with. He narrows his eyes. "I can taste it."

How to explain to someone who's not inside her own head how her mind works? How she can flick the tip of her tongue to the roof of her mouth and suddenly know something about a stranger. Minique has been keeping the secret for so long. What a day it's been for firsts.

The two of them migrate to the table, where Cadillac makes tea—dark like tar, like hers—and they scald their mouths with it as he tries to feel different things, tries to fill his body with emotion and makes her try to sense it. It's different than when someone is all worked up with something genuine, but the feelings still come across, wavering on the salty air of her cabin, and she gets it right every time. It's little more than a parlour game, but the amazed look on his face whenever she answers is too good. She wants to keep it in her memory forever, the lopsided smile of his, the eyes widening, the little laughing intake of breath.

To his credit, he doesn't slip away while she's asleep. He waits for her to wake up on the morning of the second day, and when she opens her eyes, she can see him sitting on the chair by the hearth, half dressed, feeding logs into the fire. She has a moment of discomfort, thinking about him awake and nosing around her cabin without her knowing, and she must make a sound because he turns to look at her.

He's pulling on a boot to leave, and he's not ashamed about it. And she doesn't expect him to be. But she does want to carve the look of him, right now, in her memory. He's softer, the edge of his shoulders looser, the movement of his fingers more languid. She wonders if she looks like that, if her body has undone itself in the same way. She stares hard at him, at the grease of his hair and the purse of his lips, at the hook of his nose and the way his tongue presses into his cheek and the skin below his mouth as he concentrates. She focuses on the way his tongue tastes when he leans over the bed and kisses her goodbye. On the way he doesn't say anything when he gets to the door and looks back at her, his body silhouetted. At the way he tilts his head toward her and then to one side, as if considering her. She keeps herself propped on one elbow, her hair around her like a cloud, the light in her eyes like heat, like she's staring up into the nakedness of the sun on a spring day, a halo burning. When he closes the door behind him, she feels relieved. Bereft. Less like herself than she's ever been.

The first several days are fine. Minique is used to being alone with only her thoughts. Nearly two days of lolling around means that she has plenty of things to do. She has to draw water from the well and boil it; she has to strip her linens and wash them in her tub, and then struggle to hang them over her clothesline. She has to gather chanterelles and nettles to dry and get ready for the fall; she also has to check her corn and beans. She has to start getting ready to plant pumpkins and squash, which means sorting her seeds and tilling a portion of one of her gardens. She should also be going out foraging for berries, in order to have dried fruit throughout the winter, and leaves she can turn into tea.

There is a peace to doing chores and repetitive things. She can sweep and chop and haul and lug and her mind can just unbend, give in to the burn of her muscles and the movement of her body. She launches herself into the work.

After a week, though, something shifts. The usualness of her life doesn't work in calming her down anymore. Something itchy is crawling around inside of her, something that makes her want to toss the broom to the side and howl.

To stay busy, she cleans her cabin from top to bottom. She wipes every corner free of dust and scrubs out pans and airs out her mattress and fixes a wobbly leg on her table. She darns her linens and hems a skirt she's been needing to tend to and fixes some loose yarn in her sweaters. She sweeps all the cobwebs off her rafters. She hones her axe blades and then her knives and then polishes every spoon and fork she has. She stocks her woodpile and neatens her path. She organizes her pantry, and realizes that, through the spate of trades she's done recently, she has enough food to last her for weeks and she won't need to go into town any time soon. She tries not to think about that, about having no excuse to wander the streets of Montréal and see who she can bump into. She hates this, the change from a solitary creature into someone who wants to stroll and have contact with other people. Her whole life she defined herself as alone; to have this shift, now, is disorienting. It makes her skin crawl, her neck prickle.

As the days pass, Minique starts to take walks into the woods. She hums out loud as she does, to warn off predators but also to give her mouth a chore. She tries to breathe in the green smell of the forest and let it wash over her like it normally does, but it doesn't work like it used to. Walking until her thighs are burning and her calves are twitching doesn't make her feel relaxed. Chopping wood until her arms are weak doesn't help her sleep at night. She feels like she's losing herself to something bigger than her. Whatever is taking over her body is beyond her power. Her body feels duller than it ever has, unbothered by hours of physical work, keeping her awake every night with restive fingers and fidgety legs. Her mind is weaker than it's ever been, flitting to thoughts of Cadillac and memories of his face by hers, his mouth on hers, his hands on her and in her. Every so often she gets an image of Daniel, the sun hitting his concerned face as he sits and watches her in her garden. But the details of him feel fainter and fainter the more she thinks of Cadillac. The bearded lines of Daniel's face melt into the hard strokes of Cadillac's brow, nose, jaw. Her anger at Cadillac has faded, but her anger at Daniel remains, irrationally. She's upset at herself for letting Cadillac fuck the rage out of her. She has to remember that he's as dangerous as any man, probably more than most men because of his thirst for glory. She has to remember that he lies. And yet she finds it hard to; she battles with herself to hold on to her core of ferociousness.

This is why, she tells herself as she fights the urge to go into town for no real reason, *women become weaker when they meet men*. This is one of the ways men exert power over women. They meet them, they fuck them, they charm them, and something like magic happens between their bodies, something that feeds the male and weakens the female. Something that makes a woman into a grovelling mess, someone who wants to jump when told to jump, stay when told to stay. Being alone suddenly doesn't feel good, as it mostly has for the past decade. It feels like a prison. And if it's a prison, then she's not only the prisoner but also the jailer.

When two weeks pass, Minique has had enough. The responsible thing to do would be to focus her energy on something self-protecting, something that makes her concentrate on building up her strength and her mental reserves. She could open the back of Anne's grimoire to that page, and reach for the pepper, the amber, the cedar. She could hang sage over her windows and crumble it up to sprinkle in the corners of her cabin. She could meditate, drawing on her inner reserves.

But Minique is not feeling responsible. She's not remembering conversations with Anne about putting the book down and walking away when she feels upset or overly emotional. *Nothing good can come of working when you're not in control*, Anne's voice recites in her head. And Minique had been the skeptical one, saying *if it's not real, why bother?* Anne had never answered. But it was made clear to Minique that being what some people would call a witch and some others would call a healer meant being in control of your feelings.

She ignores all of that. Anne's voice has been fainter in her head every day, though it persists. Minique still thinks about her, wonders how her life is. If she's still alive. If she stayed in the new world, or eventually went back to the continent. No letters ever came from her, or not that Minique knows of, but it's hard to address a letter to a cabin in the woods, especially given that Anne doesn't know about it. Some days, she tries not to think about Anne, about the bitter lump in her stomach that appears when she focuses too long on the image of their two bodies in the forest, the camaraderie. The long pale fingers pointing up from Anne's forehead, the howl.

Today, though, it's as if Anne is in the cabin with her, standing over the table, looking out the window. Taking stock of Minique and all that she's built. Is she finding her wanting, or does Minique pass the test?

Why did you never remarry after Alexandre? Minique had always wondered it, and finally found the guts to ask Anne as they stood side by side cleaning out the centres of lobster mushrooms, big orange blooms named after a sea creature Minique had never seen or tasted.

Anne laughed, keeping her eyes on her knife and the deft motions she was making to pare off as little of the mushroom as she could. Later, they would save the scraps and cook them with butter, to make an infusion they could drizzle on bread or eggs through the winter.

Because men are more trouble than they're worth, she said.

Why?

Anne turned to Minique then, laying her knife down on the table-top, looking her in the eye. *Every time you couple with a man, you lose part of your power. Whether he takes it from you by marrying you, or whether he sucks it from you like a vampire. You lose dominance,* she said, gesturing to Minique's body, *from between your legs.* She turned, picked up her knife again. *Don't forget that. It's a hard lesson to learn.*

I won't.

The only thing you can control, Minique, is what you do. What you make.

Minique shakes her head, trying to dislodge Anne from her mind and the corners of her cabin. She promised Anne then that she would never forget that, that she would never learn that lesson the hard way. And still she opens the grimoire to the empty pages. In the past decade, she's maybe had to cut out a page two or three times. She memorized the love tincture and the abortifacient, because those are the two things requested the most. One she can absolutely guarantee will work; the other, she tells people, is basically useless. If people still demand a love spell, even after she's said it won't work, each time her refrain is the same: *I'll make it for you, but if it doesn't work, you can't return to my door.* What she doesn't tell them is that it's all in their heads, that anything that does happen because of what she's given them is either a coincidence or something they've done themselves. She's never had someone refuse those terms, and so she sends them on their way with whatever she's created for them, and with a few bags of valerian tea also, to at least help with the sleepless nights and the anxiety. She's never asked about results; no one has ever returned to demand a refund or to complain.

As her brush swirls across the page, her palms get sweaty and her mouth fills with saliva. She feels like she could throw up or dance a jig; there's nervous energy all through her body. She knows sorcery isn't real, or at least that's what she tells herself. She knows that it's mostly in the head; she remembers Anne's words. And yet—

She draws the circle by facing east, walking clockwise, letting the salt fall from her palm onto her floor. Tomorrow, she'll sweep to make sure there's no evidence of what she's done. But for now, she can afford to be messy. She stands in the middle of the circle and looks at the things she's laid out on the tabletop. A piece of paper, a quill. A pouch, made from pieces of an old red scarf dug out from under her bed. Dried rose petals. Apple seeds. A stone she found in a creek a few summers ago. A piece of string. A bowl of sugar. Things that look harmless and sweet.

The one thing she doesn't have is red ink. She pricks her finger, and dips the quill into the welling jewel of blood. The grimoire told her to write her wish on the paper, and so she does, slowly, patiently, squeezing her fingertip every time her quill runs dry. When she's done, she puts her finger in her mouth and sucks, tasting the metal sweetness. As the bleeding slows, she makes sure her writing is dry and then folds the paper three times, slipping it into the pouch. She follows the paper with two petals, two seeds, a pinch of sugar, and the little stone. She takes the string, wishing it was a beautiful purple ribbon instead, and ties it around the mouth of the pouch, making six knots. Six, the number of giving and taking, the special number of three multiplied by two. Two people, two halves. Each knot she ties a little tighter, and she whispers her wish out loud to herself. When she's done, she holds the pouch in her hand and stares at it.

"By my will and by my word," she mumbles, feeling incredibly silly. She tucks the pouch into her shift, right next to her skin, and then she scuffs part of the salt line with her boot sole.

Three is the number people give meaning to. The fates. The furies. The holy trinity. Three times for luck. In this case, she's not sure about the luck. She's sitting at her table, sorting through her tins, trying to decide if it's time to get the blacksmith to make her some more, when suddenly he's in her clearing. There's no heralding, no greeting. He just emerges from the woods. Her breath catches in her chest, the pouch throbbing against her body like a heart. He can see her through the open window, and his eyes are set on her, his stare indeterminable.

Cadillac is different. He looks fragile in the lines of his forehead, tense around his mouth. As he moves toward her, he blinks a few times like he's surprised. Minique is frozen in place, shocked that her charm worked. She feels the hair on her arms prickling, the idea of her own untapped power a terrifying and seductive thing. When he opens the door to her cabin and steps inside, she wants to raise her hands and touch her fingers to his collar, to the ends of his hair, but she can't bring herself to move. She feels foreboding, worried by his silence and his bewilderment.

She grabs at his jerkin, yanking him toward her.

He smells like cedar smoke. Like green boughs on a fire, a trick for keeping bugs away. It's acrid, so she breathes through her nose in shallow sips. She cups one hand around the back of his neck, and pulls his mouth down to hers.

He groans into her as his hands come up to the laces of her dress. She shoves a thigh in between his legs and he pushes back at her so she's braced against the table. He still hasn't said a word. Minique digs her nails into the skin of his neck, and he grunts and bites at her in retaliation. She feels the blunt edges of his teeth along her veins; she feels one of his hands ripping at her collar. Another hand is hiking her skirts up to her waist, shoving in between her knees, then higher—

He stops moving.

She looks at him, using the table to lever herself up.

"What is this?"

She doesn't know what he's talking about until she sees the square of red in his hand.

Her stomach flies into a thousand little pieces. She's sure that he can see the pulse pounding in her neck, because she feels its drumbeat in her head so loud it's drowning out everything else.

She doesn't move and she doesn't answer.

The hand between her legs grabs at her thigh and squeezes hard.

"It's a charm," she blurts out, not knowing what else to answer. She can't think of a lie fast enough.

Without taking his eyes from her, he removes his knife from his belt, slicing open her six knots. He tips the contents out into his other palm. The seeds, the stone. The paper. Minique wants to grab it out of his hand, but when she steps toward him, he keeps her back with one hand at her collarbones, his fingertips digging into her shoulder. And then he reads it.

She wants to sink into the floor and die. She wants to crawl around at his legs and beg for forgiveness. She wants to drive her kitchen knife into his chest and watch him bleed out like her humiliation and defeat is bleeding throughout her body. Anne told her to never learn her lesson the hard way, to never give away her power, and here she stands, her face flushed and her gut sick and her shame blooming all over her skin like a brand. How can she ever look him in the eyes again after this? How can she ever have the upper hand? They're no longer equals, not with her desperation. He has turned her ordinary, like the women who come writhing to her door at night.

When she looks at him again, he's still for a moment, eyes on the paper, until he looks up at her with a snap of his head. There's no confusion in his face now. He closes his hand into a fist, and then flings the contents into the fire beside him. His gaze travels over the cabin, the grimoire she didn't have time to put away, the mess she's been living in.

The hand on her neck and shoulder tightens, pulling her body back to him. She can't tell if he's angry or upset or fearful. She can't smell it over the smoke. She can't see it in his face. He's implacable, back in his body now, not sleepwalking anymore. He leans his face close to hers and slides his tongue back between her lips. She feels like a corpse, unable to move.

"I have an idea," he says into her mouth.

"What?"

He smells like a fire. His hands are higher up her back, higher and higher, tracing along her neck and looping her braid around one of his fists, loosely, like he wants to hold her in place for another kiss. Her heart beats faster.

"An idea about how you're going to help me." He kisses her again. She can see the corners of his smile. "Now that you've finally revealed what you are," he breathes against her—she tries to push away from him, but he's too strong—"now that you've let me in on your *charms*, I think the least you can do is help me."

Minique pulls back as far as she can, her hands scrabbling against his chest.

"Help you with what?"

"Become governor," he says, his nose rubbing against her cheek, and then she smells it, the naked ambition, and she knows, then, that he's planned this. That she's allowed herself to become a pawn. She makes a sound like a wail, half caught in her throat, and shakes her head.

"Sense things for me. Spell things for me. Change things for me, to ease my way into the seat of power. Make it so that I have a good reputation and a beautiful home to bring my family over to, when I'm in charge."

Another man choosing another family over her, though at least this instance is all her own making. She can't blame anyone but herself.

"I don't know who you think I am," she says, her voice strong for how jagged she feels inside, "but I don't have those skills. I can't change the course of the future."

"But you read my palm," he says.

"I read the situation. I read the room. I used the one skill I have to cheat."

"And the charm?"

"It's not real," she says, and she doesn't know if she believes it, but

she has to in this moment. She can't have that power, because if she
does, she becomes invaluable to him in a terrifying way.

"I'm here, aren't I?"

She violently shakes her head.

"And that skill of yours—"

"What skill?" She points her chin at her cabin. "Look at me. If I
could change lives, don't you think I'd change my own?"

He stares down at her.

"And even if I could," she continues, "now that you've done this,
I wouldn't help you." What she doesn't add is: *if you hadn't done this,
maybe I would have.* What she doesn't add is: *I'm just as guilty as you
are in trying to get what I want.*

It happens quickly. She's no match for his breadth, and so he half
walks, half drags her, bends her backward onto the bed, wrestles
her down with very little effort. It's when she hears the rip of cloth,
sees the strip of red fabric in his hands from the remnants of the
scarf, that she feels genuine fear. He pins both of her wrists, and
although she fights him, although she snarls and spits and tries to
bite his fingers and kick up at his back, he lashes her to the head-
board with a shocking speed and ease.

Cadillac straddles her body, his legs on either side of her torso.
She doesn't mean to, but she freezes up. She knows, as a woman,
what he's saying with this position. Part of her wants to tell him that
nothing he can do can scare her, and another part of her wants to
curl up and cry. Wants to give up, finally.

He slaps her. It's not hard enough to bruise, but it's strong enough
that the blow makes her head turn a little. Her cheekbone reverber-
ates with shame and fury. All of the skin on her face is prickling,

like bugs crawling. There's something so intimate about a slap in the face; it repulses her that he thinks he can do this to her, and that she was so much of a fool to let him in close enough to be able to do so.

She thrashes her head back and forth so much that spit leaks out of her mouth, getting caught in the fine hairs around her face. She groans like she's been injured, tries to lift her hips as hard as she can to dislodge him. She pulls as hard as she can at her bindings. She's heard from the coureurs that you can get out of restraints if you use a blood sleeve—rub your skin so raw that you start to bleed, which serves as lubrication to slip free. But even if she did that, she'd be face to face with a giant of a man, with nowhere to go. Cornered in her own home with tattered wrists and a bloody heart.

Cadillac watches her flail, like he's waiting for her to tire herself out, and when she stops to take a breath, he grabs at her face. He makes her look at him.

"You will listen to me," he says.

I will not.

"You will listen to me," he repeats, like he's heard her thoughts. His voice is firm and steady. "You see how fast things can turn? Consider this a lesson, Minique." *A lesson.* Anne stands in the corner, aghast. Minique is aghast at her own self, at putting herself here, underneath this man. After everything she knew, after all her years of living on her own and building her walls high and foreboding, she burned it all down for a moment of pleasure and weakness. She's learned her goddamn lesson, and now her anger courses through her, pure and fierce, so much so that her cheeks burn and her teeth clench hard enough that she feels drool come down the sides of her mouth.

"God, you're stubborn," he hisses when he sees that she won't reply to him. He brings his face down low. "I'm in charge. Not you, not like you thought you were at the tavern when you marched in and tried to take control." She's shocked that he's held on to that for this long; he never let on that it was festering in his mind. She doesn't know if he's been obsessing over it like a wronged predator, or sulking over it like a little boy. *Is this all revenge for that night?* She can't believe it is. He's too mercurial for that, she thinks. And yet— does she really know him at all? And does he even know her?

"I'm the boss. I'm the man. I'm the ruler. I'm going to become governor whether you like it or not. You can stand in my way and get mowed down, or you can be by my side and help do the mowing. Which I know you've thought about." He smiles. "I can sense it. We're the same."

Are they? She wants to say *no, we are not, you're the brute and I'm the adult, you're the beast and I'm the hunter,* but how can she, pinned like this? And beyond that, in the darkest part of her heart, she knows that Cadillac is the similar, the equivalent she wished for so many years ago, whether she brought him to her or they were always going to meet.

"We are not the same," she says, gritting her teeth. "I'm not the one being unfaithful to my spouse."

He tenses up, staring down at her. "Don't talk about my wife."

"I've already written her a letter, telling her about you. And—and it's with a friend who's just waiting to send it as soon as you do me wrong."

"You have no friends!" He smiles meanly, though she thinks she sees a quiver of fear running through his mouth. "Who's going to send this letter?"

"I do have friends." It's a lie.

"Oh right, that one coureur." He looks thoughtful. "My wife is worth ten of you, and if you ever do anything that puts my relationship with her in jeopardy, I won't even give you the decency of being killed. I'll ruin you in so many other ways. I'll whip you till you're at death's door. I'll make you walk naked through town tied behind my horse. I'll burn your cabin down and you'll have nowhere to go and no one to turn to.

"And also," he continues, "who'll even believe you? It'll be my word, a man of prestige and a leader, against yours. You, the mumbling wretch in the woods!" He laughs. "Maybe we just have to have an agreement that we won't tell each other's secrets." He bends lower. "What other secrets do you have, Minique? What can ruin you?"

She thinks about the back pages of her grimoire, ointment between her fingers, and the way the moon looks at midnight.

"Do you do this to your wife, too? This woman who's worth ten of me?"

"Do I own her completely, you mean? Yes, I do. Does she do what I want when I want it? Yes, she does. That's the natural order between a man and wife."

Minique shudders. It mollifies her, in a sick way, to know that she's not alone, that Cadillac sees women as something to claim and till. She feels kinship with this unnamed wife, separated from her husband by an ocean. What terrible surprises await her in the new world? Maybe she does have to tell this woman about her husband; maybe it's her duty, as part of this difficult, dangerous sisterhood. She sees the words in her head.

She scowls so deeply at him that her face hurts.

"Ah, you try to hide the fact that it's anger that drives you. Anger's the fuel that makes the world run, Minique, and the sooner you realize that, the better. It'll be easier when you realize that." He pauses, rolling his lips. "Please." She's horrified at how his voice can turn from forceful to nearly begging. Is it real, or is it part of the act? Does he feel it, too, the string that threads and tightens? The giantness swelling inside him somewhere, threatening to take over?

He moves his hands up to the bindings, and starts to loosen one. As he does, he keeps on talking. "I'm giving you a week to think about it. A week to say yes or no to me. And I suggest that you say yes to me. I think you'll say yes to me." His fingers stray over hers, and he touches the thick metal band of her signet ring. He twists it so he can see the letter.

He laughs. "M for mine, I think."

Once the tie around her wrist is looser, he stands up before she can rear back and do any damage. She lies still, though, watching him as he puts his hat back on his head, as he walks to the door, as he nods to her as though they've just had a conversation about laundry or hunting or how best to stack wood, as he closes the door behind him.

After she gets free, she levers herself upward, ignoring the chafed wrists and the stinging cheek. She stands still in the middle of the kitchen for a long moment. Her insides are churning. Something feels like it's trying to scratch its way up her gullet. Whatever control she's kept over herself, it's slipping. What did her salt mean? What was the point of blackberry leaves and birchbark and blue thread if nothing protected her?

Everything in her body feels like it's made of hot, warping metal. Minique curls her hands into fists by her sides and tilts her head back and lets out the longest, loudest scream she can manage, letting her voice tear through the corners of her cabin, swoop out into the foliage like it has leathery wings, paint the trees red with her grief and her rage and the pain that's manifested behind her breastbone. She can feel her voice fly like the shriek of a hawk, like the rich roar of a thunderstorm, and she knows that it's reached Cadillac, wherever he is in the woods, that it's even echoed its way to Montréal and clattered around the streets and clawed at the doorways. That the fur runners and the Iroquois and the habitants and the nuns and the brothers can all hear her humiliation. Can hear that she's been fucking fooled. Her vision turns scarlet at the corners; she tastes the tang of blood on her tongue, as though she's bitten her cheek and not realized it. She screams, slavering, jagged, over and over again.

M inique spends the first night sitting by the fire just focusing on her breaths in and out, letting her mind self-soothe in the darkness of the cabin. She rubs honey into the abrasions on her wrists and wolf's bane on her cheek. She doesn't think she's bruised there, but for some reason she can still feel his palm against her.

A week is not a very long time to make a decision, let alone an important one. A year isn't even long enough. No amount of time can be enough to give her the space to unfold all of the thoughts she needs to examine, to weigh them in her hands.

After that, she pretends that nothing is wrong. She does what she always does. She sweeps her floor. She cleans out her fireplace. She decides that she does need the blacksmith to make her some new tins after all. She tries not to count the sunrises and sunsets. Maybe he'll leave her alone; maybe he only wanted to scare her off and keep her from ever contacting him again, especially if his wife and family are coming over. She lets herself believe she'll be alright. She realizes, as she watches ten men walk down the path leading to her house, how wrong she was. That men who take and take will never be changed nor tamed nor diverted. That in Cadillac's mind, she's like a piece of land or a fort: something to be clear-cut, something to carve his name into.

She wraps her cloak around herself and opens the cabin door.

She wants to laugh at their stricken faces. She knows they were expecting a fight. They're unsettled. The men stop about fifteen feet away. Barely men, basically boys, sweating underneath their hats. They didn't even bother to bring muskets, but she sees that a few of them are carrying pikes, and some of them have hatchets hanging at their waists. She wonders what would happen if she picked up her own hatchet, whether they would scatter like sparrows. But before she can reach for it, the group parts slightly, like a stream, and it feels like she's standing in cold water, like the stream has widened to become a river and she's up to her neck, because Daniel is staring at her, a raw look on his face. She feels like congélation générale, like she's blizzard-confused, hot and cold, naked in a snowstorm. She prays he's a hallucination, that he'll disappear into the shadows if she shouts his name.

That one coureur, Cadillac had said. That one friend. Minique holds Daniel's eyes for as long as he'll allow and then he looks away, gaze skittering across her shaking, fisted hands.

One of the men flicks a hand, and Daniel disappears into her cabin, slinking like a shamed animal, and her heart beats double-time. If she turns away, ignores it, maybe it won't happen. Maybe her secrets will remain buried.

The other men keep her at one end of the clearing; each of them is clearly too scared to touch her, but they scowl at her, shake their pikes at her, hold their hatchets in their damp hands. She partly feels pity for them, and partly wants to grab a pike and bash all of their young heads in. She wonders how many she would be able to kill before being subdued or killed herself; her wondering distracts her from the fright she feels at the thought of Daniel in her living space. She wants to know what he's doing in there, what he's looking for.

When Daniel steps out into the clearing, her knees buckle. It's only by sheer will and practised stubbornness that she stays upright. But her throat tightens and her guts twist, gorge rising to the back of her mouth, because he has her grimoire in his hand. He holds it out in front of his body as far as his arms will allow; his eyes are half shut and darting all around the woods, looking anywhere but at the knot of men and Minique's stricken face in the centre of them.

Anne didn't struggle when she was marched to jail, and Minique doesn't, either. She can't see Daniel out of the corners of her eyes, but she knows he's there. He's staying near the back, out of her line of sight, her book wrapped in his jerkin or in his bag. She wonders how Cadillac got him to agree to this. She wonders if Daniel and Cadillac had some sort of pact, if Daniel was always in on this. If he was watching her, tracking where she kept her grimoire. Her heart pounds at that thought, and she has to take a silent but ragged breath through her mouth. A mistake: she can suddenly smell all of the men around her, their maelstrom of emotions—panic, fear, delight, apathy. She grits her teeth to prevent it all from sinking into her and stirring her up into a froth of sweaty anxiety.

They walk into town like a grim parade, and this time, the streets are busy. It's the middle of the day, so there are people out doing their shopping, gathering at the hitching posts and the water pumps and the church steps. She recognizes some people: former classmates, now with children of their own, tugging those girls and boys behind their bodies and gaping at Minique; the merchants she has to buy her necessities from, coming out of their shops and staring at her; Claude, horrifyingly, closing up his boulangerie for the day and turning to see her shame, her being marched through the town like a criminal. She sees eyes at the windows, glass fogged from disbelieving breath, mouths open. She sees fear; she sees glee. But mostly she tries to see nothing and everything, letting her eyes touch every face. She tries to let her eyes alight on every person: *I see you, I know you, I knew you.* If she's going to die or be banished, she's going to make sure that every member of the town remembers her when she's gone.

The jail is cold and damp, so small and ramshackle that there's only one cell, just down the hall from where the jailer sits with his boots on a chair and a bottle under his desk. Because the trials in Montréal are set so quickly, the cell is empty. It's a small relief for her; she doesn't know what would have happened if there had been another prisoner, a man, in here when she arrived. When she's pushed inside and the door is locked behind her, she turns in a circle, pulling her shawl close to her body to ward off the chill. There's a low bench, a small, barred window that lets in the watery light. Instead of hovering around a corner, watching someone being brought in, now she's the doomed one. She's sure there's some other girl standing where she was a decade ago. It could be her own ghost, just as she can see Anne's ghost standing at the door of the cell, her strong hand wrapped around the bars. Minique is taken with a sudden wanting for her, a sadness that's deep and fierce. She has to close her eyes so she doesn't cry, because the worst thing in the world would be for the jailer to come around the corner and see her weeping and assume she's crying because she's scared. She's not scared. She's burned all the fear out of her damn body over the past ten years. She's frozen it in the dark winters. She's ground it away like her soft skin turning callused. She's only sad because she wishes she had Anne with her. She wishes she had someone on the outside willing to speak for her. She wishes she had someone waiting.

When she wakes up the next morning, her back aches from sleeping on the bench and her fingers and toes are so cold from the dank chill that she has to breathe into her hands and stamp her feet to get the feeling back. Her body hurts all over from her poor night's sleep, and it's making her feel like she has a fever.

There's a murmuring around the corner: two male voices, speaking so low she can't hear what they're saying. Then the door opens and closes and there's only silence. She sits as still as possible, listening. There's quiet, and then there are footsteps. One person is coming closer, will soon turn the corner to be able to come and mutter vitriol into her cell. She wonders if Cadillac has already come, if he's going to come at all. It seems too soon; surely he'll keep her here to make a point. Because even if she were to escape, where would she go? The footsteps get louder and louder and Minique wants to close her eyes and brace for impact. But she thinks of Anne meeting her fate head-on, her body standing tall and strong in the courthouse, her voice as she threatened to whip Father Etienne. So Minique keeps her eyes open and on the cell door, watching as Daniel comes into view.

He looks like shit. His face looks drawn and there are shadows under his eyes. He seems exhausted, so the two of them make a ragged and similar pair. Minique turns her head away from him and stares into the filthy corner of the cell where the slop bucket is, which she hasn't had to use yet since no one has brought her food and she's barely had any water. If she breathes through her nose, she smells the fetid, damp jail, human waste, and dried sweat. If she breathes through her mouth, she takes in the years of anguish and fear that have soaked into the walls. She wishes she had her scarf to wrap around her face.

"Minique." His voice is hoarse.

"Go away," she says, and it sounds like they're twelve years old again, her voice is that truculent.

He comes up to the cell bars and presses his face against them. "Guillame, the jailer, has left for ten minutes. I gave him money to go get a beer at the auberge."

"I don't care," she says, continuing to stare hard at the slop bucket.

"Tabernac, will you just listen?" His voice rises on the last word so much that he's almost yelling it.

She whips her head around. "Well, I don't really have a choice, do I?"

His face goes from scowling to staggered to somewhere in between. "I wanted to say I'm sorry."

Minique starts to laugh.

Daniel has to speak louder to be heard over her. "Cadillac told me he'd come after me and my family if I didn't—" He falters here, looking for the right words. "If I didn't help him."

Minique snorts.

"He told me he'd sell my wife off to one of his Frenchmen, the highest bidder, and that he'd do the same for my daughter as soon as she bled."

It's horrifying; she tries not to think about what she would have done if she had been in Daniel's place, with people she loved being so threatened. But she's spiralling after a night alone in her cell. She can't see beyond her own misery. "And so helping him meant stealing my property?"

"He told me to get that, too. Or else—or else." Daniel swallows.

"Where is it now?"

"I gave it to him."

"Did you read it?" She's not incredibly worried about Daniel seeing what's inside, since he's frankly dimmer than Cadillac, and won't question the empty pages nor the notes in the back cover. But the idea of her book with Cadillac, in his hands, his hawk eyes looking over every page—that worries her more than she can say. If she thinks about it for too long, the fear becomes so painful, like a honed knife, that she can't breathe.

"No," he says, and she knows he's telling the truth. But something else lingers at the edge of his scent, something uneasy and ripe.

Minique narrows her eyes at him.

"Did he promise you something?"

Daniel blanches. "No," he says, sounding indignant. But he's betrayed by the set of his shoulders and the wobble of his chin.

"Was it my land? Was it my house?" Her voice rises.

"No, Minique, no. I would never take your clearing."

"Then what?"

"He told me," he says, his voice wavering, "that if he became governor, I wouldn't have to register to become a voyageur. That he would see to it that I could keep running my own fur trade."

Minique wants to yell at him. She wants to stand up and put her face close to the door and yell *my god, you idiot, niais, if you could find your own way to the solution you wanted, why did you ever involve me?*

Now they've both been taken in by Cadillac.

"Fine." She's too upset to say anything else. She wants to end this conversation so she doesn't have to hear any more of his betrayal.

"Fine?"

"I don't know what else I expected."

Daniel splutters against the bars. "Expected? I *told* you not to get involved with him. I *told* you what people were saying about you. Now you really have no favour, Minique."

She stands so quickly she startles him. He backs up a little as she moves closer to the bars.

"Don't pretend that you didn't come to me in the first place to set me on him."

"I didn't ask you to do *shit*." His face is red but his eyes are panicky; she can see the whites all around his irises. She's never known him to take something on like this. Normally, his tactic is to disappear.

"Well, I did. And now I'm here," she yells back, frightened.

"You're arrested for witchcraft, and I've heard Cadillac's already called for the executioner."

She starts violently. No one has told her what she's been arrested for; she had no idea. Sorcellerie. Years ago a woman got off on those charges; she doesn't think Montréal will let it happen again. Anne was a central part of the community, for better or for worse. Minique lives in the woods, freakish and apart.

"He'll kill you!" Daniel is shouting. "Don't you care? He'll kill you like he killed that woman back in France!"

"Shut up," Minique says. She wants Daniel to stop talking. She wants to get the image of a tattered, naked corpse out of her mind.

"He has a real wife! And a family! You think he'd ever pick you over that?"

"Daniel, shut up. Shut *up*," she screams at him, her mouth so close to the door she sprays spit on him.

Just like that, the temper goes out of the room. Daniel's shoulders droop; Minique lets her head fall forward and thunk against the bars. The two of them stand there, on opposite sides of the metal that keeps them apart, and breathe. They've never had a fight like that before. The river between them widens.

Daniel clears his throat. "I'm sorry."

She doesn't laugh this time.

"I really am sorry. I didn't know what choice to make. And I'm—I shouldn't have said those things."

"It's alright," Minique mumbles.

"I'm talking to a lawyer for you," he says. "I wanted you to know that you're not alone."

But I am, she thinks. Instead, she reaches her fingers through the bars, and Daniel takes them, squeezes them tightly. There's nothing more they can say.

After he leaves, Minique sits down gingerly on the bench. She hears the jailer come back in through the front door. She hears the muted hustle and bustle of the town outside her window. Inside of her, she hears her heart galloping. She feels very, very tired. So she pulls her legs up, rearranging her cloak around her, and focuses on the darkness of her eyelids. She leans her head back against the wall and feels the coolness spread into the base of her skull. She becomes inanimate, solid and cold and still. She pretends she's earth, snake, hibernation, stone; she tries to be as silent as possible, taking up almost no space, disappearing into herself, becoming so small that eventually she'll be able to slip through the bars and out into the setting sun, and that's how Cadillac finds her when he comes to get her.

M inique opens her eyes slowly, tipping her head to the right to be able to see him better. She creaks her head back to centre, moving his figure to the periphery of her vision. Because of this, she's slow in seeing him move, slow to react when he's in front of her, bending so that his face looms in her vision, his hands gripping her upper arms. She can hear the jailer down the hall, which means Cadillac was allowed in without having to bribe or beg. So as much as she wants to believe that he can't harm her in here without someone hearing, she knows that no matter what happens, no matter what sounds come from her cell, the jailer won't come running.

It's just them.

She's repulsed at herself for remembering what he looks like under his clothes, the milkiness of skin that hasn't known the withering work of New France. She's repulsed at herself for the flicker of want she feels, even now. How can this be what she bound herself to?

"If you had only listened to me," he says, and his voice is filled with grief, raw and harsh. His fingers pulse on her arms. "If you had only." He's surprised she chose the *no* option. Like he was certain her decision would have been to join him.

"I can't listen anymore," she says. What she means is: *I've been told to listen to men my whole life and I'm done with it.* Her words make him pause. His grip flexes on her and he moves forward until his forehead comes to rest on her own. She inhales, and he's exhausted, mulish, afraid. It swirls with her own feelings.

They stay like that for a while. The two of them, locked together: one a destroyer, one a creator.

"I hate this place," Minique murmurs. She means the cell, the town, New France.

"Then we'll go," Cadillac says. There isn't comfort in his words. Wherever he's going to take her, there won't be witnesses.

She turns her head and bites into her forearm. There's just enough blood to suck into her mouth and chase away the cloying taste of his self-loathing. She traces her tongue around the bite mark; the pain clears her head. But the self-harm distresses Cadillac enough that he jerks away from her to stare. She's not sure if it feels like a win or a loss.

He puts his hands around her wrists, avoiding the spit-wet skin of her arm with a grimace, and pulls her up. She goes willingly, moving toward him until he bends at the knees and lifts her. She closes her eyes, uncaring of his movement, uncaring of the people who will see him cradling her like this. There is no word of protest from the jailer. She feels the door open, the cold air. Feels nothing. Feels hardened, inside, like her father and her aunt became over the years. Minique keeps her eyes closed and her body limp, so at least later he'll be able to pretend that she was unconscious. She looks at the red-dark of the inside of her eyelids and falls into herself.

He brings her back to the house; she smells the cold dust of it. He brings her back to the same room, puts her on the longue that he once stretched out on like a cat. Only when her body hits the fabric does she open her eyes. She imagines herself reptilian, something that curls into itself in the chill but bides its time. She watches as he lights a fire, his back tense, his shoulders near his ears. She looks around the room; how different it seems this time around, colder and more forbidding. The walls seem darker and closer to them.

Once the crackle and smell of flames fills the room, he turns around. Instead of sitting on the chair across the room like she once did, choosing to re-enact their blurry tête-à-tête, he comes down to his knees beside her. The floor shakes under his weight. She barely flinches.

"I didn't want to," he says, and there's a hitch in the middle of it. She doesn't trust that sound. His stories are unreliable. They always have been, and she was too naive to see. He was trying to control the narrative—they both were, each cagey in their own way, but he was better at it because he had more experience with people, ordering people around, captivating people. It's funny, she thinks, that the so-called witch was taken in by a true bewitcher.

She stays silent. She thinks about Tante Marie and her quiet mouth and hard eyes. If this is how Minique's going to die or be ruined, she's going to do it with some grace. Her aunt would want nothing less.

"I had to," he says, and she feels anger light up in her belly. Because it's not true: no one has to do anything. Minique didn't have to keep on living after a fever levelled the town and killed her best friend and drove her other best friend away in grief. She didn't have to live her own life, hard as it was, away from everyone else, when the easy thing would have been to give in. No one *has* to do anything; they're only tricked into thinking that they do. Mostly, they trick themselves.

The ember of anger flares into a fire so suddenly it surprises her.

She sits up so quickly she startles him, and he falls back, catching himself on a hand.

"You come to my cabin and you tie me to my own bed." Her voice trembles but she keeps going. "You threaten my only friend and tell him you're going to destroy his family if he doesn't help you." She doesn't know if she can call Daniel *friend* anymore, but it doesn't matter; she feels stronger now, picking up speed. "You make me think I'm your equal when really you're telling everyone in town how you're going to tame the witch." She should have listened to Daniel, and then none of this would have happened. "You make me think I'm your equal when all you wanted from the start was to use me to further your own goals. And for what?" She flings her arm around her, gesturing at the cold and empty house. "To be governor of this? To constantly be fighting against New France? Stupid!" She's nearly shouting. "Stupid idiot. Stupid lying sac à merde. You deserve it, then. To be governor of this place."

Minique spins the ring on her finger to focus herself, and pushes herself to her feet. She becomes upright in pieces. She straightens her legs and creaks up to her full height slowly. She can feel her muscles shaking but her feet are planted firmly on the floor. She stretches her arms out, the shadows of her fingers long and pointed in the firelight. She feels like she's as tall as the ceiling, like her hands could touch both walls. She feels monstrous and full of rage, all of it shooting red and delicious through her. Her hair has partly fallen out of its braid and clouds around her face like a dark mist, but she knows he can see her eyes because she can see his, and he looks awed.

Minique's body moves like she's not controlling it. She circles him once, twice, three times, her steps slow and measured, her boots clicking on the wooden floor. She bends over him so that her hair touches his face. Without any preamble, she shoves her fingers into his mouth, like she's a horse buyer inspecting his teeth. His eyes open wider, but he doesn't move away. He doesn't bite down, like she would have when he had her pinned to her bed. She wipes his spit on his cheeks and then on his collarbones as she rips open his jerkin and the laces keeping his breeches up. She undoes the belt around his waist and pulls it into her hands like a warm snake. He must think that she's trying to fuck him, because the expression on his face whipsaws between fear and interest.

That's not what she's here for. That's not what she wants anymore. He starts to move up toward her and she rears back.

"No," she says, her hand outstretched, her palm flat toward him. She knows that people can't force magic out through their fingertips. Magic, in that sense of the word, does not exist. A woman can't throw a man off of her with just her mind and anguished hope. A person can't bend the air to their will, set a tableau to their liking.

But there's something in the set of her hand or the set of her face, because Cadillac stops. He's frozen. She runs her tongue along the edges of her teeth, tasting her own blood.

She takes his face in one of her hands. Her palm isn't big enough to grab him the way she wants, but she tries, pushing into his flesh with her forefinger and thumb, and he hisses and sinks back down to his heels. Minique stares into his eyes, looming over him like he's tried to loom over her so many times, and she worms a finger from her other hand in between his lips, between his teeth. She pries his mouth open, and then spits into it. He swallows without any protest, without even a dark expression crossing his face, and she can feel his heartbeat under her fingers.

"Take off your jerkin and shirt." He scrambles to obey her. "Turn around," she says, and she doesn't recognize the voice, a snarling thing, but he turns.

She wonders if this is a dream, if she's going to wake up soon back in the jail, the bench hard under her and her body shivering. If it is a dream, she knows she needs to take full advantage of it. She wants to become the thing that has always danced at the periphery of her vision, the thing that people have nightmares about.

The room has changed. It glitters with her, the swell of her power that came from nowhere. She was in a jail, at people's mercy, and now she's here, like a towering pillar of fire, with a terrible and awesome plan and a rage that's pushing her. There's something about the way she's holding her body that's made him subservient to her. Like all she needed to do all this time was to pull her shoulders back like a man, hold her hips steady, keep her arms locked.

She puts a boot in the middle of his back and shoves. He falls forward and catches himself, but he doesn't turn back to look at her, nor does he say anything. She can see his breath quickening from the way the muscles of his bare back flex and relax, and so the first time she hits him, she strikes him on the exhale.

The belt makes a sharp sound that seems to bloom a few seconds after the leather hits his skin, and she's frozen by it, her rage temporarily ebbing as though it has travelled down her arm and into his body.

He doesn't move. He doesn't even make a sound. The blow's wide stripe is already painted across his skin in a delicate shade of pink, which tells her that she could strike harder. She could turn him red.

Minique hits him again, harder, and the stripe lies next to the first one. And then she hits him again, the third one the hardest yet, and the crack vibrates back up into her body, stoking something in her. She hits him again and again and again, until her arm starts to ache and sweat is in her eyebrows.

"Apologize," she says. In her mind's eye, she sees them back at the cabin, scuffling in the dirt. The two of them smiling.

"No," he says, and his voice is gravel and rust.

She doubles up on her swing, starts to strike layered over the stripes she's already given him, and now she can see his body jolt, can see that his hands are clenched in front of him, that his nails are digging into his palms. That there's a sweat also on him, sheening his body. His thighs are shaking and his hair is quivering, and so she cracks him across the middle of his back and the end of the belt wraps around his ribs like a tongue, and that's when he does cry out, a harsh thing, a plea without words.

Minique drops the belt. She's panting. She's tired. Her body's singing, pleased to have been allowed to let loose, thrilled to be bolstered with anger. She feels swathed in it, protected by it. Her eyes dart around the room; she focuses on his jerkin and shirt, crumpled by his body. From underneath the fabric, she sees the corner of something leather.

Relief courses through her. Finding the grimoire feels like a body part returning to her, like she's recovering a piece of herself. She drags it toward her with her foot, grabbing it with shaking hands and tucking it into her waistband at the back of her skirt.

She hears scraping, fabric moving against wood. The muted exhalation of someone trying not to groan. Cadillac has pushed himself up to sitting, turning to face her somewhat, half his front and half his back visible to her. He's wrecked and smeary, panting. There's a streak of his own blood across one of his cheeks, and it looks like tears spilled out of his eyes at some point. She can see, when she looks down at the crotch of his breeches, that he's hard.

"You're disgusting," she says, and she presses a booted foot into his thigh.

He makes a noise like a dying man and she presses harder, just to better hear the weakness that he's finally allowing her to see, that she's forcing out of him. As her boot digs harder into his skin, he whimpers, something manipulative-sounding, and she moves without thinking, slapping him across the face. Cadillac slumps down to the side, partly on the floor, holding himself up with a forearm.

"That's for the bed," she says, and she realizes that she's also crying. She smacks him again. "That's for lying." Again, but she can't bring herself to keep talking. *That's for the bed and that's for the bindings and that's for lying and that's for taking something from me and not being at all deserving of it.* She moves to hit him again but he holds an arm up to shield himself, trying to grab at her hand.

"Please," he says, raspy. "Please."

She wrenches her hand out of his grip. "Please what?"

"Please join me."

She imagines what life would be like if she agreed. Would he keep her in a cabin on his land in his new settlement, only a few arpents away from his family? His wife? If a woman is coming over to the new world, a new land, for her husband, she must love him. Minique won't be that person. She won't be kept on a shelf for use only once in a while. And she won't live in the shadow of someone else. And he'll never give up if he thinks she's useful to him.

There's only one way out.

She slides the heavy ring off of her finger, trying not to think about Daniel's face pressed to the bars of her cell, the timbre of his voice as he yelled at her. She tries not to see him standing in her clearing, behind Cadillac's men, staring at her. Him, standing in her clearing, laughing as he taught her to throw an axe, clapping her on the back as he walked her through skinning and cleaning her first rabbit, persuading the habitants' sons to help her build her cabin and glean her freedom. Him spinning around her at the dance, the grin in his eyes as he looked at Barbe, the flute of his laugh. His boots dangling from the apple tree as he sat above her, regaling her with stories about the nain rouge, opening up her world.

She weighs the ring in her palm. It's just a thing, after all. Things come and go; people come and go. Freedom and power are forever.

Minique takes her gloves out of her cloak and pulls them on. It's harder than usual because her hands are shaking, but she manages it. She turns to the fireplace and grabs the tongs, clamping them around the ring. The tongs are as steady as she can manage as she holds them in the embers for as long as she dares, until the ring sizzles when she holds it up to her face and spits on it to test it. It's only three steps before she's back standing over him. His eyes are full of suffering, but she's not sure how much of it she caused and how much of it was already there, begging to be lanced like a boil.

She curls her hand in the hair at the back of his head, and forces his forehead to the ground, turning his body fully over, exposing that broad span of back striped and weeping. She picks the space right at the top of his spine and over to the left, almost where the neck begins. It's skin where the belt didn't hit, where maybe if he moves a specific way, someone might see the edge of damaged skin under his shirt and wonder what happened.

The sound he makes when she presses the M of the signet ring into his skin is unholy. It's the devil, it's a howl of rage and acceptance. And then it tapers off into something more visceral, more venereal. When she pulls the tongs and the ring away, she can see it there, ugly and blistered: her mark, her victory. No matter where he goes, no matter what he does, she will be there, a presence that hangs over his shoulder. A shadow he'll remember when he changes his clothes and a hand accidentally runs over the puckered skin. Maybe he'll freeze; maybe he'll exhale. Maybe he'll get hard; maybe he'll feel sick. But she'll be there.

"M for *mine*," she says.

Minique picks up the poker again, and it trembles in her hands. She slides it into the embers. Her body aches with a cold-hot fear that starts in her armpits and her crotch. Her stomach is queasy, and she knows if she waits too long, she'll be sick.

She looks at him where he's half lying on the floor. The front of his trousers is slightly damp, and at first she wonders if he's pissed himself, but she knows that's not it. The room smells like meat. She pulls the poker out of the fire and holds it up in front of her face, watching as it changes from hottest to hotter, from hotter to hot.

"Look at me," she says. His eyes slot up to hers, still so potent even in the ruins of his body. She opens her mouth to taste one last time, her tongue flicking like a snake's. She senses it all, his self-loathing compliance, his arousal thick like honey, his anger and excitement at the belt marks, the confusion and horror and yield to the brand. And underneath it all, the acceptance that floats like the taste of sugar.

"Never, Antoine," she says, and his eyes flicker at the use of his first name. *I'll never join, I'll never let you use me again, I'll never let my gifts fall into the wrong hands.*

And then she opens her mouth and presses the hot poker to her tongue.

Minique stares out her window at the path to her clearing. It's different, now. She nailed rabbit skulls and tied antlers to all of the trees, put hawthorn branches anywhere an arm could brush or a leg could stray. She scratched nonsense marks into bark, symbols that look like some sort of evil spell but mean nothing. And it all seems to have worked. Only the bravest or the stupidest will make their way to her, and they're the ones who'll pay the most. She doesn't need a thread connecting her to Montréal anymore; she can live off of her garden, her trapline, her chickens, and her old cow.

Her mouth aches, even months later. This morning it feels itchy, even though the blisters are gone. They healed slowly; it took more than a month. She could only drink broth and eat honey, and her body became even thinner and sharper than she was used to. It felt fitting to diminish and become harder. She tried not to look at herself in the looking glass.

Now, she can barely taste anything. She isn't able to put cedar to the tip of her tongue to see if it can be picked. She isn't able to taste if her milk has spoiled. She can't taste if she's put too much sugar in a cup of tea. Even her sense of smell isn't right. She's three-quarters of the person she was before, and she accepts that, like she accepted the pain that came when she swished salt water around in her mouth to heal the blisters, when the pus ran, when her lips cracked. When the sadness was so deep in her body she could barely move, let alone care if she lived or died.

She fought so hard for her autonomy, but for the first few weeks, she didn't want to get out of bed. She didn't want to wash, didn't want to open her window to hear the grey jay or the crow or the barred owl. Her skin was grimy, her hair snarled, her eyelids oily. She felt like she could lie there and moulder into the mattress, and when the mattress rotted, part of the floor, and then when the floor peeled apart and splintered and the cabin exhaled down around her, slowly collapsing, she could become part of the earth.

She refused to get up when the sun rose. Instead, she pinned a blanket over her shuttered windows so no light could even get in through the cracks. She kept the cabin dark and hot. Her home was womb-like, pulsing with grief. She could cry and no one would hear her. She could loosen the mask. And there was the luxury: to be free, completely, angrily, in the thick-sweet rage of sadness.

She slept for hours at a time, only waking up to drink water or stumble to the outhouse before crawling back into her nest of a bed. She wouldn't even know if it was day or night until she opened the door to go relieve herself. Occasionally she ate, but hunger was mostly smothered under the exhaustion. She dreamed of nothing, a small mercy. She tried not to touch herself, not even to let her fingertips rest on any of her skin or one leg brush against the other or the backs of her hands press together under her cheek.

And then she woke up cramping, confused until she shoved a hand between her legs and her fingers came back red. As she stared at the blood, something in her shifted. It was like her body was saying *time to move, time to change*, reassuring her that there was at least one less reason to cry.

It propelled her to sit up, wiping her bloodied hand on her night-dress. It made her stumble over to the window on weak legs and pull the blanket down. It was night, and she opened the shutters to let the cool, dark air in. She tugged her nightdress over her head, look-ing at the swipes of red, and then she tossed it into the fire, smelling the rankness of days of sweat and tears and saliva start to burn. She stood in front of her window, naked, her body diminished but still there. Still upright, still flesh and bone. Still her. Just a little changed. Just angrier. Just warier. But she was breathing. She was bleeding. She was alive.

One morning, as she's braiding her hair, she feels it. Like a breath on the back of her neck or a twist in her ribs. Something unwinding itself inside of her, so she can breathe from the deepest parts of her lungs again. Cadillac has left.

Minique knew she was never going to see him again. But grief still climbs up and over her, for the other chair at her table that'll remain empty, for the feel of a paddle in her hand. She knows that whatever glory he finds for himself, he'll squander. She saw it when she first touched his hand. She knows that New France will reject him, spit him out back to where he came from. She mourns for the diminished returns other people will see once Cadillac chokes out the fur trade. She mourns for the life she didn't know she appreciated, for the fact that she can never go back and unlearn the things she knows now.

The ladder's knots are tight and weathered, but they're no match for her strong fingers, which have hauled wood and dug out roots and been burned by wicks and mugs and spoons. She sits at her kitchen table, unceremoniously, and starts to pick, unravelling the knots one by one. She doesn't say anything out loud while she does it; maybe if Anne were here, she'd know what to tell Minique—if there was a counterspell, a curse to unweave. But Anne isn't here, and Minique feels that nothing needs to be said. She loosens the white pebbles and slips them into her apron pocket. She picks out the pine bark and feels it crumble in her palms; she sweeps the dust out the door. She saves the crow feathers for last, taking them outside, walking them to the edge of the clearing, opening her hand and watching the wind pick them up and scatter them into the woods. She tosses the pebbles to join them, turning away so she can't see where they land. When she returns to her cabin, all she sees is a length of old rope on the table. She picks it up and throws it into the fireplace. She expects to feel something, like a bolt of lightning, a pain in her stomach, but she feels nothing. And that is somehow the best feeling of all.

Trouvée

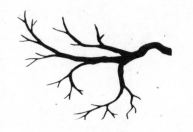

1711

For years, people have talked about the witch in the woods. Some say they remember when she used to come into town, to buy everyday things: sugar, linen, needles, tea. They swear up and down that she was normal. She didn't wear teeth on a necklace; she didn't speak backward; she didn't hiss at the cross or flinch away from the Ursulines or the Sulpicians. She kept her head high, yes, and she made eye contact with everyone who dared to cross her path, but people chalked that up to bad genes: everyone in town knew that her father was fucking his sister, who was secretly Minique's mother. Or was it that her mother, that elusive fille de roi, ran from her father? Killed herself? Got back onto a ship and returned to the continent, leaving her new husband and infant in this harsh land? Everyone in town knew that her father eventually went berserk, killing himself and three of his fur runners. Four of them. Five. That his wood runners killed him, fed up with his temper. That he moved to the woods to be with another family. That he went the way of his wife and walked away from everything, leaving his sister and his daughter to fend for themselves in town.

People have tried to ask the one coureur de bois about her, the man who played with her when they were children, the man who wanted to marry her best friend and, if some are to be believed when they talk at the pub over one too many beers, at one point maybe wanted to marry her as well. He's rarely in town as it is, preferring to live with his wife and their children as far away from Montréal as they can manage, but when he does come in to barter with a few pelts that don't reach the same price as they used to, shopkeepers try to press him as subtly as they can for details. *Is she dead? Is she mad? Is she gone?* Some people even think they know about the man who was obsessed with her, the founder of Détroit. The coureur never answers their questions, pretends not to know what they're talking about. And if he buys far too many supplies for just one family—if he buys extra sugar, a hairbrush, yards of red linen that a woman might make clothing out of—no one says anything.

Paule likes the orchard the best. She can escape there when she wants to be alone, which is often. School isn't interesting, and she hates having to learn how to spin wool and hem skirts and all the other stupid things girls are supposed to do. When she can sneak away, she comes to the orchard to climb her favourite tree.

Sometimes, she walks a few feet into the woods, just to see. It used to be a game with the children of Montréal, to see who could stand nearest to the trees and who could do it the longest. The older children talked about the witch in the woods. Sometimes they sang songs about her when they played hand-clapping games in the schoolyard. They say she cursed the founder of Détroit, and that's why he got sent back to France and thrown in the Bastille. They say he maybe loved her and she maybe loved him, but he locked her up.

They say she told him to beware the nain rouge, the demon of the strait, and he laughed at her. And then one day, when he was out walking, he met the demon and he whacked it with his walking stick. And then it all fell apart for Antoine Cadillac, sent back to the continent, thrown in chains. The red dwarf got him after all. Boys say they'll go and find the witch themselves, they'll drag her back to town by her hair, but no one ever has the guts to do it. Paule might have the guts to do it. She never feels scared of anything. Not bears, not ghost stories, not even the idea of burning in hell forever. If she was ever invited to, she could win that game of standing near to the trees. But she's never been asked to come along.

One day, when she's puttering around, sitting on a patch of moss on the forest floor and eating an apple, trying to see how much time she has left before she has to trudge home and help make dinner, she looks up at the sound of a stick snapping and realizes she's not alone.

The woman is tall and thin. Her cheekbones are high and her eyes are hooded. She has freckles on her face and neck and hands, and her skin is tanned like she spends a lot of time outdoors. She's pretty in a way no one in town is: she looks different, and a little bit wild. Her dark hair is coming out of her braid, as if she couldn't be bothered to plait it properly, and her knuckles have dirt on them. She's wearing a red dress, which Paule thinks is a strange colour for the woods.

"Hello," Paule says. She waits for the fear to come, but it doesn't. It never does. Her mouth is full and little pieces of apple spray out as she talks.

"Hello," the woman says, and her voice is like a tree creaking in the wind. Like she doesn't use it very often. Paule continues to eat her apple as the woman squats down to get on her level. She has a strange ring on her finger, something that looks half melted, and she smells like fir trees and smoke.

Paule wonders if she's about to die. "Are you a monster?"

The woman's face crinkles, and she smiles. "A monster?" She looks up at the tops of the trees, like she's lost for a moment. "Some people might think that." She looks back at Paule, and her eyes are bright like a hawk's. "You don't have to be scared."

"I'm not," Paule says, and it's true.

The woman hums like she's thinking. Her knees pop as she stands up, and she winces. When she's upright, she hesitates, and then reaches a hand down to Paule. Her palm is callused and there's dirt under her fingernails, but Paule thinks it's a nice hand, the hand of someone who works hard and knows lots of things. She thinks that maybe she can finally make a friend, even if this is the witch in the woods. She thinks she understands why a witch would want to live alone, far away from everyone else. Because Paule knows what it's like to be alone, too.

She takes her hand. "I'm Paule."

The woman pulls her up with surprising strength, and keeps her fingers wrapped around Paule's hand. She's warm.

"I'm Minique."

AUTHOR'S NOTE

This book is based on the story of Antoine de la Mothe Cadillac meeting Mère Minique, an older witch, as written in 1884 in *Legends of le Détroit*. Before that book, Minique doesn't seem to be mentioned in any written history, so I can't be sure she was a real person. Cadillac was, though, and many of the characters in this novel were based on real-life figures. Some of these people lived during the timeline of *Minique*; others have been introduced outside of their actual timelines. The same goes for a few key dates and events, as well as for the ages of some characters—for example, I shifted Cadillac and Minique's meeting earlier than documented to explore how they would react to each other as younger, more tempestuous people.

ACKNOWLEDGEMENTS

Thank you:

To my agent, Stephanie Sinclair, who knew how hard this first novel would be after all of that mess, and pulled me through with grace, backbone, and patience.

To my editor, Kelly Joseph, who saw what I was trying to do and made it ten times better with her glittering brain and her willingness to grab my hand and jump into seventeenth-century Quebec alongside me.

To my publisher, Jared Bland, who heard this idea when I blurted it out over drinks at the King Eddy and said, "Yes! But forget about his perspective—write it from hers."

To Gemma Wain for the copy edit, Kendra Ward for the proofread, and Andrew Roberts for the beautiful design work.

To Shannon Busta and Kim Magi, who had to suffer through endless group-chat messages in which I talked at length about New France laws, food, clothes, lore, professions, plants, transportation, art, and/or music. Kitties rules.

To my family, who is ever there, ever listening, and ever loving. None of this would have happened without them.

The Canada Council for the Arts provided a grant, without which this book would not have come into being.

And to all the women who have stood up to world eaters: I see you. I remember you. We persist.

© Yuli Scheidt

ANNA MAXYMIW's memoir *Dirty Work: My Gruelling, Glorious, Life-Changing Summer in the Wilderness* won the Louise de Kiriline Lawrence Award for Nonfiction. Her writing has appeared in the *Globe and Mail*, *Maclean's*, the *Washington Post*, and the *Toronto Star*, and has won a National Magazine Award. She lives in Toronto.